ALSO BY NANCY E. TURNER

These Is My Words

HARPER PERENNIAL

The Water
and the Blood

a novel

Nancy E. Turner

A hardcover edition of this book was published in 2001 by HarperCollins Publishers.

First paperback edition published 2002.

Designed by Claire Vaccaro

The Library of Congress has cataloged the hardcover edition as follows:

Turner, Nancy E., 1953–
    The water and the blood : a novel / Nancy E. Turner.—1st ed.
p.   cm.
ISBN 0-06-039430-7 (acid-free paper)
1. Young women—Fiction.   2. Texas—Fiction.   I. Title.

PS3570.U725 W38 2001
813'.54—dc21
2001041673

ISBN 0-06-098902-5 (pbk.)

12 13 14   DC/RRD   10   9

This book is dedicated to those quiet heroes who,

seeing the right way, knowing that

the path is strewn with debris,

its surface pitted,

its incline treacherous,

and its walls crumbling,

take it anyway.

And to the memory of Daisy, who was never just a dog.

acknowledgments

I would like to thank Junior Prine, whose firsthand account of the United States Marine Corps landing at Luzon is recorded here. Other combat veterans whose experiences lent detail, insight, and authenticity are too many to mention. On the home front, special thanks to my parents, Stan and Jo Groves, for innumerable minutiae; a big bouquet to John Turner for law enforcement advice. Applause goes to the Pima Air and Space Museum and its staff, who maintain a priceless trove of information. My heartfelt thanks to the scores who have shared their stories of combat, captivity, and home-front activities on the Internet, and to the unnamed soul who transcribed and posted President Franklin D. Roosevelt's Fireside Chats.

I want to thank my agent, John Ware, for continual support and encouragement.

I appreciate the gentle editing of material by Cal Morgan at Regan-Books.

Finally, I owe a debt of gratitude to www.navajopage.com, for first-hand information on Code Talkers of WWII, cultural insight, and patience. In Beauty.

. . . a great and strong wind rent the mountains . . . but the LORD was not in the wind:

and after the wind an earthquake; but the LORD was not in the earthquake:

And after the earthquake a fire; but the LORD was not in the fire:

and after the fire a still small voice.

I KINGS 19:11–12

The Water and the Blood

We set fire to the Nigra church after the junior-senior Halloween costume party. Marty Haliburton brought the gasoline. Coby Brueller brought his cigarettes and a couple boxes of matches. The Bandy twins came with two pint jars of shinney each pulling down the side pockets of their overalls, and we'd all had several tastes by the time we did it. Those four boys were the root of all evil in our town for most of their lives. But the rest of us were there, too, just as much a part as the boys who spread the gas and fanned the flames.

My friends represented a few fairly nice girls and about the sorriest collection of humans caught in the throes of pre-manhood ever scraped together. Maggy, Neomadel, and Garnelle made a little half circle with me in the middle. I guess there's something odd or poetic about me, a girl named Frosty, being in the middle of something burning on a hot October night in East Texas. That bunch of boys and girls would make up about a third of the graduating class of 1942 from Big Thicket High School, but in the fall of 1941 that event still seemed a lifetime away.

Neomadel dared me to taste the moonshine, and all the kids giggled as I took the jar. It looked just like water. I put it to my lips and just touched it with the tip of my tongue.

1

Garnelle snickered into her hand. "Coby, don't be pushing that on her," she said.

Coby looked back at her and shrugged. "Nobody's making her drink it, are they? Give it back or drink up, Frosty." He held out his open hand toward me. They were all watching closely.

"Come on," Beans Bandy said. "Gimme a swig."

"I'm not drinking after you," I said. "Just give me a second. I'll take a drink."

"She won't either," Neomadel said. "I knew she wouldn't do it."

"Nobody has to if they don't want to," Maggy said.

I guess I wasn't in the mood to be swept aside like that. I guess I had something in my craw that a good swig of liquid might wash away. I opened my mouth and gulped. The fire surged to a pit somewhere below my navel and boiled out the top, as if steam shot from my ears. My eyes watered; my nose stung; my throat closed like a large hand had reached around my neck and squeezed. From somewhere in the back of my head a little voice said, "She isn't breathing. Slap her on the back; get her to breathe."

Black sky and grass and stars and dirt rolled around in my eyes, and my face was pressed flat somewhere wet and dark and froggy-smelling. "Sit her up," the voice said again.

Voices swirling in the darkness argued for a second; then I coughed so loud and long I thought my lungs would burst. All I could think of was Garnelle's daddy coming home from the war gas and coughing his lungs out and barely breathing and what if I have to have an iron lung and live in a tube forever? After a few minutes the coughing subsided. I held my elbows tight to my ribs, and I could see the kids circling me.

"Lookit," Marty said, "We came to do something, and we're gonna do it. You all can horse around later. Pass me that shine." He took a drink, smacking his lips with a satisfied sigh. "Sissies and babies shouldn't be drinking a man's drink anyway."

Coby said, "You girls just take a little sip first, till you get the hang of it. Y'all doing all right, Frosty?"

"I'm fine," I croaked. "Your turn, Neomadel."

We passed that jar around the circle, and then we passed it again. I began to feel better than I had all day.

It was Marty's idea that we come here tonight. The Bandy boys always had their hands on shinney, so that part probably wasn't planned. Marty had a rusty yellow can full of at least three weeks' worth of gasoline, and he was circling the little shack like he had a special purpose on earth, sizing up the place, checking for anybody hiding out that might tell on us. Satisfied, he returned to our cluster and said in a whisper, "Let's do it." Then he held out his hand to Coby. "Gimme them cigarettes, Cobe."

Coby said, "Nothing doing. You pour the gas, someone else lights. Otherwise you're liable to set yourself up, too." Coby upended the first jar of shine and finished it off, smacking his lips and belching to punctuate the act. Farrell Bandy had already started on a second one. Beans had a whole one to himself.

The boys circled the little church, marching, pouring gas in arcs against the sides so the liquid left slick black hooks painted on the walls. The girls and I stepped back, watching intently as they walked round the building a second time, drizzling the gasoline into the damp ground. I took another step into the shadows cast by long pines under the watered-down moonlight. I knew there could be nothing hiding in the darkness any meaner than I was.

The scratch-puff of matches being struck made me keen in the direction of the sound. Abruptly there was a hustling noise, jostling, elbowing, and out of the darkness the boys ran, headed toward us. We waited. Nothing happened. After all the gas was gone and most of the matches, there was still only a meager flicker of flame on one side. It had rained just yesterday. The wood was soaked.

"Let's go home," Coby said. "This is no good anyhow. There's enough there to show 'em we meant business. It don't have to really burn."

Marty's face was hidden in the night, but I heard something edgy and pinched in his voice. "Gimme the last of that shine. This thing is going up tonight, or I'll know the reason why. This'll teach 'em."

Clouds were thinning overhead. Maybe I wasn't so mean after all. I felt a mosquito drilling at my ankle and heard another one annoying close at my ear where a drop of sweat moved from my temple toward my neck. I backed up one more step, jumpy and wary at the sudden croak of a bullfrog nearby.

I was on the outside looking in. Looking at these hooligan kids standing around like saps, wondering how to get themselves into trouble. The girls whispered together, not including me in their secret. Garnelle turned and stared directly at me. "Frosty? You still with us?"

"Yes, ma'am," I said, mocking her. "I don't feel so swell, though."

I smelled the char of old wood. Brackish and bitter, dirty smoke rolled at us as dense and malevolent as a freight train off its tracks. Then it shifted straight upward, propelled by silent orange tongues of fire. When I saw that, a strange relief flowed through me, as if I'd been afraid this would not really happen. I watched the other girls, whispering, barely paying attention. We were doing the worst thing I'd ever done, and they were hardly noticing—careless and easy, the way you'd just roll off a log if you were tired of the sun in your face.

When the fire was waist high, it started to get too hot to stand nearby. And it smelled awful. Worse than a wood fire ought to. The mosquitoes departed. Ash flew from the building and settled on us like silent gray rain in the starry night. The moon looked through the smoke at us. Watching me. Mother says "the man in the moon" is the face of God. I've looked a thousand times, but I don't see a face. She says it's because I'm stubborn.

The girls backed from the heat toward me. I was dizzy and stumbled farther back, where they couldn't see me. Maybe I'd just run. I was thinking about running away from home soon anyway. Maybe I'd go now. Or maybe I'd cut through the field here and head on to our church and confess all this. Maybe God would send a snake to bite me and they'd find me dead in the morning. Or they'd never find me and I'd become a hobo and jump a train and ride forever. Or I'd get pulled into the swamp by that fourteen-foot gator the Bandys' daddy was always telling about that took off a piece of his left shin bone and left the foot still on. I'd be in the paper, a Missing Person of Unknown Whereabouts.

"Frosty, what are you doing back there? Come on up here with us, and let's go watch the Catholic kids shake a leg at their party." It was Garnelle's voice.

"Oh, all right," I said. *You don't have to pretend to be my friend. You can't even see me back here.* "Anybody know what time it is?"

"Nearly eleven," Coby said.

"I have to be home by eleven-thirty," I said. "I better just go on home. You-all go watch them dance if you want to."

"You're not walking home alone *this* time of night?" Neomadel could sound so much like my mother sometimes.

"Unless you all want to walk with me." I knew good and well Garnelle Fielding, and probably Neomadel and Maggy, too, were not allowed by their parents to cross the train tracks over into the part of town where I lived. The boys, of course, went anywhere they pleased. I stared at the embers, pulsing red as if blood were coursing under a paper skin on the black wood.

Farrell reached his hand toward me and said, "Too bad you can't come with us. Maybe we'll just all go home." We walked down the street a little ways, and he said, "Better let me smell your breath. If you smell like liquor, you can chew on some lemongrass."

"I wish I had a piece of gum," Garnelle said. "I had some gum last year. I even kept the wrapper and smelled it for the longest time. It made my mouth smell like mint, Daddy said."

I'd never had a piece of gum. Deely and I chewed tar one time, pretending it was gum. It turned our teeth black along with our tongues. Mother thought we had diphtheria and gave us that brown tonic she keeps that gives me diarrhea. The whole way to my house they talked about what would take the smell of alcohol off your breath. I was thinking about the smell of my hands, though. I smelled gasoline on my hands. I don't remember touching the can; the boys spread the gas. But I could smell it.

"Let me smell, Frosty," Farrell said.

"Don't let him. He's going to try to kiss you," Garnelle said to me.

"Maybe I want to get kissed. Are you going to kiss me, Farrell?" I said. He was always hanging around me at school, giving me hound-dog eyes.

5

He backed up slightly and laughed. "These girls get some liquor in 'em and get fast real quick, don't they?"

"I'm not fast," I said. "I'm just being careful. Besides . . . well, never mind."

They all laughed as if I'd said something hysterically funny.

I turned and faced the road we'd come down, my face hard and set. The kids moved on without me. I could still see a slight glow and the murky gray smoke reaching above the trees where it spread to the south. Funny how no one came. Usually when there's a fire in town, people come running, if not to put it out then at least to watch. No one came to this one.

When I thought they were out of earshot, I took a deep breath. "You lied to me," I whispered toward the building, to all the people it represented, to the hours I'd spent on those hard split-log seats, and to my childish epiphanies born there. Familiar faces, as worn and comfortable as old shoes from constant exposure, now became strange and harsh in my memory. Unnatural. The presence of those people seemed to close in on me. "You lied," I said. "These are my best friends now." The crackling remains of the edifice answered me with a sputter and sigh. I turned my back on it and ran to join the gang.

SEEMS LIKE HAVING FRIENDS is a small thing, unless you are a lonely child, desperately poor, in a new school in a new town for the seventh time in two years. From almost the beginning of the Depression until we landed back in his hometown a few years ago, Daddy's lack of a regular job caused us to move every few months. Sometimes he had the same job but we found a new house, far from whatever place we'd been renting. Once we spent nearly half a year in a boxcar that leaned so badly off to one side that Mother put bricks under the head of the bed I shared with Deely and Opalrae to make it level. Opalrae wet the bed a lot in those days. I was never so glad as to live here and have my very own private bed.

During those years, in and out of place after place, I got real used to being the "new kid." In some ways I kind of liked it. Not so much in others.

I was nine when we moved here to Sabine. Nine and scrawny. Went barefoot most of the time; had fine, limp hair; was perpetually hungry. For some reason I felt at home right away in this little sawn-log house. It was so much nicer than the side-railed boxcar that had been home for the previous six months. Still, I mostly played alone with our yellow brindled dog in a muddy settle behind the house. Berries grew on thorny bushes around it.

On a summer's day a week after our arrival, a raggle-taggle gang of children about my age ambled by and a boy called out, "Hey, you!"

I was busy. Working on a mud face I was drawing with my finger.

"Said, 'hey, you,' " the boy shouted.

"I heard you," I said.

"Why you sitting in mud? You some kinda dummy or sumpin'?"

I stared at him, not sure whether to answer. Boys were always out looking for a fight. Stupid ones were the worst.

The boy chucked a rock, hitting my arm soundly. I gritted my teeth hard and didn't move, didn't let out a peep so he'd know how it hurt. The rock was jagged and left an immediate welt. I kept my eyes fixed on the ground between us.

"Nigga dummy! Mudpie dummy!" the boy shouted, and those around him joined in. "Say, how y'all make a mudpie? You gotta receipt for that? Take some dog shit and mix it in real good with yo' hands, dummy!"

They walked on by. Laughing. Whispering. Pointing at me. There was nothing wrong with making mud to play in. And only a hillbilly said "receipt" instead of "recipe." I had a doll I kept in the house. Outside, by myself, there wasn't much else to do that I knew. There's only so much rock throwing and running and skipping a kid can do without a ball or a jump rope or a friend to try to outdo. Besides, I was used to being kept away from other kids because of the infantile paralysis. I figured I was too old to catch anything called "infantile," but Mother and Daddy kept me alone anyway.

Two weeks later school started, and that rock-chucking boy sat right beside me in class. Marty Haliburton was his name. He kept up a steady stream of chants every time the teacher leaned away or was preoccupied. I'd hear, "Dummy. Dummy. Nigga dummy. Dog-shit dummy," all day long.

Miss Breckenridge was strict. After finding out I had to take home lessons for Deely on account of her being a big baby and catching the infantile paralysis even though we were warned not to, I figured the teacher was pretty much inclined to take my side. Still, I didn't tell her what Marty was doing just in case I had her figured wrong. I figured he probably went the opposite way home that I did; he never bothered me outside of school. Until the third week of January.

All day long he was singing, "Dummy, dummy, dog-shit dummy," in my ear, over my shoulder, under his breath. I'd had enough.

I cornered him on the playground in front of a bunch of kids. "You want to fight?"

"Who? You?"

"I'll knock you into next Tuesday," I said.

"You and whose army?"

"Just me. You're gonna quit saying that in class or I'm gonna beat the liver out of ya."

"Saying what, nigga dummy? Whatsa matter, dummy, cat got your tongue?"

"You be here at four o'clock. And come hungry. You're gonna eat a knuckle sandwich."

Marty laughed.

Four o'clock came, and everyone from the third, fourth, and fifth grades was there, standing in a ring. The air was crisp. I shivered. Most of the kids around me had on coats.

I was wearing my school dress. It was made from a cotton flour sack, more faded in front than in back. I'd gone home and put on my daddy's oldest tattered shirt, too, to protect my school dress from dirt, because I couldn't very well tell Mother I needed to wear old clothes to go have a fight. The sleeves of Daddy's shirt hung below my wrists. My hands balled up with all my might into bony fists. I lifted Daddy's holey sleeve with my whole arm, motioning to Marty. "Step up here," I said. "Step up and get your whoopin'. I'm gonna whoop you."

A murmur rippled through the spectators. Marty sauntered into the center with his three friends and looked me nose to nose. "Aw, you're shakin' like a leaf."

I held up my fists like a prizefighter and hollered out, "Just cold. You kids gonna fight four against one? We don't have those kind o' cowards where I come from." I guess the other kids were eager to see a fair fight, so they started jeering at Marty, pushing him alone into the ring.

He put his arms up, wobbling the wrists at me, and said in a high-pitched mocking voice, "I'm gonna whoop you, I'm gonna whoop . . ."

Before he finished the last word, I popped him straight on the chin and caught him cold. He teetered and sank to his knees.

He opened his eyes wide, with the help, it seemed, of arching his brows. "No fair!" he shouted. "I wasn't ready. You cheated, dummy. You're supposed to toe a line."

Standing near him, I put my hands on my hips, aware of my shadow in the dirt, the big winglike sleeves flopping clownishly with my every move. Without looking down, I knocked him again, nailing his cheek with a peck. I said, "Get up. You ready now?"

"I ain't fightin' no cheater."

"What's my name?"

He looked dumbfounded, rubbing his cheek. His tongue touched his teeth and he toned, "N-n-n," for three seconds.

The kids got quiet. "Get up. Fight, Marty," someone said.

"What's my name?" I said again, facing the crowd.

"Don't know," Marty said.

I looked right in his face, shaking my fist. "I didn't think so." A few kids laughed. "It's a pretty silly name, Frosty is. You'll get a kick out of it when you start using it." Then all of them laughed, and I turned around. It took every ounce of courage I had not to run home, and I shook so hard I thought my teeth would break against each other. At the back porch I dropped two palm-size stones I'd held in my fists all the way to and from the school. My fingers were black and blue from pounding that boy with the rock held in them, but it worked.

"What've you been doing?" Mother called from the back door.

"Some boy at school said he'd show me how to juggle these rocks if I'd show up with some smooth ones," I said. "He couldn't do it at all. Busted my knuckle trying."

"People here don't teach their kids better than to lie about what they can do," Mother said.

"Yes, ma'am."

"Get in here and sweep this floor. Your sister is driving me to distraction."

"Yes, ma'am."

SOMETIME LATER, I think it was late in February, Mother met me in the yard after school. "Looks," said Mother, "will help you make friends, especially if a girl has nice, curly hair that all the other girls wished they could have." I knew I was supposed to agree, although I didn't know if other girls wished for curly hair or not. But I did know that mine was about as limp and uncurly as if it were a wet rag all the time. Mother went on, "This afternoon I got a permanent-wave kit. They were just throwing these away from the dime store and said I could have one. Come on in the house." It was a bright, cloudless Thursday afternoon, in those balmy days of spring when winter sputters to a close in fits and starts. The weather today was joyous. I wanted to play some baseball with the kids.

That afternoon, over the space of three hours, Mother rolled my enormous bundle of slick, belligerently straight hair onto four dozen pencil-thin permanent-wave rods, which I handed to her one by one, rubber-band-side down. After all that, she applied smelly, dripping liquid that got in my eyes and burned my nose.

Then she pulled out all the curlers, which hurt so badly she ended up threatening to leave them in if I didn't stop howling. When it was all done and dried, Mother ceremoniously called the whole family into the kitchen. She turned me to face them, and I smiled my best smile. Deely and Opalrae's eyes opened wide. Opalrae started to giggle, then looked at the floor. Daddy rubbed his chin with his hand over his mouth.

"Doesn't she look pretty?" Mother prodded them. "Well, Daddy?"

"Oh, yes," he said. "Just terrific. Real pretty. Great job. Right, girls?"

My sisters mumbled, "Pretty. Yes. Real pretty."

"Next week I'll do both yours," Mother said, proudly beaming at the other girls.

I watched those two nodding as they were expected to do. They looked as if they'd been promised next week they would be peeled and boiled. I hurried to the mirror in the bathroom to get a look. My mouth opened and closed soundlessly, gulping for air, for words, for something. My skin was chapped, pale, and drawn, my eyes and nose blood-red and weepy. Oh, the hair. Rather than being curly, it stood out from my head like a giant rusted orange steel-wool pad, its entire length suspended in a crown of matted, damaged-looking sponge. The bangs, too short anyway, stood up in front like melted doll's hair, wiry, brittle, fried. Some hair was burned right off at my scalp, making pink bald lines. When words finally came, they were unintelligible groaning noises. A great sound came from my stomach, like a belching roar coupled with a wild animal's cry.

Daddy came running, flung open the door, and said, "What the devil is the matter with you?"

"Look at my hair!" I shrieked, spittle running down my raw-feeling chin, tears burning the chapped skin on my cheeks. "I'll pull it out. Cut it off. Please, cut it off, all of it. Please, Daddy, cut it! I can't go to school tomorrow looking like this. Cut it"—I jerked at the hair—"off." I stretched my arm to the ends of the hair, standing out like a clown's collar from my head.

Daddy's face was softening in recognition of my plight. When Mother reached the bathroom door, though, his face grew suddenly cold. He said, "That's no way to talk when Mother has just spent the entire evening doing something nice for you. It looks real nice. Stop carrying on, or I'll get the belt. You tell your mother you're sorry. Now.

Tell your mother 'thank you' and that you like it," he said, his jaw tightly clamped.

I looked back and forth between them. "I'm sorry." My lips were dark rose above a chin that I clenched so hard it hurt. I said, "Thank you, Mother. It's very nice. I think I'll go to bed now. I'm very tired. Thank you. I like it a lot. You can give Deely my supper." Maybe it would go down by morning.

I undressed in the dark in my room. I had to do a lot of dressing in the dark in order not to wake Deely, so I knew where everything was without light. I put my aching head on the pillow and reached up to touch it, feeling the stubbly strip of baldness at my right temple. The dawning inside me became brighter; they hated me—wanted me to be publicly humiliated, beaten, taunted by the kids at school. They loved only Deely, whom I'd had to give every freedom to and for because of her polio. (If only I'd had polio and she had this hair!) If they could look at this and say it was nice-looking, they would lie about anything. Anything. I cried myself to sleep, muffling the sounds into my pillow, until I racked with heaving and thought I might vomit in my bed. I forced myself to stop crying and turned over to face the ceiling, dry-eyed, unsleeping, wishing I could die before the sun rose.

Breakfast was a silent trial, no one looking in my direction. Mother soaked the hair down with water and dried it again, but it still looked the same. "I know what will fix it," Mother said, jumping up from her coffee cup and rushing toward the bedroom. So even Mother realized it needed fixing, though there would never be any admission that it was a bad job. Good intentions were all that really mattered.

My face was nearly touching the cold oatmeal in my bowl. The smell of Daddy's cup of chicory and coffee lingered in the air. The solution Mother came up with was to tie a large scarf about the hair, the way she wore it when she worked on her parents' farm as a girl. But the hair would not lie down or be tamed. It bobbed around in its new binding, perpendicular to my head, and the scarf crawled halfway down, tied just tight enough not to be able to slide across the massive ends.

By that time, Delia and Opalrae had already left for school, early, so Delia could walk slowly. I was going to be late and have to take a note from Mother. Plus, I would have to walk in late, getting everybody's full attention. As Mother bent to place her customary morning peck against my cheek, I stuck my tongue out at my reflection in the window of the front door. "Here, Mother," I said, pulling the scarf from my hair. Several strands came with it. "It'll be all right without it." I turned to the little window in the front door, my reflection in it bright from the angle of the sun. I looked away.

"I don't mind you wearing it," Mother called. "It'll stay put if you just tie it better."

"It won't stay on." I looked at the scarf, hanging from my hand, and at the many long, burned-looking strands of hair that came with it. "The bell just rang. Here—it might fall off without me knowing it. Might get careless." I ran in the direction of the school without looking back or saying good-bye, without a note for being late, without my lunch. All the way there I saw a bizarre shadow in the slanted morning light, gaunt and long, a giant bouffant of hair bobbing with every step. When I opened the door, the second bell rang startlingly loud. I stared into the middle distance, praying that the woman in that kitchen holding the ugly yellow scarf could hear the kids taunting, see them pointing.

All day I held tightly to the hope that Mother would be overcome with horror at the way the other children treated me, rush to the school, whisk me all the way to Beaumont to a real beauty shop, and pay gobs of money to have my hair repaired or at least shaved off. Afterward we'd have ice cream sundaes like I read somebody did in last year's Reading Robins book. By lunchtime I'd thought of another possibility: Mother could meet me at the end of the day, weeping, begging forgiveness, and offering to let me go to a different school, maybe after taking six months off to let the mess grow out. Then Daddy could drive me to Miss Emily's Metropolis in Toullange for the latest Hollywood style.

All the way home I watched my feet, taking slow, tiny steps so as not to rush and miss Mother driving this way in the Smiths' borrowed

Studebaker. When I finally got to the front porch, Mother was plucking feathers off a chicken in front of a scalding kettle. The stench of burned feathers and chicken guts hovered around the door.

Delia and Opalrae did not receive permanent waves.

WHEN I THINK of that hairdo, I remember the smell of sulfur and the weepy, raw feeling of my face and eyes. Mostly I remember falling in love with the Missionary Way Evangelical Tabernacle and Mrs. Jasper and Reverend Swan.

The first time I laid eyes on Reverend Swan, I was amazed at his enormous smile. He had large ivory teeth and fleshy, plum-colored lips on a dark face laced with the fervent passion of preaching that rang the people sitting in the stuffy little building like bells on ropes. He was lean, the very definition of the word; a secondhand suit coat swung on his shoulders as loose as if he were a scarecrow in a field. Mrs. Jasper was the opposite: round and short, warm and steamy like a little teapot. She always smelled of cooked rice. She was one person I wanted to see as soon as I could get over there.

It was that very Sunday that I'd discovered Missionary Way. I had gone through the rest of the week, jeered at in school and repeatedly warned by my teacher to keep quiet. I would have torn out my own tongue rather than say a word in class those days; the kids around me couldn't keep still. Sunday morning, just after Sunday school started, Mrs. Brady told me it was my turn to take the roll book to the church office. As soon as I took it from her hands, it slipped from my fingers to the floor. I bent to retrieve it, and the drooping scarf my mother had again tied around my head slid off. The hair pillowed out from it, waving about my head in springs of coppery wool and crimped brass wire.

Laughter billowed around me in waves, and Mrs. Brady was forced to thump her cane on the floor again and again. When quiet was finally restored, Mrs. Brady frowned at me. I searched her face for sympathy. I was always fond of her. I could not tell what I saw there. "Frosty Summers," she said sternly. "Go to the lavatory and put some water on that and see if you can flatten it *down*."

I went to the lavatory. I ran the water and put my hands under it. Feeling the coolness. Seeing it go down the sink. With the roll book clapped under one arm, I cupped the water and drank, and it wasn't as cool in my mouth as it felt on my hands. I balanced the roll book on the corner of the porcelain sink so I could get a bigger handful to lift to my hair. When I pulled my hands back, the book fell into the sink and the water washed away the checkmarks on the edge of the "Class Five" page. Sure that I'd now ruined the roll book, I felt the hounds of hell at my feet as I turned off the faucet and ran for my life.

I tore through the knee-high grass and weeds, found I was at the edge of the churchyard, and slipped through a thicket of mayhaw before I reached the pine woods.

The woods near the church were thin, and pine went to hickory in a few steps; then a sudden opening in the trees revealed a small meadow, clumped with weeds and low boggy places, bristling with green bottle flies. I stumped on across the meadow, tripping over an old limestone foundation still sticking up where it marked a large rectangle on the ground, and found a narrow wooden picket fence at its far edge. There, two magnolia trees drooped with their load of yeasty, glistening blossoms, lemon-smelling and big as a plate. I stopped running and turned back to see where I'd come. I could not see the Sunday school building or the separate church house. But I heard preaching.

A singsong voice bounced among the trees, calling, almost trembling in urgency, and voices answered it in chorus, "Glory, Lord. Come, Jesus. Come on, Jesus. Hallelujah. Amen and amen."

Out of breath and frantic, I knew I could not run back across the field and show up in Sunday school without the roll book and with dirty socks and mud-caked shoes to complement my squirrel's-nest hair. But I was expected to be in church, and my parents were strangely lax in knowing my whereabouts as long as they'd seen us to the church grounds and rounded us up to go home to dinner. I tiptoed toward the

door and read the neat hand-painted letters over its frame. MISSIONARY
WAY EVANGELICLE TABERNACLE. ALL WELCOME. Reading was my best
subject in school. ALL WELCOME included frazzle-haired kids with dirty
socks, because ALL meant *all.*

Tall people were standing inside, singing: a song I knew, but different somehow. ". . . Safe and secure from all alarms," they sang without
organ or piano. By the time they got to the last "Leaning on the everlasting arms," I found a spot wide enough to slip into and piped in with
"everlasting arms."

The congregation sat. It was quiet, but murmury-quiet. A man, thin
as the rail fence I'd squeezed through, taller than Abraham Lincoln,
came to the pulpit. I was startled to see he was a Nigra man. I never
knew a church to have a colored man stand up in the front, only tuck-
ing around back dusting and fixing things when church was out.

I wondered if I should be scared of him, because he was a little bit
raggedy-looking. Like my daddy said, watch out for hoboes, swamp Cajuns, and raggedy colored folks. Watch out, and if they talk to you, run.
But I didn't run. This fellow began to talk again, but he wasn't real
raggedy, just poor—heaven knows we were all poor in 1933—and his
voice was that of the sing-talking preacher I'd heard. Wide. Warm. He
recited something from the book of Proverbs and had just held up a
miraculously long, bony finger toward heaven when he glanced in my
direction. I nodded toward him like girls and women were supposed to
do to show you were paying attention to the preaching. Men could say
Amen, out loud. The serious look left his face, and he leaned his head a
little sideways. He looked worried, then something else. I wasn't sure
what. He smiled. "God love us!" he shouted. "God will"—he smiled
again and turned directly to me—"God will love . . . you . . . too."

Amens came from all around me. Then whispery sounds. Then
chuckling, gurgling sounds. Even that tall, thin colored man was laughing. Suddenly I felt, more than saw, dozens of pairs of eyes on me. I
turned my head and looked around. I was surrounded by Nigra people.
I'd never been near so many black-skinned people together in one place.
Still, I didn't run. They weren't scary; they were laughing.

16

Then I remembered my hair. I touched it with one hand. The volume increased with the movement of my hand, as electricity jumped from my palm to the frizz. Tears filled my eyes. The lump that had been in my throat since I first looked in the mirror that morning threatened to strangle me. I tried to put a smile on my face and said, "Don't worry. It ain't catching."

The little church rang with laughter. I'd been brave as long as I could. The tears brimmed over and flooded down my cheeks. The place got quiet. I sniffed. The tall, lean man stepped toward me. "Why did you come here, child?" he said.

It took a few seconds to find the words. "Your sign said 'all welcome.'"

I guess I'll never forget the look that came over his face. He worked his big lower lip in and out, making it slick and red. Then he stuck it way out. For a second he looked at the floor. He looked at the ceiling. He said loudly, "Suffer the little children to come, Lord."

"Yes, Lord," came the response.

"All welcome! I mean *a-a-all.* A, double L! Thank you, Lord," he called.

"Thank you, Jesus," the people hollered back.

"Sending us this lamb to remind us," he said.

"Lamb. Lamb of God. Come on, Jesus," the people said.

"Sisters," he called, "can we help this child?"

"Yes, Lord."

"Sisters, who'll step forward? Come on up here. Come on up!"

Hands took my shoulders. Hard hands, bearing down on me. Suddenly I had to pee.

"Hallelujah!" the preacher bellowed.

"Hallelujah! Come on, Jesus. Come on, Jesus," they all started chanting. Pretty soon it broke into a song, just like that; without anyone calling out a page number, all these colored people were singing "glory hallelujah" and "amen and amen." It was the most wonderful thing I'd ever heard.

"Come here," a woman said to me. She was gray-haired and fat. Her

17

fingers were swollen and short, and her glasses were so thick her eyeballs looked like brown eggs bobbling around behind the lenses. "It's just a little old girl. Come here, little thing, come on." She pulled at me, and her hands started tugging on my hair, raking her fingers through it, pulling and jerking. I thought she was going to rip it all out, and really I was glad of that. The whole place seemed to grow quiet, waiting, watching her pulling her hands through my hair. She spoke into my head, loudly, her nose just above my brains, "Lurinda? Give me a bob-pin. Lord knows you got forty-'leven of 'em in that setup. Here we go. Looka there in that window."

She turned me brusquely away from her so that I faced a glass window with sunshine streaming through it. My hair had been transformed into two rolling, crownlike braids, one on each side. Thick, tight, they encircled my head like a halo of even, perfect coils. Applause erupted. I felt that woman's hands planted firmly on each of my shoulders. She leaned heavily on me to lift herself to her feet, muttering, "Jesus, Jesus. Praise Jesus," the whole time.

Then she began to sing. That was the first time I heard Mrs. Jasper dole out "Rock of Ages" like it was heavy chocolate cake. She leaned on me as we swayed to the rhythm. People hummed as if the whole place were one glorious choir. I'd never heard such a sound, and it carried me on its shoulders, lifting me from the floor.

When the song was over, Reverend Swan called out, "Will we have a collection today? Y'all remembers, could be angels about unawares. Could be a lost lamb come, but 's really a angel. Not saying so, but could be. Will there be a offering for the Lord?"

The people shouted, "Yes, yes, there will," and when the plate passed by me, I had the presence of mind to reach into my sock and take out the penny I'd been given for the offering and put it in. The plate lingered just long enough under my nose for me to see two quarters and eight dimes and about twenty pennies. Then it was over. People milled toward the door. Why, these colored folks acted in church just like we did. They all talked the same, too, when they weren't calling back to the preacher. And children, too. I'd never in my life seen a Negro child do anything but hide.

I was so relieved. All the time Mother had warned me against talk-ing to these people, and they were just fine. Just kind and neighborly as could be. Now the only thing left on my list of people to look out for were men with tattoos and hoboes. Mother would be glad when I told her there was nothing to worry about with colored people anymore.

At the door a little line formed to shake the preacher's hand, just like at our church. Mrs. Jasper pushed me ahead of her. A light-brown-colored man blocked the way for a minute. He was facing the preacher, leaning on two canes, looking older—my grandmother Summers would say—than Methuselah. "We can't have that white child here," he said, loud enough that I heard it easily. "It ain't right. Ain't. Gonna bring 'em down. All 'em down on us."

Reverend Swan shook the man's hand. His face turned gentle, and so sympathetic I thought he would shed tears right then and there. He held the man's hand warmly, putting his other hand on his arm, and said, "Brother Luke, the sign says 'all welcome.' I can't turn anyone away from the Lord. It's gon' be all right. You'll see."

Brother Luke, behind Reverend Swan as he bent in my direction, said again, "It'll bring trouble. You know it'll bring trouble."

Reverend Swan said to me, "Trouble brings itself. But we'll not turn out any child comes in the door without malice. Mizz Jasper, thank you. Will you explain to your little friend?"

"Sure enough," Mrs. Jasper said. And she tried to, I suppose. Mostly what I got out of her explanation was that my folks would be worried sick if I was missing and they'd be angry if they found me fooling around outside of my *own* Sunday school where I *belonged*.

"Thank y'all for my hair," I said. "People been laughing at me all week since my home permanent wave. They even sent me home from school with a note saying I was a disruption."

"Your mother did a permanent wave in your hair?"

"She's not my real mother," I said bitterly. "I wish I could always wear these braids. Mother and Daddy will say I been up to something if I come home this way, though."

Mrs. Jasper adjusted her glasses, which sent her eyes rolling around on her face unnaturally through them. "You know where Porter Lane is?" she said.

"No'm," I said. Our side of town had streets and avenues. Their side had lanes and ways. Both of us had roads here and there.

"You know where Ricker's is, that lane run past a old cut-down cypress stump?"

Every kid in town knew the cypress stump: a place of dangerous roots and hiding holes, and once or twice a hobo had been run off after sleeping underneath it. "Yes, ma'am."

"You keep on going down 'at lane until you come to a bottle tree. First one you see. That my house. If you get there before school, I'll fix your hair for you. You takes it out before you get home. Then the chil'ren won't laugh."

Mrs. Jasper changed my life. I went across Ricker's Road to colored town every morning for three weeks. And I brought Mrs. Jasper treasures my young mind told me she needed. A real brass pen nib I found that had been swept behind a doorjamb. Paper from my tablet. A brand-new green crayon. A cube of fool's gold we were given for paying attention to a science lecture on rocks. Two marbles I won from one of Lucetta Moroni's brothers. Mrs. Jasper told me she saved string to crochet doilies, so I began scrounging string from the tops of flour sacks, feed sacks, anything. Despite my joy, I did not mention my discovery to anyone. In a blatantly selfish bargain with God, I decided I would keep these friends for my own.

After that, I showed up at the Missionary Way services pretty regularly. I loved how everyone moved to the music. Everything, even the prayers, were sung in a rolling chant that had a rhythm to it. I got to know the beat of it all, the weight of the responses that were expected. I met Mrs. Jasper's grandson, Junior, a boy my age. He told me he went to school, but not the white kids' school. He'd never owned a pencil of his own, a fact that amazed me no end. I made it part of my bargain with God to locate every pencil I could find and bring them all to Junior.

I remember now, being allowed to touch the single possession Mother held dear. It was a hair comb, simple, but carved from real tortoiseshell. "Be cautious, there," she would always add as she laid it in our eager and admiring hands. "Those are real pearls." Sixteen graduated blue-gray pearls. A hand-carved tortoiseshell comb for her hair, which she never, ever wore.

I stole it from Mother. Carried it in my pocket to Mrs. Jasper. She wouldn't touch it; told me to put it back where I got it and *don't never steal nothin' again or a boogie man'll th'ow you in the swamp*. On my way to school, though, I put it in my braided hair, imagining I was a princess going to a ball, taking it out when I got to class. Then, all day long, I carried it in my pocket. But when I got home, it was *gone*. I walked back and forth to school, heartsick, searching every inch of the way. Mother never asked anyone about it. I never told.

Getting to school was easier than it might have been. Those were the weeks, on and off, Deely was most sick and didn't go at all. And Mother took to walking Opalrae, so I made the excuse of leaving early to go by Deely's classroom to pick up work for her or report to her teacher on her progress. So no one walked with me or knew I'd not left the house in the perfectly coiled braids I was seen in at school. I took my hair down every day on the way home and fluffed it with my hands into the mass they would be expecting.

At Missionary Way I became part of the rhythm. Part of the sway of bodies that prayed like one voice and talked right up with *Amens* and *Come on, Jesus* during the sermon, and didn't a solitary soul laugh at me. It was the first place I ever thought I belonged. Of course I didn't.

IN THE END I let myself in the front door that night without doing anything about my breath. Mother and Daddy had gone to bed, but their light was on. Mother called from the room in a hoarse whisper, "That you, Frosty?"

"Yes, ma'am," I said.

"Delia got home fifteen minutes ago," she said.

"Yes, ma'am. Delia went with Raylene to listen to records. I walked with kids from my class."

21

"Why're you so late then?" Mother's voice came from their room.

"They had a bonfire. We watched it for a while."

"Who lit a bonfire?"

"Well, just the boys. They said they wanted one. It kept the mosquitoes away."

"That's what I smelled. Well, you can't take a bath tonight, you'll wake the whole house. Better do it in the morning."

"Yes, ma'am," I said. Her light went dark. I felt my way to my room.

Sheriff John Moultrie blew through his teeth and pursed lips, making a sound more akin to a steaming teapot than a whistle. The tune was "On the Road to Alabam'," a melody he'd picked up from watching gangs of gandy dancers as a child; he'd forgotten the words, but the ditty remained part of his grain. As he stepped carefully, the tune floated without pause through the air over a parched square of earth, the only blot in a field green and thick with weeds and grasses. The colored folks' church had burned to the ground the night before. It was a tired old building to be sure, lit by coal-oil lamps and candles since before his granddaddy's day, when it had been a plantation outbuilding.

Moultrie breathed deeply, parsing odors into corridors of recognition in his brain, and stepped toward the leaning picket fence under the magnolias. He hooked his rear over the flattest part of a post and brushed his hair from his forehead with the back of his hand as he lifted his hat. Something wasn't right, but he couldn't quite put his finger on it. The sun was hot. Nearly noon. Old Brother Swan had looked him up at first light. He settled his hat, and at the same moment a glimmer of metal shining in the ashes darted at him. He moved his head back and forth, finding the angle at which the flash remained constant, and, lifting himself from the catch of the fence, he advanced toward the beam of light.

In the cinders he reached down for what looked like a coin. Moultrie pulled, chain and all, a pocket watch. The case was worn smooth from handling. Popping its catch, he found that the face of it was darkened, its hands still. Words had been etched into the case lid. He pulled his handkerchief and rubbed it delicately across the engraving. "Our humble and eternal gratitude to Lucius Thomas Blye for the rescue of Adam Moultrie III." The watch had belonged to old Luke Blye, his granddaddy's butler. Adam Moultrie III was his own daddy. Luke had been a family slave as a child and stayed in their employ until he crippled up from age a dozen years ago. Moultrie knew the story: his daddy had been rescued from the bayou's edge, then tromped on his stomach across Luke Blye's bony knees until the water lurched out of him and the air rushed back in. John himself had sat at Luke Blye's feet as a boy, listening to him weave endless tales about the past, some stories taller than the pines around their home. To John Moultrie, Luke Blye had always been Uncle Blye, puller of boyish splinters, confidant of his young manhood's dreams. Uncle Blye had to be over ninety, maybe a hundred years old.

Moultrie scowled at the watch and shut it tenderly. He pushed his hat back, squatted in the ash, and began gently pushing aside what looked like the remnant of a singed burlap bag.

November winds swept harshly against the dark sandstone monuments that pinned the steppes of northern Arizona to the continental surface. Snug within a six-sided hogan, out of the chill blast that sent powdery, grainy snowflakes obliquely against its mud-chinked wall, eleven men stared into dim red coals banked low under a smoky fire. Their faces were taut, their chins grimly pressed against army-surplus blankets. One younger face peered above the coals, above the flame itself, watching the movement of the blanket over the doorway as the wind tugged and pushed at it.

"Gordon," his uncle, Old Bill Tsosie, said. "The Uncles are sure of this. It's prophesied."

"I don't know of prophecy," Gordon said in English.

"Speak in our words. Diné words. Confusion."

Gordon wasn't sure if Uncle Bill was worrying about confusing the old men in the circle or the spirits they all thought howled in the wind. It had been a long time since he'd given thought to spirits' feelings. Next to him, his seventeen-year-old cousin Young Billy Tsosie squirmed, popping his head turtlelike from the cocoon of his blanket. Being the youngest, Billy had been given a particularly holey and rat-eaten one, stained with something brown.

"I never heard such a thing in school," Gordon said. "The radio said the president is right now negotiating peaceful treaties with the Japanese." He was still annoyed that they'd gone to such trouble to locate him and bring him home. After months alone and hungry, he'd found a job at Joe Babbitt's Hardware in Flagstaff and had just been put on full-time when Young Billy showed up with the note.

"Treaties," said one of the old men. "Paper words."

Gordon went on, "It's only war in Europe. Across the water. It won't come here."

Another elderly man began to sing, very softly.

Uncle Bill said, "It is already decided. We will go as a clan. We will fight the coming Enemy. We will sing the Enemy Way."

"And you want me to get all the young boys to join the United States Army? Who'd listen to me? Besides, we don't owe the government soldiers anything. If they're going to die, let them die."

"This is about our clan," Uncle Bill said, "not about the white soldiers. If you had not gone away to white school, you would know this. It's only because you've been gone that it's hard for you to believe." His voice trailed off, leaving unsaid any judgment against Bill's sister, Gordon's mother, for failing to give Gordon enough sense of tradition.

Gordon frowned. Maybe a lot of things would have been different if he hadn't gone to the white school. All he could think of was that he'd lost his job for this: old men scaring each other around a fire.

Bill was his mother's older brother, the closest man he'd known since his father had died when Gordon was thirteen. Those were the hungry months, the mourning months. The Department of Indian Affairs chief, John Collier, said the people's vast herds of sheep were killing the land, so the animals were shot dozens at a time, their carcasses dumped in pits, doused with kerosene, and set ablaze. Three days after the bloodbath Gordon's father, Ned Benally, crawled onto his blanket to weep and stayed there for eighteen days. On the nineteenth day of sorrow he walked four miles to the top of Needle Grass Hill and stepped off the edge of a basalt skirt that had flowed from the center of the earth before the Diné came to the surface world.

But when the sheep people were gone and the fences erected, the land did not heal. Without the open space to be shared by all the four-footed people, the remaining sheep didn't thrive. Without the large sheep herds to crop and fertilize the bunchgrass and needle grass and bitterweed, the land mourned and died, too. Then the starvation came. Old people quit eating so their children could survive. New babies shriveled in their mothers' arms, held hopelessly against dry breasts on bony ribs. So the government came with wagons, then buses, and took the children, because they said the Indian parents weren't taking care of them either.

Gordon learned to do long division in the Holyoke Indian School in Gallup, New Mexico, eight days' walk from his home. He learned the Gettysburg Address and that George Washington had chopped down a cherry tree, that brave Pilgrims helped Indians out so the grateful redskins taught them to grind corn and smoke tobacco, that the cotton gin and the industrial revolution were the beginnings of civilization. He excelled in school, lapping up the white man's knowledge with a gnawing, hollow hunger.

After he graduated from high school, he found a job busting horses for Raymond Fitzgerald at the K-Bar-J ranch near Puerco Creek. When fall roundup was done that year, Mr. Fitzgerald kept on a few of the hands, but not all of them.

The men at the fireside were no longer paying attention to him. They were singing, a gentle rhythm that took him back to his father's knee where he was very small and frightened of something in the dark. The song was old and yet new: familiar melody; ominous, unfamiliar words.

"Children must always eat on their feet, in their shoes, ready to run," his father's voice said. "Keep your knife at your side, for the Enemy Who Comes at Last may be on the next breeze." He wanted to get a job, maybe take part in the industrial revolution, not fight in some war between white tribes. When he had lost his job on the ranch, Gordon found a sign in the window of a gas station advertising that extras were needed in a motion picture production; he got a month's pay for a week's work from the producers and a ride to Flagstaff. He'd finally found a job at the hardware store, only to be summoned from the brink of his new life by Uncle Bill. "Children must learn not to cry no matter what, in case the Enemy is listening in the dark," his mother's voice added in his other ear. "This is not the time to cry. There will be time for that someday." There was never a time for that.

Young Billy, only son of his Uncle Bill, nodded as if sleepy; then he, too, started humming along under his breath. As if stepping through a shift in time, forty-eight hours after Uncle Bill's note arrived, here were the uncles—all the men of their clan—singing war songs at a round fire. Including him for the first time in a council. Telling him to prepare for the Final Enemy. Believing in old prophecy like it was gospel. Gordon stiffened his back. Try as he might, the songs were coming in his ears. He could not turn them back or soften their effect.

East Texas probably has more churches per square mile than any place on earth. Sabine, a squatty little sawmill town three miles down a dead-end dirt road from Toullange, which was forty-one miles southeast of Longview, still had Holiness Gospel Homecoming Church and a little Catholic place right next door, High-Way Bound Freewill Church, Little Hope Primitive Baptist Church, Ebenezer Church of the Gospel, and the Methodists. There were two Southern Baptists—First Southern, an imposing white-front, redbrick edifice, and Siloam Springs, to which my family and I belonged. No telling how many churches the colored folks had. I knew only of the one.

Our lives revolved around church. It was the main source of what I had long accepted as my duplicity of purpose: I worshiped faithfully, deeply; wept openly at stories of lost children dying and spending eternity in hell because no Born-Again-Baptized-in-the-Blood-of-the-Lamb Christian had come to their rescue. I read my Sunday school lessons every Saturday night, underlining passages. During Sunday school, however, I filled the margins of my lesson book with versions of my name connected somehow with Wilbur Fielding's: *Mrs. Wilbur (Frosty) Fielding, at home;* or *Mrs. W.F.;* or *Frosty Fielding, wife of prominent citizen, wins presidential recognition.* Garnelle's brother, Wilbur, had never said more than two words to me in my life, but I'd made it my goal in seventh grade to be permanently connected to him, and by now it was a habit. On my good side I could sing by heart every song in the hymnal, and the alto lines, too. Maybe being just plain full of the devil led me to memorizing Bible verses to the tunes of radio jingles for fine-tasting filter cigarettes.

Having reached high school age, I slowly began to understand that when people said of me, "Nevertheless, she knows her Bible," it was a backhanded compliment. When I wasn't paying attention to the sermon—which was most of the time, since Brother Miner had gotten on a "damnation" jag lately—I stayed busy contemplating what exactly preceded the "nevertheless."

My sister Delia was just under nineteen, a year and half older than me; both of us were in the senior class of Big Thicket High School. Delia had taken polio in the spring of 1930, right after my birthday that year. It was a mild case—on the surface hardly more than the grippe—but ever since then she had constantly suffered bouts of indefinable ailments that kept her from school. Mother and Daddy tried to keep her current with her classmates, having me haul her lessons home every night. It seemed to be my lot in life to drag two sets of books and homework all over creation. Meanwhile, Deely clumped around on leg braces until last year. She still walked slowly, but I guess she was glad to have those metal things off. They hung behind our bedroom door, and she never looked at them, but she always looked sad for a minute if someone opened the door wide enough to clunk into them.

Mother's misgivings that my sisters and I were doomed, determined to be "the nastiest tramps since Jezebel killed her children," drove her to hound us night and day for signs of debauchery. She found out last night after supper that I had gotten Miss McMurphy, the Home Ec teacher, to help me put a gusset in my brassiere to allow more room. Like everything Mother finds out about me, Deely was behind it. I don't think it was the sewing that got me whooped as much as the way Deely put it, insinuating that how tight my dresses were getting was intentional craftiness on my part. Deely actually believed I was consciously trying to outbosom her.

The next morning we dressed in silence. My arms and legs were ribboned with red welts. Mother had really laid into me this time. My back had one large, solid, purplish bruise across it and a clear imprint of the prong and half circle of a belt buckle under one shoulder blade. I'd seen them with the hand mirror in the bathroom. Opalrae was watching me as I brushed my hair. I kept seeing her eyes in the mirror over my shoulder until finally I said, "What are you staring at?"

She said, "How come you can get a whooping and not make any noise? Don't it hurt?"

"Just practice, I guess." I was thinking, *No wonder Grandmother Summers despises Mother.* Being a good Bab-diss, Grandmother wasn't allowed to hate anyone, she always told me. But despising, she didn't mind despising. That woman in the kitchen, hostile as a raw burn, could no more be my real mother than a fence post could.

Delia said cheerily, "Today's the day I'm getting the Bandys' old roadster to drive. For my very own. It'll be after school. Of course, I'll have to drive it to the dime store tomorrow to work my shift. But afterward we could go for a drive. Want to?" Delia bristled with excitement. Her own car—something better than all the other kids had in Sabine. In Sunday school, people had taken up a collection to get the money—fifty dollars. The De Soto arrived at Bart Bandy's, prepaid and brand-new, two years after the crash of '29. It was all over town about his new car coming. A week later the sawmill in Sabine had just ground to a halt; there was no gas. Necessity being what it is, he found that the moonshine he brewed on the side made the auto run fairly well. To any who didn't bother to smell the fuel line, Bandy was making a living delivering furs from the backseat. Ten years later he got a new one, so a month ago he tacked up a scribbled-on scrap of paper in the post office offering it for sale.

"No." My forgiveness was not for sale that cheaply.

"Are you going to the pictures tomorrow? I could come by and ride y'all home. Your friends, too. I'll carry everyone home."

"I'm probably not going."

"Well. If you change your mind, sweetie, I'll be glad to carry you home." After a while Delia gave it another try. "I'm leaving. Do you want to walk together?"

"Nope."

Mother's voice came through the door. "You will too walk together. All the way to and from school. Don't either one of you come home without the other. That clear?"

"Yes, ma'am," we said together toward the closed door.

Halfway there, Garnelle Fielding caught up with us and hugged me the way she usually did. I recoiled with pain, and tears welled in my eyes for a second. "I hurt my arm yesterday," I lied. "Fell over Bosco onto the short wood fence and bruised everything." Daddy had come home with him in his pocket a couple of years ago, saying he'd found him in a little pail. He's not my dog.

"Stupid dog," Garnelle said.

Delia bristled. "Bosco is not stupid. He's smarter than some people I know."

Garnelle grimaced at Delia. "No kidding. So let me see it."

"No," I said. "It's just a bruise."

"I wondered why you're wearing long sleeves. Can you believe how hot it is for November? Daddy said it must be forty degrees warmer than yesterday."

"Was that the first bell or the second?" I said. "I think we're running late."

"Only first. We've got time. You're walking slow, though," Garnelle said, then chatted on merrily about a gift she was making for her mother for Christmas.

Soon enough, I told myself, it would be Deely's turn to suffer. Although her turns came less often than mine, on account of her infirmities, she still had them. For the moment I would be bound to sit between my parents in church for a month, until they got tired of that or forgot how angry they were or something. Then I would be freed to once again sit in the tiny balcony with my friends. Or, as happened more often than not, to merely make an appearance and slip out the side door. From there I could tiptoe from that little pine clapboard building, sure that even the grass would rattle and give me away, and made for the Missionary Way Evangelical Tabernacle, where Mrs. Jasper or someone else might be singing and Reverend Swan would preach in that "tunin'" way that just took me right straight to the throne room of heaven.

The air, musty with the sweat of those recently washed with Ivory soap and a few less recently washed, suspended dust particles in the sharp rays of light over the eyes of tranced children. They pretended to fan but were really watching the dust motes swirl. The adults' fans moved randomly at first; then they took up the beat, subtle as it was, as Mrs. Ronelle Jasper caressed each note of "Have Thine Own Way" in a seductive lullaby. If I let my mind loose, I could feel the feet move, shuffling between the pews in what has to have been a dance passed on by collective memory. It didn't take much imagination, watching those halted, stiff legs moving under the wildly gesturing arms and shouting faces, to feel and hear the cobbled rattle of chains holding them together. But that was just imagination. Colored people were never chained in my lifetime.

We had an understanding, Mrs. Jasper and me. She was old and so very fat I remember thinking if it wasn't for her feet pushing against the floor she'd tip right out of the hard, backless pews at Missionary Way. She had a way of shaking her head slowly at me and saying, "Frosty Summers. Mmm, mmm," that bespoke a sort of pity for my circumstance, dread for my future, and sympathy all at once.

BY MID-NOVEMBER a drenching rain had pelted our little house for five straight days. The world was settling down for winter with a never-ending wind that came from the northwest. I used to wonder if the trash that blew out of town during the summer was stored against a great wall north of Lavarre County somewhere, and when the wind changed in winter it might blow it all back into place. A chill in the air that day made everything seem odd. Christmassy. Little kids at school made paper cutouts of snowflakes and round, white-ball snowmen, even though the closest anyone I knew had ever gotten to snow was scraping the ice off the side of the cooler in Ricker's Grocery.

Thursday after school I finally gave up and washed my hair, which meant we got to turn on the grate heater until it was dry. I sat in the floor in front of it, brushing my hair, and wished I were darker and olive-skinned like Grandmother always told me her husband was. French, she would say, with that fine molding of features and that sultry skin and dark, heavy hair. Not Cajun, you understand, she would add, but what she would call "old country" French, always said with a wistful sigh. Myself, I was freckled and ivory-colored, and my hair went almost red in the summer and a tawny shade this side of clay other times. My mother's fault, Grandmother Summers would say with a sniff. "It's that Irish coming through." Like it was some congenital aberration.

The telephone rang, and soon Mother appeared at the door to our room. The look on her face was a mixture of distrust and anticipation.

"Girls, there's a boy on the telephone. I knew this day would come soon enough. A boy on the telephone for one of you."

We were both bowed over books, doing homework.

"Well, Mother, who?" Deely said.

"It's Danny Poquette." Deely brightened like someone had thrown the switch on a spotlight inside her. Mother said, "He wants to talk to Frosty."

"Oh," I said.

Deely looked away.

"Well, he's waiting," Mother said.

I walked toward the door and the telephone in the hall, and just as I passed Mother, she whispered, "You ask him to come have dessert with us after service Sunday night if you'd like."

Danny and I were in the same geometry class, and he had forgotten part of a formula. When I returned to the bedroom, Mother was sitting on my bed and Deely was on hers, looking blotchy-faced, her nose swollen from blowing it. "What's the matter?" I said.

"Oh, well," Mother said. "Is he coming for dessert?"

"I didn't ask. It was just a geometry problem."

Mother turned to Deely and spread her hands. "See there? He'll call. He probably meant to, and got nervous at the last minute and asked for Frosty instead. It was safer to make up something about geometry. It probably scares him to death to talk to you, honey. You know what I'll do?" Mother said, her posture suddenly ramrod straight, her expression radiant. "I'll call Mrs. Poquette and invite the whole family for dessert Sunday. We haven't had company in quite a while. That's what I'll do. And, Deely, you'll bake a pie. That way you'll show off your cooking. There's nothing like a flaky piecrust. That's what." She left in mid-thought, already laying out the whole evening in her mind, I was sure.

Deely sank back onto her pillow. "I don't feel well," she said.

I said, "Say, next time he calls like that, I'll just let you talk instead."

Deely had flunked out of geometry twice, because of her illness. She had been granted the option of taking an extra quarter of home economics instead of geometry. This, to my thinking, brought her cooking up to the level of her geometry skills.

After finishing my homework, I had chores to do. I was keeping everything caught up and then some—doing my penance, although I dared not use that word or risk my sentence being quadrupled. In our family there were layers of sin to which you could sink before you fell into total damnation. As long as you stayed a committed Southern Bab-diss, you were headed for heaven. Anyone who wasn't Bab-diss was Lost, with a capital L. There might be a few practicing Methodists admitted by the skin of their teeth. No one else was invited.

Mother came home the next day from the houses in town where she did ironing twice a week, with a new bra for me. It was bought from the dime store and presented in a brown paper bag as if it were a gift. It was, I knew, a token of my atonement. My siege was over. So the Sunday before Thanksgiving, freed of their presence, I sat through Sunday school between Deely and Raylene on one side and Maggy and Neomadel on the other—the five of us in our best clothes looking like charms on a bracelet. Marty Haliburton was elected chairman of the Youth for Home Club and got his ribbon that day. He talked about how he wanted everyone to join in taking care of old folks in town. Then we had Bible study and a closing song. When we were dismissed, I headed over toward Missionary Way to see if anything was left.

Halfway there I stopped in my tracks, stricken. The smell of wet ash clung to the Sunday-morning air. But the familiar voices calling out "Come on, Jesus," and "Hallelujah, Lord," following Brother Swan, still drifted across the meadow. They were all out in the field. I turned, fran-tic that someone might have seen me, and ran.

There was a time, in the beginning, when we could have put the fire out. It was hard to start, first of all. We had to start it again and again, and it would sure have been easier to give up. Marty dribbled the gas out slow, and gradually the old wood soaked it in, and up it went.

Retracing my steps, I opened the vestibule door at Siloam Springs church and stepped inside. Sweat drizzled down the middle of my back. My head swam. I backed out and closed the door just as my stomach lurched, and my breakfast hit a nearly leafless rosebush. A few minutes later I made my way as quietly as possible to the pew where Mother and Daddy sat, singing "Trust and Obey."

"Mother," I whispered, "I'm vomiting. I'm going home to lie down."

Impatience showed on her face, quickly replaced with concern. "You do look ill. Do you want me to come with you?"

"If you want to. I think I'll just walk real slow."

"Delia is singing a duet this morning with Sister Miner. I can't miss it."

Delia's singing could make an alley cat's teeth stand on edge, but I knew I'd best sound sincerely apologetic. "I hate to miss it, too. I'm going to be sick again," I said, and headed for the door. I waited several minutes. She did not follow.

It took me nearly twenty minutes to get home, and by then I felt a little better. I drank some water and stripped down to my slip, lying on my bed, hoping this feeling in my insides—like I'd drunk something from the bottom of the bayou—would leave me.

In a little while I got down on my knees, intending to pray, but started crying. I meant to run away from home Halloween night. But I'd gotten scared. Tired. Something. Chickened out. I got back on the bed and stared up at the ceiling, wondering just exactly how stained and blackened my soul really was. I had a feeling God was sitting just on the other side, above the mildew-stained white planks, shaking His head and saying, "Nevertheless, Frosty."

The first week of December, Deely drove herself to school, so Opalrae suddenly took it upon herself to walk home with me and the kids. We all paused at the window of the dime store and automatically shaded our eyes with our hands like we were watching a penny arcade show.

"Take a look at that baseball glove, Brueller," Marty said. "It's just waiting for my folks to buy it for me. What a beaut."

Coby obediently peered in and whistled two notes. "When'd they put that in there?"

"There's a set of sixteen colored pencils there I want for Christmas," Opalrae said. "I asked Mother and Daddy for them." I was still annoyed with her for including herself in our gang, like she didn't have her own friends. I wished she'd go on home.

I had a strange feeling someone was standing behind us; seconds later I heard a man clear his throat. "I'd like to have a few words with you all, if you've got the time."

It was Sheriff Moultrie. I felt some kind of weight go from the back of my head to my stomach, like the sinking of a rock in a well. The boys stuffed their hands in their pockets, looking innocent as newborn lambs. I lost all my manners. "What for?"

Neomadel stared, her mouth open, her face blushed magenta shades. Her elbow caught me in the side. Garnelle giggled and hid her face behind her books.

"Nothing particularly official, kids. Yet, that is. I just know sometimes the youngsters in town got their ear to the ground better than the grown-ups, so you might have heard. Wondered if you all knew the Missionary church burnt down?"

"The nigger church?" Marty said. "Well, I'll swan." He hooked his thumbs into his suspenders and wrinkled his forehead, shaking his head like he was deep in surprised thought.

I grasped my history book to my chest. "No," I said. "Well, I'd heard. But I didn't know it for sure. We've got to get along, Opalrae. Mother's waiting on us. Bye, y'all. Bye-bye." I tugged on my sister's arm and hurried down the road.

Suddenly a wide shadow joined ours, moving ahead of us on the dirt road. " 'Scuse me, ladies," the sheriff said. "I know you're in a hurry, so I'll walk with you a bit if y'all don't mind. Miss Frosty? You said you heard about the fire. Who from?"

"Oh, you know how people talk," I said. "I don't remember exactly." I picked up my pace.

Sheriff Moultrie nodded slowly but kept up with us effortlessly, scratching at his head under his hat brim. "How 'bout you?" he said to Opalrae.

"No, sir. I don't know anything," she said. Then she blurted out, "Frosty had some smoky clothes she was washing out. She mighta walked right by it and didn't notice."

I stared at her for three seconds before I realized my mouth was open. "Well, that was from the Halloween bonfire, s-silly. That's all."

"I heard from Mizz Fielding that her girl was at a bonfire. I forget where she said it was at," he said. "Y'all remember where?"

I said, "Um, no, sir, not really. It was pretty dark. We just went along where the mill had this pile of trash. We lit . . . trash." I could spill the whole thing right now. Me and the kids would be on the chain gang by morning doing ninety-nine to life. The weight in my stomach made me lean forward as I walked.

"Don't know what road it was near?"

I guess even on the chain gang the kids would all blame me. A sound caught in my throat, and I coughed softly. "No, sir. We went through some trees. Kind of, off over toward the mill road somewhere."

"I see. Seems like someone said it mighta been down around the short-spur tracks."

"Oh. Well, maybe it was. I forget," I said.

" 'Cause I didn't find any cinders near the tracks." He hitched up his pants at the waist. "Well, you kids hear anything about it, y'all let me know, awright? Hope this weather breaks and we get some rain. Cool down a little so it'll seem like it's Christmas." As he strolled away from us, he began flipping the chain he carried the courthouse keys on, around in a circle in the air. All the links on the chain made gray wheels before him. Wheels within wheels.

Opalrae and I hurried off toward our house. I'd done it. Gotten away with it without having to tell on my best friends or go to prison or anything. And I didn't even have to lie exactly, just forget about it.

Everybody forgets now and then. It's over. Soon forgotten. Just an old shack anyway.

When we were a ways down the road, I said to Opalrae, "What did you have to say that for about my clothes? Mother'd beat the living daylights out of you for talking about laundry to the sheriff. You better not mention it to her what you said."

"Well, it was the truth. Ain't we supposed to tell the truth?"

"It doesn't mean you just blab everything you know. You *don't* talk about underwear with a strange man. Mother'd brain you if she knew." My heart thudded—hollow—under my ribs.

She smiled and swung her books by the strap they were bound with. "I never mentioned underwear. And he wasn't strange, he's the sheriff. So were you-all at the bonfire for real?"

"Sure. I just forget where it was, is all."

THIS YEAR I've been working two afternoons a week at the post office, and on Saturdays I clean house for Mrs. Tucker and Mrs. Fielding, Garnelle's mother. Garnelle is always gone Saturday mornings when I'm there; she takes piano lessons from Miss Breckenridge, who quit teaching school to marry Mr. Phipps from the sawmill. Marty is after me to add Mrs. Beaudrin to the list without being paid, on account of the Youth Club he's doing. That morning Mother had gone to help with the flower committee doing something up at church for the Azalea Festival. So when I heard Central put through our ring on the party line, I picked it up at the Fieldings' house, pushing my hair away from my ear. As I was about to say hello, I heard Mother's voice say it instead. Grandmother Summers's unmistakably nasal voice was on the other end. "Where are you at? You're late." I frowned, putting my hand over the mouthpiece.

"I've got another headache. You'll have to do the flowers without me this time," Mother said.

"You just get yourself down here. We're waiting on you."

"I'm not dressed." Mother sounded upset.

"Well, if you take too long, I just might have time to do some rem-

37

iniscing here. I'm sure these ladies would love to hear about how you came to be married into this family."

"You've been threatening that for twenty years. I've got a terrible headache. I'm not dressed."

"Get your lazy self down here. You planning to try my patience?"

"No. I'll be there in ten minutes." I'd never heard Mother so resigned.

I grew up in a land and with a people peppered with injustice, hard work, shattered dreams. When that slow crucifixion of the human spirit called the Depression came, I was a child, but even then I saw something discernible change in my daddy's manner. He was not the same man when I was eighteen as he was when I was eight. Mother had always seemed the same to me, always on the alert, ready to strike, never this meek, submissive voice on the phone.

I had always known there was bad blood between my mother and Daddy's mother, but I'd always thought Grandmother Summers was the innocent victim of Mother's bile. This was the first time I'd had a reason to suspect it might not be so. I hung up the phone earpiece very gently, trying to remember every word they'd just said.

"Frosty, was that for you?" Mrs. Fielding called. "Have you changed those sheets yet?"

SATURDAY AFTERNOON I went to the movie show as usual. It cost a whole dime. I always did everything I could to make sure I had a dime, but I never wasted money on popcorn or lemonade, no matter how good it smelled. If I had an extra dime or two, it went into my Honey Doll for my eventual flight out of here.

That afternoon's double feature was an all-western show. After the first feature there were two MovieTone newsreels and a cartoon. Even the cartoon was about Nazis. All the newsreels anymore were about Germans attacking somebody new. The second feature was a Roy Rogers western, with real stars in it instead of just anybody who owned a ten-gallon hat. I would have stayed to watch them again, but Deely was outside honking the horn of her new car, making a big scene.

Maybe it seems odd that in a family as dyed-in-the-wool Baptist as ours, Deely and I were allowed to see movie shows. That was on account of the polio, too. The year Deely had the polio changed our entire world. She was too sick and weak to play, too weary even to read. It was the doctor's suggestion that she be taken to a movie show now and then for a diversion. Deely could not, by some Southern holy commandment, go alone; Mother would rather have shown up downtown in her house shoes, and Daddy had to earn a living. So I was ordered to accompany her.

Now that she could drive and find other ways to amuse herself, I got to go on my own. The pictures were my other life. If only for a few minutes, to be someone else, living a life far removed from Sabine. They were the only time I felt and saw and thought everything.

Deely was jerking the gearshift lever around this way and that, her skinny knuckles white.

"Hey, are you ready?" I said.

"I'm just waiting on you. Hurry up or I'll leave you here." Deely said. She fidgeted the lever back into the center of its track.

"What in heaven's name have you got on?"

"Don't shut the door so hard. You'll break the window."

"Sorry, I thought it was isinglass. So, what's with the chapeau, Deely?"

"Drivers wear these."

"They do?"

"In France."

"How much driving did you do in France?"

"You should go on vaudeville, honest. First I have to set the choke. I have to set the choke and put down the clutch and adjust the gear lever." The little auto sputtered and shook, then settled into a steady rumbling. "So how was the picture?" Delia said.

"Just fine," I said.

"What was it about?"

"Cowboys and Indians. Same old stuff."

I sighed. Silence was my solace, too. Deely couldn't stand a moment not filled with conversation. As we pulled into the worn pathway that led to the place next to the well where Deely parked her car, a grinding started in the back of my head. Deely made a big commotion of putting on the parking brake and turning off the motor. As she was stepping out, the wind spun Deely's French driving hat from her head. I sat in the car, watching her run, arms outstretched, as the chapeau rolled like a coin toward the backyard.

Our town is always clean-swept-looking, but it isn't because people are so tidy, it's just the wind that never quits. When it's really hot in the summer, the wind sucks the life out of you. It was said by some that if a person was to be outside in that summer wind—on those scorching days when the dogs hide in any speck of shade there is and the only things moving are mosquitoes and seven-year locusts—and take a deep breath of that wind facing into it, letting it out started something in your lungs so the air would keep on blowing out until you strangled and died.

The house we had lived in ever since we moved into Sabine had never been painted. Seeing as it was so close to the tracks, I used to think it had been something romantic in the olden days, like a depot where people stepped off to parts unknown. But it was only a tiny house, always a house. Always a poor person's house. A half-dovetail, double-pen log house, it had been built with timbers thrown out from the mill as too short for building and too bent for railroad ties. The ground falls off steep in back, so the pilings at the front are two feet high, but off the back the porch is nearly five feet up in the air. When we were very young, the nine crooked and splintering steps were my playground to jump or fall from or to cause us to spend hours upon hours in ladylike promenade. We were southern ladies just arriving at a ball, a cotillion, or simply dressed in our antebellum splendor with skirts spreading like broad silken bells. I truly thought that to be a southern belle meant to wear the bell-shaped dresses where your legs became a clapper and the gown swung around you prettily as you walked up and down stairs.

On those steps long ago Deely and I imagined ourselves dressed in finery, descending to the soft clink of delicate Parisian china touched by fine-polished silver, in a dining room of unsurpassed elegance. We sometimes let Opalrae be our train bearer or some other lackey. On nine rickety stairs we were ladies of the manse, admired throughout the county for style, glamour, charm, beauty, and renowned parties at which we entertained the cream of society, including no person, living or dead, who had ever resided in Sabine. No, these were kings of France and Spain—and when Deely found out something about a country called Switzerland, of course the king of Switz had to come, too. We spent the soirées constantly dashing up those nine red-and-gold-carpeted steps in our voluminous gowns to make sure the guards in blue satin uniforms at the doors didn't allow any of the wrong sort of people in. Other residents of Sabine, who were never invited to the parties, crowded humbly at our draperied windows to peer in at the grandeur; with a snap of our fingers we sent them away, only to find them meekly applying at the kitchen door for table scraps or a job shoeing our famous riding ponies. Of course we refused. We were far too grand to bother with that kind of person.

In our scruffy little downtown theater, somewhere among twenty rows of folding opera seats just like at church, all kinds of pageantry unfolded before our eyes. I snuck in to see *Gone With the Wind* when it came to town and saw it nine more times, sometimes paying admission. Never mind the conniving heroine or the harsh tale of marriage gone bad—that was not its appeal to me. It was the beautiful clothes, the balls, and the staircases that made that story mine. I had a staircase. I was already partway there.

There was a time, for a couple of years, when I waited for my music to start, when the reels of my life would start turning, accompanied by the theme song that should be mine. I wasn't sure what it would sound like, but I felt positive I would know it. Lately, though, I figured the only sound my life would ever have was the whistle at the mill and the vibration of the log train on the floorboards of our house.

"Hey!" Deely yelled. She was standing between the car and the house, red-faced, her hat in her hands. "Are you daydreaming again? Aren't you getting out?"

"Yes, ma'am," I said numbly, and stepped out in front of our house on tufted grass, gone to seed, that will never make a lawn.

The Sunday afternoon of the impending company dessert, Deely took another bath for at least two hours. It was going on four o'clock before she went into the kitchen to start her pie baking for that evening. I was reading my Western Civ book, sprawled across my bed, taking notes for my senior paper. I wrote the date in block letters at the left margin of my notebook, December 7, 1941. I had just gotten to the list of Caesars and was trying to sort out the Augustuses from the Juliuses when Deely came in, her face pale, a hand over her eyes.

She sat at the edge of her bed. "My bathwater was too hot. I think I'm going to faint."

"Lie down," I said.

"Mother!" she called.

Mother came running after her. "Delia," she said. "Delia?"

"It's that weakness that comes over me. I'm just feeble, that's all. I'll never be able to get married or—or anything."

"Oh, forever more! Why, sure you will," Mother said. "Of course you will. You'll get stronger and stronger. You'll see."

Caligula and Constantine. *Now, there's a pair of bookends,* I thought. That's what I'd do my senior paper on, comparing those two. I started putting some notes on the margin of my book, about things that I might want to include. I had to get this read before the Gene Autry show came on the radio. There aren't many programs I tried hard not to miss, but that was one.

The only other one was even more special, but hard to plan. That was a Fireside Chat. President Roosevelt has been president all my life—for all time, as far as I was concerned. I always found a way to stay up for a Fireside Chat. I imagined the president sitting here in our front room, in the best chair, with a cup of coffee—maybe the pale green china cup with the white rim—and talking about everything in the world with us. I'd offer up the single silver spoon that comprised most of the hope in my hope chest for him to stir in the sugar we'd offer freely, even if we had to save up a month of stamps for it. My father, who art in Washington, blessed be thy name.

I knew what was brewing around me without even watching the scene. Vivien Leigh had nothing to worry about, but this one was spectacular: Deely's Thoroughly Wretched Melodrama. All the play lacked were some rolling diminished chords from a wheezy organ like the one our Aunt Uvalia played at the Golden Melodia Theater in Toullange. All Deely needed was a torn bodice and black charcoal circles around her eyes.

"Frosty," Mother said, "you're so quick at it, why don't you help your sister out and whip up a pie? It's getting late, and it'll taste so good. I'll peel some apples for you, and we'll have it out in jig time."

I puffed out my cheeks. Piecrust or Caligula. What a choice. Old Caligula would be waiting here in these pages, shooting flaming arrows into the crowd at the Colosseum, while I made my sister's piecrust in a bid for redemption.

I had the pie in the oven in about thirty minutes, held up only by the peeling of the apples. I showed Mother how I could carve a peel in one piece from an entire apple, and we got to tasting a couple of them, and we started trying to see who could make the longest strip of apple peel without breaking it. Mother won that one, easy. That was redemption, too. Of a different sort. I never knew if I really could peel an apple better or faster than she did, but what counted in that contest was something far less tangible than winning.

The pie hadn't even started to smell good yet when Deely came into the room and dragged herself to a rush chair. "I'm feeling better now," she said.

I looked at the clock. I'd missed Gene Autry. I pictured Deely in a rowboat down at Little Moss Bayou near Magnolia Springs, shrouded in curtains of Spanish moss. Fainted away, posed as only she could do, in a little canoe. After a while she would get tired of waiting to be rescued and sit up, maybe even look for a paddle. And that was when a big old gator . . .

There was a thundering bang on the front door, so hard the glass rattled in the window over the kitchen sink. The door opened before anyone could get to it—my father sitting on the divan just five or six feet away—and there were Junior Jasper and Coby Brueller standing in our doorway, looking as if they'd run the entire half mile from Coby's house to ours.

"No one can get through on the phones," Coby blurted out. "Me and Junior came to tell y'all."

"What's the meaning of this, young man?" said Daddy.

"Yes, sir," Junior said "Excuse us, sir, for—" He stopped, looking startled at his own effrontery. Young colored men did not address white adults without being asked a specific question.

"Mr. Summers, sorry, sir. But"—Coby paused and puffed—"y'all might want to put on your wireless. It's all over town. And I was going to call all the kids, but the phones are just busier than golly!"

By then we'd all gotten to the room, and we stared at Coby as if he'd lost his mind. Our phone hadn't rung, but the other lines had jangled nonstop. We owned a telephone by the grace of God and the will of the Dallas Telephone Exchange. In order to run lines across the country from Dallas to Baton Rouge and onward, Toullange, Kirbyville, and Sabine had to be crossed like clothespins on that line. Our aldermen ran on the issues of Rural Electrification and the Dallas Telephone Exchange. As long as your house was in a straight line with Baton Rouge, you qualified for the free phone. Junior looked at me for a split second, then focused on Daddy. His face was hard to read as stone.

"All over town?" Daddy said. "Not polio again? What is it, influenza?"

Coby caught his breath and swallowed. Junior looked at the floor, ducking his head. Coby said, "No, sir. It's *war*. The president and Congress have declared war. I was listening to the radio, and I was sittin' real close because you can't hear through the static from this blasted wind. Excuse me, this hard wind, sir. And they came right on, just as the show was starting, and said, 'We interrupt this program,' just like that. Right on the Gene Autry program. Man, oh, man!"

We stood in a circle like confused children. Mother reacted first. "It's not time for *Fireside*. They never announced it."

Junior sniffed. "War, ma'am. There's war, sure enough. The Japs have bombed us. Don't y'all have your radio playing? Pearl Harbor is blown to smithereens and back, and all our navy is sunk. All our sailors killed, ever' last one. Dead and drowned. Ever' last one. The Japs are coming this way. Gonna land on California soil, is what the news fellow said after it."

Coby broke in. "I'm gonna sign up. Me and all the gang. Found Junior here running to tell folks, too, and we're gonna go. Everybody. We're gonna whoop them Japs back to where they belong, that's what. That's what I was going to tell you-all. We're signing up first thing in the morning. Head straight west to stop 'em in their tracks." Then, like the wind they blew in on, Coby and Junior were out the door and leaped our rickety picket fence headed toward the road.

Daddy found a station that had a newsman on. He talked about the ships that sank, the lives lost. We watched the speaker screen like it was a mouth announcing the end of the world.

Americans, dead on the bottom of the ocean—murdered by enemies from a foreign land. Nazis on the East. Now Japanese on the West. America was going to die. All of us would be slaughtered. I had no idea how far Hawaii was from California, but I knew it was an island in the ocean, and islands are always off the coast of something. California, most likely. American ships were torpedoed somewhere between San Francisco and Hawaii, and the submarines and bombers were on their way. Congress was declaring war.

I thought of Hollywood. All the movie stars will die first. Then they'll come after us with hideous brutality, newsreel-worthy aggression, shooting flaming arrows into the crowds. But there will be no one to make newsreels of our dying, because all the moviemaking people will be dead first.

Deely and Mother started to cry. Tears were running down my face, but I didn't feel the clenching of crying. In the background the reporter's voice droned on. I could hear us all breathing, like terrified animals—listening and breathing. Daddy hung his head and put his hand over the back of his neck, like he did the day the doctor told us Deely had polio.

The potent air stirred by the reporter's voice gave way to bristly static, and after a while someone at the station said, "We now return you to your regularly scheduled broadcast." There was a lesser static before another voice chimed in: ". . . our Family Gospel Hour choir. Sing along with them, won't you?" When they got to the words "and the water and the blood, from thy wounded side which flowed," Daddy turned the radio off.

In the quiet the wind took up the last pitch I'd heard from the choir and moaned around the house with it, sweeping in, chilling me with the eerie harmony.

The wind-up kitchen timer racketed around in Mother's pocket, making us all jump.

"I'll go check it," I said, moving quickly. I burned my thumb on the rack and stood at the back door looking out, sucking on it and blowing it cool.

How strange Gordon felt to have returned to the old way as simply as that. One Blessingway ceremony, and it was as if he'd never left to go to the white school. It was good to be in his mother's house once more. He'd set so many things aside. And now he had to leave again, but it felt different. His mother would be sad for now, but he would send money from the Marines to her, and she would have plenty of food from then on. She would be proud, too. Mothers really never understood war. They always wanted you to come home. He smiled.

In the shade cast by the two-room wooden house, Gordon sat on a milk crate and played with one of Na'atlo'ii's dogs. The dog was mostly black, lithe and quick, with long hair that made him look like more dog than he was. Gordon held out a piece of meat from the lunch stew.

"Hey," a young woman's voice said behind him, "some people are going to spoil other people's dogs, make them not work anymore." Her eyes twinkled when she spoke.

"A dog ought to be paid for working so hard. There's not much left of that dog, just a lot of hair." He grinned as he said it.

"Maybe someone can borrow it."

"The hair?" The dog was licking his fingers thoroughly.

She laughed. Gordon turned to see her face. Na'atlo'ii had done her hair in a loose bob, the way all the girls at the white school wore it. "You're a little behind in growing out your hair, Hashke," she said. "Ask that dog. Maybe he'll let you have some." She had on a gathered skirt but wore her school blouse over it, tucked in loosely. She was his sister's best friend from school.

"Maybe he wants to come along himself," Gordon said. "Join the Marines. See the world."

"He seen the world. He likes it fine here." She whistled, and the dog sat.

"Anybody thinking about waiting for me to come back?" he said.

"P-ss-sh," she said with a wave of her hand. "All the boys are going. Nothing to do but sewing. Nobody getting married anytime soon I know of."

He nodded. She bowed her head until her hair fell forward, then she looked through it to his face and smiled. He grinned, too. He wiped his wet fingers on his pants. "Better feed this dog pretty good."

Na'atlo'ii nodded.

Delia has had her eyes on Danny Poquette ever since we moved here. Her many and varied plans to trap him into proposing to her took on a frenzied pace by our senior year in high school, so great was her fear of being labeled an old maid. Thank goodness there were other boys around, or I would have seriously considered turning Catholic and becoming a nun, but the other boys were older than me and had already graduated. Garnelle's brother, Wilbur, for instance. I kept hoping he'd be around when I was cleaning Mrs. Fielding's house, or that if I were really nice to Garnelle she'd pass me a note from him like I'm doing for her and Coby. Now that he's gone to fight the Nazis, I feel extra lonesome for him.

Danny Poquette came to our house that evening after church, along with a bunch of the kids. More than we'd ever had—ever expected— scrunched together in our tiny front room like it was suddenly all right to associate with us because of the war. Sunday nights we always went to someone else's house. We talked of nothing but the war until we were drained. Eventually Maggy asked, "What shall we sing tonight?"

Garnelle Fielding said, "My brother joined the army three weeks ago. He's already in boot camp, and his unit is going to the front. He isn't allowed to say where. So I'd like to play something for him." She played a piece I'd heard her practice before, some little étude or something by Chopin, ethereal and doleful. She did a pretty good job of it until the last couple of bars, when she dropped her face into her fists and shook all over, quietly.

"Garnelle," said Coby, "old Wilbur is a scrapper, and he's smarter than any Kraut alive. Play something happy. Don't be thinking sad stuff. There's nothing to be sad about. Now that America is really throwing her hat in the ring, you know, it's all over but the cheering."

Farrell Bandy pulled Mother's Baptist hymnal from the top dust runner over the upright piano and opened it. "These aren't hard," he said. "Give it a shot."

All the kids gathered around as Garnelle clumsily banged out a couple of songs. Pretty soon they were singing so badly that the gloom lifted. Someone laughed right out loud as Farrell was trying to sing harmony on "When the Roll Is Called Up Yonder." Danny had been sitting on the divan near where I was standing. I excused myself between verses to make some more coffee. He offered to help, but I told him, "The kids need you. Sing with Farrell, or we'll have to choke him."

When I was in the kitchen, Mother leaned over to me and said, "How is it going?" as if she were a spy on a mission.

I put a blank look on my face and said, "Fine, I suppose."

"Well," she whispered, "that Danny. He's kind of flirting with you."

"Yes. I guess he is."

"Say 'suppose.' "

"I suppose he is."

"Well, you know, honey, I know it's hard to not get your feelings hurt. And you and Delia are at that vulnerable age. But he is closer to Delia's age than yours, and . . . and all that."

"And all what, Mother?"

"It's just that he might be trying to go through you to get to Delia. You know . . . to make friends with her little sister in hopes that she'll notice him. It's just more normal for the older sister to marry first. And she's his age. It makes sense he'd be wanting to date her."

I shrugged. As if you could not just date somebody or go to a movie without its meaning something eternal. "Well, I don't think he's flirting. Besides"—I banged the percolator's grounds into the crock we kept under the sink to hold wet trash—"I don't care."

"Well, I thought you were friends."

"We are, Mother. We've known him since we first moved here. If he wants to go out with Deely, he should just ask her."

"That's just not the way it's done. Some people take their time. Lead into things more carefully. Now, be sure to turn all the cup handles away from you as you fill." Mother read *Crosspoint's Etiquette* at least as often as the Bible, mindful of the day when we would entertain at lavish dinner parties as young wives.

"Well," I said, running the water until it came out clear and turning it over the open pot's mouth, "I'll just tell him to ask her out."

"You can't do that. Honestly, Frosty, I don't know how you ever expect to get married. The way you act. Like you haven't got a brain in your head sometimes." She gave me one of her melting stares, like I was the stupidest thing that ever walked on earth. She huffed toward the door, set her face in her company smile, and went through it.

The next day President Roosevelt himself talked to me through the screen in our radio. ". . . the United States of America was suddenly and deliberately attacked . . ." At ten the next night he spoke for over an hour. I didn't sleep until after the clock chimed one in the morning. It rang, *War.* I believed somewhere in my imagination that President Roosevelt was my true father, sending me letters from home during those Fireside Chats; that I was some poor wandering soul, and he was doing all he could do to send me his concern from afar, through the round, cloth-covered hole in the wireless radio. Just weeks ago he'd warned us about Hitler and what Hitler was doing to the poor English people. Now that father was rising up from the fireside easy chair, where I usually sat basking in love at his feet, speaking out in righteous anger like a commanding wrathful God striking at the barbarous Philistines.

It was only five days until Christmas vacation, but we didn't do much all week except the same thing the second-graders did: find Hawaii on a map and every day locate it again like we were surprised it was still there. I used my thumb to place off inches between Pearl Harbor and California, and Pearl Harbor and Japan, even though we each had to look it up in the atlas and get the real distance. I kept hearing President Roosevelt's words. *Somewhere between Hawaii and San Francisco, California.*

Teachers brought their wireless radios right into the classrooms, and no one kept up with any schedules. I left my homework half done in my notebook, and no one asked for it. Everything was suspended until after vacation.

Sometimes at night I cried into my pillow. Deely didn't hear me crying, or if she did, she didn't ask. When I did sleep, I dreamed about Japanese soldiers in Roman chariots. They drove in circles, shooting flaming arrows into everyone I knew, their audience held spellbound in a church where each pew had chains beneath it, into which the worshipers had willingly fixed themselves. First as part of the audience, then in the role of bearer of the flaming arrows, I searched the stands for a merciful or forgiving face. There were people I'd known all my life— my family, my neighbors—but there was no sentiment or connection between them and myself. Just anger or fear, first on my part, then theirs. I woke sweating, my teeth chattering, feeling feverish.

After the fourth night in a row of that dream, I made up my mind to quit sleeping. I listened to the wind, moaning through the chinks in the house. At a certain bowed place at the top of the wall next to my bed, sand from the dirt roads and sand hills west of our end of town would periodically collect, forced there by the never-ending, thickly moving air. When the little pile reached the point where its own weight and bulk overwhelmed its natural want to stay put, it would dribble right down the wall, a little sandfall, and make a new pile of itself on the floor. I reached over and felt the side of the bed, adjusting the sheets away from the possibility of sand.

What would happen if bombs fell here, if soldiers lined us up in the streets and marched us away? Wasn't that kind of judgment reserved for evil places like Sodom and Gomorrah? Sabine, at least on the face of it, was a place where people helped each other out in times of trouble. Didn't the whole town show up and help paint the Fieldings' house just a couple of years ago? And when a hurricane killed sixteen people in Kirbyville the summer before, every store owner in town opened his doors to folks, free.

Sabine was that kind of place. Of course, Sabine was also a place where Negroes better be on their side of town most of the time and not show a face on our side after sundown, a town on whose only lighted street—straight through clear from Dallas and Toullange, onward to Kirbyville, eventually to Lafayette, Louisiana—were posted signs warning NIGGER! DON'T LET THE SUN GO DOWN ON YOU IN THIS TOWN! The threat was lettered over a big, ugly, cartoon Negro face through which someone had done target practice, so the eyes on the sign were hollow and the mouth was open forever in a silent, jagged metal shriek.

I waited for the sandfall. Fearful of Japanese banging at the door and not wanting to be caught blind in the dark, Mother had defied the blackout ordinance and left the light on in the hallway near the picture of the angel and the lost children. The wind howled around the house. It was turning into a real storm, not just the normal sound. I sat up in bed, leaning against the wall, watching the blackout blanket breathing against the windowpane in time with the changing pitch of the wind. I reached under my pillow and pulled out my battered rag doll. Now and then, out of the sighs and moans, I heard a wisp of "Have Thine Own Way, Lord." I held Honey Doll to my cheek. "You're going to take me out of here, aren't you?" I whispered to her. "You'll let me know when it's time to go. I know you will. I know you will." Years ago I found a dime under some leaves next to a fence post and put it in my pocket, and I dreamed all day long of the places it could take me. Eventually, in search of a better hiding place for my wealth, I found a little frayed spot on the hip of my rag doll and pushed dimes and nickels and pennies into her leg. I called her my Honey Doll. The rhyme reminded me of money.

My yearning for escape had begun before we came here, during the boxcar days. It came back to me tonight as clearly as if it had just happened. Maybe because I was scared down to my core—fraught with the feeling that something large had already been lost, no matter what the eventual outcome of the war. I reached toward my memory with my thoughts, afraid to touch it because I knew it was there and as alive as a fresh burn. I did touch it, from time to time—like pressing a sore finger—just for the pain of it.

That year, when Palm Sunday came, along with her polio Deely took the pneumonia. Mother came and got me out of school, and she and I and Deely and Opalrae rode in the backseat of the visiting nurse's jalopy all the way to Kirbyville, to the hospital. Opalrae bawled the whole time and wet her pants, which got my legs wet. Daddy came and got me and Opalrae, but Mother stayed at the hospital with Deely. I mumbled, scared. Daddy said, "Hush up. The Lord giveth and the Lord taketh away. If you've got something to say, it better be in a prayer."

A couple of days later Mother came home and sewed Deely a new Easter dress. All the while she sewed, she cried. Then she folded that dress and put it in a box and slid it under my bed. Then she and Daddy, the both of them, said they were going to go bring Deely home for good, so while they were gone, Opalrae and I cried, because to us that sounded like she was dead. When they brought her in, she wasn't dead at all, but she was put right in bed nevertheless, and we weren't allowed to talk to her, only to smile at her and bring her things.

Back then, I had a small dog that followed me everywhere. Daisy didn't know about Deely; she didn't know to feel sorry anyone was sick. Daisy was bulging with puppies so bad her teats dragged on the floor. The next morning I went to school for the last day before Easter vacation. I remember the class stopped to have a prayer for Delia Summers right after the morning bell. When I got home, Mother was so mad she was pounding the whole tomato garden she'd just planted into a green mush on the ground. Deely was safe in bed, pale, but sitting up, looking at some paper dolls one of the neighbors had brought her. The box under my bed was gone. Deely's new flowered dress was gone. Daisy was gone.

Mother said she'd run away. I called that dog for days, looking far into the woods past every boundary I was supposed to stick to, calling her name. Daddy told me sometimes a dog will go off to have puppies and not come back. I cried for hours at school and called that dog until I couldn't even eat, until on Easter Day, Mother pointed her finger at me. "You should be thankful your sister is going to live, instead of moping over a worthless mutt. Now, eat your dinner, or I'll hold your jaws open and shove it in. I won't have another child sick from not eating." Then she pinched my cheeks together and jammed a handful of peas in my mouth and held her hand over my face until I gagged.

I don't remember getting into bed, but that's where I woke up the next morning. When I was fully awake, without making a sound I crawled under the springs, curling as far out of sight as I could get against the dirty floorboards, watching sunlight from the window as it cast a long yellow mark under the bed that moved slowly toward the door. It touched a fresh scrape mark that curved to the leg of the bed and a tiny, dime-size, crooked dot of blood. I didn't ask Mother again where my dog went.

All these memories were sand. Toward the very small hours of the night the sand fell from the crooked timber over my head, dribbling down the wall next to my elbow. It caught the sleeve of my pajamas, and I shook it off as fiercely as if it had been an insect.

To stay awake, I made plans. I could switch my Home Economics class to Nursing; then I could go in the army, the Women's Army Auxiliary. Maybe I'd save somebody's life or something, and he'd fall in love with me and propose marriage, and I'd never come back here as long as I lived. Maybe if I was a nurse, if I saved lots of soldiers, someday President Roosevelt would be just stopping by, checking up on the troops, and happen to see me and say, "Well done, thou good and faithful servant, and why don't you come live in the White House? Eleanor and I would love to have you stay just as long as you like. Make yourself at home."

Two days before Christmas, Sheriff Moultrie finally found it necessary to don the only coat he owned and pinned his badge to the outside of the old woolen overcoat. The ring of men who normally occupied the steps and porch of the courthouse had moved with their checker games and dominoes to the Masonic Lodge's front parlor. Moultrie liked the smell of the lodge. Old tobacco and whiskey and something buttery and stale: his daddy had earned his degrees in that lodge, so the fragrance reminded him of his daddy, the feeling of holding on to rough overalls, running beside long legs, was still imprinted in his hands and feet.

"Well, if it ain't Mitchell Haliburton," Moultrie said, slapping hands as they shook. "Ain't seen you in a while. What're we drinking, boys? I'm off duty."

Someone said, "Well, pass that man a beer."

Moultrie accepted the glass and drank carefully, taking his time so that it looked like a good, hearty swallow. He licked the foam from his lip. "Don't y'all know it's a sacrilege to drink beer in the Masonic Hall? Nobody but some backwater swamp rats would allow anything less than good twelve-year-old Kentucky through these doors." The men laughed.

Someone said, "This building has been temporarily reassigned due to circumstances beyond our control," and laughed.

Moultrie continued, "Say, then, you're just the boys I need to talk to. I'd like to know if there've been any meetings in the last few months. Any . . . well, activities you might call obvious."

The men looked uncomfortably from one to another. Mitch Haliburton said, "Meetings, that's all. We keep asking you to join in, Moultrie. Ain't it about time you did?"

Moultrie smiled. "Well, my angel is right particular about what happens with her sheets."

The men laughed again. Haliburton said, "What you gettin' at, Sheriff?"

"Just wanted to know who lit the Missionary Way Tabernacle. After all, that's the last place you'd find any threat from those people. Those folks don't mean no harm. And someone went and . . ."

"Well, sir, it wasn't us," the men all said. "No, nope."

"That the gospel?" Moultrie said, mulling it over. "I didn't really think so. Didn't have the feel of Klan business. You boys got any ideas who?"

Their heads wagged in silence. Knowing these men all his life, Moultrie had seen plenty of Klan arsons, and they didn't have the feel of this one at all. He left out telling them about the murder. But with a smile and a wave of his hand he bid them Merry Christmas and set his half-full glass on the table by the door. "Y'all get wind of anything, you'll pass it along?"

"Sure enough. Merry Christmas, Sheriff," they called.

Marty had wrangled a couple of the kids over to Mrs. Beaudrin's to help out one afternoon. Only Neomadel and I showed up. Neomadel waved at him from the road. I think she's too flirty, particularly with Marty. He was out in the yard. He leaned the scythe he'd been using to cut Mrs. Beaudrin's grass against the rail on the porch. She'd set a pitcher of water on a wicker table, and condensation had made a deep ring around it. He called us over and said we girls were to do the dishes. Then he lifted the glass of water to drink. It was decidedly grimy. I pushed open the screen door. "Miz Beaudrin?" Marty called. We could see her nodding on the rocking chair.

When I saw through to the kitchen, I made a face at Neomadel. The place was piled with several weeks' worth of dirty dishes. "Now, Frosty," she said, "be nice."

I didn't want to be nice. I didn't want to do someone else's dishes who thought she was too good to speak to me or my mother and sister at Women's Missionary Union meetings. "Marty," I said, "where are the other kids?"

"No one else could make it. It's up to you girls to step up to the call." He patted Neomadel's arm. She grinned. Then he picked up the scythe and returned to the yard.

Mrs. Beaudrin woke up after we got her kitchen cleaned. She offered to pay us each a dime; I held out my hand, but Neomadel slapped it down, saying we were doing it for the Lord.

BEFORE CHRISTMAS CAME, all the boys in high school had discovered they couldn't just leave and go off to fight the war; they'd have to finish up and graduate first. There were age limits to get in the service, no matter how good a shot you were. Lying about it was out of the question, too, since all of the parents in town got together and swore to tattle on any of their children that tried it. The boys all wanted to load in a pickup truck and start taking potshots at attacking Japanese. To soothe their disappointment, on Christmas Eve they drove around the county doing Rebel yells all night long, shooting at the moon.

The only one stupid enough to go lying to the army recruiter was Beans. Beans Bandy's real name was Jarrell; he was a twin with Farrell, although they were as unalike as any two brothers ever thought about being. Especially after Beans's hunting accident four years ago. Mostly Jarrell changed on the inside of his head, but after a while his very face began to look different from his brother's.

According to Coby, he and Beans were hunting with Farrell and his daddy, Bart Bandy. Beans found this set of calling antlers and was marching along whacking them like a drummer when he spotted his brother and daddy through the trees. Coby had both their rifles and saw Mr. Bandy, too. Beans put the antlers on either side of his head and said, "Watch me trick 'em with this." He leaned out from behind a tree once, then again, far enough to see around it with his eyes.

Coby heard a rifle report. The usual *pe-whing* had a stutter in it, a sort of thud. Beans fell to the ground. Coby yelled, "Mr. Bandy! Beans is shot! Somebody shot Beans. God Almighty, Beans is shot in the head! Mr. Bandy!" Bart Bandy came running, rifle still hot, a whiff of smoke streaming from the barrel.

The upshot of it was that Beans lived. A doctor in Shreveport made him a piece of skull out of a silver dollar flattened out with a hammer. His dad was awful sorry and felt real guilty, but by the time Beans was up and around again, it seemed he was going to be fine and there were no hard feelings. He and Farrell and the rest of the Bandys all said Beans wasn't much different than before, just ate less and snored more. Having known Beans Bandy most of my life, I'd have guessed that there was nothing but bone in his head, but since they put in a plate, I'd say that bullet hit an air pocket in there and just bounced right out. Leastwise he got away with goofing off in class and never doing any homework, but nobody cared much. He'd probably just go on living at home and working at the lumber mill like everyone else here does. By the time he was a senior in Big Thicket High School, Beans had had a silver plate in his head for four years.

The boys collected tin cans and old pump handles and wire for the war. We saved cans and paper and had a big tub for grease that we took to a big drum kept in the back room at Ricker's Grocery, where everyone started bringing their old grease. What a smell that place took on.

WHEN SCHOOL STARTED back up after Christmas vacation, we all got a big shock. The Government and Economics teacher, Mr. Hicks, had gone and enlisted in the navy with a commission and everything. Everyone is required to take those classes before they graduate, and all of us who were seniors were counting on him to teach us for the last two quarters. Mr. Hicks was also the teacher for Western Civilizations, so both his classes were combined and held in the biggest classroom in the school, the room that had held the third-graders before Christmas. That meant everyone in the whole senior class was now in one room for one class, with only one chance of a grade instead of three. Those of us on thin ice grade-wise always hoped to dilute the stench of any particular score in a volume of others. Then again, I thought, if Mr. Hicks was gone, maybe we'd get excused from our senior papers for Western Civ.

By the time we settled into our seats, I saw standing at the front of the room a lady in a long, old-fashioned navy blue dress with a starched lace collar like I've seen on pictures of ladies during the Civil War. "Ladies and gentlemen," she began. The boys in the back of the room were whispering, and Beans was turned around in his seat making faces at anyone who'd look. The teacher walked down an aisle and without raising her voice said again, "Ladies and gentlemen, your attention, please." With the word "please," she whipped the blackboard pointer stick out from behind her back and whopped Beans across the shoulder with it so fast and snappy that it sang like a whip and didn't break.

"Ow!" Beans said, rubbing his shoulder. "What'd you do that for?"

"I will have your attention, young man. Perhaps if the term 'gentleman' does not apply to you, you may not have known I was addressing you. In this one instance that will be forgiven. In future, however, you may assume that when I ask for the class's attention, it does include you."

Her name was not Mrs. Fine. It was Dr. Fine. Or we might politely address her as Professor Fine, she said. My mouth dropped open. In a strangling kind of accent she told us in about three quick sentences how she and her husband had refugeed clear from London, England, on account of the bombing. Her two sons, who were both medical doctors, had stayed in England to care for wounded people. Her husband, Dr. Fine, had a specialty in some kind of tropical East African diseases, and even though he was retired he was needed at the little six-room hospital in Kirbyville because we were rampant with mosquito larvae and fungus. And she herself was a doctor, but not like we'd ever heard of before. A doctor of the philosophy of letters, she said, from Cambridge University by special grant.

Then she got down to business. First she arranged how she wanted us to sit, very obviously putting all the straight-A kids in the back of the room and the poorer students in front. That in itself had never been done in all my years in school. I was pretty much a straight-C student, averaging it out with a few D-pluses and a couple of C-minuses, and hung around the last two rows in every classroom for my entire life. Suddenly I was in the second row, behind Beans Bandy instead of in front of him. I could see the two big scars that made an upside-down Y on his head.

Then she dropped a bomb on us all. She snapped that pointer in her hand two times, then held it tightly and pinched her lips together. "In my eleven years teaching," she said, "it has been my experience that certain ideologies, when held up to the light of practical procedure, are ineffective in producing adequate education in young people. I know that you were told you would have to prepare a senior paper for this class. You will have two weeks from today to complete that assignment. There is precious little time to try to get through the mountain of material we have left to cover before I release you on the world."

Shocked looks went up on everyone's face. Dr. Fine continued, "Put your hands down. There will be no questions about this. I understand that typically these papers are due the week before graduation. You know good and well you weren't going to begin working on them until three days before that. The work kept in your files here appears abysmal in nature, so this assignment will be a good place for us to begin. You will be graded on content and grammar, punctuation, linguistic style, and form. Until two weeks from today during class time we will concentrate on structures of global economics while you are preparing your papers as homework."

This new professor said we could go on with the subjects that Mr. Hicks had agreed to, since we got to choose our own subject for a change and most of them were all right. She talked for the rest of the hour on the difference between a thesis, a research paper, and an essay, and what kind of margins to use, not to even bother writing a paragraph without an introductory clause, and how to do footnotes, which were going to be absolutely required because how could we possibly maintain our theories without citing some known publication? We were to use the research we'd do in order to back up our points, and each of our subjects was to be tied in to some issue in modern politics.

I'd never heard of such a miserably difficult assignment in my entire life. I tried to take notes on all she was saying, but she went so fast I know I lost parts of it. It was like a nightmare had stalked into Mr. Hicks's comfortable old class, where we were all expecting to slide through toward summer. Her accent was so strange I could hardly understand what she was saying. As I stood to leave the room when the bell rang, my knees quivered and my foot hung against the leg of the chair. I nearly tumbled on my face. She descended on me, popping that pointer into her palm with the end of every sentence.

"Posture! Young lady, your posture is abominable. No wonder your feet cannot bear you up. Lift your shoulders, straighten your spine. Watch where you put your feet, and you won't trip over them!" She aimed the pointer directly at my face.

From the corner of my eye I could see the other kids dashing from the room, glancing toward me with that horrified I'm-glad-it's-you-and-not-me-that's-getting-it look. I hated her instantly. Oh, I hated that woman with a bristly lace, navy blue hate that stung my eyes and made them want to water so that I cried right in front of her.

"What do you say when an adult addresses you, young lady?"

"Yes, ma'am," I said. Tears dripped off my chin. All the other kids were already out of the room. I just wanted out of there, and fast. She was now standing between me and the door. "Ma'am," I added, "excuse me. I—I have another class."

"Pick up your feet when you walk. Don't blunder around my classroom like a great donkey."

"Yes'm," I said, and ran, squeezing my books into my chest.

I don't think I've ever worked so hard and sweated such earnest drops of blood over an assignment in my life. I had already taken some notes about those Roman emperors before Christmas, planning to do a report like all the others I'd done. Comparing ancient Rome to modern politics, not to mention coming up with my own thoughts about it all, was about the most trying thing I've ever attempted. I worked on it from the minute I got done with the dishes until late at night every night for two weeks. Mother even complained that I had too much homework, more than was healthy. She added that I should have started sooner and not waited until the last minute, until Deely for once stood up for me and explained how neither of us had gotten any warning about it.

That weekend in Sunday school I sat with Maggy Sips and Neomadel Blaylock. Raylene and Delia were in the pew in front of us; according to Delia, this was so they wouldn't be "distracted nor disgusted," I presumed she meant by us. Garnelle went to First Southern. Most of the kids I talked with at school went to church either here at Siloam Springs or to First Southern. Sitting next to the Bandy twins and Marty and Coby was Danny, a general flirt but polite to people's parents, good-looking but shorter than I was. I know that Danny kept a plug of chaw in his coat pocket. From the corner of my eye I saw Deely pass a note to him. I was thinking only about my essay for Dr. Fine. Oh, the notes I'd taken these two weeks—my middle finger had a knot on the last knuckle from holding a pencil and writing like crazy for a solid hour and fifteen minutes every day in her class, besides working on my homework and the paper.

Walking past Sheriff Moultrie on the way to the door, I craned my neck, looking hard for Coby so I could hand him Garnelle's latest note. I was so busy looking for Coby I didn't have time to say hello politely to the sheriff. I heard him say behind me, "Now, Miss Delia Summers, don't you look pretty," but I didn't turn around.

Sunday night, I copied and recopied pages of my essay in ink, finding one stupid mistake after another, always at the bottom of a page so I'd have to start over. Each time I put the pen to the paper, it was a new chance for the ink to dribble out, or for my hand to shake, or for me to misspell some word I've known how to spell for a thousand years. I didn't go to bed until after midnight; the last forty-five minutes were spent searching for three matching brass brads for the holes I'd carefully cut in the sides of the paper.

At breakfast I was still checking page numbers and making sure I had my "ibid"s and citations perfect. I didn't have any expectations of getting a good grade, but I surely didn't want that woman to call me up in front of the class to show just how awful a paper could be. My fingers were blue with ink worked into the skin and sore with writing cramp. My eyes burned. If that horrible Dr. Fine failed me on this paper, I could fail the class, and if I failed the class, I wouldn't even graduate. So much for the WAACs. So much for getting out of here. That afternoon, as soon as school was out, I went and applied at the dime store, and told Mr. Jakes there that I would be dropping out of school any day now and could start right away. He was shorthanded now since his son, Hardy Jakes, had joined the army and headed off to France or Switzerland or somewhere.

The next morning I was so nervous I couldn't eat breakfast. Delia wanted to drive her car to school, and I actually asked her to give me a ride. I sat through first-hour Nursing in a daze, and when she and I had to go to Dr. Fine's room, I walked behind Deely and Raylene. I was terrified at what new assignment that horrible teacher might think up next.

Upside down on our desks were our papers. Already graded? How could that be? I knew mine from the kinds of brads I used—one had long tabs and the other two were short, and I'd had a problem bending one, so it had a wrinkle in it. There was a red pencil mark under the last bibliography entry. We sat without a sound, more solemn than any of these kids had ever been in church.

Dr. Fine had on the same navy blue dress that she'd worn the first time I saw her. The pointer was safely leaning against the side of her square, battered oak desk. Instead, in her hand she wielded a cardboard-backed tablet of paper with writing across it, all in red pencil. We sat like stones. The bell rang. Before its echo died, she said, "This was, without doubt, the most appalling— Don't touch your paper, young man, until I tell you to turn them over. Class? One person—only one— turned in an essay. The rest were mere *reports*, without deliberation or weight, simplistic recitations of mundane data of the sort one might expect from children, not young men and women. Only one individual in this class followed the directions and actually thought about what she was writing. These grades will be entered on your records. However, because of the paramount importance of this class, it behooves me to require you to make up the work you have failed so completely. Miss Philadelphia Christine Summers, stand and hold up your paper."

Oh, God, don't let her do this. In front of the entire senior class. It's always worse to be either the first to be ashamed or the last. Kids were already snickering because of my name. Every eye followed my movements as I stood, lifted the paper from my desk by the wrinkled brad, and held it, shaking like a leaf. I started to turn it over to see the grade, but she kept talking before I did.

"The only A in this class went to Miss Summers. Not only was the paper well researched, analyzed, and cited, but she alone turned in a true essay. Congratulations."

I've never earned an A on anything in my life. A. Excellent. Professor Fine, with the stuck-up accent and the boy-whacking pointer— "Witch Doctor" we'd called her—had given me an A.

"Miss Summers, I want you to read your exemplary paper aloud to the class. You may have fifteen minutes to look it over and practice it silently in the hall."

"Yes, ma'am," I said, and dutifully went to the door. My face burned with a glory of Old Testament proportions. I could no more read my paper to myself in the hall than I could tap-dance. I listened instead through the door to what she said to the rest of the class.

63

"The rest of you have until Friday to turn in an essay. Naturally, your grades will be lowered, because you've already missed the deadline. I will not go over the lecture I gave you; you had your chance to take notes. Apparently only one of you was capable of doing that.

"And now I must ask three girls, please, to stand. Neomadel Blaylock. Margaret Anne Sips. Raylene Smith. Each of you seems to have turned in, absolutely word for word, the same document. Did you think I wouldn't read them? How dare you insult the integrity of this classroom and the endeavors of your fellow students by descending to the loathsome deceit of plagiarism? How dare you insult me? You three will get letters home to your parents about this, and—and what, Miss Blaylock?"

Neomadel's daddy was head of the trustees of the school. She'd never had anything but straight A's her whole life. Same with Maggy and Raylene, whose fathers were also on the board. Suddenly dizzy, I leaned against the door; then, thinking about my posture, I stood up. I hardly cared if those three had copied off each other again. They'd been doing that as long as anyone knew. What really mattered was the paper in my hand.

When I stood in front of the class, a roaring in my ears made it hard to hear my own voice. Dr. Fine had said, "Nice projection, but next time mind your diction." I positively floated through the rest of the day.

During last hour I was summoned again to Professor Fine's room after school, by a fourth-grader with a folded note passed to my English teacher. "Yes, ma'am? You wanted to see me?" I said with a shy smile. Dr. Fine still looked ominous behind that beaten old desk where Mr. Hicks had rested his feet while we read in class last fall, before I had an A.

"You've proved something, Miss Summers."

"Ma'am?"

"The reports handed to me regarding the students in this class listed you as a mediocre student at best. How do you explain that?"

"I don't know, ma'am. I tried to do my best, but I never got an A before."

"Your English needs work. You have never *received* an A before. I

64

will require equal effort for the remainder of the semester. Do not expect that you have simply filled the vacancy for school pet left by those three delightful offspring of the school board. Is that clear?"

"Yes, ma'am."

"Have you given thought to what you will do after graduating?"

"No, ma'am. Well, yes, a little. I thought I might join the W-A-A-C. Or get a job at the dime store."

"What else do you do—besides school, that is?"

"Collect grease, ma'am."

She rolled her eyes in disgust. "I'm talking about your talents and interests. Have you considered higher education? Perhaps a career. You have a persuasive way with the written word. What about studying literature, or law?"

"Ma'am?"

"Yes. Do you know what a solicitor, a lawyer, is?"

"Well, ma'am, that's for boys."

"Nonsense. It may be true that the higher professions have been closed to women, but they are opening, here in the United States particularly. It won't be easy, but nothing worth doing ever is."

"Don't lawyers have to talk in public?"

"Yes. They speak in public."

"It says in the Bible for women to be quiet in public."

She sighed and frowned at me. She rolled her eyes again with an exasperated shrug. "Paul's letter to the Corinthians does call for *certain* women to pipe down after being caught disturbing the worship service with gossip. There is nothing in the Bible about women not being able to do public work. One of Paul's great friends was an orator and deaconess named Phoebe, for whom I was named."

Phoebe Fine. Her name was Phoebe Fine. It made me smile just thinking about the feel of it in my mouth. "I could never do a boy's job, Mrs., Dr. Feeb—Dr. Fine."

"A boy's job. A boy's job? What exactly . . . ? Did you know that Miss Amelia Earhart was a personal friend of mine? People thought flying was a 'boy's job,' too."

"No, ma'am. I didn't."

"Miss Summers, I want you to write another essay. You shall have a day's head start on the other students, but they will be up all night, I expect, trying to complete today's assignment before I give them the new one tomorrow. I will expect greater effort on your part because of it. You've shown some interest in the Bible; therefore, you will write an essay on the meaning of Galatians three, beginning in verse twenty-six and going through twenty-eight. You will include how it applies to people of all races, notably Jewish and Negro people in this country. And most particularly to yourself. And"——she stressed the word, looking down her bony nose at me, squinting her eyes——"you shall apply it to the manner in which you may personally make a vast difference in the world. Those three verses have been the towers of my life, my stay when I feel daunted, so I will expect thoroughness. I will not ask you to read this essay aloud in class, so you may be sure to address the subject wholly and without reservation. When that's done, perhaps you will think differently about your prospects."

"Yes, ma'am. My prospects."

"And you will drop that ridiculous nickname from your homework. You have been given a noble name. There is no benefit in covering it up with some absurd equivocation."

I have always disliked the name Frosty, particularly attached as it was to the surname Summers. My parents had bestowed upon me my dead grandmother's middle name and Mother's given name. During the second winter of my life apparently I had attempted to pronounce myself to the world, and Philadelphia Christine became fused into Frosty. It stuck to me the way childish names do, and I couldn't shake it. My older sister had it easier: she got Daddy's mother's and sister's first names, Delia Louise. Opalrae is saddled with Cornelia as a middle name. I envied girls named Beth.

In March of 1942, in a farther corner of the world than any citizen of Sabine, Texas, could ever imagine——farther in cultural remoteness even than Japan or Germany or France——a group of men signed papers that made them part of the United States Marine Corps. That place, which they called Spring-on-the-Plain, lay close to the Lukachukai Mountains in northern Arizona. Wizened warriors, their long gray hair caught up in tightly formed buns at the backs of their heads, lined up with quiet eagerness next to boys obviously too young to qualify. The recruiters were astonished at the turnout. The Indians arrived ready to leave, their belongings rolled in blankets or tucked in leather bags. They carried knives, hunting rifles, and pistols in oiled leather. One old man, weathered and dark as walnut bark, held a quiver of arrows and a bow.

Diné Hashke' Yitah Deeya', Fierce One Who Walks Among Enemies, clan of Hashk'aa Hadzoho, born for Tabaahi, contemplated how to fill out his military form. Known at school as Gordon Benally, he was older than some of them and taller than most. Some of the boys were thirteen or fourteen, but none of the others spoke up to refute their claims of being twenty. Everyone there gave his age as twenty, even Uncle Bill. The white man smiled at Gordon when he said he was twenty-one. "Old fella, aren't you?" the man said. "No one else here is a day over twenty."

His cousin Billy Tsosie handed him a stub of pencil. "What's the matter, Hasteen?"

"Trying to figure out how to get my name in this little line. They've got two inches here."

"Give them your school name. It's all right."

"I was thinking this was more important than school, though. I want it to have the outfit name on it, in case."

"Maybe. They can't say it anyway, you know."

The taller man smiled and wrote "Benally, Gordon," and for a middle name he squeezed in "Tadechiini." Under religious preference he spelled out "Presbyterian." Tsosie watched patiently over his shoulder while he wrote.

"That looks pretty good, brother," Tsosie said. "I wasn't going to put all that stuff down. What did you write for 'address'?"

"Tse Giizhi," he said. "My mother lives at Mexican Water, but I gave the address of the gas station at Fort Defiance."

The bus got to the reservation just as the sun was going down. The men filed on quietly, and as it started rolling, most of them immediately fell asleep. Gordon and Billy were near the back. Gordon stared out the rear window, watching the red sand play in wispy designs on the outside of the glass. The slanting rays of light made strands of rice grass and alkali grass loom long and red as blood against black earth.

Gordon was exhausted and exhilarated at the same time. Stretching his legs as far as he could under the seat in front of them, he slouched against the window glass. It had been a long farewell. He'd felt uneasy ever since the Enemy Way ceremony—wary. It felt odd and old and superstitious, but at the same time comforting. If nothing else, it was good to know that those around him cared so much. The ceremony had cost his mother a lot, and not just in food. He'd been so full of good food he thought he'd never eat again. It occurred to Gordon now that he was not afraid of the Enemy Who Came at Last, the Final Enemy who would take away what little the white government had left them. Every meal he'd ever eaten as a child had been in a crouched stance, preparatory for flight, knife at his side, shoes on his feet; now, at last, he was going to fight. He was not afraid of death either, except for a mild worry that his ghost would go crazy and bother people he cared about. It would be a good thing to leave his ghost in a far land, where if it chose to molest, its victims would be Enemy people. In a lump tucked against his chest was a very full corn-pollen bundle. That part wasn't superstition. He knew the power of it; a warm place on his skin proved it.

After the day Professor Fine asked me to read my essay aloud in class, Neomadel never spoke to me unless some adult was around to chide her for being rude. Maggy, either. Raylene suddenly got all coy and cozy, as if I was her new best friend. They got their straight-A bottoms sat right in the front row for a while, because they each got a big fat F on that assignment. The only person who really surprised me was Beans Bandy. Instead of having him writing his paper over, Dr. Fine gave him some assignment different from the rest of ours. By the end of school Beans was actually getting B's on some of his work; he was really proud.

It seemed Dr. Fine thought nothing of giving each person what she considered was just the right assignment for them. All the kids hated her, including Deely. Except me. And it's not like I had it easy. She could pull an assignment out of some storehouse she held in her head, like an arsenal of weapons against our sloth and spare time. I did a ten-page report on Amelia Earhart for a topic Dr. Fine called "Worthy Persons of Note." Dr. Fine loved to give out C's too, but I got more B's than ever before. When I walked home, instead of conversation, I thought a lot about my posture and my feet.

I guess I liked Garnelle because she said things I was thinking. As far as I could tell, people with money were allowed to say pretty much anything, and people just agreed with them. If people like me or Deely complained, we were just ungrateful. It was like a girl's figure: If she was rich, she was slender. If she was poor, she was just skinny. I remember everyone being skinny when I was a child. Negroes looking starved and bug-eyed drifted down the road. I remember always being hungry. Breakfast was unsalted black-eyed peas and crawdad. Sometimes you could find salsify to put in it. Supper was black-eyed peas and crawdad, with okra and a little salt. We'd not have had that if a neighbor whose crop came in good hadn't let us go in and glean. Mother said we were fulfilling a verse from the Bible, like Ruth and Naomi. She said Ruth was happily married to Boaz—who most of the time Mother forgot and called "Beau"—because she gleaned up his field. Only she got wheat, which meant they made bread from it. I asked Mother couldn't we grind the dried peas and make flour and have cake for supper, and she boxed my head. Every time she read that story, I kept thinking they were only happy to be poor because they had all the spoon bread and biscuits anybody could want. All we got was black-eyed peas and okra. I guess mostly without crawdad, although I remember those dinners best when there was a 'dad tail or two in the pot. Once there was a bacon rind. That was Christmas. That was one of the times Mother chased colored folks, two of them, from under our porch with a broom in her hands and threats of the sheriff. She suspected they smelled the bacon and came to steal us blind.

Now and then us kids would find a plump body down by the tracks or up on the Indian trail to Turkey Creek, both of which were not far from our house. We'd hear about folks going off in the swamp to fish or hunt alligator and never coming out, or after a heavy rain a bleached, gorged carcass would wash up that looked like it had been under the swamp awhile. When it was pretty much whole like that, with some little fish nibbles on it, the kids at school called it an "alligator plug." Gators will take you down and plug a hole with you and let you get good and rotten before they'll eat you.

Poor we had always been, and unless I really did get an invitation to the White House, that's all I expected I'd be. But regardless of our current low economic standing, we Summerses had a slim claim to a blue-blooded Southern Heritage, of which the entire family was persistently proud. Grandmother Summers's maiden name was Ratcliffe. "English!" she'd say. "Not Irish." And one afternoon, as school let out, I sought Dr. Fine to tell her about this little link, this common English ground between us. "My grandmother Summers is descended from James Ratcliffe, the Englishman who founded our first colony, Jamestown," I said proudly. "It was named after him."

She peered at me over her long nose. "I don't think so, Miss Summers."

"Yes, ma'am. Sure enough."

"It would be better, Miss Summers, were you not to carry that tale with you."

"Everybody already knows."

Without another word Dr. Fine strode to large rack of books she kept behind her desk. They had a look of holiness about them. She handed me a huge volume. "Peradventure you might take a moment to look up that name, Ratcliffe. Settlement of the colonies and the ensuing revolt. Alphabetical. Take notes."

I nodded and did as she said. "Jamestown, Virginia. Begun in 1606 by order of King James I of England." I looked up Ratcliffe, James. "Indentured servant credited with being a governor of the town called Jamestown after servitude. Like most slaves, he took on the name of the master of the house, Ratcliffe, while in service . . . died, unmarried, at the age of twenty-four." I closed the book. I said, "I suppose, then, it couldn't be." I had a few things to think about on the way home. We were descended either from the illegitimate child of a slave or from someone else entirely.

BEFORE I KNEW IT, graduation came and went. I got a B in Government and Economics. Almost everyone else took home a C, except Marty Haliburton, who failed.

Neomadel Blaylock had been up for valedictorian until she got into Dr. Fine's class, where she had to work for a grade. Everyone on the board of trustees had a son or daughter who'd been affected by Dr. Fine. That couldn't be tolerated, no, sirree. Those little angels deserved straight A's, and the trustees were going to hire only teachers that gave them to the right pupils. If Daddy had been a trustee instead of in sewer and water pipe repair, I'd have had more A's all along, though I guess none of them would have felt like the one I got. The next thing that happened was Dr. Fine got fired. That week Marty got his diploma hand-carried to him by the principal.

As part of their weekly meetings, the ladies of the WMU held a reception tea to welcome the high school graduates. The thing I dreaded most about graduating was that I would be forced by my new adult status to go to WMU meetings instead of the Girls' Auxiliary. At least the GA was geared at having a little fun.

At my first official Thursday morning, sweet and dressed up and white-gloved as we all were, I noticed that there seemed to be two factions of ladies who circulated around each other but didn't mingle. When seats were taken, the Fieldings, Smiths, Mrs. Brady, and some of the other ladies all clustered together, and the rest of us, the poorer side of town, were seated in another room, straining to hear. While Neomadel's mother began droning on and on about missionaries' birthdays and reading something aloud from the Baptist Foreign Mission Board— we were a captive audience—I started thinking about where everyone lived in town, and I figured out you could tell the distance people lived from the railroad tracks by where they were sitting in the room. Mother sat next to me during the whole thing, smiling, a cheerful look on her face. Grandmother Summers sat with the "tony" ladies, but in the last seat, nearest us. I wondered what she would think if she knew a little more about her heritage.

As summer wore on, all I could think about was the WAACs. I heard girls were going down to Sweetwater to fly planes. Like Amelia Earhart. One morning, before I went to Raylene's, I walked uptown to the two-story houses to see if I could locate Dr. Fine. Maybe she'd tell me what to do with myself. But she and her husband had been renting the top floor of the Phippses' house and had left shortly after school was out. Miss Breckenridge, who is now Mrs. Phipps and out to here in a family way, said *Mr.* Dr. Fine told her they didn't belong in this town and that any school who thought they were too good for *Mrs.* Dr. Fine had just cost the town the best of medical *and* educational care. And wasn't that uppity? And the nerve of those people, just because they believed in kings and queens instead of God and the president like we had!

Mrs. Phipps had been my teacher in sixth grade; until now I'd never thought it was possible for a teacher to be stupid.

Coby Brueller got his Greetings from Uncle Sam two weeks after graduation. Three weeks later Beans, Danny, and Marty were called. They had three days to get to Port Arthur and report in. Beans Bandy was sent home with 4-F on his card. Marty said the idiot cried in the bus all the way home.

RAYLENE AND I WERE in the yard catching a ball—she let me use her new baseball mitt—when here came Marty toting his daddy's supper pail. He didn't have to pass our house on his way to the mill; he had to come on purpose. Mitch Haliburton had come back from the first war—not all staved up with coughing fits like old Hal Fielding or missing any pieces like some of those old men who spent their days playing checkers in front of the sawmill—and promptly fathered seven children as fast as his wife could bear them. Marty was the youngest of these.

"Hey, y'all," Marty called out.

"Hey back, y'all," we chimed at the same time.

"Reckon I'm going to go see my Uncle Sam."

"That a fact?" I said. "What'd y'all get on your physical?"

"Frosty!" Raylene said, "You can't ask a boy that."

"He's just bustin' to tell us. What'd you get, Marty?" I threw the ball at Raylene, so she couldn't turn toward him to watch him answer.

Marty cleared his throat. "Well, One-A. Top-notch, I guess."

Raylene tossed *him* the ball. "That means y'all will go right away?"

"Yup." He tossed the ball at me; I missed it and ran after it.

"I guess Farrell's going, too, finally," Raylene said. "Are you boys going to be in the same division? Do you think you'll catch up with Wilbur Fielding?"

"Maybe. A division is awful big, you know. Thousands." Marty shrugged, his daddy's supper swinging in his hand. He looked as though he wasn't sure it was worth setting her straight. "Put it here, Frosty, and this time when I throw it, catch it. It's a shame they'd take Farrell and leave Beans. If I was the Bandys and had to have only one son left, I'd rather it was Farrell. Besides, the army could've saved money on a helmet. He's already got that metal head and all."

Raylene giggled.

Marty looked pleased. "I'm leaving Thursday at five in the morning for Port Arthur. Reckon I'll be killing Japs before the summer's over."

Raylene said, "You be careful there, Marty. If you see Wilbur, tell him I miss him."

Marty went on down the road, kicking dirt up with each step, intentionally making a cloud that followed him.

"What do you think he wanted, coming here?" I said.

"Saying so long, I guess," she said.

I laughed. "You've got your cap set for Wilbur Fielding just like all the other girls."

WHEN MARTY GOT HOME from Raylene's, he found his mother pouring ice water for the sheriff. "Hey there, Sheriff Moultrie," he said when he was greeted. "I'm starved, Mama. Y'all excuse me, I'll be in the kitchen."

"Martin," his mother called from her chair in the parlor, "you don't know anything about any children in town committing vandalisms, do you?"

He hollered over his shoulder, head in the icebox, "No, ma'am. Is there any of that cake left from last night?"

"Martin? Come in here, please. You know good and well, Sheriff, we have never had any truck with the kind of people who'd raise juvenile delinquents. My husband has been a deacon for twenty-five years. I've known your wife all my life. You know what kind of people we are."

"Of course, Miz Haliburton," Moultrie said. "I just hoped your boy Martin might have heard some rumor. Not that he'd have had anything to do with an actual crime. There's just no time like the present to put a lid on things. Things"—he paused to give the word weight—"have been

74

real quiet for a long time. I know there's been some riots lately, and some of the boys in the Knights are keeping a eagle eye out for trouble on the home front, so to speak. I just don't want any trouble in this town."

Mrs. Haliburton nodded, fixing her eyes on the rose border of her tablecloth in the kitchen, where Marty sat over a plate of buttermilk cake. "Martin? Don't you know one or two of the rougher boys—by reputation, that is?"

Marty appeared at the doorway, licking his lips. He began to nod, as if searching his memory. "Well, now. Well, Sheriff, I seem to remember that Brueller boy—isn't his real name Adolf, just like Hitler?—being into something a year ago. Didn't he and the Bandy twins and one of those lowland boys from Louisiana get into some ruckus? Steal a car or something?"

Moultrie thought. "Went for a joyride on a mill wagon, is all." He studied Martin Haliburton carefully. "What is it the Brueller boy goes by? Coby?"

Marty shrugged. "I think that's it. I've got packing to do, Mama. Off to the war, praying and hoping I'll come home and all. My patriotic sacrifice. May I be excused?"

AFTER MARTY LEFT, Raylene and I got to talking about the girls from school who got married within a month of graduation. Jean-Marie was pushing things to wear white, and everybody knew it. The sad part was that she was instantly left single again, just like the other two, mooning at home, staring at their rings, because every one of their husbands got drafted by the end of the month. I still had my jobs cleaning two houses and helping out a few hours a week at the post office. If I didn't find a way to get into the WAACs or something, that's all I'd ever do. I had more freedom and money than I'd ever known, but I'd been so busy trying to get work done for Dr. Fine's class that I'd forgotten about leaving home. Until now. I wished Dr. Fine was around to tell me what to do next.

By the time Deely came to ride me home, it was raining. "Deely, you better slow down," I said.

"Shut up. I know how to drive," Deely said.

"For crying out loud, you're too close to the edge. You're going to go off into the bar ditch and flip us over like I saw on a newsreel."

"That's in the movies. These things don't turn over."

"Stop this car."

"No. You wanted a ride from Raylene's. Now, shut your mouth before I slap you."

I clutched at the leather seat with one hand, trying to stabilize myself with the other against the dash as we fishtailed all over the road. I decided to try more diplomacy. "Please. Delia. Please slow down." Rain battered the little blue-black car as it pushed through the gummy, sucking clay.

"If I go slower, it'll get stuck, and you'll be the one who walks to get help. This is my car, and I'm the driver, and I know what I'm doing."

"What was that? A bump. I felt a bump. You hit an animal."

"No I didn't. That's just a rut in the road."

"You squashed a dog!"

"No I didn't."

"Stop. I'm going to see if it's still alive."

"I'm not stopping until I get to Delaware Street. Then you can get out and get sucked up by a hurricane or washed away in a flood for all I care."

"You hit a dog."

"Get out." Delia stopped the car, ramming her foot onto the brake and clutch pedals so fast that my head beat against the windshield. "If I get stuck here, you're paying to have my car fixed." When her tires caught traction, the car lurched forward, spattering mud, fishing around, rushing into the darkness.

"Deely!" I wailed as she vanished in the rain. I shook with anger as I watched the tiny red lights of her car flicker and disappear. I felt my way to the side of the road, banked on one side with a berm and on the other with a ditch lined with fence wire. The dog I thought I'd seen in the dim light was gone. Maybe it was a turtle or something else, but it looked like a yellow dog. I started home, now and then kicking out with

76

my right foot in the darkness for the berm at the edge of the road, trying to maintain my bearings.

The depth of night that accompanies thunderstorms in East Texas can be surprising, as if the atmosphere had left the ground and the blackness of space had descended in its place. The wind and rain and blowing leaves and bits of grass completed the oppressive pall. I hate being rained on. I always have. I don't begrudge the rain itself; it's all right if I'm in a house or under an awning, even an umbrella or a big hat. But rain on my head, my face, my shoulders, can bring me to the point of desolation.

I gulped and shielded my eyes, trying to make out some landmark. I had two choices: either to take to the middle and risk being hit or to stay on the edge and risk washing away. Still, having left the storm of neuroses that was Deely behind was a consolation. Eventually I recognized our yard through the rain and gray, although the house was only a few shades darker gray than the rain. Bosco came running and barking, slopping through the water, but stopped and wagged his tail when he recognized me.

There was a light on in our front window on the porch. Deely's car was parked against the side of the house, driven right up to the porch, so when she got out she wouldn't get wet. It didn't do any good to be mad at her. It was better to take the chance that my bedraggled appearance at our front door would hit some sympathetic chord with Mother. Anything, human or animal, caught in a situation of sudden pathos did it, and I was certainly that.

Daddy was in the front room behind a newspaper, with the radio going loudly. It was his retreat from our world. As soon as my mother got a look at me, it was clear that tonight was Deely's turn. Her turn for the lecture that went on into the night. Her turn for the slapped face, too. Opalrae had been whipped this afternoon for leaving the house without a slip under her dress. Deely never gets whippings, but she gets her face slapped and a double dose of Mother's relentless tirades. If I'd walked home on a balmy, lovely morning, of course, nothing at all would have been said except an offhand remark about my being so lazy as to want a ride everywhere I went. As it was, I hid in the bathroom, taking a warm bath and emerging still damp into the sultry atmosphere of our house.

Both my sisters were on their hands and knees scrubbing penitently, Deely in the kitchen and Opalrae on the screened back porch. I asked Mother what she wanted me to help with for supper and got the chore of frying okra and shucking crawdads. I whacked the tails off them with a knife and threw the tops in the wet-trash jug with the rims of the okra and some black-eyed peas that had turned sour in the icebox yesterday.

"Well, that Fielding girl has gone to sign up for airplanes."

"Garnelle enlisted?" I plopped the crawdads into the hot water. Airplane school. She'd be flying airplanes with wings spread like the great egrets from the swamp, saying things like "Contact!", her hair billowing and glamorous beneath that tight leather cap and those goony goggles. As I tried to picture her, I spied a few discarded crawdad bodies trying to escape the garbage. I knocked them back into the mess with the edge of the lid and clamped it down tight.

At midnight Marty Haliburton sat on the foot of his bed, staring into the dark. Sweat soaked his pajamas and sheets, and as he sat in the warm, humid room, chill bumps crusted his skin like hard scales. He shook, trembled actually, and for a second thought he'd be sick; he thought he might be fainting, although he didn't know what fainting was like.

Somewhere in the woods outside, somebody's hound had treed a squirrel or possum or something. The dog bayed, and Marty felt his mouth water like he was about to vomit. He stood and opened the window, leaning his head out to try to take in fresh air. How long would it be before he'd go hunting? How long before he got home? *If* he got home, that was. His daddy's hunting dogs were sleeping on the porch, sprawled like only a hound dog can, jowls flopped and bellies upturned, feet twitching in some dream chase.

Katydids chirped. Something moved in the woods that crowded in on their backyard. Could have been anything. Gator. Deer. Nigger. Some old Cajun moonshiner like old man Bandy, crazy, running through the woods toward the swamp draped in hanging moss like veils from some whorehouse window. Not Japs anyway. Not out there. He slapped at a mosquito boldly drilling through his pajamas into his arm. A drop of blood blossomed on the cloth around the crumpled bronze insect.

Marty found his clothes and dressed in the dark. He took his hunting rifle from behind the door where it leaned in the corner. He thought about calling the dogs but changed his mind. The moon was high and bright. It was a cold moon, even for summer. Not the usual warm vanilla color, but distant and silver and ugly. It was bright, though. He pushed his hat down around his ears and slipped off the porch quietly, rifle in hand. Making his way through the shadows, he stuck the butt of the rifle behind the farthest row on the woodpile to make sure there were no rattlesnakes or anything back there. Satisfied with the silence, he reached in and gingerly brought out a pint-size mason jar nearly full of clear liquid.

He opened the lid and sipped. His throat ignited, every wet membrane from his lips down shocked with the fluid fire. He wheezed. He bit his lips hard to keep from coughing. He took a longer drink, walking into the woods with the jar in one hand, the lid pinched between two fingers like a cigarette, the rifle swinging lazy arcs in the other hand. Keeping to a worn footpath the kids called "Indian Trail," Marty stalked the broken moonlight, quickening his steps where the trees obscured it, stopping to listen, wary of the huffing of a misplaced alligator. An owl startled him, calling overhead, moving on soundless wings across the path. The jar bobbled in his hand, and he cleared his throat. Beyond a bend and a high point on the trail, he leaped up on a rocky outcropping of black, smooth stones. It was only four feet higher than the land around it, but it gave him a place to observe and sit above the world.

Propping his back against the rock's surface, Marty worked the lid of the jar loose and let it slide off. He took a drink and stealthily set the jar at a place where it balanced. Then he took aim with the rifle at the moon. When the jar was emptied by about a quarter of its contents, Marty started to cry. After a while he stopped. He blew his nose loud against the rock with one finger over each nostril. He took another drink. His head was about to explode. Japanese soldiers could be in these woods right now. They'd do terrible things to you if they caught you. He wasn't coming back, he knew it. His skin puckered with chill bumps so hard it hurt, but he wasn't cold. He was sweating great drops that rolled from his head and down his back. Terror clung to his entrails and crushed the breath from him so that he could not cry out, though he tried, his mouth opened in a grimace of anguish. He picked up his rifle and aimed it at the treetop across the trail from him. Then he pointed it down at his right boot.

He heard the trigger click in place. And the world turned white and silver and cold.

Alone in my room, I pulled out my cardboard hope chest and read, word for word, the essays I'd written for Dr. Fine. I tried to recall everything she'd said to me, as if Dr. Fine were talking to me, snapping that pointer against her palm. There were things in my hand that I didn't even remember writing. I took out my paper on Galatians. She said those verses were her mainstay when she was troubled. For the life of me I didn't know why. I'd tried to get something out of them, but I just couldn't. She'd given me a C on that one. I felt as if I'd failed utterly. One thing about Dr. Fine was that you always knew exactly what she was thinking. People around these parts are used to things being a lot mistier and more tangled.

We heard that three people had been killed over in Toullange from the tornado that hit the night we had the terrible storm. Although a few houses lost their gas and lights for a couple of weeks and two alligators were chased out of people's yards back to the bayous, there was nothing in the way of permanent damage to anyone we knew. If it was God's judgment, He sent it on down the road. Daddy was convinced that the only reason we were spared was that we had been praying away the judgment hand of righteousness.

I was sorting stamps in the slotted drawer at the post office when Garnelle Fielding came in to send a little package to Wilbur. She said she'd gone and signed up for the WAFS, and her mother and daddy drove her down to Sweetwater to take a test at Avenger Field, where the government was training hundreds and hundreds of women to be pilots. Trouble was, she didn't pass her physical because they said she was too short and too thin for the service. Her mother rushed her to a doctor in Toullange the next day and tried to get him to write her a letter so she could join the navy instead, but he wouldn't do it. He told her the service was no place for a girl, and she'd be better off to wait home for someone brave to come marry her.

Garnelle hung around until four o'clock when my hours were up, then walked with me to my house. "You should have seen my mother," she said. "Better yet, you should have heard her. She fussed and fumed the whole way home about how women in her family had fought in every war this country has ever had, right up from loading muskets in the Revolution to she herself driving a staff car in North Carolina during the Great War. I tell you, she would have made a better recruiter than any of those movie star speeches I've ever heard. My mother doesn't sell kisses in a low-cut basque. She preaches pure patriotism like an evangelist in a tent revival. If she'd had a tambourine, we could have stopped the car and held a meeting." We laughed. "I'm still mad, though," she said.

"Hello!" I hollered as I opened our front door. I didn't tell Garnelle I felt relieved she wasn't going to fly without me. The house was eerie, too quiet. "Well, I'm still thinking about the WAACs," I said. "Only I haven't said anything to Mother and Daddy yet. I don't know how to tell them. But I'm planning to, maybe in a couple of weeks. I really want to *do* something. Maybe you can go with me then. We can learn to fix army jeeps or something." Maybe I'd just get up the courage and go one day without telling them, I thought, until I was across the country somewhere and signed on, so that I couldn't go home even if I changed my mind.

Garnelle sat on my bed, bending one leg under her and swinging the other off the side. "Got any new magazines?" She flipped a couple of pages on my old issue of *Life*.

I let out my breath. "Nope. Say, maybe there's some kind of job around that men don't want."

"Flower committee chairman for the WMU."

"Want to stay for supper?" I said.

"I'll check with Mama. Then I'll help you set the table. Maybe I can muster up enough feminine bravery to put the knives and forks down without cutting an artery or something."

"If you do, I'll whip out my Junior First Aid Kit and we'll play nursies." I laughed, but inside I shuddered. In my last two quarters of the spring semester I'd taken Introduction to Nursing in the Twentieth Century, like a lot of other girls in school. We dissected pigs and worms and frogs. We looked at pictures of compound fractures and kids with smallpox. That class had cured me of ever wanting to get near a white uniform. Anything that involved blood, bones, or any fluid coming out of someone's mouth was beyond my gastric tolerance. I thought it was exciting that Garnelle wanted to fly airplanes, but I couldn't picture myself doing that either. I typed about five words a minute, as long as there were letters on the keys. Some of those girls, I read in the paper, could do over fifty and sixty words. I didn't know how I'd ever get in the WAACs.

At supper Mother and Daddy said they were just as thankful Garnelle wouldn't be going in the service. Daddy explained in great detail to her that women didn't belong in the air corps and that he would never consider letting his girls fight in a war. It wasn't ladylike.

I could tell Garnelle was bristling underneath. "Men are needed to fight the war," she said, "but women are needed to fly supplies."

Daddy was having none of it. "Now, nursing. There's where a girl is the one thing in a war. You girls took that course in school. Why don't you see if they need some more nurses?"

"Mr. Summers, I don't want to be a nurse."

"Why not? You want to help our boys in uniform, that's how you can help. Girls should be nurses. It's in their nature."

"I just couldn't do it. Cleaning wounds, changing filthy beds, mopping up—"

"There's more to nursing than the hard part, Garnelle. You should know that," Mother said. "There's writing letters for hurt boys. And helping them eat soup. I don't see why you wouldn't want to see a poor hurt boy get some soup."

Garnelle smiled. She looked at me from the corner of her eyes. "Oh, I do, Mrs. Summers."

While we did the dishes, Deely disappeared to use the phone. She came back into the kitchen somberly, shaking her head. "Oh, I hope you girls are praying for your friend Neomadel Blaylock," she said. "You know she needs it now more than ever." I was glad for the change of subject but caught off guard. Deely sought each face earnestly before she continued. "Well, it was told to me in the form of a prayer request, mind you. Poor Neomadel. It's so awful. Her daddy's run off. Said he was going to join the navy, but he was found in Toullange with some woman. Now we'll have to—and this is another prayer request—find a new treasurer for the WMU. Neomadel told Raylene her mother is looking for . . . a *job*." Garnelle and I elbowed each other at the same time.

Mother said, "But Eugenia Blaylock has been the treasurer for twelve years. The very idea."

I closed my eyes and tried to picture Mrs. Blaylock, previous wife of the chairman of the school board, sitting humbly in the back at the WMU meetings with the rest of us.

AT CHURCH the weekend of July Fourth you'd have thought the war was already over. We had a group from the Scrappin' Valley Glee Club in to sing patriotic songs. We had an all-day picnic planned. During the sermon Pastor Miner read Roosevelt's speech aloud like he'd thought of it himself, after which for forty-five minutes he exhorted us to rise to the occasion like David in the face of the Philistine army. "What do you want to be caught doing," he warned, "when a bomb falls from the sky and in the single beat of a heart you go from this world to the judgment seat of God? Don't let God find you in a place you have to explain." I figured he was referring to drinking halls where terrible men hung out, waiting for loose girls to dance with them. "Satan," he intoned, finger pointed at the back door, "will take you further than you want to go, keep you longer than you want to stay, and charge you more than you want to pay!" Brother Miner used that motto so often I mouthed the words along with him. When the glee club sang "The Battle Hymn of the Republic," I felt overcome, my emotions acute and threadbare, like I was supposed to *know* something. Exactly what, I wasn't sure.

Church was over. Everyone stood around looking stunned for a few minutes. Nervous, like they'd put money down on something and were already having second thoughts. We were so patriotic our blood flowed in red, white, and blue ribbons. No one wanted to break the spell.

Then someone hollered "Amen!" and people laughed, and it was broken. We hurried home to retrieve our fried chicken and watermelon and jugs of iced lemonade and get back to the picnic. On the way back Opalrae and I lugged armloads of tablecloths and a blanket to put on the grass, with a picnic basket borrowed from Grandma Summers between us. A large black automobile came down the road in our direction and slowed as we approached. Junior Jasper was driving it. Without thinking, I smiled and lifted the fingers of my right hand from the bundle of tablecloths. He had the window down and nodded to my folks first. "Good morning, Mr. and Miz Summers. Fine day, ain' it, folks?"

"Hey-ho, Junior," I said. "We're off to a picnic."

"Yes, ma'am. I've got me a job driving Mr. Ricker's automobile here. He sent me to get some ice for y'all's picnic from the grocery. Gonna make ice cream."

Deely and Mother and I had been up until ten-thirty putting the hem in Deely's new dress and getting all the facings to lie down flat. The dress was organdy with little orange flowers, and it was flowing and ruffled so that wisps of it brushed against her legs. Mother kept saying it would have been perfect if only she had some silk stockings, but there weren't any to be had—not that we could afford, anyway—and so she had to wear ankle socks with her pumps. She looked pretty as a picture, Daddy said, and as if to prove it he got out the Kodak and made her pose in front of the mimosa tree this way and that several times.

Deely came to me after we got the food laid out. She exclaimed loudly how wonderful the message was and how it convicted her deep within her soul. She said, "I believe I'll embroider a hand towel with today's scripture verse to keep in my hope chest. To remind me of this propitious day."

I looked at Deely, her eyes bulging, her face radiant, mouth darting around the word "propitious," feeling it again and liking it. "Oh, good idea," I said. Satisfied, she turned and sauntered away. When she was running high like this, any contrary word from me would have brought immediate orders to stop trying to make Delia feel bad. I thought she mostly looked haunted and distracted, positively floating around like her whole body, not just her mind, was no longer connected to the earth. Her eyes shot this way and that, looking longingly toward the sky the way she always did in church. She believed she set a pace for me to follow, but she was always pathetic and lost, and at the same time zealous and ferocious without foundation. She somehow managed to be zealous in her very pathos.

I do have to admit that Deely looked good. She flitted around the picnic in her pale orange flowers like a butterfly, never lighting long enough to have a decent conversation—not even with Raylene. She and Raylene always had an "understanding," meaning that Delia forgave Raylene for being a whole year younger and spoke to her as if she were a real person. That day they just exchanged glances, their noses upturned, their righteousness glowing like neon even in broad daylight.

Beans Bandy was giving Deely the eye like anyone could see it, and if she sat anyplace for more than a few seconds, he was right there beside her, drooling. She ignored him with a masterful skill, staying out of his range and out of his line of vision slick as a sylph on a moonlit pond. I could sort of picture her with Beans. Him with that silver-dollar skull and her with her airy orangeness, both of them together making a big old splash in their little puddles of life.

After finding a place to balance a plateful of salads and fried chicken, I waited for Marty's cousin Rich to come over and talk to me, which he did after at least an hour of cutting his eyes this way to see if maybe I was likely to try to bite him or something. For somebody who was such a tough guy in the army, he seemed pretty shaky. He'd graduated last year, from Kirbyville High School. Got drafted three months ago and had two days leave before going over. He hadn't seen any combat yet, but to hear him tell it, life in boot camp was as rough as any field soldier ever saw.

I sat there listening to him go on and on about all the brave stuff he did, watching him smoking cigarettes like it was the most important thing he could do at that moment. I started concentrating on the way he would hold it in his lips and inhale like he was taking a mighty effort to come clean with his story, only the story flowed out without a break, as if he were rehearsing lines for a radio program. Sometimes he would let out all the smoke in a puff, and sometimes little wisps of smoke came out with his words like a chugging train engine. He took the pack from his pocket again and held it toward me. "Go ahead," he said, "they're real mild. I could sure use a case of these in the trenches."

"No thanks," I told him. "It's just something I'm not used to doing."

"Well," Rich said, "you won't get used to it if you don't do it." He smiled and winked at me.

"I guess I'm not interested," I said. I suddenly saw him the way I'd known him from before, in a plaid shirt and his daddy's holey work pants, cutting grass in their front yard with a push mower. He'd always have the shirt hanging clear open without a single button closed, like his chest was something we were all just dying to see, and a baseball hat on his head pushed way back, and he'd have a cigarette behind one ear as if he was just about to smoke it. "I think I'd better go see if Mother wants me to help do dishes or something," I said.

I left him looking puzzled as a puppy staring into a mirror, and I found Mother and asked her, "Doesn't Deely look good today?" which of course delighted her. She told me to run and visit with the young folks while there was still time.

D elia knew she was every bit a southern lady at last. She was radiant in her new dress on this sparklingly hot day as she held the image of a formal debut in her heart that was undiminished by the rustic setting. She knew she would have the last laugh, and that it would be demure and flirtatious and beautiful.

Raylene was trying her best to make some time with Danny Poquette, who was leaving at six in the morning for Fort Bliss. He was more engrossed in a plate of pie than any man had reason to be. Meanwhile, Delia imagined Danny, cold and shivering, fighting Germans, eating rations from a can. He was short and sturdy of build, boyish of face. His curly hair made him even more childish-looking, and he reminded her of the angel in the picture in the hallway at home. Danny had the same expression on his face as the little boy in the picture, the same hair, curly, soft, vulnerable, not at all ready for the evils of the world.

It was of utmost importance, on this day of days, for Delia to show Danny her most ladylike qualities. Thus, of course, to further emphasize his manliness. To let him see her for what she was, a combination of virtue and allure, all the while charming him with the beauty she felt was exuding from every pore. Poised where she could follow Raylene's one-sided conversation, she breathed a huge sigh of relief when at last Raylene gave up and left in search of some potato salad. "Would you like to rest a little?" she whispered to him. "Why don't you slip into the church and put your feet up on a pew? Get away from all the commotion." Delia smiled sympathetically. "You go on and don't make a fuss or anything, and I'll bring you some iced tea." She felt bristly with the singular importance of it all, carrying the jingling iced tea with its paper-thin sliver of lemon perched on the rim. As she got to the threshold, she stopped to make sure no one was watching, then kissed the rim of the glass before opening the door.

Inside the church it was quiet and stuffy, with the smells of worship heavy in the still air. The holy fragrance made her feel sanctified, puri-fied, glorious. It was candle wax and hymnbooks and colored glass windows and the glory of God shining down directly for her from the light over the pulpit on Sunday mornings. A whispery place, safe and above the world around it. "Here you go," she said. "Do you want lemon?"

"Sure. Thanks." He drank most of the tea in one draft.

"It's nice in here, isn't it?"

"Yeah. Yes, ma'am, I mean."

"Hard to settle down with all that silliness outside. This is my fa-vorite place in the world to be. Close to God, you know. No one can come before the throne of God and not feel His presence."

Danny nodded. He drained the tea and stretched out his legs on a pew, rubbing his thighs as if to stir the blood in them.

"I suppose it would be all right to tell you—that is, to confess, here in church," she cleared her throat and stood. Sighting a glimmer of sun-light pouring through a pale blue fragment of glass on a west window, she tiptoed near it and looked reverently to the picture in the colored glass. "I'll miss you while you are away."

"Oh? Thanks. That's nice."

"Personally, I mean. I suppose you'll be really lonely."

"I dunno. There's lots of guys around."

Delia knew her position in front of the window would be useless if he would not face her. She reached toward the windowsill, pushed at a tray left there to catch runoff from flowers if a pot were set upon it. Feeling the air thicken around her, she pushed the small metal tray off the sill and it clattered to the floor.

Danny came quickly to her side. "Let me get that for you, Miss Delia."

She laughed sweetly. "Miss? Call me Delia, Danny. We've known each other since childhood. There's no reason for formality now."

"Delia," he said obediently. "Here." He handed her the tray; she put it in place as if it were a holy relic.

"Danny? I'll wait for you until you're safely home."

"Thanks. I guess I'll take a walk outside now," he said.

She weighed the advantages of walking with him, the chances for more conversation. But she also knew that her beautiful dress and her elegance, so profound this day, could best be seen from afar. She judged that a memorable pose would surely cling to the heart of a lonely soldier longer than a few silly words. She reached toward the pulpit with fervent hands and paused to turn her face to him. "I'll be out shortly," she said, and bowed her head.

Sheriff Moultrie sipped lemonade and watched the crowd. His wife stood behind one of the tables laden with food, dishing up a plate for him. He put the toe of his boot discreetly on the front corner of the chair Bart Bandy was sitting in. Bart was concentrating on some of the boys Indian-wrestling toe to toe in the midst of a circle of squealing girls. "Hey, Bart," Moultrie said softly.

"Hey youse'f, Moultrie." Bandy shoved a mouthful in, saluting with his empty fork.

"How's business?" Moultrie said, not specifying whether he meant the legitimate one.

"Business fine. That missus o' your make a fine lemon meringue."

"That she does. Your boys look to be fine boys. They ever give you any trouble?"

"No, sir. No troubles. Got me four boy and t'ree girl. All *bon* chil'ren."

"Not everyone in this town is so lucky. There's some folks got kids even a black-strap whipping won't fix. Hell, you know the type." A long silence fell while each man thought of children past and present who fit the sheriff's description. After no one spoke, Moultrie went on, "I know you travel around town on business more than most people. Something's been on my mind—you know how you get to thinking about a puzzle and you just can't let go of it? It ain't important, but it racks my mind at times. So since you get around, I wondered if you heard anyone talking about lighting a fire? Maybe it wasn't kids that did it, but I think some of the older kids know about it. I mean, bigger than a campfire. Like burning down a shed or a woodpile or anything?"

Bandy chewed thoughtfully, staring at Moultrie's boot. "No, sir. Ain't heard o' that. What done burned?"

"Aw, just that old colored church. You know the one used to stand yonder through those trees. Found some gasoline cans inside." And a body. "It's nothing serious, just what they call public nuisance, but still, if it was kids that did it, they ought to get caught before they grow up to be criminals."

"Sho' got 'nough crim'nals in de world."

"Sure enough. That's a fact."

"Wisht I knew to tell you, Sheriff, I surely do. That ain't a fit thing to do. I pretty sure 'twaren't my boys. You ast 'em if you want. Mebbe dem Klan boys done it. Prob'ly dey did."

"Well, here's my angel with enough food for two men. Darlin', you think I'm still a growing boy?"

The beach-landing craft lurched through the choppy waters early in the morning to drop its great tongue wide and let them rush to the sandy atoll. Corporal Benally leaned into the sand on Wake Island. The world became a grisly motion picture, unfocused around the edges. Gordon leaped from the landing craft into a waist-deep tidal pool awash with bodies, floating in the tide like dead minnows in a bucket. Machine guns rattled like the strum of a stick on a rough rock. Everywhere the sky was perforated with the crash of artillery, sprays of pink sand, taste of bitter salt. The bulky radio pack had weighed him down as they swayed, crammed like cattle in the craft, but now its sixty-five pounds were lighter than air. All through the training days of hiking and running with the huge radio pack on his back, Gordon had felt the burgeoning weight of it, the weight of the words he had to learn, the technology that went into the talking box and brought other words from afar. He believed in his task in ways he could hardly have explained. He wanted to strike blows against the Enemy and was pleasantly amazed at the military's understanding of the power of words to do so. Benally fired his weapon and exultantly pierced the air with war cries as he plunged through the brine.

Over the vast ocean, each of the twenty-one days since Hawaii, he had offered prayers to the Ocean People. A couple of men threatened to throw him overboard if he didn't stop singing, calling him "flathead nigger Indian." A young white boy he'd talked to only briefly, Private Coby Brueller, turned defiantly to fight them one day when someone criticized Gordon for praying. Brueller had made them eat their words, in a scrap that the officers either didn't see or ignored. The men stopped making fun and left him alone. From that day Gordon had included Coby in his prayer and hoped they would give each other strength. He told Coby he would fight beside him all the way up the beach. He knew, however, that this was beyond the Ocean People's power to control. This war was something evil from another world.

In the chaos on the beach Gordon wondered about his cousin. Billy was carrying a radio, too, and Billy was a lot smaller. Not as strong, Gordon worried. Tough, but not as big. They were in the same unit but purposely spread far apart during the landing, so that in the event one was killed, the other would still carry on with the equipment. "Diné Tsosie!" Gordon yelled, then closed his mouth. To call a name! To point out a victim for death to take! That was an old men's superstition, he knew, but they'd brought him so surely back to their world with that ceremony it was as if he'd thought of nothing but old ways all his life. "Rosie-posey!" he called at the top of his lungs. "Running nosey!"—any words to throw off the mistake. People yelled back, but their words were lost in the maelstrom.

Next to him, roaring like a human lion, was Coby, a quiet young man, only nineteen or so, from the South somewhere. A voice cried out in pain behind him, but he focused only on getting through the water. Once on the sandy shelf he could do little but lean forward and fall under the weight of the heavy radio unit he was hauling. Something carried him forward. Lunging and kicking against the sand, he went up the beach through the tumult, forced by will and muscles beyond his control. He was a Marine, in either world, a warrior.

Coby flopped next to him in the sand, a pistol in his hand. He carried the only Browning automatic rifle the troop had been issued, and he, too, was burdened and clumsy, with ammunition in canvas bags attached to a woven belt.

A pause in the firing made Gordon raise his head to look around them, and he pushed Coby's shoulder. "Let's move up," he said. "Now's our chance."

Coby nodded. His face was white, his eyes wide as if in terror, but his jaw set. "Follow me," he said, and scooted forward without waiting for an answer. Coby crawled ahead ten yards. Then fifteen. Then he got to a low crouch and rushed forward through a barrage of small-arms fire. From somewhere directly in their paths a grenade arched toward Coby. He rolled right, hid his face, and disappeared for a few moments in the dust and shrapnel. Gordon breathed slowly for five counts and threw three grenades in the direction of the firing that had Coby pinned down. In a moment's silence Brueller rolled onto his side and looked back, grinning, holding his helmet on with both hands.

Gordon slithered through the sand, wary of letting it fill his rifle's barrel. "I thought you were done for," he said. He spit sand, but it still made grinding sounds in his teeth. "I'm heading up for those trees there," he said, and crawled past. His eyes burned and watered, but he couldn't make his hands leave the stock of the rifle to rub them.

Brueller slapped the side of his helmet. "Say what? Dang. I can't hear you. That was something. Look, they're moving." Coby reached Gordon's side and at that second a bullet glanced off Benally's helmet and against the pack on his back, to bury itself in the sand beside them. Coby arched up to a kneeling position and fired five shots over Gordon's head. Three Japanese soldiers, one of whom was still aiming at them, wilted and fell to the ground. Coby stood and ran past Gordon a few feet, then dropped to his knees, shouting over his shoulder, "Y'all stay in my tracks. We'll get through the barbed wire there, but there's mines."

Gordon stayed in Coby's tracks. They reached a place where the sand was hot and dry. The tides rarely touched this high on the beach, and the whitened sand below gave way to bleached, acid-smelling scrabble full of stiffened black seaweed and sharp-edged shells. "Let me go first this time," Gordon said. A mortar landed near them and peppered them with pebbles and stinging, salty sand. It rocked two tank barriers strung with coiled razor wire up onto one leg like a giant's game of jacks. The springlike coil stretched and rose in the air, forming an arch under which they could have walked standing up if not for the machine-gun fire coming at them. His head was filled with a loud buzzing. Some giant insect must live on this island. They shouted over the high-pitched, grinding whine in their ears.

"I'm going to take out that Jap MG nest or know the reason why," Coby yelled. "Y'all just stay down!" He moved, five paces, two paces, now seven, now ten. Another round of machine-gun fire put them on their faces in the sand. Coby said, "Y'awright, Benally? Damn it. My ears are ringing like crazy. Stick with me. I'm going up."

Benally grasped Brueller by his pants leg and jerked him back to the ground. "No, not yet. Look. Look around us. We're alone."

Coby raised his head slightly. They were very alone. Completely cut off from the rest. They lay in a shallow depression formed by a previous blast. The bridge of wire where they'd breached the line still hung suspended, but no one followed them. Far up the beachhead, Allied soldiers had reached the hot, dry sand and were inching toward the jungle, some of them now and then obscured by smoke and dust. But close to their position, all other men were pinned against the wet sand, motionless, frozen in time in the midst of a skewed danse macabre.

Gordon breathed the breath from the bitter sand. It thirsted for blood. He could not feel the corn pollen beneath his chest. Maybe it had been torn off as he edged up the beach on his stomach with the radio on his back. The only firing in their area was coming from the thick trees. His ears rang with a noise dense and loud enough to deafen him, but when Coby spoke, Gordon heard him through the din.

"Shit. Cover fire. And I'm going up there. See that rock? Betcha there's another MG nest back there. I'll lob a grenade in on those sons a bitches." Coby raised himself to a crouched run, scuttling to within ten yards of the low plants that edged the jungle growth.

Gordon fired bursts at the foliage and saw Coby sink to the sand and wave him up. He tried to shrink in his own skin and ran in the same steps as Coby had. As if in slow motion, he saw Japanese soldiers rise from the green plants ahead and aim straight at him as he ran. Brueller shot them, so close to Benally's side that the movement of the bullets through the air made him shiver. Each of the enemies raised their arms in stunned disbelief, weapons still at the ready, and, sneering without crying out, fell as dead weight to the ground. In less time than it took for the last one to sink, Coby pulled the pin on a grenade and pitched it over the low wall of sandbags they could now see through the trees. The concussion threw the body of another man into the air along with a machine gun, its snakelike bandolier tangled around the flying man's right arm.

Gordon crawled on his hands and knees to Coby's side and dropped heavily beside him. "Thanks, man," Gordon said. "Don't know what I was doing running like that."

"Y'all don't do it again, awright, Benally? I'm trying to save ammo." He was giddy. "Here, keep this for luck." He tossed the ring from the grenade.

Gordon caught it and locked eyes for a moment with the white man. The pack took weight again. It pressed him low into the blistering sand. It crushed the breath out of him.

"Benally," said Coby, "I want cover. I'm going up there, and you stay in my tracks."

"Gotcha."

"There, about ten o'clock. Where these sons a bitches keep coming from," Coby said, and scuttled forward on his belly. Then he said, "Do you hear something?"

Machine-gun fire sounded again, and this time the very air around their helmets whizzed with leaden mosquitoes. Gordon caught up again. "Mortars. We're close enough to hear them launch."

"God . . ." said Coby.

The ground around them shook violently. Sand buried Gordon's head, and it felt as if the earth abruptly gave way; his stomach slid into a hole that opened up beneath him. His ears rang, louder than any waterfall, and a drone filled his head again, this time accompanied with swirling darkness. He wondered if he'd died. The crushing radio pack sank on his ribs.

A few minutes of darkness held him; then, gingerly, without moving anything but his tongue, Gordon spit acidic grit from his mouth. The sound in his ears darkened his vision. Numbed his mind. He tried to take stock, knowing that Japanese gunners might still be watching him for signs of life, and minutely shifted his head in its awkward position, higher than his swayed back, pinned down under the equipment in a depression in the sand. Coby's body lay next to him, its mouth still open, forming the words he would never say. His helmet was gone, along with the top of his head. Only the face remained. Gordon turned away from it.

Beyond him another mortar rumbled the earth, and from behind a shout came, thin and frail against the violent blackness in his ears. Marines were coming up the beach, but at great distance from where he'd come ashore. Five more craft opened maws, and now the men were gaining foothold at the line of tank barricades suspending hooked wire coils. But they were moving farther and farther down the beach. The firing around him stopped. It concentrated on the Marines some two hundred yards or so away, and Gordon was alone under the radio, a tortoise under a great shell, next to the body of Coby.

He jerked the equipment upward and found his feet beneath him willing to move. He found a dense, brushy place to crouch and wait and try to hear what was happening around him. He'd left the Browning. He could hear Sergeant Andrews berating the squad for that. But the sergeant was dead; so was the squad, and Coby. Everyone except him. He felt his every sense keening. Most of the trees close at hand were unclimbable stalks without branches, but not far away he saw another bushy cluster that might be good hiding. Aware of the direction of the firing, he pushed aside bushes and moved into the thicket. It closed around him, and Gordon pulled the radio from his back.

The dead stretched like paving stones on a gruesome pathway from where they had first landed to where he now hid. A branch cracked, and a Japanese bayonet thrust through the leaves close to his face. Gordon held his breath. Voices spoke in a strange tongue, and several more forms moved stealthily beside the brush enclave where he hid. Not daring to move even to see them, Gordon waited to turn his eyes until there were no more sounds of motion.

He pulled his knife and, intensely aware of every minute sound, pushed it into the mossy ground beneath his feet. Little by little he dug himself a hole. First it was enough to crouch into, a fist's depth of wet soil. Then it was a foot or so deep, the sand piled upon clumps of moss he removed and placed, wet side down, around his tiny bunker. He thought of stories he'd heard as a child. So wise were the grandmothers and aunts and grandfathers and uncles. So many stories of Rabbit and how he eluded the Coyote, and Snake, how he waited for his prey, nudging aside the soil, unhurried, to find a place that would serve as both lair and stronghold.

By evening the sounds of battle were far away. Now and then the earth trembled with mortar rain, but it was a distant thunder. Heat from the day's sun left the sand quickly, and fleas attacked him in the hole. Merciless as the enemy whose land they owned. Gordon rubbed at them, aware of making sound, and consoled himself with asking them also to bite and make itch the hides of all the enemies who still walked on the land.

When darkness took hold of the island, quiet seemed to come with it. The battle, which had rumbled on for hour upon hour, now stopped utterly. The stillness was dense. Once again rhythmic brushing among the leaves alerted Benally to the passing of a small line of soldiers. They didn't talk, but he knew they were enemies, for they moved past him confidently. Americans would not yet be confident in this thick jungle.

He considered signaling with the radio, but he wasn't sure how far away the enemies were. He decided it was too risky to make a sound. And he knew he must find a way to go back and retrieve the Browning before it fell into enemy hands. Slipping his knife again from its sheath, he felt for a pebble from the soil he'd piled around himself and rubbed it slowly against the edge of the blade.

Hours later Gordon edged himself from the protection of his hiding place, covering the radio with brush and moss, filling the hole he'd dug with branches that would be easy to remove when he came back. A quiet voice spoke, not far off. He adjusted the helmet on his head and crouched. The branches he'd stuck into the netting caught in a vine and pulled at the helmet, and the unexpected tug made cold sweat break over his back. With one hand Gordon touched the place under his shirt where the corn pollen should have been. It was still there. He'd been afraid it had torn away, but it was still there.

In the direction the enemies had gone he found a small clearing about ten feet across. He skirted it, staying out of the moonlight, until he came to the tree he estimated was directly in line with his hiding place. There, bent low at its base, he felt their presence before he saw them and moved stealthily around the tree trunk. Suddenly he was face to face with enemy soldiers. Two of them, small men with brown skin and dark eyes, knelt over a small kit, eating from it. They looked up in surprise, reaching for their rifles. Gordon nodded at them, held a finger to his lips. The men's expressions and stance instantly relaxed. They crouched again, and one of them said something to him. Gordon nodded again and stepped sideways into the foliage. He'd been told they had black hair, and he saw a flicker of recognition in their eyes, as if he were one of them. Good. If they didn't recognize him as a GI, he would last longer.

He made his way back around the edge of the clearing. There, hunched at the place where he had crept from the thicket of brush, another enemy soldier seemed to be looking into the hole. Gordon's knife was quiet. But as the man fell from his hands, Gordon felt a terrible urge to shout. He shuddered, realizing he'd been shouting all day, every step of the way; he'd crossed every grain of sand with a rage of noise.

From his shallow hiding place he watched and listened. The two Japanese soldiers stayed in place, apparently keeping guard. He wasn't sure why they accepted his presence, but he wasn't taking any chances. He waited, one hour and then another, until at last one of the men leaned against a tree and slept. The other kept ready, rifle poised, but after a while he raised himself to look around. Gordon was waiting behind him. The man fell silently to the ground. Gordon dispatched the other in his sleep, but he was not so quiet, making one choking moan under the blade before he, too, was silent.

Moving around the place where he had stashed the radio, Gordon made a wide circle. He was alone, as far as he could tell. A bright light appeared over his shoulder. It was the moon, watching people warring on this island. Benally wondered for a moment if it could really be the same moon he'd always known, and he moved his eyes to see it. For the first time in many hours he felt calm. Insects chirped, and a strange thudding sound made him start. He pushed at a large, waxy leaf and uncovered a toad. He let out his breath. The toad slipped under the brush.

Gordon slowly pulled out the radio's antenna and cranked the spark handle. A crackle of static broke the air. Alarmed at the noise, Gordon pulled off his shirt and wrapped the receiver in it, cupping it over his mouth and head so he could hear and speak. Fleas and gnats attacked his bare arms and back with a vengeance, but he got across his position as near as he could figure it. He was the last one of Charlie Company. From where Gordon reported his location, the voice on the other end assured him he was now at least half a mile behind enemy lines.

Someone crept past him just before dawn, so soundless as to arouse his admiration along with suspicion. Just like the games the boys used to play, hiding from each other, camping on the ridge at Black Mountain

Sitting Up. That was the summer of long nights, when he'd entered his first rodeo, the summer his sister went to the women's side. Billy should be in the group that landed in the second wave far up the beach, going in under the barrage of shelling from ships offshore. Gordon was proud of his mission, proud for all his ancestors and his children who might follow, that he had this chance to do something of such magnitude. He only had to stay alive long enough to have a few children, he thought with a smile.

He mashed a mosquito against his left forearm with the thumb of his right hand. The insect was gorged, and Gordon's blood smeared into the sand and sweat on his skin. Maybe he wasn't in such a hurry to leave his ghost behind on this dank and sultry island.

I keep thinking there has to be something more I can do about this war than pray. Collect grease. Save cans. Do without sugar when heaven knew we'd been doing without it for so long we didn't know how to do *with* it. I'd begun reading the paper zealously, sitting next to Daddy as he finished the front page, eager to pore over it before Mother and Deely cut coupons and store ads. And Monday morning's paper had an article about children being saved from bombing in England. Mothers, it said, were throwing their own bodies in front of fleeing rescuers to make them take their children. Babies were being rounded up by the hundreds, taken to safe places in Ireland, France, Canada, and even America.

Then I saw another article on the opinions editor's page. Dub Evertt, from out on Stobbs Avenue past the mill, had written in that he didn't believe there was any crime in what the Germans were doing as long as they stayed in their own country to do it. Dub said that last week's *Life* had said that the Germans wanted to kick all the Jews out of their country, so if all they were doing was to kick squatters off their land, they had a perfect right to. The editor, Henry Scoville, answered him right back—his words were in italic writing, which he always set up to show he was *The Editor* and had only done folks a favor printing their letters anyway—and told Dub there in the paper that the Germans weren't kicking Jews out, they were shooting them down in the streets, bombing them in their beds. People there were fleeing for their lives, he said, and suggested Dub put on a uniform like Scoville's boy Arvin had and go see the facts firsthand.

"Daddy," I said, pushing my piece of newspaper onto the table and speaking toward the shield made of his, "do you think the Germans are killing Jewish people? Do you think they kill them all? Or just the soldiers?"

"I think what we've got to worry about here in the States is the Japs. I've got to go to work."

I followed him toward the front door, where he stopped to smooth his moth-eaten fedora as importantly as if it had been new. I held his lunch in an oiled paper bag. "There's a boiled egg in there I made for you," I said.

"That's one of the good things about having you girls graduated. You've got more time to help your mother."

I nodded. When I went back to the table, I looked again at the aerial photographs printed in the paper. I put the sections side by side. Under the one that said "London," was a smaller title "The Youngest Refugees." Later that day Mother had me clean out our bedroom and sweep under the beds, moving everything. I found a church fan made during the Christmas program, lost off the edge of the bed; it had lain, collecting dust, since before Christmas. It had a picture of Jesus, a tiny blond-haired baby lying in a soft-looking bin of hay. I blew the dust from the fan and tucked it in between the bedsprings and the mattress, then went on with my dusting.

Sweeping, I hummed a Christmas carol. After I'd gone through "O Come All Ye Faithful," I remembered the pageant we'd done at school, after Pearl Harbor and before the siege of Dr. Fine had begun. Marty had stood in a costume made from his daddy's bathrobe and hollered, "Hail, all hail. 'Where is He that is born King of the . . .'" Suddenly I sat on the bed, so heavily that it groaned in the springs. "'. . . Jews,'" I finished.

Even back then, soldiers had been sent to slaughter baby Jews, killing them in the streets. I mouthed my lines from the play, "'And there was heard in Ramah, Rachel weeping for her children.'" Then I saw my face in the mirror and gulped. "It is a sign." My mind raced around the thought so quickly I stood and walked a tight circle around the room. If English children could be saved from random bombing, somebody, surely *somebody*, must be saving the baby Jews from the slaughter. The same as the Passover. The same as the Exodus, baby Jesus in the manger, and Moses in the bulrushes. "Mother!" I fairly screamed. "I have to go to church. I have to find Brother Miner!"

I put on my Sunday dress, the only one that would do for this mission. I started to put on my Sunday shoes but decided they were too fragile for the pace I intended to make. Mother's voice was still calling, "What in heaven's name are you doing?" when I heard the screen door slam against the jamb.

Breathlessly, I explained the plight to Brother Miner, how I wanted to help rescue those children. He listened, even appeared interested, then leaned forward, and said, so sincerely, so lovingly, "Sister Frosty, we cannot do anything to thwart the will of God. You are talking about a race of people who rejected the Savior. Until they face Jesus, there is no saving them."

"But, Brother Miner, I'm just talking about the children. They haven't had a chance to reject anything. Somebody must be saving the children. I just thought you might know who. I just want to know if they're saving the babies. I've thought all the way here. They have a Project Airlift; I want to call this Project Moses."

He looked at me as if I were just let out of some mental asylum. "Sister Frosty, this is something that's not your business. Be a good girl and go home."

I felt defiant, like I wanted to write an essay to Henry Scoville.

"How can it not be our business to save those children? Americans are saving British children. We have to do something."

"Don't be sassing me, girl. The British are Christian children. Totally different. Now, I'm the first one to appreciate charity, but let it come from someone who's spent a little time in the Word and reflected on the whole picture, Sister Frosty. Not just chasing some wild hare. You just take it to the Lord in prayer, and you'll see that *all* those who reject the Savior are in danger of hellfire." He put his hand on my shoulder and propelled my immobile form toward the door to his office. "It's called *judgment*." When I reached the threshold and he could do it without actually hitting me with the door, he closed it against my back, saying, "Read the Word, you'll see right."

I went to the Methodist minister, the Full Gospel preachers, even the fancy office of Brother Ambrose Caney at First Southern—where I could only explain my dilemma to his secretary—and finally, screwing up all my courage, to the Catholic church. A lady in a long black dress asked me if I wanted to see "the Father" and I said, "No, I want to talk to your preacher." She shrugged and walked away, muttering. Eventually, though, a man came out, wearing pretty much the same long black dress that she'd worn. I was terrified but desperate. So I told him my story, too.

He said, "I don't know of anyone doing that. You need to find a Jewish congregation. It's called a synagogue, just like in the Old Testament. You find a Jewish rabbi; maybe they've got something going already."

"Where?"

"Over to Baton Rouge, I think they've got some Jews there."

"How do I find them?"

"That I don't know. They don't just hang a sign on their door. Sometimes they get people throwing eggs at them and such like. Sometimes you can see one of those little markers on the door."

I couldn't possibly walk the streets of Baton Rouge looking for people who'd rather not be found. I wrote about my plan to Henry Scoville and took the letter to him personally. He told me he wasn't about to run that letter. Discouraged, I ambled home, dragging my hand against flowers and weeds in full array, staying clear of the thistle heads. The more I walked, though, the more excited I grew. Project Moses would lift those babies out of the war. Maybe I'd even get little baskets to carry them all in. And a blue blanket for each one. Unless they were too big for a blanket. Oh, it would be such a wonderful work, such a successful, magnificent thing, that when people finally found out it was me that started it all, I'd be something then. Remembered, a famous missionary like Corrie ten Boom or Lottie Mae, or like Babe Ruth or that man who invented the Boy Scouts. There would be a Frosty Summers Fund collected each year to help orphans in wars from this day forward, cited by President Roosevelt. This day was just the beginning; I wasn't done. I'd call Mayvis Plinkle, the central telephone operator, and see if she knew where to find some Jews who could help me start saving the children. All great things have a rough beginning, I knew that. The passion made me tremble.

Mother grabbed my sleeve and twisted me around where I stood. "I just had a call from Brother and Sister Miner," she said.

THE NEXT MORNING Deely was moping around the house lamenting the fact that she was out of gasoline and that Mr. Ricker asked her to donate her tires to the rubber drive, telling her she didn't need to drive around a town that was walking distance even for Mrs. Brady. "What does he think I am," she said, "some kind of mule?" I went out to the garden to pull weeds, trying to stay as far from Mother as possible. I was wearing a batch of red welts on my arms and legs and back, plus what felt like a bruise on my left cheek, though it didn't show. I put all that out of my mind. Other missionaries with a purpose before them had been tortured, put in chains, starved. I'd wait for a chance to call Mayvis.

There were hornworms on the tomatoes, so I went after those ugly things with two crossed sticks. Mother always just yanked them off with her hands, but I couldn't stand the feel of them. I stabbed the hornworms with my stick, gouging them mercilessly. I flung them over the garden fence as close to the tracks as they'd go. It was near time for the morning train, and sure enough, before too long the whistle blew its usual two shorts and a long when it crossed the road above the Knob.

The train came charging by, going faster than I'd ever seen it. I waved to the engineer like I always do, but there was no wave back. I saw through the trees around the curve in the tracks that there was something on top of the cars. Soldiers, with machine guns; they pointed them straight at me, so that I was terrified to move. I backed away, feeling behind myself with my hands until I came to the garden fence. I ran to the porch, up the stairs two at a time. All my life I'd been hearing how we're all blood-guilty, as sin-ridden as the most devilish murderer. I felt as if they'd come for me at last. Discovered, tried and convicted, ready for execution. I wondered what it would feel like to be shot, particularly if I were shot for smuggling Jewish babies into America—so, as Mother had underscored with the strop, that they would grow up and rot our country and turn people away from Jesus Christ as I was bound and determined to have them do. I imagined a bullet going into my heart. Punching in, heavily but deeper than a fist. The sigh, like in the movies; the dramatic rolling to the side with a look of peaceful resignation. It never seemed to hurt if they were hit in the heart. That was curious. I went and stared down the tracks. I wondered where I would have to stand so that the machine gun would go straight for the heart.

"Frosty! You have work to do!" Mother's voice shouted.

MAYVIS PLINKLE DIDN'T mind at all, looking up total strangers. It was just another chance for her to snoop into people's business. A few days later she connected me to a man who said his name was Rabbi Levy. When I told him what I wanted to do, he was silent for so long I thought he'd hung up the phone.

"That isn't possible," he said at last.

"I know it'll take money—" I started.

"Our children will die with their parents. It's that simple."

There was nothing I could do to convince him otherwise. When I hung up, I felt deflated. It was a good plan. How could people not accept something so obviously meant to help? How could they refuse? For nearly two weeks I believed I'd found my whole purpose for living. Now I had nothing to do.

IN THE FIRST WEEK of August 1942, when the rain left us and the whole earth seemed to be in the clenches of a relentless heat wave, two men with neat, new-looking black suits came to Sabine. They got off the three o'clock bus with nothing but briefcases, and they put up posters all over town about a "National Patriotic Meeting" the next day, in the Sanctuary of First Southern Baptist Church. Everyone in town was urged to attend. It's not like they'd have to ask twice; none of the girls in town—except Raylene, who sits in the Smiths' front room with Marty—has been on a date since the war started. This is such a boring little town that they could have gotten just as good a turnout if they'd announced a reading of the Fort Worth telephone book.

Four third-graders were rounded up to sing "My Country 'Tis of Thee," and Coby Brueller's little brother carried in the United States flag while they did. Old men in the crowd saluted. We actually had six really old fellows who'd served in the Confederate Army, and one of them wore his gray cap and coat even though it was hotter than all get-out inside the building.

Marty Haliburton was across the room from me, his foot still in a bandage that looked bigger than his thigh, his crutches at his side, next to his mother. When we stood to sing "The Star-Spangled Banner," tears streamed down his face, and he kept his hand at a salute, even though he'd never made it to the army, where he was meant to go. No one was sure if anyone would ever track down the colored men that tried to break into the Haliburtons' house that night.

Poor Marty had chased the two men and lost them in the dark of the low woods that led to swampy land west of their place. In the dark he'd waited on Sugar Loaf Rock with his rifle, and when the moon came out and he saw one of them, he'd accidentally shot off his own big toe. The men left him there to die, too. If it wasn't for his hunting dogs finding him the next morning, passed out from pain, he'd have bled to death. I smiled at Marty, weeping there with patriotic fervor. The Calling surged inside me, making my head feel light and my eyes water with unexpected tears.

Brother Ambrose Caney from First Southern stood solemnly and intoned all of heaven to witness our devotion to God and our country. Deely didn't stand but sat fanning herself long before the "Amen" from Brother Caney was chorused all around with heartier voices shouting "Amen!" The visiting men tacked posters around the table on the stage: pictures of muscular women with kerchiefs on their heads and tools in their hands, sleeves rolled up like a farmer and wearing pants like a man. WE CAN DO IT! the posters announced, and KEEPING THE HOME FIRES ALIVE! and AMERICA'S WOMEN WORK WITH PRIDE! All around the room fans broke out just like it was church; the flutter of cardboard and painted paper looked as if a host of butterflies had been invited to the laps of the people as the first of the three men got up to speak. Lots of people nodded off to nap—also not unlike church.

One man stood, put his fingertips together, and looked sadly at the floor of the stage. He shook his head, took an audible breath, and somberly drew letters on a portable blackboard, two feet high: H-O-P-E. He spoke slowly, richly, as if he were on a movie set. "Hope. America was built on it. Our mothers, whose tender nurturing has seen us through childhood; dads, whose example led us to to adulthood; babies at this moment lying in their cradles, trusting that we the people of America will protect them until the terror of this day is over. The courageous spirit that forged this country out of a savage wilderness must not let hope be shattered. Now," he said, and paused. Then he drew a big slash through the word "HOPE" with the side of the chalk. "Picture everyone you love, everyone you ever knew—your grandmother so feeble she cannot walk, your tiniest newborn infant still suckling under a blanket—dragged in chains to be imprisoned. Brought down by Fifth Columnists, Nazis, and the tyranny of Imperial Japan. Tortured . . . defiled . . . executed." How hopeless my hope chest would be if I were marched away to a prison camp. "The United States is almost out of airplanes, bombs, and tools.

The factories in California are desperate for girls and women to learn to rivet metal, cut steel, to build engines and airplanes and bombs. We're desperate, ladies, desperate."

When they asked for questions, Marty was first to raise his hand. "How are you going to teach girls to do that?" he said. "Women can't build bombs."

One of the men behind the table adjusted his tie and smiled. "Oh, yes, young man. I see you've already paid your price. We've implemented a program using women and girls from all over the country. They are hard at work as we speak, making tremendous inroads, carrying out—"

"Putting men out of work!" someone shouted from behind my head.

"No!" the recruiter answered. "Men who have jobs that can't be done by women are still employed, but every woman who fills a desk job or a factory assembly line puts another trained, armed soldier on the fighting line." The man chuckled and said, "I don't suppose you'd want to put a pretty girl in petticoats in a trench with a fifty-caliber machine gun?" The crowd laughed. "I didn't think so," he said with a handsome smile. I liked the way he talked. His words were clear and crystalline, his language as foreign as if he'd come from a far country—every bit as strange as Dr. Fine's speech. Maybe to us in Sabine, Texas, California was as foreign a country as England.

My heart was hammering against my ribs. I was ready to swim the ocean with a dagger held in my teeth. People kept asking the stupidest things. Someone wanted to know who were the corporate heads of Boeing and Lockheed, and why aren't they in uniform serving their country? I was going to pass out from the sheer stupidity of their questions. All I needed to know was how fast I could get to California.

After twenty minutes of questions at last there was a silence. The man said, "Look, folks, we are losing ground to their advances. I don't know if you've heard about Midway Island yet. Have you? Thousands—" His voice cracked. His face reddened, and a tear moved down his cheek. "Thousands of our boys poured out their life's blood trying to gain a foothold on Japanese soil. If we can't get the people to help . . . well, I hate to think where we'll hide. But I *believe* in the people of

America. I believe that the young women of this country will not let her go down in flames." A burst of applause followed. The man continued, smiling with those white teeth. He dabbed his cheek with a handkerchief. He said, "How about it, girls? If you can run a sewing machine, you can run a steel punch. Can you see yourself learning to operate machinery and being paid good wages to do it?"

I could go to California. God's voice was calling me from across the country. I raised my hand—it shook so hard it looked like I was waving—and stood on trembling knees. Yes. My whole body vibrated with the urgency I felt. Yes. I stammered, "Sir, I will come and build airplanes. I'll go."

For five beats of my heart, louder than the roaring in my ears, there was wooden silence. Then rustling, and at least a dozen others stood, one by one. We formed a line and one at a time signed our names to the roster. They handed out papers with directions, the names of boardinghouses, and the guarantees of pay, promotions, dozens of other things I didn't understand. Each of us received a coupon for a free bus ticket or a voucher for twenty-five gallons of gasoline for transportation.

My family trundled home, talking quietly. I clutched my papers in my hand until they drooped with humidity and sweat. As we walked, Mother was going on and on about how Maureen Dobbs's cousin Beatrice signed up to work in the Naval Yard at Port Arthur, a few hours' drive south of here, and got herself in trouble in a month. And how Aunt Uvalia's son Donny was off in Europe and his wife was down at Sweetwater, wearing pants and fixing airplane engines just like a man. I couldn't tell by her tone if that was shocking or exciting or maybe some of each. When we walked in our front door, she took off her hat and held it as if it bore some significance to the subject. "California is far away," she said. "So far."

I went into the kitchen and started measuring pinto beans to put on to soak for tomorrow's supper. Delia was washing dishes left behind from supper without a single hint of protest. My papers were spread across the kitchen tablecloth. It looked like someone had made a quilt with a blue-and-white-checked background, spreading white rectangles at different angles across it, like birds, soaring.

"Well, Frosty, that was a brave thing you did," Deely said.

Mother stood behind us. "It was. Very brave," Mother said. "Volunteering like that. You caused a lot of people to chip in to help the war effort. That was a good thing to do. I'm proud of you."

"Thanks, Mother. Thanks. I guess it's just over a week until I have to be packed up to go. I'm really a little nervous."

"What are you talking about?" Mother said.

"About being on my own in a strange place. I'm glad they'll have rooming houses ready for the girls that are going." Maybe I'd take my silver spoon.

"Well, young lady, what makes you think you're actually *going* to California? I said it was a good thing you did getting all those people to volunteer. But you can't think you're going alone to California to run wild."

"But I promised," I said.

"Well, that wasn't a real promise. That was just a—a something else."

"What? What does that mean?" If I didn't go to California, what would be left for me? Working at the post office and doing dishes? Waiting to marry someone like Beans Bandy or Marty Haliburton?

"Oh, you know."

"No, I don't. I had every intention of doing what I said I'd do. I meant it. You've always told us to stand for what's right. I was—I *am* sincere. I want to help."

"Well, the best way to help is for you to stay here and act like a lady and quit trying to find excuses to run off and go wild and turn into some kind of trash like Beatrice Dobbs."

"Mother," I started.

"Don't sass me, young lady. Get that done there, and then you get in and scrub that bathroom like it never was before. I want the whole place to shine like it was new."

"No."

"What did you say?"

"I said no, Mother."

"No. No? I want that bathroom cleaned this minute!"

"I'll do the bathroom, but, no, ma'am, Mother. I've been feeling this way ever since Deely went up in church and said she was devoted to the war effort. I was, too, but I didn't know what I'd do, so I didn't say anything. I signed up to build airplanes. I intend to do it."

At the sound of our raised voices Daddy came to the door to assess the situation. I had every expectation of being skinned alive, but I held my ground, standing determinedly over the bowl of wet pinto beans. I sank both my hands into the bowl, pinching beans between my fingers to hold them still while I waited for the explosion, the sound of thunder. Here I was talking back to my mother while clawed, swastika-tattooed hands reached for innocent American babies. I took a deep breath. My jaw was trembling. "I have to go. The war is real. It takes all of us. All of us, that man said." Any second now and God's mighty hand would smash me like a mosquito. Either way I'd be free of this place.

Mother's mouth opened two or three times, and finally, her eyes drilling into me in disbelief, she shouted "Earl! Come here, quick!" not seeing Daddy standing behind her.

Deely nodded at me, looking sincere. "Mother and Daddy only want God's will for your life, dear." She turned toward the sink, filling a pitcher with water. "Let's us pray over this issue." Deely brought the water to the table and filled glasses with ice, serving them to each of us as if we were sitting in the diner. Daddy looked surprised when she handed him the glass, spilling it down the side.

The telephone rang. I heard Mother's voice in the hall saying, "Yes, that's true. Very patriotic. Yes. And brave. Just fine, thank you. Yes, I'll tell her. She'll do that. Sure enough. Bye, now."

I said to Daddy, "I just have to do something besides sit here and be scared all the time."

Mother returned, her expression softened, a warm blush on her collarbones.

Deely cleared her throat and folded her hands in front of herself on the tablecloth. "I think y'all should let her go. I think it's very noble," Deely said. "My own calling is toward something much more humble."

More ladylike was what she meant. I turned to Deely. I couldn't read what I saw in her face. She was smiling so tenderly at me, and yet her eyes were so chilling at the same time. An unexpected ally, regardless of her motives. "You know, Mother," I said, watching Deely, "if God had asked me to join the Women's Air Force, I'd be really afraid. But this is safe. Working in a factory, living in a dormitory with other girls. I've heard the news about the war. We can't be sure we'll even win." I drank my water. "It's going to take more than rolling bandages."

"Psshh. It isn't really that bad," Mother said. "Tell her, Earl."

"Maybe it is that bad," he mumbled.

"What?" She was not used to being contradicted by Daddy.

"I read the paper," he said.

"Lands. You can't believe those papers. They make stuff up."

"You can't make up those pictures. If all three of those men from California say it's that bad . . . well, maybe it's that bad. America could lose."

Mother said, "Lands' sakes alive."

That night was probably the first time in my life that I'd ever felt any persuasive power with my parents. I don't know how much of it had to do with Deely's complicity in this, nor what my service would gain her, but at the moment I didn't care. In the end we went to bed, satisfied that I would be going to California for three months. A trial period, they called it. And I was to write home every other day and find someone, maybe that recruiting man, whom they could count on to let them know if I was showing signs of running wild. When I hit the pillow, I slept hard for an hour or so; then, in the small hours of the early morning, I awoke as if an alarm had gone off in my head. Lying there staring at the uneven wall over my bed as if I'd never seen it before, I made mental notes of everything I intended to take with me.

That week Garnelle Fielding got really busy—doing what, I couldn't figure out. She was just never home if I called, too busy at work to stop and speak to me, and never came by the post office to talk to me anymore. Never had time for a movie matinee either. Time was closing in on my date to leave, and I wasn't going to get a chance to say so long to her. Deely told me not to be proud, that Garnelle was probably sad to be losing a friend. "It isn't much of a way to show it," I said.

I went by Mrs. Fielding's on Saturday to clean her house for the last

111

time. Garnelle was in her room, the door locked. She hollered through it, "You don't have to bother cleaning in here. I'm busy."

"Well, I'm going to California. This is the last time I'll be here."

"Sure enough," she said.

I leaned toward the door. "I just wanted to say good-bye."

"Bye."

"So long. I'll send you my address if you want to write."

There was nothing but silence from the other side of the door. I gritted my teeth. My jaw hurt as if I ought to be crying, but tears did not come. I couldn't stop my nose from running as I swept. I got to their telephone table in the hallway with the broom, holding my breath, thinking any second she'd come out of there and act like she was sorry I was leaving. It took me an hour and a half extra to clean that day, taking my time, waiting. She never came out of her room.

The same week Raylene came to show Deely and me a letter from Danny. My thoughts were deep into a map I'd gotten at the filling station and spent the better part of the morning studying. Deely got all steamed about that letter, I could tell.

John Moultrie held a handkerchief over his nose. Somebody had run downtown in the middle of the night, broken into an old, unused outhouse at the Phippses' place, and thrown kerosene and a match down the hole. The loss of the outhouse didn't amount to anything, but it was a sorry thing to do. Every household on the block would be tasting it in their food for two weeks, he guessed. Phipps was a loyal member of the Knights of the White Magnolia. They didn't do this to their own. Adding to the commotion, a fairly good-size bat, resident of the former outhouse, had flown into the Phippses' open bedroom window. If this kept up, Sabine was going to have to organize a real, honest-to-goodness fire brigade.

Delia shifted through the stubborn gears, pushing her foot into it, gaining momentum for the short but steep climb up the Knob outside of town. Danny Poquette had written a letter to that simpering Raylene Smith, and Raylene had it in her pocket as she bicycled to their house today, haughtily displaying it, reading aloud. Rubbing Delia's nose in the fact that he'd not gotten around to writing her yet. She felt a bitter exultation in the roar of the motor.

In daylight the top of the Knob was a place to see, for one moment, beyond the trees that crowded in on Sabine, all the way to the bare patch of stubble around the logging office and sawmill. The sun had just settled into the cushion of pines in the distance. The wan remaining light was thin and ocher-colored with dust. Clouds clumped together at the treetops. Trace lightning scudded through them. Usually she paused there on top of the Knob, taking in that higher-than-everything feeling. But Raylene's sneering face pressed at her back. Raylene's pale green plaid summer dress billowing in the breeze around her bicycle tires. Raylene's thoughtless and calculated method of making her feel bad, knowing full well how crazy Delia was about Danny. No doubt the whole town knew how Delia Summers was longing for Danny to come back and take up their romance right where they left off, heading toward a lifetime of happiness together.

Delia flicked on the headlamps with one hand, pulled the clutch out a little more. Down the hill she sped, over the little rise where the railroad tracks ran like a zipper that separated the white from the colored side of Sabine. Her car sailed over the tracks so fast she bumped off the seat. Angrily settling, she jammed her foot against the pedal, mashing it to the floor. An indistinct grumbling from the sky rolled from her right to left, and she checked the speed. The gauge was probably wrong.

At the bottom of the hill a tangle of thorny raspberry bushes crowded the right edge of the road. The bushes were flanked by a low stone fence that screened a culvert, perennially oozing water that stayed

113

murky and dank and peppered with mosquito larvae. After it rained, water ran through the culvert, but at the moment it was still, alive with dragonflies and gnats. The insects were loud enough that she could hear them over the sound of the car's engine. Delia thumped the speed gauge with her knuckles; she rubbed the edge of a handkerchief on its dusty face and thumped it again. She looked up just as the car made a shuddering lurch to the left and banged something incredibly heavy. She was just past the lowest place in the road, and the shadow of the Knob itself made the deepest area indistinct. She stopped the car, her entire body trembling.

Dust encircled the car, obscuring, then forming beacon shapes in front of the small dim headlights. Sweat rose up on her lip, and she stepped out, searching timidly while hanging on to the car door to support herself. Insects sawed at the air. A toad called, and another one, farther away, answered it. Frantically, she jumped back into the driver's seat. It felt as if she'd hit a brick wall, yet she had seen nothing. She tried to put the car in reverse. Only it wouldn't catch. Stupid Bandys' old car. Never would go backward. The Bandys had obviously done something to the reverse gear in this car.

She put it in first gear but sat for several minutes. Wondering what was in the road that she couldn't see. Wondering if something were still there. Some alligator. An old turtle or something The car inched forward in the dust. The headlights were dim, and with the blackout paint on half their surface like some diameter measurement in a schoolbook, anything could have been out of the half circle of their small beams. A few dozen flying insects took up temporary residence at the headlights. A dragonfly disturbed from sleep came to the windshield, hovering inches from her face, glaring menacingly through the glass. Lightning flashed overhead, accompanied by a simultaneous burst of thunder. For an instant the roadway was illuminated brighter than daylight. She saw a place in the raspberries that had been parted roughly. It looked as though something had run pell-mell through them. Delia's heart battered her ribs. Her throat threatened alternately to close up and strangle her or to offer up her lunch into her lap. Whatever it was she'd hit, it was gone through the bushes. Delia stopped the car again and set the brake. Trembling, she opened the door and slowly inched toward the front of the car. In another brilliant burst of lightning she saw with horror that the right front fender of the car was hanging askew, gnarled into a coil.

"You stupid car!" she wailed. "Mother and Daddy will just— Oh! I can't let Daddy see that." She put her foot against the fender and tried it. It wagged up and down, uncoiling slightly like an insect's proboscis, curling when she took her foot away. The metal was bent badly there, and, weakened by years of rust, it peeled away. Now it was hanging on by a small flange of twisted metal around a single bolt. She put her foot on it again and stomped downward. With a loud complaint it resisted and then gave way. Delicately, she lifted the coiled fender between her thumb and forefinger and tiptoed to the far side of the road. With all her strength she flung the metal hunk into the culvert, low and foreboding, under the depth of the roadside. Tympanic thunder burst through the air without lightning, so close it rattled her bones.

Delia stepped backward and looked at the car, staring hard, trying to pick out its outline in the velvety black by the remnants of spiderweb lightning flickering through the clouds overhead. Everything seemed fine now, except for the missing fender. Maybe she could argue that something else had hit her and not the other way round. Just what the offending creature was, she wasn't sure, but Daddy and Mother would be upset unless she could find a way to explain that it was in no way her fault. "Could have been an alligator," she said loudly. The words echoed, a clap of thunder obscuring the end of it. "I risked my life just getting out of the car to see some alligator in the shadows where no one could see it jump out. I'da been dragged off to who knows where by morning." Convinced that even the black of night believed her very plausible story, Delia got in her car and locked the door behind her. She sat for another five minutes, shaking, feeling more victimized each moment.

The moist humidity earlier had been replaced by an effusion of swampy dankness and molasses-colored vapor that was as hard to see through as it was to breathe. Between the bursts of lightning that shimmered above the cloud cover, dark settled in fully, cottony and impene-trable. The first drops of misty rain made her face glisten, and a salty droplet rolled from her forehead and curved in a path across her cheek, finding its way to her lips. A katydid screeched close to the car, making chills rise on her arms and neck. Somewhere in the woods a coon dog bayed, followed by two or three more canine howls. Eerie and echo-ing, the clamor seemed to hang on the air, swirling pale sulfur. Delia shuddered. She drove the rest of the way home, never taking it out of second gear.

In the morning Delia went to the car, parked with its right side tight against the barn wall. The night's rain had washed it clean. All seemed well, but staring at the place where the torn-off fender should have been, she suddenly noticed a little strip of cloth hanging from some bolts and a spring behind the tire. Her heart made several charging, horrible beats. Perspiration bloomed on her upper lip and forehead. She held her head between her hands and said, "This can't be happening to me." Sickened, she leaned against the barn wall. She made a stern face, pinching her lips.

Delia tugged on the faded shred of fabric a second before it let go. Past the barn and out of sight from the house, an abandoned well that served the original homeowners stood with a cover over its mouth. It was spiderwebbed in place, overgrown with brambles and running blackberry vines that they never trimmed or picked. She took a stick from what had been a trellis by the well for the vine and pried at the wooden lid.

Terrified that there might be a bat or some equally creepy thing in the well that would flutter up at her face, Delia gingerly held out the stick while stepping away. She thought she heard a movement and let it slam shut. Shaking, trembling, she wedged the lid open a second time. With one hand holding the wooden prop, she hastily wrapped the shred of cloth around a rock, slipped it through the gap, and pushed it over the rocky side. It splashed. Lowering the lid back into place, she tossed the stick away and brushed the dirt from her fingers.

On her way back to the house, she stopped at the garden to gaze at the vegetables. She took measured breaths, quieting her heart, counting the rows. By the time she'd gone through the chicken coop and picked up a few eggs, she'd decided to write a letter to Danny. She might just write one to Raylene, too, and explain things, in sort of a nice way, about her relationship with Danny. That would do it. Mother always said a nice letter was the polite thing to do.

Daddy was waiting at the door. He knew about the missing fender. Only the way he put it, asking matter-of-factly at breakfast what happened to the car, Mother couldn't jump on her first. He was mostly curious about where she'd gotten the gasoline—and it better not have been from Bart Bandy.

Delia pushed back her chair and burst into tears. "I was so scared! I didn't want to tell you for fear you'd worry about me!"

A N D   W E   H E A R D for about an hour about the "thing" that came from nowhere and bumped into her car in the night.

I still didn't quite believe the whole story. Never mind, though; I had more important things to think about. Two more days until I got on that bus.

On Friday, Mother sat at the table shucking corn for lunch, and I was slicing tomatoes, distracted, wondering about California. Mother said without looking up, "Just be sure you don't end up like that actress, that Caroline Lombarg or whatever."

"Carole Lombard? Why, Mother?"

"She's dead, you know."

"Yes, Mother. But she died in a plane crash on a war-bond tour. I'm not going to ride in airplanes. Just build parts and things. Maybe all I'll do is work in an office. You can't get killed from answering telephones."

"Don't talk to any of them movie people. If you see any of them, you just keep on going. You don't owe them a polite return. Remember you're a Christian. Remember how you were brought up."

"Yes, ma'am," I said.

Deely came in from the chicken coop with half a dozen eggs propped in her skirt, held in a loop. I was sitting at the table. Mother was at the sink. Deely looked from Mother to me.

"Frosty," Deely said with a sigh, "I want to give you my car. To drive to California. I'm only sorry I'm not strong enough to go with you. But you take it. It's my contribution."

Mother stared in disbelief. Tears formed in her eyes. "Lands. That's the most generous thing. Didn't I always tell you, you girls should love each other? Isn't that something? Giving away your car. Oh, Delia, you are a loving sister. Just the way, just— Lands' sakes alive."

I have to admit that I, too, could have shed a tear at Deely's gesture. Anyone who has her own car and doesn't take the free bus ticket to California would get all that free gas instead. "Do you mean it? Are you sure, Delia?"

She nodded. "I want you to have it, honey," she said.

One of the eggs in her skirt slipped through the fold where she was holding them all down on one side, and in slow motion it plummeted to the floor, making a soft crushing sound when it hit.

Hunger and the need for sleep dogged Corporal Benally. He knew that the Allies were on the island, but they'd moved leeward. The pillbox inland from his hiding position had proved impenetrable, and the offshore artillery concentrated somewhere to the west. He buried the radio at night and slipped toward the enemy camp he'd seen before, but there was no trace of it. There was left, however, in the remnants of a fire pit, a tin pan with burned rice stuck in the bottom. Carefully he extended his knife and poked through the sand under the pan for a mine or other device. Nothing. He slipped the knife under the crimped edge of the pan and tugged.

Sliding over the sand, the pan sounded quick and silver and too empty to hope for much. His mouth watered. He no sooner put his hand into the crusty rice than a movement softer than a shadow behind him made him freeze in place. A voice said something in a language he didn't know. Japanese. Feet appeared in front of him. He didn't look up. One of them took the knife from his hand.

John Moultrie climbed the steps of a small veranda crowded with people. Most of the congregation of Missionary Way Evangelical Tabernacle was in the yard of a small, neat-framed but unpainted house. Seated, standing, all dressed in their finest mourning, they were fanning themselves with new, identical fans. A confederation of old colored women, teary-eyed but for one, sat shoulder to shoulder just inside the door, creating a dismal receiving line. He pulled his hat from his head and extended his hand to each of the women, lifting their fingers respectfully. "Mrs. Paul. Mrs. MacFee. Mrs. Lamont. Mrs. Wiggins." To the last lady he not only raised her hand but covered it with his other one. "Mrs. Jasper. I just heard. Poor old boy."

She alone was dry-eyed. "Old folks like us just be in the way."

"No, no. Don't say that. I'm sure it was an accident."

Mrs. MacFee leaned forward. "Wa'n't no accident, Sheriff. Somebody runned him down in the road after he out visiting the Wigginses' sick grandbaby. Up all night with that child, and he's walking home, and like that"—she slapped her hand against her thigh—"he's gone, too. Don't matter how it happened. Who killed ol' Rever'n' Swan, 'at's what you got to ast."

"Hush, hush now," Mrs. Jasper said. "Don't be saying that right here in the house. You'll be calling up a haunt."

Moultrie knelt before them, his starched uniform starting to show a ring of sweat at the neck. A certain memory-tinged odor came from the tiny kitchen, where he could see that the body had been laid out on the dining table, the only place in the house large enough to accommodate it. "Miss Ronelle," he said to Mrs. Jasper, "if any of you ladies knows anything about this that I need to know, you be sure and tell me. But for now let's just say it was an accident. Well"—he patted her arm and stood, his left knee grinding audibly—"I better pay my respects. The coach will be here any minute. I passed them on the lane." The ladies nodded.

In the kitchen the smell was stronger. Death mingled with algae and naphthalene. A man stood at the head of the table, swaying, his eyes closed as if deep in prayer. Moultrie hesitated. When two minutes passed with no sound other than those from the front room and the incessant nagging of bottle flies, he cleared his throat. " 'Scuse me."

The man opened his eyes, popped them open wider, narrowed them quickly. "Sir?"

"May I look at the body?"

"Shore, sir. They he is."

"I mean, may I *look*?"

"Oh. Yes, sir, Sheriff. You go right ahead. Been too long, though. I'se Boston Peters from Peterses' Burial. I set up the body. No bullet holes. Not even a busted neck, just a goose egg at the back o' his head. Lef' leg is broke. What I figure is somebody knocked him on the head, th'owed him in the ditch, and lef' him for dead. Drownded himself in that nasty water before he come to. Tell you truth, it wasn't easy getting him in that coffin. If you move him, no telling . . . Just sayin', be wary."

"Thanks, I will. If you'll close the door on the way out." Moultrie caught himself giving orders and tried to adjust his tone of voice. "Much obliged."

"I'll be waiting here by the door. If anything . . . if you need me, just holler out."

"Will do."

Under the cloth covering Reverend Swan's face, pennies had been laid on his eyes, a silver dime on his lips. These were tied rather unceremoniously in place with twine. The skin was bulging in places that made the man hard to recognize.

THE WHOLE TOWN must have tried to squeeze into First Southern Baptist Church's sanctuary for the funeral of Reverend Swan. My family got to stand along the wall, pressed tightly but thankfully near an open window. Over the steady fluttering of fans, Pastor Ambrose gave a fine message about what a righteous man Brother Swan had been, what a good example to every Christian, and that tragedy doesn't need war to bring it on; life was always precious, tenuous, valuable.

As I wept, I heard Brother Swan preaching in my head, his voice, melodic and earnest, ringing through the pines. If I could turn back the clock and hear him just once more, I could go to California on wings with his voice lifting me. If I could, I would stop those boys—stop myself— from watching Reverend Swan's church burn. If I only had another chance.

MOULTRIE CARRIED THE somber mood of the funeral with him through the week. He had followed the mule-drawn hearse in his auto, ferrying Mrs. Jasper and two of the other older ladies. Something she'd said kept him awake at night. *Death always visited in threes.* "He always got three picked out," she said. "Someone else going. Not that sick grandbaby, but someone else."

He thought she meant herself. Politeness kept him from bringing it up, but what struck him was the acceptance in her voice. Luke Blye, Reverend Swan, and Ronelle Jasper were the last three of the truly old folks on the colored side of town. The last three that had been born slaves to slaves, freed as children, but mature enough to understand what that meant. Reverend Swan had died violently, but whether it was intentional or not, Moultrie couldn't prove.

Tuesday, Moultrie put in calls to the five sheriffs' offices in neighboring counties, checking on any upsurge in Klan carrying-on. Nobody knew of any local boys up to anything. That fact just made the whole damn thing harder to figure.

Miss Frosty?" A voice startled me. I was sitting on the back porch swinging my legs off the edge, staring into the air.

"Hey, Farrell," I said. I liked how I was "Miss Frosty" now that I'd grown up.

"Heard y'all are off to California." He waited, as if he had something he had to work up courage to say. "Well, I wondered if anybody ever showed you how to find the reverse gear in the old '31?"

"Oh," I said. "No. Are you offering me a driving lesson? I hadn't even thought of that. I've watched Delia do it."

He grinned and motioned me forward. "Come on, kid." He held the door for me and went around it to get in, stopping at the missing fender. "Jeez-o-mighty, Fros. What'd you do to my car?"

"Delia hit an alligator. Now she's scared to death of driving and won't go near it."

"Alligator, my grandpa's left shoe. She had to have hit something taller than that. A wall or something. Well, you know how to start it? Show me where your clutch is and put your foot on the brake."

For over an hour Farrell cringed as I learned the rhythm of clutch-shift-gas-release. I felt like a windup toy, hands and feet moving and eyes watching all sides. He put his hand on my hand over the shift lever, working me through the gears until I could find them all by feeling notches in the machinery.

We drove around the yard, then around the courthouse and Masonic Lodge and back. He'd been collecting stuff for the rubber drive and swapped me the old spare Deely had never used for one that was nearly new. Hers wouldn't even hold a puff of air, but he said it didn't matter about the hole because it had as much rubber as the good one, just not in the right place to drive on.

Then he coached me back down the road to my house, and sitting there by the porch, next to me in the car, he said, "Well, that ought to get you down the road. Doesn't that even deserve a little kiss? After all, I've been drafted, and I'm leaving a week after you are."

That surprised me more than anything he could have said. "Well, no," I said. I laughed. It felt like a scene from a movie. "Besides," I told him, "if I were to kiss you now and you go off to the war, why you'd just break my little old heart all to pieces."

"Dopey." He winked at me and got out, tapping twice on the hood. "Be careful driving," he said as he held my door.

"I will. Want me to carry y'all home?"

"No, I'm walking. Taking in things, you know, in case I don't come home for a few years. Hey, Frosty," he said, reluctance in his tone, "be seeing you."

"Maybe I'll kiss you then," I said.

"I'd come back for that."

"If I offered you a plate of pan gravy and biscuits, you'd come runnin' just as fast."

"Maybe."

"So, let's make a bargain. When the war's over, we'll meet right here. After all, I owe you a tire."

"Gol-durn right, you owe me. I still might take a kiss for it, though."

"When it's over."

"When it's over," he said, and waved. He put his hands in his pockets and whistled on down the road without looking back. The sight of his back, growing smaller as he went, filled me with a lonesome ache, a sort of homesickness for a home I hadn't left. Like nothing would ever be the same again.

"WHAT HAVE YOU been up to?" Mother said the second I came in the door. "I saw you drive up with that Bandy boy."

"Yes, Mother. He was teaching me to drive."

She peered at me as if I were translucent, squinting her eyes. "What else he teach you?"

"Nothing, Mother. He gave me a tire."

"Well, that wasn't free. What did you do?" With the word "do" her hand struck my cheek hard enough to cut my lip against my teeth.

All my resolve disappeared, and I sobbed noisily as she berated me. It seemed like hours went by—Mother screaming caustic accusations, me wailing innocence. Finally, tired of the inquisition, I abruptly left the room. I went to the bedroom to finish the last of my packing. Delia sat on the chair with a WMU magazine, watching me, turning her eyes away from Mother at the doorway as she stared after me, incredulous at my sudden escape to the bedroom, like it threw off her rhythm. Only when we heard pans rattling on the kitchen stove did Deely say anything. "Mother believes the Bandys are of low moral repute."

I looked at my face in the dressing-table mirror on the bureau where I stood. I considered being honest with Deely. Or telling her to just shut up. But rankling her now . . . I needed her compliance in my escape if it were to happen. "I understand that," I said.

"Well, you shouldn't have been out driving with one of them, then, should you?"

"Farrell was teaching me how to shift the gears. It was his car first, you know. Nothing more than that."

"Are you sure?"

"Delia," I said, "I've been to the movies. I think I'd know a pass if I saw one."

"Didn't he even ask for a kiss good-bye or anything? He's usually pretty fresh."

"No. He said he'd see me when the war's over."

"Daddy found you another suitcase. It's there by the door."

AT 6:00 A.M. on Saturday I watched myself telling each of them that I'd write them and miss them and let them know the minute I got to California. Daddy warned me about fifty times to "be careful over there," as if I was going off to war. He said one false slip and I'd come to no good, because "California is full of skirt-chasing movie actors and Republicans."

"By tomorrow," he said, "you find yourself a house of God. Don't you be traveling on Sunday. And don't give rides to hoboes. Or *any* men. Remember what we told you about places to stay. You should have found someone to travel with."

"Well, remember, we thought I was taking the bus. Don't worry, I've got all the papers and the map and the list of places to stay. It's going to be just fine."

In the yard Mother squeezed my neck, stiffly. Opalrae and Deely followed suit. I didn't have words to say to them. "You got your Bible and your Sunday school quarterly?" Mother said.

"Yes, ma'am."

"Did you remember to take the hymnbook, in case they haven't got a decent one?"

"Yes, Mother."

"Don't go losing it. Bring it back."

"I will."

The last thing Delia told me was that when I saw the ocean I should sell her car and buy a war bond. I watched her, wondering if she could tell I wasn't planning to come back. Daddy said quietly, "Well, Frosty, if anybody in this family could do it, you'd be the one."

I drove the car off the yard and onto the humpbacked road. Suddenly Washington Street looked like a broad thoroughfare. It opened up wide like a great bridge to some unknown place. I didn't know what Daddy meant by what he said. I guess he had faith in me. Faith that I'd turn out all right—or maybe faith that I'd run wild. But I chose to take my encouragement when I found it, so I picked out the words I wanted and put them where I wanted them and promised myself that I wouldn't let Daddy down.

When I got to the Knob, I slowed the car and looked at the road before me. Down to the left was the cypress stump that marked the turn off Ricker's Road to Mrs. Jasper's house, where she used to do my hair every morning to save me from being laughed at. I eased the car into first gear and felt it chug as I started down the hill, like a log wagon straining against a chain. It occurred to me that I might say good-bye to her. About a year had passed since I'd seen her. Maybe she wasn't even alive anymore.

When I slowed down, I could hear a low hum over the engine of the car. The mill was running full bore. I guess everybody had a job now. I could at least stop and see if Junior was in the army, I thought, just to be polite. But the Jaspers' friendship was never what I thought. I couldn't forget that they'd been responsible for everyone finding out I'd been sneaking off to Missionary Way, making me the butt of every joke in town for months. And Garnelle never said good-bye to me. Looks like I never had any real friends at all.

I pushed my foot into the gas. Something hurt in my chest as I passed the cypress stump. I was trying to quit the habit of being an idiot. When I got to the paved part of the road out of town, I stopped the car and waited until the dust settled before getting out. In a week or two the September rains would come and weigh the grit down, but in August the scant showers did little except mess up laundry on a line or windows with flecks of dirty water, so the dust flew thick and orange around the car, coating the windshield.

I stood, trembling, facing the path I'd just come along. At last I was going to do something. The only thing more frightening than going on down the road was turning back to go home. I drove well over the speed limit until I ran nearly out of gas at Nacogdoches—which was the wrong direction, I found out—and stopped at a little place to fill up. It took two days to catch up with Route 66 in Texola. Then I pointed the steering wheel toward the Pacific Ocean and drove like one possessed.

OVER THE NEXT few days I found that if I stopped and explained to folks where I was going and why . . . well, sure enough someone would offer to let me sleep in their spare room or parlor or even on the screened porch because it was hot. I had to pull over five times for convoys of dark green trucks and jeeps. I considered it my American duty to wave at every single boy on his way to the war. One time someone yelled from off the back of a tarp-covered truck, "Marry me, sweetheart!"

Every time I came to a town or a gas station, I filled up the gas tank and the water bottles I was carrying, always looking for the Route 66 signs—my road to freedom. I got to making a habit of stopping every two hours to cool and refill the radiator. Consequently I made terrible progress. I sang every song I knew several times over. When I crossed the New Mexico state line, the car thanked me by spewing water out its nose from the radiator like Mount Vesuvius.

One time four great big trucks came by, all covered in tarps of dark green, with splotches on them and huge barrels like cannon sticking out the back. Sitting atop of each of the trucks was a man with a machine gun on a stand like the ones on top of the train back home. These seemed so much closer they scared me; they made me feel beaten some-how—as if the threat of being killed for one false move made my every move false. I drove slowly for the next two hours, making sure I didn't catch up with them. Now and then I'd cross a railroad; for several miles the highway ran right alongside one. Train after train would sail down the rails, topped with men and machine guns, alert as if they were under attack right here in the middle of the United States.

I remember the first seagull I saw, over the sweltering farm fields of El Centro. I remember the first smell of California—at once friendly and exotic, forbidden and flourishing. I'd made up my mind about stay-ing in California long before I got there. Saturday morning, a week after I'd started, Route 66 brought me almost to the city limits of San Diego. Even the name of the place was so foreign, so full of romance and flow-ers, with a crisp, electrical feeling. I'd read the map so many times that the names of California rambled deliciously, like multicolored gumballs in my mind. Fullerton, Anaheim, Santa Barbara, Cucamonga, San Bernardino. The air here was golden.

SO MANY PEOPLE, so many cars! I was lost. I ran through a traf-fic light that turned red. Horns honked at me. Looking back at the light swinging from a wire stretched across the street, I nearly hit a man in a crosswalk at the next block. Everywhere there were sidewalks, making it impossible to pull over. At home you could drive off the street any-where. At the first low place I came to in the sidewalk, I drove in and parked, frantic and shaking. *The first thing I've done is make everyone here mad at me,* I thought. *I might as well go home.*

A sign on the front of this place said Rexall Drugs. I'd heard about how rich people in California took drugs sometimes—sleeping pills for movie stars. Who would have thought they'd just hang out a sign? I watched the front door from the car, expecting to see drowsy people stumbling out, dressed in zoot suits with long chains dangling from their pockets. Out came a woman in about the smartest green polka dot dress I've ever seen, holding the door for two little boys licking for all they were worth on some double-scoop ice cream cones, smiling and saying, "There we go. Is that good, fellas?" Knowing full well that Mother would turn inside out if she saw me under a sign that advertised drugs for sale, I decided to take a look in the door.

"Can I get you something, sweetheart?" said a woman's voice.

"No, ma'am. I'm just taking a look."

"Well, come on in. It doesn't cost to look." Right by the door was a soda fountain, gleaming and polished with pink and gold decorations and big knobs for pouring soda, just like in the movies. At least ten round, pink-seated stools hugged the counter like at the saloon in a cowboy show. The woman behind it was about my height, older than I but not nearly as old as my folks. "Just get in town?" She had a name tag that said SYLVIA, with a flowered hanky tucked under it.

I smiled. "Yes, ma'am. It smells good in here."

"That's the grease we use. Nothing but the best. Almost pure lard. You take that cheapskate place two blocks down. They fry their chicken in petroleum jelly. It's a fact."

"Oh. I thought I smelled perfume."

"Well. That, too. Get you something? We make a good milkshake. Chili-con-carney?"

"How much does it cost for a glass of water?"

"Nothing. Here's a menu. Look it over with your water."

"Thank you, ma'am. Actually, I have to find the . . . the Morrison Kellogg Tool Company." It was the first time I said the name aloud. "I have a job."

"Sure, kid. Try these french fries. Just a sample. Where'd you say?"

"I'll go get my papers."

I got almost to the door when Sylvia said, "I don't know just what kind of small-town, cracker-hillbilly place you're from, honey, but this is California." She nodded at my purse on the counter. "Take that with you if you want to hold on to it."

"Yes, ma'am." I might not have dressed like the people here, but I was no cracker and I'd never even been near a hillbilly, much less been called one. I grabbed the purse and went to my car. In a few seconds I had my envelope of papers with MKTC in broad letters across the top. "Here's the address, ma'am. They said there'd be a dormitory where I can stay. I've got a map, but I'm completely turned around."

"Hey, you're not sore about what I said, are you?"

"No, ma'am."

" 'Cause you had a look on your face. And will you nix it on the 'ma'am'? Makes me feel old."

"Yes, ma'am. Yes." I tried to smile.

"There's dozens of 'em. I don't know where this place is." Sylvia leaned over the counter and shouted toward the rows of shelves. "Hey, Mil. Where's 9336 Del Mar? Is that up at Lomita or farther down by Mission?"

"Yeah. Lomita. Pretty sure." The voice came from somewhere between the aisles.

"There you go, kid. Take a right out of here, another right on Del Mar. You can't miss it."

"Thanks." I collected my papers. Folded the envelope in half and stuck it in my purse. I was so tired. I'd find Lomita on the map and get out of here. The smell of chili and those french fries I didn't eat was clawing at my stomach.

"Remember," Sylvia said with a motherly finger raised in my direction, "you're not in Kansas anymore, Dorothy. You remember to lock your doors and windows at night. It's the big city, now. See you around, kid."

"Yes, ma'am. Thanks, I mean."

Big city. *I'm not a cracker. Lock my doors. What does she think I am?* The address on the envelope was blurry when I looked at it. Blinking hard, I pulled out into the traffic when there was a break and traveled up the road in the direction I'd been going when I pulled in. I passed Del Mar and circled around a block to get back to it. Out of pure luck I found Lomita but didn't see the company's sign until I was past it. The second time around the block there was a tree blocking my view; all I could see was Mor— —ogg T— —ny. *I'm here.* I got out of the car. The wind was cool, although the air felt sun-baked and warm. It was a warmth I wasn't accustomed to—a far cry from the sultry delta afternoons. This was a homey, oven-full-of-cookies warmth, dry and lingering, with the fragrance of some distant, indistinct blossom.

Delia sniffed. All around her the ladies of the WMU cut sheets and rolled them into bandages. Mrs. Brueller was telling them all for the third time about a letter she'd gotten from Coby. "He said, 'Don't worry about me, Mama'—you see he calls me 'Mama' like a little boy. He said, 'I've got a message right here for Tojo, written in lead.' Such a brave boy."

"Mrs. Poquette," Delia said, "have you heard from Danny at all? I've written him loads of letters, but he must be awfully busy."

"He's at Fort Dix, dear. Sometimes they work him night and day in that kitchen."

Delia nodded. Her back was going to absolutely spasm in half if she didn't get up and move around. "I think I'd enjoy some fresh tea. May I make some for you ladies?"

There was a little sink and a two-burner stove in the church basement. Delia stopped at the threshold, thought better of it, and tiptoed to the doorway to listen in case they said anything about her when she was gone. Someone said, "I hear her sister's off to California." "Lots of girls are doing that. I'd go too, if George would let me. Imagine!" "Raylene, tell them what *you've* done." Raylene told everyone how she had convinced Marty Haliburton he was the only person in town who could lead the Civil Defense Committee. "He's going to go down this week and start organizing drills." Delia descended the steps to the chill of the basement. A roach slithered under the bottom step when she reached it.

I sent a postcard home to my folks, telling them I'd arrived safe and sound and got the job right away. And that I'd write more soon, Love, Frosty. It took me about four hours to get my job and get sent to a row of small, flat-roofed houses, all painted white, connected back and forth like a chain of paper dolls, and filled, for the most part, with girls just like me. They called it a "complex." I loved my new home the minute the landlord opened the door. It smelled a little dank, but a good scrub with some vinegar cured that. I didn't have a roommate like lots of the girls, so it seemed roomy compared to being at home. Some of the girls worked opposite shifts from their roommates, so they were never home at the same time, and that way they could use the same bed and dishes.

I loved dusting my apple-crate table, putting my hands on things and knowing I could move them or clean them or not, as I chose. Cooking meant heating soup in the can it came in, and eating toast or jelly sandwiches on a napkin. I had no furniture, but there was an iron bed and a stove, and the former renter had left a chair that had one leg wrapped with package-tying twine like we used to use at the post office. I was scared that if I took the twine off, the chair would fall apart, so I left it on. I had a few quilts and blankets from home. Someday, a mattress would have to come out of the money from selling Delia's car. In a jar under the sink I kept the cash I was saving for bonds, someday.

At work I found a bulletin board by the time clock where postcards advertised things for sale and put mine next to a note from someone wanting to buy a piano for twenty dollars. I didn't know what to put for a price, so I wrote, "1931 DeSoto. Dependable—Broken in—Make an offer. Frosty Summers, Section A, Graveyard Shift." Deely told me she had paid fifty dollars for it, but I had put a lot of hard miles on it; plus, now it had a fender missing, a conked place on the roof, and a misfit tire that didn't match the others. I don't think the gas tank was full either, although I hadn't started it since I parked it in front of the storage room at my little apartment.

The factory was chugging around the clock. It was wrapped with canvas tarps painted to look like little houses with curtains in the windows. I started out the first week deburring the lead edge of loading pawls, which pulled chains holding ammunition, smoothing all the edges with sandpaper on a small stick. The pawls have this little bent thing on them, right under the hole over the notch, where metal flecks got stuck. Eventually, I got moved to disintegrating belts, and some newer girls were doing the pawl smoothing. All day long, snakes of machine-gun belts squirmed on the table in front of me. Check the belt for burrs, make sure it fits on the lug attached to the end of this little post on the table without snagging, roll 'em up, pack 'em five in a stack, stack 'em in the box, box goes down the ramp. Mr. Yount gave everybody a sheet of statistics we were supposed to memorize. We quizzed each other at lunchtime, our shoeless feet in each other's laps.

The girls who worked in the room below, down that ramp, had a scarier job. They did everything from cleaning and loading brass cartridges to filling the belts with the fifty- and thirty-caliber rounds. Sharmayne, a girl I met the first day, worked at a table down there, putting rounds of ammunition in the belts. Sharmayne was from Chicago and had a college degree in mathematics. Molly Barnes, who'd never finished ninth grade, worked in the office filing papers. I met a girl named Julia who lived in my same complex. She and Marge from the dorm stood on either side of me at work. Julia said she had a sewing machine and told me she could show me how to fix the pants of the uniforms I was given so they didn't fit so baggy in the waist. They were all cut for men, she said, straight up and down.

I learned about terms like "killing range" and "effectiveness curves" and "accuracy tables." There were posters on every wall, making us so proud of ourselves. We recited things to make the work go by: poems from school, songs from the radio, hymns from church. On dinner breaks they played the evening news on the radio, and they played it anytime President Roosevelt or Winston Churchill came on for any reason at all. Everything would get quiet, but we'd still work. One time after the news Julia picked up a box of machine-gun belts I'd just loaded and shook them at the radio speaker, shouting "Hey, Hitler! Your Christmas present is in the mail!" Everyone cheered. Julia believed that her aunts and uncles in Poland were all dead. I never knew a Jewish girl before. I watched her, wondering what was different. Sometimes I felt a terrible tugging at my heart over the mystery of people who'd rather their children died with them than in some foreign land. It was a pride of knowing what you were all about. I think Garnelle had it to some extent. Maybe everyone but me did, too.

A man from the delivery section bought Deely's car from me. I waited until Sunday afternoon to call, when I knew they'd all be home from church. I kept hearing noises in the line and new operators getting on as they strung the connection from San Diego to Sabine. Finally a louder voice said, "Your connection, ma'am," and I heard the longs and shorts of our line: the phone under the picture in the hall.

Opalrae's voice said, "Summers residence."

"Hello," I said. "It's Frosty."

"Frosty? Hey, seen any movie stars over there yet?" she shouted.

"No. Hollywood is a long way from here. I'm in San Diego. It's—"

Daddy's voice broke in. "Well, I'll be. Frosty's calling from California, everyone."

"Hi, Daddy. I only have five minutes. I called to tell you I sold Delia's car."

"You get a job yet?"

"Oh, yes," I said. "Right away. I have a little apartment and a place on the graveyard shift. In a month I get to go to swing shift. It's great, Daddy; it feels like I'm really doing something—"

"Here's your mother," he said.

"Hello, Mother. I sold Delia's car. I have a great apartment and a job in Morrison Kellogg—"

"Are you ready to come home?"

"No, Mother. I just got here. I found a job and a place to live. It's real nice."

"You've been gone near four weeks. Seems like that's long enough."

"Mother, it took me a whole week to get here. It's a long drive. I just started working—for the war effort. We talked about me doing this, remember? I'll be staying for a while."

"How long?"

"A couple more months at least. Remember?"

"I think you'd better just get on home. Nothing there you can't do right here at home."

"But, Mother, there aren't factories in Sabine. Just the mill. I can't work in the mill. Besides, I called to tell you all I've sold the car."

"There's a place right down in Beaumont. You can just get down there and work now and then if you want. You could help Delia at the dime store. Heaven knows there's plenty of work around this house to keep you happy."

"That isn't the way it is, Mother. This is a War Industry Plant. They count on me to be here."

"Here's Daddy," she said abruptly. I could hear voices in the background over the static.

"Daddy, please tell Mother about having a job. I can't just stay for a week and go home."

He said, "Your sister Delia wants to talk to you about the car."

"Hello, Deely. I sold the car like you said. I got more than you paid for it, so I'll send you the extra money."

"No, thank you. I'd rather forget I ever had that car. Besides, I don't think it's very ladylike to drive. I'd rather just let the man do it."

"What man?"

"When I get married. There's no reason for a wife to drive when her husband can."

"You don't want me to send you the money?"

"Keep it. I don't want any memory of that car. You promised you'd buy a bond. Get our boys home sooner. You know, Danny and all of them."

"I will." Maybe. "Mother said she wants me to come home already."

"Mm-hmm. She's pretty upset, at the way you fooled around and tricked everybody."

"About what?"

Mayvis Plinkle broke in, "Five minutes are up, Miss Delia, Miss Frosty."

"I have to go; the line will go down. Good-bye, Deely. Tell everyone for me. Good-bye."

"Good—" was all she said. I don't remember if the operator disconnected me or if I pressed on the lever in the middle of her word.

Moultrie, I'd like to see this through, but I tell you what, you can't prove any of it. And, there's not going to be a jury brought against any white kids on account of a hunnert-year-old colored fella. You're all het up 'cause he was your grand-daddy's. Try a piece of this cornbread?"

"Thanks. I'm just not putting up with killing in my county, I don't care who it is." He stopped to take a bite of the cornbread. Bobby Lee Baker was the county attorney in Jasper County. The office was paneled with walnut. A large gas globe burned on the desk although it was noon. Between the men, on a scrap of newspaper, were the sooty remains of a burlap bag and a piece of coiled rope. "That isn't all, you know it, Bobby Lee. It wasn't any accident. That there's a noose if I ever saw one. Since when do we ignore flat-out murder?"

"More coffee?" Bobby Lee held the pot forward and raised his brows. "Trouble is, with what you've got, you still haven't got enough to make anything stick. You can prove who's dead, and maybe you can prove it wasn't an accident, but you can't put anyone at the scene."

"I can. I've got three families that owned up to having someone at a bonfire. Only there isn't any sign of anything burned except that old church."

"How long ago?"

"Last fall."

"Been there lately? Ever seen a place in this county that weeds didn't take over in a week or two? Before another month is out, you'll have a hard time even *finding* the place."

Silence fell between them. Moultrie finished his coffee. "Damn. Circumstantial evidence, that's all I've got. Good as nothing."

Baker nodded. "You're going to have to find someone willing to testify, under oath, that saw the whole thing. Who put the knots in the rope, who put the gas on the floor, who struck the match."

"I got another one, too."

"Hell you say."

Anytime a bunch of us got together, which seemed to happen a lot, we made cookies or taffy or popcorn and talked about boys and laughed and played records. I met people from as far away as Maine and one girl from right near home in Toullange. Beulah Davenport taught me how to lindy hop and jitterbug and swing. I suspected she might be Catholic; she just always had so much fun. We had camp-outs on the grassy lawns at the apartments, and everybody'd turn their radios to the windows, set them on the same station with the volume all the way up. We ate bologna sandwiches and tried recipes on each other. We formed book-reading clubs and movie-critic clubs and sewing circles and home-care circles for girls who got sick. When I caught a cold, Julia made me chicken soup and Sharmayne brought biscuits and greens. I used to think people never really lived like it seemed in the movie shows, but I was so happy every day I felt that's what I was doing. By the end of September I thought I'd lived in San Diego my whole life.

Before long I got another spot on the line, packing things up to be sent down the road to Consolidated Aircraft. The interesting jobs—putting rifling slots in barrels, assembling the whole thing, testing with the aligning gauges—you had to work up to. What I did was take stuff from our floor to the Section B people. As I stacked a row of heavy metal cylinders in front of me, lining up the flash guards, the powder shields, the cylinders, a gloom came over me like a solitary cloud crossing the sun. I glanced at the door, as if expecting to see that someone had passed through it and blocked the light. I had this horrible feeling that my stay in California might be cut short at any time. Boring or not, I wanted with every bone in my body to be here. Some days I watched the door, expecting to see my parents.

Years before, the summer before high school, Mother and Daddy sent me off to Girls' Auxiliary Camp in Kirbyville for two weeks; five days later there they were in a borrowed car to pick me up. There was an embarrassing flurry of dragging me by one arm from my lunch and telling me in front of the entire camp cafeteria I didn't deserve to be there, cramming my meager clothes into a paper bag and throwing the Genuine Sioux Indian braided moccasins project I had half finished into the trash can by the Wah-me-Tika Lodge's door. All I ever understood of my crime was that I was off in the woods having fun and not doing my regular chores. After all, I had a sister with polio and a younger sister who didn't get to go, and was disappointed about it; and there, wasn't I ashamed of myself? Now every letter I wrote home was filled with details about the taxing life I led: laundry done in a metal tub by hand, hung about the bathroom I shared with the girls next door down; long hours, bumped shins, skinned knuckles. It would be all right with my folks for me to give of skin and exhaustion to the war, but to have fun while I was doing it would have them at my door in a heartbeat.

"Summers, wake up and watch what you're doing!" Mr. Yount's voice rattled my ribs.

I looked at the table in front of me, and at that moment the whole string of components jiggled, toppled like dominoes, and rolled helter-skelter to the floor. The crashing noise caused a dimple of hushed quiet at my table that spread through the area like ripples on a pond. "I'm so sorry," I said. Tears formed a knot in my throat.

"Get that derned dreamy look off your face and do your job, or I'll put you outside cutting grass. This is no place for daydreaming! Jee—Jumping Jehoshaphat! Get this cleaned up and get in my office."

Oh, *no*. "Yes, sir."

Ten minutes later I watched myself go to the door to his office. I tapped lightly on the glass. But I didn't get fired. He told me he'd come to see me that day because I worked really fast—*usually*—and he wanted to make me part of the later assembly. It needed someone with dexterity, he said, and I had it, when I wasn't daydreaming. I was going to Section B. I'd have to come half an hour early tomorrow and learn the way it went from the girl on the swing shift. *Now get back to work. We have quotas to meet, orders to ship. And quit daydreaming.* Yes, sir. I went back to my station and started again, my face red, my throat full and tight with emotion. I was getting a promotion, but I'd also made a big mistake and could just as easily have been thrown out the door.

M artin Devoe Haliburton, you swear to keep all this secret upon your life and eternal soul, so help you God?"

"I do swear it, in the name of the Father, the Son, and the Holy Ghost, upon my life and soul, Brother Thompkins."

"Be seated, then."

The room was close and dark, lit with twelve small candles. Cigarette and pipe smoke condensed over the shoulders of the men, packed tightly together. It took less than half an hour for the questioning; nobody doubted his sincerity. And he astounded and energized his newly pledged brothers by encouraging them to join him in church. He explained, "I feel God's will in this. My eyes have been opened by the atrocity that kept me from military service. Why, I don't mind telling you that I've spent my last cent purchasing no less than twelve books put out by the Sunday school board on preaching, teaching, reaching a community. It's not too late to turn this country around. I believe God is making His way known. There's a great spiritual revolution waiting to happen. It can start right here in our midst. We have to hold strong together."

"Amen!" someone said. "A upstandin' Christian," said another. "He's got a point." "Preach on, Brother."

Marty lowered his voice, watching them for the reaction. It pleased him, the way they leaned forward in their seats. "You see, everything works together for good, to them that serve the Lord. This country is fighting wars all over the world when what we ought to be attending to is right here under our noses. I hope I can count on you brother Knights to stand by me in this fight against evil."

"Hell," Marty's father said, "we ought to start with the poll tax and the reading tests. Get that back on the goddamn ballot by next year. Get them niggers out of the voting booth."

"Please, Daddy," Marty said. "I'd appreciate y'all's keeping the language clean. I'm surrendered to God's call."

I could stay in California forever. The smell of the ocean seemed to remind me of someplace I'd been. The mild temperature and breeze were better. But the best part of California was the anonymity of it. It was the joy of not being who I was in Sabine. I'd come here as unknown as all the other girls on the line and become part of something much bigger than myself or my past. I wasn't automatically associated with the brands of childhood, the flaming accusations haloed forever in my permanently scorch-waved hair. New ones—better ones, I hoped.

Fall was in the air. My parents' trial period of three months was up, but everything was working out fine, so I wrote home that I'd be staying a bit longer. Life was full and wonderful.

The girls from our section planned a picnic, and I was invited to go along, starting out early Saturday morning. Several of us had yet to see the Pacific Ocean. Everybody met at a garage on Lomita, and after all the girls had jimmied up fifteen cents for gasoline, Julia filled her broken-down truck with gas and with us. We laughed and joked as it trudged down the road. On the way we started singing and waving at people from the back of the big old truck. It wouldn't go more than twenty miles an hour, and we sang songs as we went along, waving brazenly from the back at soldiers and little kids. A carload of boys went by—soldiers, by the look of them, probably from Camp Pendleton close by. The honking and waving went on for two blocks before we had to turn off the road. I tried hard to remember the route we took; I wanted to come back.

Beulah knew all the words to "Pinup Girl," which was a pretty racy song.

"What does that mean?" I shouted over the roar of the motor. Our knees were touching, but sitting in the back end of the truck was as loud as the punching machines in the factory. " 'The chassis that made Lassie come home'—what does that mean?"

"Get back," she said. "Don't you know Lassie? Babe, you've got to go to the movies!"

I didn't say anything. As we bumped up the curved incline, I saw the ocean for the first time. At first a thin blue line, just a vague hint on the horizon, it widened as we climbed the rolling hills until it was at least as deep as the city below us. We could see its waves far distant, bursting white against a rocky prominence of black jutting up from the white shoreline. Julia pulled to a stop at a little bluff high above it, where there was plenty of flat space. Eventually, I vowed, standing in the back of that old truck, eyes fixed on the ocean, I will go there and put my feet in it. Swim in it, too. Maybe.

Although it was a warm October, it was cool on the hills where we were. We walked farther up, finding some fairly level areas to blanket with our tablecloths and old towels, anything to set our food on. We carried our sandwiches and jars of tea to the middle. We talked all afternoon, the ocean moving below us. Now and then we could hear it, the sound of traffic on a busy street.

I don't remember how many other Saturdays I sat up there, often enduring a wind fierce as a tornado and downright cold to my southern blood. By the end of November, though, the other girls had begun to come sporadically, finding the cold too harsh. It was too far to walk. But if I couldn't go, I felt empty and cheated. I found myself wishing I'd kept Deely's car. Those war bonds I'd bought with it were nice, but I couldn't ride them to the shore.

On a bright Sunday afternoon someone tapped at my door. I felt my heart lurch and a cold chill surge into my hands and feet. Girls from the factory didn't knock quietly. They always banged on a door and loudly whistled or called out "Yoo-hoo! Anybody home?" The person rapped again. I couldn't breathe. I moved toward the kitchen and the slender door that led to my empty storage room. It had to be them, come to get me and make me go home. I tiptoed around the far edge of the building and then ran to the front corner and peeked around. There, by my front stoop, stood Garnelle Fielding, three huge suitcases at her feet.

"Garnelle, it's you!" I called. "I was just out checking on my laundry. Give me a hug. Oh, I'm so glad it's you. I mean . . . I'm so glad to see you. Oh, come in!"

I showed her everything, and she got a job quick as a wink in my same factory, in a section where they made flexible mounts for the fifty-calibers. I was glad to share my apartment. We could split the twenty-five dollars a month rent and the light bill, giving us each nearly a hundred dollars left for groceries and savings. I found a divan at a secondhand store that folded down when the backrest was leaned forward. We made Garnelle a bed out of the divan, and instead of making it up every morning, she took up her sheets, pulled the back up, and it was a sofa again. Two suitcases with a board across them became our coffee table.

On the second Saturday of December we worked back-to-back shifts, straight through until Saturday night at eight. Garnelle didn't get off until nine-thirty, and so it was ten before we got to our little apartment. When Sunday came, we lingered late over breakfast, while a stiff breeze rattled the plush and stickery bougainvillea against the kitchen window. She went down to get a newspaper from Love's grocery store while I washed my hair and did some laundry. I'd finally figured out how to do a fairly good Ginger Rogers pageboy.

When Garnelle was done reading the paper, I had an idea. I took the funny papers and the skinny little dowels we used to keep the windows shut. Then I went next door and asked about "borrowing" some glue. Pretty silly—it's not like you could give it back when you were done—but the favor would come back, another way. At any rate, I took a lot of care to be sure to make a kite that wouldn't ruin the dowels, so they could be removed afterward and returned to their places of safekeeping in the jalousie windows. "Let's get the bicycles," I said. "This is ready."

"I'm too tired," Garnelle said. "Why don't we wait till next week?"

But I would not wait. Could not. I still hadn't made it to the ocean, but I had to get to the hills that day. Garnelle came along grudgingly, a battered romance novel stuffed in the brown paper sack we used for a picnic basket. We ate sandwiches while I prepared the kite. The wind never stopped coming up from the shore, there on those hills; like Texas.

"You know," she said to me, "if you want to go down to the beach, why don't you just go?"

"I don't know," I said. "I'm scared of it."

"That doesn't make much sense," she said.

"I guess not."

"You weren't scared to drive across the country all by yourself. You weren't scared to pop Marty Haliburton in the mouth in third grade. Why be scared of looking at the ocean?"

I had to think about it. I felt like it was pulling me, but how could I tell her that? "I'm scared all the time," I said.

"No you're not. You might say that to some boy to make him put his arm around you, but you don't fool me."

"I don't think of driving to California as particularly brave. It would've been harder to stay in Sabine and pretend to like Women's Missionary Union meetings. Besides, you came, too."

"I came on a bus, just for something to do. Mama said I ought to try it for a while and get a grip. Do something besides write long mash notes to Coby Brueller."

I laughed. "Next time you write one, let me read it, all right?"

"I will not."

"Come on," I wheedled, like Opalrae used to do.

"Write your own."

"Nobody I want to mash with."

She laughed. "I saw Elwood Peebles giving you the eye. Flat Foot Floogie."

"Well, now I have to throw up."

"Hold your silly string." After holding the kite while I ran and got it started, Garnelle dove into her novel, lying on her stomach on the blanket.

I hadn't made a kite in years, and I'd never been expert at flying one. But I liked to watch it, feel it tugging me. The kite wobbled about twenty feet off the ground, spun a quick circle before it dipped and plunged to the earth. I added another two feet of scraps torn into bows on a string tail. The next time I sent it up, it rose straight up as if it had always intended to be there, poised, a bright shape nearly still in the pale blue over the grassy, straw-colored hillside. Like a patch on heaven.

The most recent letter I'd had from home mentioned expecting me for Christmas. It was on my kitchen table like week-old fish at that very moment. I held out no hope that Mother would understand they might give me only a day or two off for Christmas. Two days on a bus wouldn't even get me to Albuquerque, much less Sabine. No one from here was going home; we were on our own for Christmas and had been busy doing goofy things to make it happy right where we are. I was on the colored-paper-chain committee, and we were daily hanging longer and longer swags around the Section B room. I hadn't decided how to explain that to Mother.

When the kite crashed, I remembered noticing the man who rescued it. I'd seen him when we first arrived. Since then I'd been looking skyward. He walked—well, more like trudged—upward, holding the kite with its broken arm flopping. Garnelle and I both recognized the Marine Corps uniform from the soldiers in town; we giggled behind their backs when they did heel-toe turns in the dime store. This Marine seemed to move with effort. When he was at the level place we'd staked out for our picnic, he held forth my paper dreams.

"This came to me," he said sadly, as if he'd caused it to fall. "Sorry."

"Oh, I'm sorry, mister. I should have been paying more attention and reeled it in some."

"That's pretty nice. What d'you call it?"

"A kite. Haven't you ever seen a kite?"

"Yes. No. I guess not up close. It's busted. Can you fix it?"

"Sure. Thanks. Would you like something to eat?"

"No, thank you."

"You're sure?" Suddenly words spilled from my mouth, as if to justify our very presence on the hill. "We've got lots. Chicken salad sandwiches. Garnelle wanted to make tuna fish, but I don't like fish. There's two apiece, if you're hungry. We can't possibly eat all this ourselves. Please have some."

The man took his hat off. He had short black hair, cut so close his skin showed through on the sides. His face was sort of smoothly browned, like some Cajuns I'd seen who spent a lot of time outdoors. He looked like he was weighing something in his mind.

"If you've got plenty, then yes, I'm hungry."

That was all it took. He shook our hands, gently. He said his name was Gordon Benally. "Oh," I said, "like my mother's maiden name is Connally. She's French-Irish." Suddenly that sounded stupid. Connally was just Irish-Irish, nothing else. He would think I was idiotic, or at the very least trying to snub his name or something. We introduced ourselves.

The Marine helped us polish off the sandwiches and sponge cake, which we ate with our hands, breaking off chunks. Almost as soon as the food was gone, Gordon Benally stood. "Good food. Thanks very much." He smiled and lifted his hand in a slight wave, said, "I'm not Irish," and walked away. Garnelle and I raised our eyebrows, looked at each other, and giggled.

All day at work I found myself replaying that strange scene. *I'm not Irish,* I kept hearing. As if it were the most funny, profound thing anyone had ever said to me.

The following Saturday, Garnelle didn't want to go to the hills again; the temperature had dropped, and it looked like it might rain. But I'd fixed my kite, so I went alone, my picnic basket full of expectation, banging my left knee as it swung from the bike's handlebars. And the smooth-brown Marine was there again, lingering below. The part of the hill where he was sitting was clifflike, full of steep precipices and loose rocks. He perched atop a large boulder watching the sea for a long time. I read. Ate. Flew my patched kite. I'd brought an extra sandwich and a second mason jar filled with lemonade. By midday the ice was melting into little white lozenges. He watched the sea. I wondered if he was asleep. I wondered what a Marine was doing out here on Saturdays watching the ocean move.

Late in the afternoon he came up the cliff, again moving as if a heavy weight were atop him. He nodded, walked slowly to the roadway, and kept walking. He still walked oddly; his was not the smooth and oiled gait of other soldiers I'd seen in town. He never even stopped.

I went back to the apartment, feeling about halfway sad and blue, halfway stupid. It was as good a time as any to write home. I explained how much I loved and missed everybody, but there was no closing down the factory for Christmas. In fact, we were all working overtime and then some. As a precaution, I quoted a direct order from Mr. Yount not to take more than Christmas day off. I put a stamp on it and took it to the mailbox. They would get it just a couple of days before Christmas. I told them I'd telephone them Christmas day, after church. We'd have a nice visit on the phone. I might make it until New Year's before they showed up.

I got a letter from Farrell Bandy, all the way from Africa. It made me cry, even though it wasn't sad. Just good old Farrell, telling about camels and sand and nomads and stuff he was going to bring home after they got done with the German army there. I sent him a letter all about the factory and Garnelle coming to live here and the bad fudge we made.

On Christmas Eve we cut off at the factory early, and Mr. Yount himself gave us cocoa and doughnuts. There was a sort of impromptu party right there on the assembly line, and then we got to go home by six, and I'd been there only two hours. The next day I waited until the afternoon and called home.

I could picture them while we talked, Mother and Daddy both trying to listen to the earpiece at once, talking at the same time. Mother wanted to know when I was coming home, and I repeated everything I'd already written in the letter, word for word. Daddy wanted to know if "this fellow Yount" was Jewish, "not letting us out for Christmas."

"I'm not in prison, Daddy," I said. "They're not holding us captive. He's just trying to keep up the quotas. We've retooled for some new machinery that goes on the Mustang fighter planes. Have you heard of those?" I told myself not to make it sound too important or interesting, or they'd find a way to drag me home. At any rate, it wasn't a bad conversation, considering. Merry Christmases all around. *Miss you . . . take care . . .* all that. When I hung up, my heart was pounding so hard my ribs rattled.

Back in my apartment it was warm and yellow and bright inside against the gray December world through the windows. It smelled slightly of gas from the stove and the chicken and yams we'd put on to roast an hour ago. "Garnelle," I said, "they asked me about five times where you and I go to church, and were we witnessing to the girls in the factory. I lied and said we were. I hate doing that, asking people about their most private, important thoughts, like someone is going to just blurt out to a total stranger, 'Oh, yes, thank you; my eternal soul is soaked in gin and blacker than tar. And how are you today?' "

Garnelle laughed and curled her legs up under herself on the divan.

"Well, howdy, Miss Davenport, nice to meet you. You dried out that soul yet?"

"I didn't mean anyone we know."

"Oh, come on. Don't be naive. These girls aren't the kind to worry about. They're pretty nice."

"But why would you say that about Beulah?"

" 'Cause, dopey. Gosh, you really don't know?"

I looked at her. I could hear that something in her tone of voice that people so often used toward me. "What? Is she on the make?"

"Gee whiz, Fros. Open your eyes. You think everyone alive is hard-shell Baptist? I didn't see you turning her away in righteous indignation when she was teaching you to jitterbug. You tell your folks you can do the snake-bottom?"

"Is she fast?"

"Who knows? Maybe a little quicker than us, is all. Haven't you ever thought about it? How Beulah has a date every weekend, and not ever with the same guy three times in a row?"

"I just thought she was friendly. I thought maybe she could play the piano."

"Nevertheless, Frosty. A girl can be friendly on the one hand and shifting gears with the other. What she's playing isn't Brahms." Garnelle smiled. "Close your mouth, you're catching flies."

"We should stay away from her. The Bible says not to associate with the worldly."

"Jesus ate lunch with prostitutes." She had me there. "Let's buy a radio," she said. "It's too quiet around here."

"I like it quiet," I said.

That night I pushed my little old Honey Doll into the corner of my bed and laid my hand on her as I said my prayers. *Now I lay me down to sleep*—my mind raced beside itself, chiding my heart for the sentimentality of it, changing the words—*childish girlhood in a heap*. I guess it was about time I stopped reciting that rhyme. I squeezed the doll. Honey Doll's entire legs and arms were now stuffed with dimes, flat-wise, as if they were paper coin rolls. Only the tips of the toes and hands were still sawdust. Her middle had been quarters, but they were bulging out and tearing loose, so I'd recently traded them for paper notes, which I folded and tucked back into her middle. I gave a dollar a week to the Allied Relief Fund, too. I had ninety dollars—bus fare to pretty much anywhere—inside Honey Doll.

Wilbur Fielding sweated under the wool blankets that hung heavy upon him, while over his face, anonymous in the row of faces in the field hospital, hung a small cloud of vapor formed by his breathing. It was winter in France. A ballroom in an old hotel had been spared its roof, though the walls crumbled and plaster sifted down on the green blankets mimicking the snow sifting onto unlit streets outside. The man in the cot next to him had urinated under his blankets, and for a while a cloud formed over the man's legs, directly above the puddle under the cot. It had ceased forming over the man's face. It cooled and dissipated over the rest of the cot, too, and orderlies came and carried him—blanket, cot, and all—away.

Wilbur thought about having a cigarette. If he could have moved his lips, he would have liked to ask for a smoke. He didn't actually smoke, but he felt he should now. He wasn't sure why his lips didn't move. While Wilbur closed his eyes, a new soldier in a different but identical cot and blanket was carried in and placed over the puddle. After a while he spoke. "You know, Joe, they say the USO is bringing a Christmas show here to the hospital, outside there in the street area. They're settin' up bleachers right now. Ain't that great?"

"My name's Fielding. Wilbur. Fielding," Wilbur spoke with much effort, tonguing the words against his teeth, between his stiff lips.

"Ralph Davis. Sure is gonna be great. All them great-looking gals, singing and dancing. I hear they kiss the fellows in the front two rows. Do you think that's so?"

"Thirty-fifth Infantry. C Company."

"Man, I hope if I get a kiss it's a blonde. Course I wouldn't mind a brunette. Some of them get around. You know what I mean?"

"I dunno."

"Bet a girl in a show like that gets around. Maybe there's a nice one, though. Man. I'd like to be kissed by a nice blond girl for Christmas. You got a girl—home, I mean?"

"Maybe," said Wilbur. A long quiet fell between them, and Wilbur tried to think about getting kissed, as he knew he must, but he couldn't remember being kissed before, and he wasn't sure if he couldn't remember because he hadn't been kissed, or only imagined it, or if his lips were gone, too, and with them the memory of all that had happened to them. He inhaled pensively, careful of the barbs he felt with each breath. "I don't think she knows I like her."

"Man, looks like you took it bad. I guess they'll put you right in the front row, huh?"

Wilbur sighed, exhausted by the energy coming at him from the next cot. He turned his head toward the corrugated metal wall two feet from his left side, which hid the recovery area from the surgery. It hid only the sights, however, not the sounds, played like a radio drama with too many sound effects and not enough script. Gurgling liquid, grinding that made him dream of sawing wood. The anguish of young boys sobbing for their mothers. To blunt the sounds, he counted out loud, making as much noise in his throat as he could muster. He counted anything—sometimes he counted the number of times he'd counted things. Mostly he stared at the corrugated wall. Twenty-nine ins, thirty-one outs. "When is it?"

"Christmas, Joe. Tomorrow. Hey, I got this shrapnel here in my neck, and it didn't even hit anything. Practically just got a new whistle hole is all, but nothing hurt. Hooked me a three-week tour in one rotten field hospital after another. Say, pal, where're you from?"

"Texas. Little town. Sabine."

"Is that near Houston? I been to Houston once. You gonna smoke those?"

"No."

"Mind?"

"No. How about you? Where from?"

"Boise, Idaho. Spud capital of the world, I guess," he muttered it with the cigarette between his lips, making the tip of it fly around just as he held the match to it. He made a production, then, out of cupping his hands around the flame and letting out a large puff, which extinguished the match. "Oh, man," he said, shaking his head and settling back onto the cot.

The quiet grew around them. The smell of the smoke took Wilbur home, to the back porch in sleepy Sabine. The smoke from Dad's cigarette would linger around them—hardworking men and boys perched in various degrees of slouch on the old furniture relegated to the veranda—swirling blue in the golden evening air like haunting spirits too heavy to rise to heaven and too good to go to hell.

He'd wanted to smoke, too, but even when he'd tried it, the nausea stopped him, until all the thought or smell of a cigarette carried for him was an unmet yearning to be like the two men he cared most for in the world and a ghastly repulsion at what it took to be like them. Uncle Beau would jeer, saying, "Do it, boy. Make a man out of ya." His dad would just wave a hand, stub perfectly poised between two fingers as if manliness were indeed connected to effortless tobacco use, and mutter "Leave him be, Beau. Coffin nails is all." Dad never got his lungs back after the fields of Europe and the gas. The cryptic words were how he addressed everything that had to do with anything besides farming. On the subjects of weevils, rust, rot, drought, and migrant workers he became a virtual poet, but when it came to Wilbur, his words were only slightly more numerous than those he used when it concerned Mama.

"Want a drag, Bud?" said Ralph.

"No, thanks."

"Mind if I take another for later?"

The Christmas show came after a month-long day, and as Wilbur watched, Ralph sauntered eagerly out, pushing another fellow in a wheelchair. Two orderlies came and tried to lift Wilbur's cot, but when they moved toward the door, pain shot through the morphine and seared his legs and ribs and the stump of his right arm; he wailed, and they took him back to his place in a hurried, hushed, and disappointed rush.

When the siege of agony lifted and Wilbur could look about again, he found that he was completely alone. He strained his ears. There was no sound but a faucet dripping into a bucket somewhere beyond the corrugated metal. No moaning. No sawing. Was this sudden quiet a Christmas gift? There were no smells of holiday breads and pies full of cinnamon and raisins, no aroma of pine tree and candles. Only the lingering hospital smells: rubbing alcohol, various excrements, and, hovering attendant to everything, the sweetish brown smell of blood.

Wilbur seemed to wait five years in the darkness. He must have slept, because when he opened his eyes he found that someone had rolled a piano—one of those upright oak giants like his mother's parlor piano—against the far wall of corrugated metal. It even had a lace dust-runner across the top and a little rose in a bud vase on top of that. Maybe the show was coming inside, he thought, although there was no sound of singing or people moving in. Instead, what he saw was a lone figure moving toward the piano at the end of the room. It was a girl—a young woman—slender and small, with wide cheekbones and large eyes and long brown hair.

"Hello," he said. She didn't respond, and he wondered if she could hear him. Maybe she was too far away. Anyway, she was intent on the piano and seemed not to notice anything else in the room. "I'm sorry about the smell in here," he ventured again. "They try, but it's just awful." She was wearing a long dress of dark calico with tiny pale flowers in clumps; it reminded him of one of the patches worked into the quilt on his bed in his room at his parents' farmhouse, where the sun would break through the window on a bleak morning, lighting the little flower clumps like stars in the night.

Soundlessly, she scooted a small bench into place. She lifted her hair in both hands and resettled it on her back. Softly at first, then confidently, she touched the keys of the old piano. She played "Silent Night," and he wasn't sure if she played it several times or if she played it so slowly that it took him an hour to hear it. Throughout the song a single note of the tune was missing, just like the F in the middle octave that stuck in cool weather on his mother's parlor piano.

"Sorry about that key that sticks, miss," he called out. She played on, oblivious to both the sticking key and his words.

When the tune came to the last line, where the words were "Sleep in heavenly peace," he began to shake a little and felt glad he was covered in the blanket so she wouldn't see his wounds and be repulsed by him, and glad she had come to bring him Christmas, and hopeful that she might come kiss him and that she didn't get around, at least not much, and that maybe she would marry him and play the piano in his mother's parlor next Christmas just this very exact same way.

After Christmas it rained for three weekends in a row. San Diego took on a gray cast. I made sure to write plenty of letters. Mother and Daddy didn't come. Garnelle and I went two weekends in a row to First Southern Baptist Church, where we saw a few of the other factory girls we knew. It was a pretty nice place. On the last of those rainy Sundays we decided not to go out in the cold and slept the afternoon away.

I dreamed that I was a man I saw on a Laurel and Hardy short, spinning ten plates on poles, balancing them all. Sitting atop each of the plates was someone I knew. Even Bosco, the dog back home. At my feet were chains in coils. There was nothing frightening about the chains themselves, but I was desperately trying to keep the people on the plates from falling on the chains, even though I walked among the coils, repeatedly pushing them aside with my feet, and they sprang back like snakes into a spiral. I woke halfway through the dream each night and prayed deliriously. *Dear President Roosevelt, please save us.*

TWO WEEKS LATER the weather broke, and a sparkling day, with temperatures supposed to reach sixty-eight, was forecast on our radio. On Saturday, Garnelle and I went to the hillside again, and this time that Marine-who-was-not-Irish came immediately up the cliff and sat with us without more than a hello. This weekend was between paychecks, and our lunch was just a few tomatoes and an orange each, with a leftover roll from breakfast. Garnelle shot me a look; we both knew politeness dictated we should once again invite this acquaintance to share. Still, it was a little pushy for him just to sit himself down like we owed him or something. I'd brought him an extra sandwich last time he wouldn't show his face, and now this week that we were scrimping to the last penny, he was here for a handout.

Oh, I see, this is about Garnelle, I thought, as if I were saying the words aloud. *Not me.* That's why he didn't even say hello when I was here before. I felt irritated, but I smiled. "Hello," I said. "We were just about to have lunch. There isn't much, but I'll share my half with you, if you like." I was hoping he'd say, "No, thanks, I'm not hungry," but of course that couldn't happen. We ate slowly, without talking, trying to make the one tomato last awhile.

"It's a pretty nice wind there," he said at last. "Will you show me how to sail the paper cross? If you don't mind."

"No. I don't mind." Garnelle read another romantic novel. She slept. Gordon Benally and I flew the paper cross of red and yellow funnies against the bleached blue California sky until the sun started to settle and the ocean mist thickened. Going through the motions of getting the kite launched eased my annoyance at him. When it was finally soaring overhead, he held the stick with the string attached and I sat on the ground, leaning back on my elbows.

"It's like you're up there with it," I said.

He nodded very, very slowly. Such a small movement of his head that I wasn't quite sure I caught it at all. He held the stick in his hands as if it would take him with it. I watched him for a while. A silent Marine, unfamiliar with something so silly as a kite, mesmerized. Caramel.

After a long time he said, "It's yours. Do you want to hold it?"

"If you're ready to let go, I'll take it," I said.

When he gave it to me, he let go of the stick as if it held him. His hands touched mine more than I expected, and the slight, unintentional intimacy of the act affected my heart's pace. More than I expected. Then I remembered—he was here to see Garnelle. He hadn't as much as looked her way. *But that's how men could be,* Daddy would say, *chasing one quail until another got close enough to catch.* I'd probably go home and find Danny Poquette married to Deely, just like Mother always said.

As soon as I took the stick, the kite dove and jerked in the air and started to fall. I clambered to my feet and pulled at it, tugging this way and that, stepping back, reeling out more string. The paper rattled and grew limp, then taut again. After circling a few more times, it rose, having adjusted to the new hands on its tether. He smiled. "You are a good person," he said.

"Thanks," I said. I'd never in my life heard such a blunt, unanswerable compliment. There was no room for demurely passing it away, no shyness about the way it was offered.

"I have to go back to the base soon. Have to do a four-hour program this evening. Thank you for the lunch."

"It wasn't much," I said. "Do you have time to help me pull in the kite?"

"You have to pull it in?"

"Well, usually, unless it crashes. I guess that's the only way you've seen me land it. Actually, you're supposed to reel it in and catch it. It's a lot easier with two people. Here." I handed the string stick to him. "You start winding it in, and I'll try to catch it. Just wind smoothly and evenly, and it'll come down. I'll get under it. When it gets close, I'll reach up and take it."

We brought the kite in as if we were old hands at grounding large aircraft together. He wound the string around the stick. Handing it back to me, he said, "I'm glad your friend came so we could talk."

"Oh?" I knew he wanted to talk to her.

"I thought it would be more polite to have an extra person here with us, since we don't know each other very well. I can't stay much longer. Thanks for letting me fly it."

When he was gone, Garnelle rolled up onto her elbow and smirked at me. "He kiss you yet?"

"No!" I said. "What a thing to say."

"Look, I was pretending to be asleep so long I really fell asleep. Did he ask you out?"

"No."

"Well, did you hint around that you'd go if he did?"

"Gee whiz, Garnelle. No."

"Well, next time be ready. Have something you need to do that you need a lift for. Like, to shop for a birthday present for someone. You know the kind of stuff to say."

"He's not here to talk to me anyway."

"I see."

"He ignored me completely the day you weren't here. I thought you could have been nice and at least acted interested."

"Frosty Benally. It's an improvement over Frosty Summers."

"Cut that out."

"He's a corporal. They make pretty good money. Compared to my brother."

"Wilbur's a great guy."

"Yeah, but he's not in the army to get rich."

"I like Wilbur. I like him a lot."

"You can still go to a movie with Gordon What's-his-name, if you'd just get him to ask you."

"Gee whiz."

"Look at this. I've got ink from this book on my arm. I bet it's on my face, too. Is it on my face? See what you've done? You know you get all mushy-looking when he comes and sits down."

"I've got laundry to do."

"No you don't."

ordon pressed the healing wounds in his stomach, sensing the dull, tightened feeling of stitches pulling against organs. He was hungry. The sky was thick with clouds all around but open overhead, like he was in a bucket looking up. Walking from his office to the PX at midnight, he was struck by the vivid images in the clouds. Lightning splintered across the sky. The thunder was distant and indistinct, a slow rolling of heavy boulders rather than a boom. The storm had put conditions right for the vivid sunset colors to appear near the coast. *Changing Woman must be waiting,* he thought.

It was useless to disturb his bunkmates; too much coffee, too many things tumbling through his thoughts. He signed out a jeep and headed off the base to the place where he'd met Frosty. But his mind was not on her. After his regular job he'd filled in at the listening station and right before shift change had taken a message of a supply transport sunk at sea: food, clothing, and all hands lost, four reports of devastation to American forces, and one list of casualties. Final Enemy was relentless. Without the tumult of sunlight, the sound of waves came clearly to the rolling cliffs overlooking Mission Bay. He watched clouds, lightning striking simultaneously from the four corners of the heavens. He saw in the sky a great buffalo of cloud, a single great buffalo that filled the sky. The white buffalo went to its knees, heavily, like a cow wounded or bearing a calf. It roared. Then tears began to flow from its eyes, and Gordon could see a gaping red wound in its side. Blood ran there. Dripped from the sky to the ground. On the ground in a heap was a cloth of colors. Red and white stripes. Blue with white stars. The flag was on the dirt, stained and smeared with grime, and the blood of the white buffalo soaked into it.

Gordon began to sing. His song was of clan and of power and strong living; it was long, older than his great-grandfather's great-grandfather. He sang a war song and a feet-upon-the-land-of-my-enemy song. Then his heart was lightened, and he sang up the sun. He took off his shirt and showed the sun his wounds. He blessed the earth and took soil in his hands and pressed it to his stomach, under the corn-pollen bundle. Changing Woman must have smiled, because the clouds split and the sun broke upon the land and covered him with a warm yellow light.

Garnelle's mother wrote her and told her to call home as soon as possible. Garnelle was afraid it was bad news about Wilbur, and she made me go with her to the Rexall store, where she made the call. She kept saying, "Yes, ma'am. Yes, ma'am," into the phone. When she hung up, she took my arm and squeezed it like she was trying to choke the life out of me through my arm.

"What is it?" I said. "Is Wilbur all right?"

"Far as I know, Wilbur is fine."

"Are you going to tell me?"

"When we get back to the apartment. Just hang on to me until then."

Hang on? I couldn't have peeled her hands off my arm with a foot-long knife. We squashed into each other trying to get through the door, and she finally let go. She curled her hands into fists and held them against her chin while she told me everything her mother had said. Then she ran and threw herself on the bed and covered her face with her hands. For a second I pictured Deely. Garnelle told me, between racking sobs, that two men in uniforms went to the front porch of Carl Brueller's house, halfway down the row of two-story Victorians on Potomac Road in Sabine. They presented Carl and Marie Brueller with a small blue flag with a gold star embroidered on it and a tassel hanging from it.

I stood in the bedroom of our little apartment while she lay across the bed where I usually slept. I held on to the window sash as she wept, her face buried in my old pillow. The creaky springs on the bed groaned with every sob. I kept telling myself I should think of some Bible verses to say, to comfort her, but nothing came to mind. I put my hand on her shoulder and said, "The Lord works in mysterious ways, Garnelle," and she nearly took off my head, shouting something unintelligible at me.

Her face was twisted, crimson. "You don't know anything. *You don't know anything!*"

"You're right," I said. I looked out the window to the grassy area beyond. Somebody whose clothes looked familiar, although I couldn't see her face, was walking with a huge laundry basket across the lawn, her hair in pincurls wrapped with a blue-checked scarf. "I don't have any idea how bad you feel. I'm really sorry, Garnelle. I'm sorry I said something so ridiculous. Maybe there's a mistake." I sat on the edge of the bed, patting her shoulder for half an hour. At last I rose, stiff from holding myself on to the tippy old spring bed with my toes pressed against the floor. She didn't move.

The next day Garnelle walked all the way to work without a word. She did at least pause before we parted at the door to thank me for sitting with her so long, and to tell me how much it meant to her. I still couldn't grasp that someone I knew, someone my age, was dead. I had nothing to say to fix this. And no praying would undo it. I sighed when she left. For a moment Garnelle's behavior caused me to think about Deely's old flinging-herself-on-the-bed act. Maybe Deely really did need sympathy, I mused. But then again, maybe people who get sympathy oughtn't to torture the people they want to receive it from.

I felt bad about Coby, too, although what was going through Garnelle's mind was something far beyond what I felt. Is there anyone I'd feel that terrible about losing? Would I care about this odd Marine Gordon that much? I thought so. I wanted to. But part of my brain told me I'd never hold on that tightly to anyone or anything. Everything in my life was made for letting go. Disposable. Especially boys like Coby Brueller and Wilbur Fielding and Gordon Benally. In the eyes of Uncle Sam, I suppose Gordon was no boy, but a man. Where I come from, everyone was a boy until he got some gray hair and kids and a house and all. Were all the young men dressed like soldiers, like Coby, just disposable to God, like ants on a busy sidewalk? What was the point of all those Sunday school lessons pounded into my head——that God had a plan for me alone, that I was among His chosen? What was the point of praying anyhow? After all, weren't people all over the country praying that their son or brother or father wouldn't get killed? Weren't they dying like flies and rumors going around the factory that Uncle Sam would start to draft us girls to fight? Was I disposable, too?

THAT WEEK Garnelle and I cut each other's hair from a step-by-step picture illustration in *Redbook* magazine. We gave ourselves smelly home permanents and followed the directions carefully——Garnelle let me give her one first, to prove to me it would work——so we both ended up with pretty nice results rather than burned frizz. "Wow, am I amazed," I said.

"You look real smart, kiddo," she told me.

I giggled, staring in the mirror. "You do, too."

"We're a couple of peaches."

"I wish I had a Kodak. I'd send my folks a picture."

"Let's go shopping!" she said. "Mama always said nothing dries a tear like a ten-dollar bill."

We went to the May Company store, and I bought a little Brownie camera. Garnelle got a smart hat with a bow on the side and a piece of net on the front. She spent over twenty-five dollars. We bought new sheets and pillows and some cute dish towels with red birds on the ends. We ate lunch at the little fountain in the store, tried on lipstick and powder. I kept telling myself that I'd better keep this money, but I got swept up in the fun of picking out things to have for my own. She bought nail polish, a color called Cherry Kissed.

"I don't know," I said. "I just don't think I could do that. Wear nail polish."

"Why not? It's just for fun."

"Pretty racy for me," I said.

"Your family was never crazy about having fun, were they?" I gave her a look. "Oh, I'm sorry. I didn't mean anything by it, you know?" Garnelle suddenly wanted to do all kinds of stuff. We had a telephone put in the apartment and split the cost of it. So she would never again have to wait two weeks for news, Garnelle said. I didn't mind, except it meant I had to call my folks and tell them, because she was going to tell hers, and news travels fast in Sabine.

Garnelle never cried again about Coby that I knew of. But one of the girls from her area, Zoe Archibald, told me that Garnelle never let a band of fifty-caliber rounds out of her hands without a kiss on the first one that would catch the pawl and be shoved into the chamber. "That's the one that the boy handling it will touch," she said. "That's for luck."

"That's kind of strange," I whispered to Zoe.

"Not so much," she said. "I'd piss on every one of them, just to send a little American goodwill along with the lead. Except I'd get canned for it."

"Well, and somebody would have to touch it."

"Yeah. But if they knew, I don't think they'd care."

I nodded and wrote down figures for the stack as she loaded them into the boxes in front of her. I couldn't imagine such rage. The more I thought about it, the scarier it seemed. I said, "You know, we could mark the boxes 'P' or 'no-P.' "

Zoe laughed, and every time we saw each other for a while we each asked the other if she was marking the boxes correctly.

Garnelle, who used to talk about Coby all the time, started dating LeRoy Hobbs from Engineering four weeks later. He was nice enough; skinny, and 4-F because of his asthma and nearsightedness. But LeRoy had a car, and he didn't mind driving us around.

IN MAY I GOT MOVED to the day shift. Garnelle still worked swing, but she said she might trade with someone and get days, too. The weather turned warm the second week. As for me, I spent my time off with Gordon, if he could get away from work. And time just went by. Gordon worked a lot—sometimes twelve hours a day—training new guys to use radio equipment. It was complicated work, he said, and didn't explain much. If I asked anything he'd just smile and say, "You know what happens to loose lips?"

"No, I don't," I'd say back.

"Me neither," he'd say. "I guess you have to start keeping them in your coat pocket."

One evening he was at our place and had brought us a paper bag full of raw peanuts. We spread them on a cookie sheet, put them in the stove, and sat around like we were watching a puppet show, opening the door to check every minute or two. Garnelle chattered away about work, about getting her hair done, about buying a pair of nylon stockings. She dashed from the room to go get them and show them off to us.

He nodded and smiled when she left. Gordon was so quiet sometimes, and I wondered what he was thinking. Being around him was so different from anything I'd known. At Mother and Daddy's house there was never a time, unless in the bathroom or asleep in bed, when I wasn't being constantly talked to. I remember going to the movies with the kids, and Marty Haliburton had never once stopped talking the whole time, about how he knew stuff about the show, and the actors, and on and on.

"Looks like it's time," Gordon said. "Smells good." We put the cookie sheet on the makeshift coffee table and sat on the floor in front of it like children, burning our fingers on the peanuts. "You like movies?" Gordon asked me.

"Sure. Pretty much any kind except those mobster ones."

"Like cowboys and Indians?"

I opened my mouth and closed it again, caught off guard. "I guess," I said.

"You know, sometimes they got those actors riding a barrel on ropes, not a horse. You can tell by the sway." Then he smiled a little. "And unless you got a horse that's hard of hearing, you never shoot from the back of a horse. They don't put up with it—they'll toss you off." He laughed. "Those are specially trained horses; you can practically shoot off a bomb and they won't spook."

"How do you know all that?"

"Where I live, lots of producers come and make movies. I knew people who got bit parts just hanging around looking hopeful. I've been in two movies already. They always need Indians to die."

I felt myself wanting to cry. "Oh."

"Hey, don't look so sad. They pay good money, and all I had to do was fall off a horse. We used to—sometimes we played tricks on them, too." There was a long silence. "Someday I'd like to go home and put up a fence so they can't drive trucks across our graveyards. But we usually had a lot of fun."

"They drove trucks across graveyards?"

He nodded. "Nothing is marked, like churches do it. But the old people, they know where they are, and they don't like it. They tell us young ones not to cooperate with the movie producers. But then the money we make is what feeds some of them. It's all pretty complicated." He waited a long time while I thought about his words, before going on.

"Well, on that cheery note, I'm off to the powder room," Garnelle said. "Too much lemonade."

When she was behind the closed door, Gordon leaned toward me. "Here's the last one. Let's share it." He opened the peanut, identical dark-skinned kernels cradled in the shell in his open palm.

My heart swelled and my throat felt tight. A *good* girl never says "I love you" first; I knew it makes you fast. I reached out and plucked a nut from one end of the shell. "Thank you," I said. Then something came over me, and I lifted the peanut to his lips and fed it to him. The smile left Gordon's face, replaced with a look of great tenderness and warmth. He took the other peanut and fed it to me. So I knew. We didn't have to say a thing to know.

From that moment on, being with him changed. Our talk was warmer, whispered, pressed between our clasped hands. He told me stories. He told stories like you'd tell a little child, animal stories. Only they weren't really about animals, they were about people. The best times were spent not talking at all. I'd never been around anyone that it felt comfortable just to sit with and say nothing. One evening we went to see Bette Davis's new picture, and he bought us sodas and popcorn. I thought all boys were supposed to try to get fresh, so you could resist them, so they'd know you were a good girl. A kind of dating litmus paper was how hard you said no. But when the credits rolled at the end and he leaned close to me and kissed my cheek, I smiled at him and didn't turn away.

He held my hand as we walked to my apartment. "Gordon, you've never told me what you do in the Marines," I said.

"Nothing much to tell."

"The girls at work ask me what you do. They think you're imaginary because I don't know. Zoe's boyfriend is a navigator."

"Tell them I train new guys to use radio equipment."

"You told me once that only Navajo men were in your classes."

"I shouldn't have said that."

"Is it a—a *color* thing?"

"It's a language thing."

That made sense. Maybe some of the men had to learn English after they were drafted. Odd that they'd put men on the radios who spoke another language. "Well," I said, "I'm proud that you know enough to train other people. It must mean you're pretty smart."

"Not smart enough. Let's get some spaghetti at the diner."

ONE JUNE MORNING I looked at myself in the mirror as I headed out the door and realized, for the first time in my entire life, I liked the image that looked back at me. I had a purpose in my life, a reason to head out the door; I made my own money and took care of my expenses; I had friends who cared about me and a nice boy to spend time with. I refused to let myself think about the whirlwind of distant horrors that had brought me to this place and time, but I wished it could go on forever.

The first weekend Garnelle got on day shift, she and I invited some other girls to come over at night and make victory fudge. Everybody was coming—Julia and Sharmayne and Beulah and half the girls from the "bullet bunch." There were no words that I could come up with that described how good that made me feel. We pooled everything we had to come up with some ingredients. Then, for a couple of hours, we laughed and talked and cooked and argued about what to do when.

We brought our droopy, scorched-smelling fudge and a jar full of spoons into the little sitting room where Garnelle usually slept. We sat in a circle in the floor cooing over our efforts, discussing the men in our lives, our families back home—anything but the war. We put each other's hair in curlers. Sharmayne brought her violin and played for us—classical things and sad songs and even new ones. Then one of the girls turned on the radio, and Julia started singing. We sang together and made ourselves sick on fudge. If there'd been enough room to dance, we probably would have cut up the rug.

As I went to the kitchen to refill the water pitcher, I happened to glance over my shoulder at the nine young women crowded together in our tiny sitting room, laughing at some silly mistake Julia had made in a song. She had about the prettiest voice I'd ever heard in my life. I started wondering what God meant by bringing us all together. How could I be the meanest thing my family ever knew and have this many friends? If Deely were here, would she conspire with Mabel and Fae to get Alvin McCloud to ask Fae for a date? Would she let a Negro girl like Sharmayne play a joke on her and laugh? Or were we all only part of each other's lives for a moment, putting down our swords long enough to win a war against a common enemy? Would we be friends if we'd met any other way? Julia was a Jew. If she ever brought her lovely voice to grace the Siloam Springs Baptist Church, they'd never again let Deely caterwaul from the podium.

The three girls roared with laughter and clasped arms about each other. They swamped Sharmayne, who was holding a wooden spoon full of fudge in the air over their heads, and all of them ended up sprawled on the floor, laughing hysterically in a tangle of many-colored arms and legs.

Tears formed in my eyes and spilled over, too quick to catch. They landed in the pitcher of water just as I reached the door with it.

"What's wrong, sweetie?" Mabel called out.

"Nothing," I said, laughing. "The water shot out of the faucet and stung my eyes."

"Are you making coffee?" Julia asked.

"Yes, ma'am," I said. I left the room again quickly and put on the coffeepot. Someone's voice drifted in, singing some old, sad song. When I smelled the warm aroma of the coffee in the can, it filled my mind with the presence of Gordon. The thought came to me like a revelation of sorts, that all the world would be better if people were blind. Everyone. Or if we could always have a huge war or something to work against, so that people could just sing and eat fudge in their living rooms with anyone they wanted to.

John Moultrie rubbed the bottom half of his face with one large hand. He had spread before him on the desk two volumes of law, a Big Red tablet in which he was taking notes, and a cold thermos of coffee. He read and reread a case history about a lynching in West Virginia, circa 1901. Even though the man hanged was a Negro, a jury had found six men—members of the local Order of the KKK—guilty. But they'd changed the charge from murder to involuntary manslaughter, on account of the Negro had annoyed one of them by driving his mule in the middle of the road, allowing no passage on either side.

Junior Jasper and a couple of the boys had offered up all the information they had, which wasn't much. Luke Blye had been a devoted lamp-keeper at the little congregation. Each week, depending on which day he felt well enough to walk to the church house, he let himself in and trimmed the wicks, polished the chimneys, and filled the reservoirs of the coal-oil lamps that illuminated Missionary Way. It might have been any day of the week, and therefore it was unlikely that someone had lain in wait for the old man. The only thing Blye owned that he valued at all was found in the ashes, still next to the heart that cared about it, so that took out robbery. And it didn't seem to be revenge for anything, for Moultrie couldn't locate anybody with a grudge against the old man.

Uncle Blye had surprised someone, or been surprised by someone, in the act of something. Burning the church had to have been intentional. Whether it was what cost Luke Blye his life or was meant to cover it up was another question. Evidence that made the death a murder was locked in a file cabinet in his office: a singed hunk of rope, a tarry scrap of burlap impregnated with a pinhead-size dot of pure gold from a filling in a tooth—the Moultrie family had made sure Uncle Blye had seen the dentist as often as he cared to. On top of the file stood two large, square metal cans. One was old, dented and rusted, and had been upright under the pelvic bone in the middle of the blackened debris; the other was found just inside a window. It was nearly new, smelled like the exhaust pipe on a car, and was painted under the layer of soot, with the yellow and dark blue insignia of Doxol Petroleum. One of the shoulders of the can, just to the right of the spout, had been flattened with what looked like strokes of a ball-peen hammer, and during some subsequent use that he couldn't discern, paint had worn off that corner, giving it the baring effect of a girl seductively letting her dress down.

Moultrie tapped his fingers on the word "involuntary" in the court description on the page in front of him. Whatever Uncle Luke could have done to annoy some smart-ass kids was immaterial. The thing that counted was whether the sheriff could get a witness to come forward on the stand. He had a confession, so to speak, that came in the mail that morning. And something about the boy's story didn't add up.

He pulled a wrinkled and folded paper from his shirt pocket. "*Dear Sir*," it started.

> *I know there's plenty of what the chaplin calls battlefield vocations going on around here. We're taking the beach tomorrow at oh-dark-thirty, and nobody is planning to sleep, and lots are writing their girls, mother, etc. I got a letter off to Mama and Pop, don't you worry about*

that. But I don't want to meet Jesus with this here, the chaplin says be-smirch, on my name. So here it is, taking my licks like a man. I take the blame for lighting up the nigger church last fall. I know there was some other kids around they didn't do nothing and it was just pure meanness on my part. I don't reckon I meant any real harm, and likely it was the corn liquor calling the shots there. We had come from the Halloween Party and we shuffled around awhile thinking maybe we'd go bust in on the Catholic kids' dance party, but Marty Haliburton says, lets go down here, I've got an idea. He had this Doxol can and started talking about what he could do with it. Course, naturally the Bandy boys had some shinney, I figure you know that isn't any secret I'm spilling about them. I tell you I had my share of it, and it filled me with the devil. I had matches in my pocket on account of I was try-ing to learn to smoke. Don't go blaming any of the other kids. No use them suffering about it. Here enclosed is the last three dollars I got on me, I want you to give it to them folks for building their church back together and tell them I'm real sorry, just sorry as I could be. So if I get through tomorrow, I remain yours truly, Coby Brueller.

P.S.: Mama and Pop don't know anything about this, and if you can keep it quiet, it'll be a blessing. Thanks, Sheriff M.

A week after the postmark on the envelope, the Brueller folks had got a visit from the War Department. There was nothing more sacred than a soldier's last confession, and if the Brueller kid was going to own up to the fire and leave out the murder, then it just plain sounded to him like the boy didn't know anything about the man inside. Moultrie didn't dare telephone Bobby Lee Baker. Mayvis Plinkle was more of a reporter than Henry Scoville at the paper. He'd have to drive.

The three dollars had not found their way to the envelope. Maybe he'd forgotten it before "oh-dark-thirty." Moultrie leaned up in his chair and tugged his wallet from his back pocket. He fished out three one-dollar bills and tossed them on the law book.

Hey, Fros," said Gordon's voice on the phone. "About this weekend."

I was instantly gloomy; it sounded like he was canceling our date. "You're going to work instead?"

"No, but maybe change our plans. A friend of mine's got some horses. I was wondering if you'd like to go riding some. I guess he has to come, too. Actually, he offered for him and me to take them, but I asked if he'd let me have another for you, too."

My mind started racing. I'd been horseback riding once, the summer I went to Girls' Auxiliary Camp for five days. My camp counselor had made us each pay thirty cents for the privilege of blistered bottoms and being drenched with the smell of sweaty horses. I was too short for the stirrups, and the horse I chose because it was pretty went on a one-horse crusade to scare the life out of me, biting at my feet and legs, jumping up on the other horses. The GA leader had said the animal was hard to control "because he was a boy." Of course a couple of years later I figured out what he was trying to do, but I remember telling my parents after that day to keep me away from "scallions" for the rest of my life.

I nodded at the phone. "Sure, Gordon. Um, I'm not very good at it, though. I—I, hey, I just had an idea. Do you think your friend would mind Garnelle coming along, too? We could have a picnic. She just broke up with a boy she was crazy about, and it'd be nice . . . the four of us."

"I'll see if he's got another. You're coming, though?"

"Yeah. Yes. If it's just the three of us, I'll still bring some sandwiches."

Saturday morning dawned overcast and dreary, with a smell of rain in the air and lumpy clouds shouldering each other for room over the parched land. Dust had been swirling around for two days, preceding the weather front, and from daybreak, Garnelle became sicker by the hour. She rolled out of bed looking and sounding miserable. I heard her in the bathroom coughing, and in a loud voice she wailed, "Dot that, too," just before the flush.

"Frosty," she said, shaking her head, "I just cad't go. I'b too stuffed up, ad I feel like by head will explode, ad dow I'be got the curse."

"Oh, no," I said. "You do look dreadful. I mean, like you feel terrible."

"Well, I do. I'b goige back to bed." And with that she crawled onto her bed on the couch, pulled the sheets over her head, and scrunched herself toward the back cushion.

"I'm so sorry, Garnelle." I was about to offer to stay in the apartment with her when I stopped short. "I haven't seen Gordon in a week. He'll be here in half an hour; he's probably already left the base. Do you want me to make you some tea? Shall I leave you the extra sandwich for lunch?"

"If you wadt. I do't care."

I pulled out the pin curls in my hair with one hand while I filled the kettle and lit the stove with the other. I brushed my hair while the water came to a boil. By the time Gordon came to the door, a light mist was falling on the kitchen window, and Garnelle had poked her head out of the sheet on the davenport and was balancing the teacup uneasily in her hands.

"You look good," she said between sips. "Thags for the tea."

I had on a pair of her brother's old dungarees, cut off at the hem and rolled up almost to my knees, and a pretty pullover sweater, light green, that had a kind of nap to it so it moved one way and another when you brushed your hand across it. "Thanks, Garnelle. I sure hope you feel better. Maybe the rain will settle the dust."

She nodded and sipped more tea. "Wish it would take away the curse, that's all. Behave yourself, girl." She stared into the cup, concentrating on her tea.

I opened the door with the makings of our picnic in a cumbersome cardboard box held out in front of me. I pushed the screen door with it; he would need to take it from me and return to the pickup without seeing Garnelle on the couch. "Hi," I said. "Here's the food. Garnelle can't come. She's not well at all." I looked over my shoulder at her. She smiled and raised the cup. I closed the door.

"That's too bad," he said. "Do we still need all this?"

"Well, I left her some, if that's what you mean."

"Pete couldn't come either. He had to pull a shift all day and won't be done until two or so. He said he might come up later, though."

We sat in the pickup for a second before he started it up. "Well," I said, pushing my voice over the sudden grinding of the engine, "it might rain."

"Maybe. It's a good thing. Hills are too dry." He chucked the gearshift into reverse and concentrated on backing into the street.

I let out a sigh. It was so like him not to say the picnic should be postponed because of the threat of rain. If I knew Gordy, it would still be a picnic if all we did was sit in this truck and watch the rain. "Are we still getting the horses?"

"Sure."

I smiled. "I hope you picked me out a real calm one. I had a bad experience before with a two-year-old stallion."

"Yeah. I got you one 'at's lame on three legs."

"One good leg? That's good enough."

"No. It's only got three legs."

"And they're all lame?"

He smiled at me and stretched. Absently, he touched the scars on his left arm with his right hand between shifting the gearbox from second to third.

I leaned toward him and said, "You're just scared I'll outrun yours."

"These are pretty sorry old nags. I guess they'd be glue by now if he didn't want to feed 'em."

"That's bad," I said. Actually, I was relieved. At least if they couldn't run or jump, I should be able to maintain some decorum.

"Or dinner. You can eat horses, you know."

"Oh, Gordon!"

" 'S true."

"You never ate a horse."

"Yeah."

"Well. Oh, that's just awful." I saw his eyes cut this way for a minute and that almost-dimple break in his cheek. I made a face at him and pushed out my chin. "You didn't either. Did it make you want to eat hay for dessert? Well? So how was it?"

"Tastes like chicken."

"Jeez."

"Them Injuns, you know."

"Cut it out, Gordy." I pushed at his shoulder and left my hand atop the box between us. His hand covered mine and stayed there, except for the time it took him to shift the gears of the old truck, until we got to his friend Pete's stables.

Two smallish horses were saddled and waiting for us, and a man with a heavy Spanish accent led them to the gate, telling us Pete had wished us a good time. They didn't look anything like the spry stallion of my youth, so I was much more confident as I swung into the saddle of one and let the man adjust the stirrups. Our lunch was transferred into a canvas bag slung over the saddle horn on Gordon's horse, and we were off. It didn't dawn on me that we would be alone together until we were out of sight of the stable.

The rain stopped, but the air was thick with it, dense to breathe, smelling of damp soil and brush, with a slight whiff of horse now and then. We weren't very creative. We rode around a little bit and ended back up on the same hill we always sat at before. The clouds hung low, partly obscuring the horizon. Everything was misty, and though the air was warm, I kept thinking I should feel cold. I pulled my sweater tight around me but almost immediately loosened it again.

We spread our picnic on the dried grass. Gordon tied the horses' reins together and fastened one end of the reins to a rock so they could graze while we ate. The air smelled alive and potent. The horses' snuffling was like distant music, a rhythm in the air. And the food tasted remarkable. It was just a chicken sandwich and some cold baked beans, but nothing served in any elegant restaurant could have tasted better.

We didn't talk, and even the ocean seemed quiet. The breeze that had plagued us was gone, and this misty cloying air was too wet to be comfortable but too warm to make us want to seek shelter. The day drifted by, clouds obscuring the sun's passage. Gordon found a little wildflower growing in the shadow of a dead weed and pulled it, holding it toward me between his thumb and forefinger.

"It's beautiful," I said. "It's so incredibly small." It was a white blossom no bigger than one of the freckles on my hand, perfectly symmetrical, delicate as lace.

Gordon smiled. He leaned back on his elbows and looked toward the sky. "There are flowers like that where my family lives. Some rocky places, they are the only thing that grows."

"What town are you from?"

"It's not a town, really. Just a place. On a road near Chinle."

"I never heard of that, Chin-lee."

"Not much to hear of. Just a filling station and a Coke machine. Place to meet someone, mostly. Get some gas and go somewhere else."

"You've spent a lot of time on horses, haven't you?"

"Some, I guess. Used to rodeo. Pretty stupid, though. After a while I smartened up and quit getting thrown."

"What do you mean? Did you get better at riding?"

"Got better at staying on the fence."

I smiled and nodded. I was used to lying in the grass, watching the clouds, talking to Gordon. I guess he was used to it, too. We put the waxed paper wrappers in the canvas bag and brushed the crumbs from the tablecloth. We lay side by side, holding hands, looking at the clouds for a long time. After a while he leaned over me with the tiny flower and held it to my cheek. He said something to me in a language I'd never heard before.

"What does that mean?" I said.

Gordon spoke again in Navajo. *"This flower is made beautiful by your skin."*

"That tickles," I said.

"It should hide its face, compared to yours."

"I wish I knew what you are saying. Teach me your language. That tickles my face."

"I can never forget you as long as I walk on this earth. I feel such love for you, if you only knew how much greater it is than the sky."

"Gordon, tell me in English."

"English is sometimes not enough," he said, still in his own language.

"You know, our parents will both be angry at us."

"Sometimes I feel like the war will never be over for us. And the next minute I feel that it has never happened. Your face is soft as a petal."

"Teach me to say this?" I said. He didn't answer. I just smiled at him. Whatever game he was playing, or whatever he was actually saying, was written in his expression in some indecipherable code. He curled his arm under my head and quit talking for a while.

I felt myself getting drowsy enough to fall asleep, but I forced myself to stay awake. I rolled onto my stomach and asked, "Do those horses have names?"

He answered in English. "Yeah. That one," he said, nodding toward the closest one to us, the horse he'd been riding, "is Daisy. The one you had is Bub."

"Bub." It was a cowboy name for a horse, all right. "Daisy is a cute name. I used to have a dog named Daisy." I turned over again, talking upward to the low gray sky. "I called her Daisy Crockett. We ran all over town pretending it was the wild woods. I used to pretend she was Davy Crockett and I . . . I was a beautiful Indian maiden and we hunted grizzly bears together."

He raised up onto his elbow and looked at me intently. "Why did you hunt bears?"

"It was just pretend."

"Why?"

"I don't know."

"Sure. Why would Davy Crockett and some Indian girl hunt bears?"

I was uncomfortable; was I really going to have to defend some childhood game? "Well, to save all the people from the bear." I looked earnestly at his face for signs this was another of his jokes. He was very serious. "It was eating people and killing all the cows and horses and sheep and chickens, and none of the soldiers in the fort could get it, so they called up Davy Crockett and his trusty long rifle. And of course the beautiful Indian maiden showed him where to find food in the forest and how to find the bear."

"Oh."

"Besides, it wasn't just *some* Indian girl. It was the Beautiful Indian Maiden. Me."

Gordon kissed me. He kissed me gently but urgently, and as I kissed him back, my mind reeled. The gentleness, the sweetness of his lips was more than I had ever guessed or pretended, passionately kissing the back of my own hand, hoping to know some handsome young prince with a kiss ready to wake the princess. His broad hands were first on both sides of my face, then under my shoulders as he scooped me to him. The weight of his body on mine should have taken the air out of me. It should have pushed me into the rocks and uneven dirt under the tablecloth. But all I knew was his kiss. The pounding of my heart, the steaming in my veins, and I was quickly covered in sweat.

He moved his head to the curl of my neck, and in the same motion he was directly on top of me. I wrapped my arms around his back. We kissed for a long time, or what seemed that way.

"You are the Beautiful Indian Maiden," he said.

"Well, I don't know."

"You could be."

"Maybe so."

"It's raining."

"I thought it was me," I said.

"Mostly it's rain."

"I like it."

He nodded and lay comfortably to one side and said in my ear, "Frosty, will you be my Beautiful Indian Maiden?"

I turned and looked in his face, almost nose to nose. "I'd like that," I said. Suddenly a raindrop landed squarely in my eye, and I rubbed at it, squinting. "This is so strange. This rain is warm," I said.

174

"It feels like a good thing. Like a live thing. It is Female Rain. The earth needs this water."

"I love it," I said.

"I do, too. Frosty," he said, then inhaled deeply, "I love you."

My eyes closed. I was mesmerized by the sound of those words. "I. think," I began slowly, "that I have loved you for a long time. I feel like we've known each other forever. Like I can't remember not knowing you. I can't imagine not having you near."

"Frosty Summers. My mother's name is Bernice."

I could not help raising my eyebrows. "Why did you say that now?"

"Maybe it's time to trust you with secrets. Names are usually secret until you know someone. I have another name. Besides Benally. And—" He made a sound like a sigh, then started again. "And you should have a name. A name chosen for you, but no one can do that except me. Would you let me choose a secret name for you?"

"All right. If you want, I suppose that would be . . . that would be a very nice thing. What would you pick?"

"Say this. Haigo áhbínígo. It means Winter Morning."

"Winter Morning?"

"You don't like it?"

"I don't understand it."

"Frosty. Winter Morning. I thought about it a long time. There's a different kind of cleanness, beauty, in a cold winter's morning. A reminder to rest, to tell stories to children, to prepare for the active time of spring and summer. A clear frosty morning is a gift to anyone who will take it. It comes from the Mother. A gift from the earth to her children. You are a gift to me."

"Oh, Gordon. That's beautiful. Tell me your name, too. Teach me to say it correctly."

Only he didn't. He kissed me again. Rain fell. We were drenched, sopping, and we kissed in the warm rain until it became part of us. And I was the morning, and he was strong hands and brown skin and gentle longing kisses, and we melted together on that tablecloth in the warm California rain, wrapped in each other's arms. Like some supernatural character in a play, carried upon the wide blue back of the hill to the clouds. Gray and hovering, clouds touched us, kissed us, soothed and urged us into each other until there was nothing but the skin-temperature rain and the smell of wet grass and the light whiff of horses. The horses nuzzled the earth around us. And I drowned in the whirlpool in my head, pulled under by the thundering weight of the one that had been us.

We slept until our wet skins began to shiver. The rain had cooled, and now it fell with more urgency. It was time to leave. I moved heavily, the way I suspect drunken people move and feel. Numb. Tingling. Exhilarated and exhausted and anxious and somewhat sore. I could not get the sodden dungarees on without his help, they were so thick and clumsy.

We didn't speak. We led the horses back to the stables, thanked the hired man, started the engine of the old pickup. He drove to my apartment and did not kiss me but squeezed my hand as I left him.

When I opened the door, Garnelle came from the kitchen. She had made up her bed but had stayed indoors, wearing some beat-up khaki trousers and a slouchy plaid shirt. She looked like she was feeling better. I closed the front door and stood there, not dripping but soggy, on the mat. "Hi, Garnelle. You feeling better?"

Her indrawn breath was a loud gasp. "Look at you! Lands. Will you just look at you? You look like— Oh, my God, Frosty. You've gone and done it."

"Done what?" I knew my face was immediately suspect. That same "you did it" feeling from when I was a child. I kept thinking of sophomore chemistry class, when Neomadel had dared me to drop a cup of sugar into a glass of sulfuric acid to see what would happen.

"It. You know."

"No I don't. I haven't done anything."

"Just look at you, kidderoo. Frosty, Frosty. I guess they won't call you Frosty the Freezer now. Gloriosky."

"I don't know what you're talking about." I was suddenly violently

176

angry. I glowered, gritting my teeth. They chattered when I said, "Cut it out, Garnelle."

"Of course you don't. Oh, you've done it all right. You just look it. You've done it sure's I'm standing here. Good golly God. Frosty Summers, you just reek with it."

"Horses. That's all you smell."

"Well, did you do something? You're not going to go having a baby or anything are you?"

That sudden change from teasing reprimand to blasting reality hit me like a fist. I burst into tears. "I didn't mean to. Oh, Garnelle, I didn't mean to. It was just raining. And all that. Oh, if only you'd come like you said you would. I swear I didn't mean to."

"Now, don't cry." She dropped the motherly attitude and came to me, putting her arms around me. "I'm sure you didn't mean to. Heck, honey, nobody hardly does until they're married. It happens to a lot of girls. Lots. It's always the rain or the sun in your eyes or something like that. You're just in love and it happens."

"I'm a slut!" The horror of my words took the strength from my legs, and I sat, directly over where my feet were planted, dropping like a heavily weighted sack. I could feel Mother's fists on my shoulders. Feel her words sinking like knives into my ribs.

"No you're not. You just made a mistake. Nobody hardly ever has a baby from the first time either. Did he say he wants to marry you?"

"Well, yes. Sort of." I squeezed my arms tight around my chest, fending off the stabbing feeling.

"Oh, crud, that's what they always say. Only if they really mean it, you know it, not just 'sort of.' "

"Well, he did. Sort of."

She pulled me roughly to my feet and just as roughly shoved me toward the bathroom door. "Come in here and take a really hot bath. You're probably going to catch a cold, first of all. You'll most likely take care of catching anything else this way, too. When you get out, you get that calendar off the wall and we'll count up the days. We'll watch for a

177

few days and keep our fingers crossed, and you take hot baths every day. And you'll see. You'll be all right."

I followed her directions, dismal and dragging with the weight of my crime. I prayed while the water filled the tub. I made it so hot that it scalded my feet red when I stepped in. I wept bitterly, longing for what I'd lost. That knowledge—that smug knowing that I was a virgin was gone. Now I was just like . . . Jean Marie? Beulah? Who else? Maybe Garnelle herself?

In the tub I tried holding my face underwater, hoping I'd drown, but I surfaced bursting for air, unable to give up and surrender to the water. I stayed until the water began to get cold, then dried off, avoiding the mirror, and went to get my warmest, raggediest old flannel nightgown.

I cried every day for the next six days, distraught with my sin, ravaged with guilt. When I was alone, in the bathroom or somewhere, I cried silently, tearlessly—the most hideously painful sorrow I'd ever felt—and while I cried, I punched my fists into my thighs, mouthing the words "I hate you" over and over, hearing the words in my mother's voice. I picked myself up, splashed cold water on my face, and left the bathroom as if nothing had happened. And deep into each night I touched my belly, wondering if within the mysteries of my body a baby was growing. When the thought grew large enough, I felt the creases smooth in my own face, felt the weighted wonder with only a small, indescribable joy. In the darkness, freed from the terror of the condemnation I would surely receive, I held the idea of a baby close to me, warming me, suckling the notion with arms crossed over my breasts. I was at peace until the light of day came and brought with it stark reality and the rush to clock in at Line Twelve, where I imagined every moment that my terrible sin would have me dragged in front of a taunting crowd and stoned to death.

On the seventh day I knew there would be no baby of Gordon's to tell my parents about, and I cried about that, too. I knew I really was no good, because I wanted that baby that I didn't have. That day I quit punching my fists into my legs.

I tried to hate Gordon and blame him, and I started reading my

Bible, finding all the passages I knew about vengeance and punishment for evildoers and Judgment Day, just to torture myself. Sometimes I read a verse and pinched my own arm just to make it sink in.

"And you call yourself a Christian? What a liar," I said to my reflection in the mirror in the little bathroom. I had been feeling so full of myself, so confident, so in control. I had wanted this time of my life to go on forever, and yet nothing could simply stop. Not even for a second. "What a slutty liar."

I got to thinking about another thing, too. How I used to hear about Garnelle being a "maybe" girl. How she was so crazy about Coby Brueller. Maybe Coby was the maybe in her life. She never said. She could have told me to go straight to hell without passing GO, or written to my parents, or any number of things. If she felt about Coby the way I felt about Gordon, everything else she said made a new kind of sense. It was like a light went on in a little, unused, amazing room in my brain. Coby and Garnelle all at once seemed like some romantic young couple in a picture show. Deely had always thought me trashy by nature; Garnelle's forgiveness didn't erase what I'd done, but it helped me live without feeling like I had to hold my head underwater.

Nine full days went by without hearing from Gordon, and I didn't call him or go to find him at the base. I could have tried to explain my worries or to insist that we marry instantly to hide my shame. I was done with men forever. I was certainly done with Gordon Benally. I wanted to see him and tell him so. I wanted to see him.

Gordon didn't disappear like Garnelle said he would. Nor did he insist on more of the same or act as if our accidental tryst had changed me in his eyes at all. He was still there every single evening after that brief absence, looking at the world with his odd imperturbability and sly humor. He chided me and teased me a little that I should have worried so much, so alone, and made me promise never to try to shoulder such a burden by myself when he was there for the asking to take it for me.

"Sure," I said. But I had no idea how he could take a burden for me. I'd never gone through any sad or hard experience alongside anyone. Alone was all I knew.

179

And then one night as he walked me home from the library, we saw people hurrying down the sidewalk, passing us right and left like there was something chasing them. "Hey, where's the fire?" Gordon called to a little boy.

"Down there, mister. The Fox Theater!"

We rushed with everyone else, stopping at the edge of the crowd, pressing in behind a red fire truck. A group of men at the back end were working a pump handle, and others held a long hose that ended someplace deep inside the building. Smoke billowed from the doorway. We waited until three firemen came out, dragging the business end of the hose. They smiled and waved at everyone. "Grease fire in the popcorn machine, folks. Nothing big. All taken care of in time for tomorrow's matinee."

"Hey," someone yelled from across the crowd, "they said that movie was hot!" He pointed to the marquee where TOO HOT TO HANDLE was edged in soot. Everyone laughed, except me.

"Gordon, let's go." Get me away from this place. "I hate the smell." That night I dreamed of Gordon and me, caught in a burning popcorn machine. Mother and Daddy were outside looking for me, but when they looked in, they couldn't find me. They saw only Gordon, and they wouldn't pull him out of the flames.

Gordon had to work Sunday, but Garnelle and I went to church. On our way home I asked her, "Do you ever feel bad about stuff you've done?"

"What stuff?" She looked at me warily.

"You know, little things. Like—like when we all had that . . . bonfire on Halloween."

She looked at me as if I'd suddenly started speaking a foreign language. "So? Just go talk to the preacher and get it off your chest. I don't think it's anything to worry about. Nobody was hurt, and there were plenty of other shacks around the Nigras could use for church. That wasn't anything. I thought you were talking about Gordon. What's eating you?"

"Nothing." The Fieldings were a family of high standing; surely if that fire were something to feel guilty over, Garnelle would know. Was there something wrong with me, that I wasn't as concerned about my fornication as about this old childish woe?

A COUPLE OF DAYS LATER Gordon stood stiffly uncomfortable in our tiny kitchen, shifting his feet. "Fros," he said, looking at the doorway, "I need to talk to you. Please, Garnelle, I'd like you to stay. I want you to hear, too. Frosty, you mean so much to me." His eyes were fixed on distant space in front of him.

I tried to ignore Garnelle's sudden breath. We'd talked about the many ways that boys can dump a girl they're tired of. She knew so many things, and by the set of her lips I was sure she was thinking this was going to be a brush-off. I felt tears already starting. She had been right. I had been used. I was disposable.

"I want to marry you. At least, that would be my wish if this war were not happening. But I cannot marry you and then leave you to be a widow if I die somewhere. I have to go. I've been reassigned, and I'm going back into action. You've heard about the buildup on the radio; it's not secret. I got my orders this afternoon. No more training; I have to go back to the Pacific. There's nothing I can do to make this better. It's war, and I'm a warrior. I'm leaving tomorrow. I will not ask you to wait for me. If your heart makes you wait, you will. Truthfully, I should never have allowed our relationship to come to this place, but that's beside the point. Please."

"Stop it," I said. "Just stop." I dropped my face to my hands. Tears didn't fall, but I'd never needed to cry so hard that my whole face hurt like that. "You're just dumping me."

"No," he said. His face looked hurt. "No."

"I deserve it, after all. That's what you came to say. You only want a good girl, right?"

"What does that mean? I'm just hoping you might wait for me to come home," he said.

"Tell me why."

"Maybe we'll get married. I was worried about finding you if you aren't here."

"So let's get married. Now." Nice girls don't say this. They wait for the boy. But he was leaving.

"No. It can't be that way. If we did that, you know your people and mine would begin our lives together angry at us. It will be hard enough as it is. There is no reason to add that trouble to our future. If I don't come back, you'll be as free as before."

"What makes you think I'd ever be free? I love you," I said softly.

Garnelle stood up and practically marched toward the kitchen door. She stood under the doorjamb, breathing fast, so loud I could hear her. Without turning back toward us she shouted, "You men don't understand what it is to wait. I'd rather go fight in the war than wait here. The least you could do . . ." She slapped the wall with the flat of her hand. On the other side the flyswatter hopped off its little tack where we hung it by the door and fell to the floor.

Gordon looked from my face to Garnelle's back. "What?"

"I guess I'm interfering."

"People who care about each other can speak their minds."

"Well, if I was Frosty, I'd rather get married, too, that's all. You don't know what it's like to be waiting and waiting and—nothing . . . that's all. Do you know what address she can write to you at?"

"You probably can't write. Not for a while. Not unless we're successful. It really is secret; that wasn't a joke. I don't know how long it will be. I'll write to you. Just be sure, if you move or anything, to leave notice at the post office. Then you'll get my letters no matter where you go."

Garnelle said, "I'm going to make coffee," and disappeared into the kitchen.

Gordon and I sat up all night, even after Garnelle finally fell asleep on my bed. We kissed and held hands. We talked about a thousand little things—how he liked lemon meringue pie warm instead of cold, how I once went fishing at the Neches River with my crazy Uncle Steven and actually caught a fish. We made more coffee. We talked about God and war and heaven and hell. We watched the sun come up. I called in sick to work while Garnelle got ready and left. Finally we settled, stonelike, silently watching people walk past the window, watching the hands of the clock turn like wheels on a car. And then, too quickly, he had to go. I could not seem to force myself to cry.

Stay outside, looking in. See those two poor people. Sad girl. Sad boy. Sadder than a movie, two people parting. My heart was behind a huge concrete dam with no gates, no opening, not even a hairline crack. On this side those people only look sad. They feel no pain. On this side.

I promised Garnelle that after Gordon left I'd go to the factory, even if it was afternoon, and tell them I was better. But I stayed home all day and moped and ached and hugged a pillow to my chest trying to fill up the hole he left in it. I got really, terribly angry. More furious than I think I've ever been in my life. Who was he to decide my future? Who was he? He and Garnelle, discussing what would be best for me as if I were some demented child in another room who could neither hear nor decide for herself. What gave him the right to dole out wisdom like he knew everything? What kind of bloated self-pride made someone able to declare, "Oh, it's better not to get married"? "Why can't I have that?" I screamed at God, as if He were sitting there above the ceiling in that apartment building. There was no answer.

I wanted to do something unexpected. Something, too, that had nothing to do with being "good" or "easy," but was about who I could be, if I were fated to be alone.

I picked up a tablet of letter paper and wrote four pages to Mother, with mingled defiance and thirst for approval.

I've learned a lot here, doing new things, meeting new people. And the thing is, when I think about my whole life and the reasons I'm here, I believe God led me here to learn I can succeed at work. So I was thinking, because Dr. Fine once told me I could become a lawyer, that I plan to look into what it takes. I have a friend my age who has a college degree. Maybe she'll tell me how she did it, so I can go, too, and become someone you'll be proud of. I've failed in the past, but I've decided to start again on the right foot. Very, very sincerely, love, Frosty

Then I wrote Farrell and told him the same thing.

Seven days later I got a letter from Mother. *"You are living a lie,"* she wrote. *"It's time for you to get back to reality and get on with life."* It was left unclear which reality I was supposed to live in, what life would hold for me if I "got on" with it. *"You have a good home and people here that care about you. Your sisters are both ashamed of you. You'll never make this right with them if you . . ."* I opened the oven door and held the pages over the pilot light, holding on far too long.

GARNELLE GOT A CALL from her parents at the end of September. They hadn't known he was missing, but Wilbur was found. Wounded, being sent home. They had been receiving letters from him, but it turned out they were written by hospital nurses; he'd been recuperating for nine months, never having told them exactly what had happened. Sympathetic nurses had obediently written only what he'd asked, until a doctor intervened and notified the War Department, then arranged for him to be shipped home.

We'd just found out we had to gear up again and pick up production, when that very day at lunch break Garnelle told me that she was going home. All the girls pitched in and gave her twenty-nine dollars for travel money. She had LeRoy Hobbs drive her to the bus station with me in the backseat of his car. They said good-bye with a handshake. He drove me back to the apartment. He and I said nice things back and forth, like "I hope Garnelle will be happy" and "She's a really nice girl" and "I hope her brother's all right and comes home soon."

THAT NIGHT Mabel called and said Mary Jane had just found out her husband was missing in action. Somehow, walking as fast as I could—in my work shoes, with a flashlight—to go to a friend's house to offer comfort suddenly felt very real.

I did my laundry early Sunday morning, because the laundry room at the apartments was empty then. *Maybe I should go home,* I thought.

But I can't get there on a bicycle, and I can't take my bike on a bus. I'd been acquiring stuff that I couldn't possibly take home, I realized.

When Julia moved in with a new roommate who had a nicer radio set, she'd sold me hers for three dollars. Now I could sit alone and listen to music or anything else I wanted. Most of the time I left it off. But that afternoon the newsman said that American soldiers had taken Peleliu, another little coral island I'd never heard of. *Maybe Gordon is there,* I thought. Maybe Mary Jane's husband was there, and Gordon would rescue him. Then, when they came home we'd all be friends, and go to movies together, and have each other over for spaghetti dinners.

Two weeks later I got another letter from Mother, almost identical to the last one. The sentences were clipped and to the point, written with deep indentations on the paper from the pencil, as if the accusatory finger were thumping my chest with each one.

Then one Friday afternoon, just like old times, my apartment was filled with girls, almost every one of them feeling the same way for some guy in a uniform that she could not get to or talk to or even write to. We collaborated on a cookie debacle: raisin, chocolate, vanilla, orange rind, and cinnamon all went into the bowl, resulting in great-smelling but weird-tasting globs that failed to deliver on the promises of their aroma. While we cleaned up, declaring the experiment a failure, and munched them down like famine victims, Julia turned the radio on to some news. Suddenly the bright and happy feeling in the room changed to darkness. There were terrible casualties, in places I'd never heard of, all over the world. They named battles that had now been days and weeks old on tiny Islands in the Pacific. Names I couldn't possibly spell. I kept a pencil and paper by the davenport, on which I wrote the names of strange places in the world where disposable men in uniforms of different designs were desperately trying to kill each other. It was eleven-thirty at night. The radio station signed off and played the national anthem. And then it played taps.

Everybody cried. The wound in my chest opened up and hurt like it was new, and that whole evening of his farewell rushed through my mind again in the flash of a few seconds.

"You know something?" I said. "Let's all just spend the night. Please.

All of you. We can make some cheese sandwiches. It's warm, and we don't need blankets. Let's stay together."

The next morning we awakened slowly. Sharmayne was in the kitchen making coffee. Her hair stood out cockeyed from her head on one side, and the sight of it made me drag my fingers through my own hair, in case it was in a similar condition.

"Gordon is on Peleliu," I whispered to Sharmayne.

"You heard from him? Oh, honey, I'm so glad."

"Yes," I lied. "He's just fine. Everything is fine, even though it was a tough fight. He can't wait to see me, he said."

"You've been writing to him all this time, without an answer?"

"Um-hmm." That much at least was true.

"You must have been worried sick."

"Yes, but now I'm not. Everything is fine." Maybe I really would get a letter soon.

"Well, I have news, too. I'm quitting the factory. Joining the navy. There's a whole colored regiment of WAVES now, and they're calling everybody. And, hey, some of the girls are getting together at my place tonight. Come on over."

"Count me in. What should I bring?"

"Whatever you've got, hon. And, say, I need you to do a favor for me."

"Just name it."

"I'll give you some money and the address and a box of packing stuff. If you'd just mail my violin home?"

I'd meant to ask her how to get into law school, but everything was over so quick I never found the chance. I tried looking it up in the library, but all I could find were things about so-called Ivy League schools in places like New Jersey and strict regulations about how men got accepted. I just wanted somewhere I could go to after work in the evenings.

A BLACKOUT CURTAIN HAD FALLEN across my life. Gordon had vanished like the mist off the beach, leaving me wondering if he'd even been real. Coby was dead. No telling about the other boys I knew at home. Wilbur was hurt, they didn't say how badly—but he was coming home, not being patched up to go on fighting, so I knew it must be serious. I got moved to another section where I didn't know anyone. The days grayed and melded into one another. The next time the girls had a party, I told them I had a cold and stayed home and moped until I fell asleep listening to the radio. Trying to forget Gordon. Missing Wilbur and Farrell and Opalrae. Even Deely. Missing home.

ctober 1943. Wilbur braced himself for the opening of the door. Although he didn't feel it, he knew that it was chilly out and that the sputtering heated air flowing weakly from the vents in the front of the car would be inadequate to deal with the frost. Mostly what he felt was not cold but dread. He had seen enough stares, whispers, averted eyes, to last a lifetime, though his lifetime was only beginning. For three-quarters of a year he had moved from hospital to hospital, beating the odds, amazing the doctors. Always ahead of his parents' letters. And for what? To survive only to come home half a man. A cripple with a reconstructed face. A thing to be pitied and clucked over and hidden.

His mother murmured and cooed at every word he said. She and Dad had arrived at the train station in a new automobile they'd purchased, he surmised, to carry him around. They'd never before owned a car. And, by God, there was nothing wrong with his legs, but without an arm they felt he should at least have a car to drive. Of course, since his right arm was the one that was missing, they would be there to drive it for him.

Garnelle slumped away from him, looking as if she were lost in the comfort of the seat. She looked toward him now and then and smiled wanly, then went back into her thoughts. If this were the old days, when he was simply a big brother, she would have tackled him like a linebacker, bruising both of them as they grappled for the upper hand. He sometimes let her gain it, too, but now and then he pinned her to the floor to prove it, just like wet carpet. Wilbur smiled at the thought.

"What, Wil?" Garnelle said. "What are you smiling about?"

His mother in the front seat turned with expectancy, her brows raised. Wilbur winced. It was the same look she used when he was a small boy and down with some cold or other, and she believed that ingesting copious amounts of tapioca and chicken broth was his only hope.

"Nothing much, I guess," he said.

Disappointed, his mother turned back to the front. "Watch the road there, Hal. Watch out for those bushes there."

His father waved his hand at her. "I've got it under control. I've been driving this thing for two weeks to get ready for this, now leave me be. You're probably just glad to be home, right, boy? Are you? I was thinking we could have some of your friends over. You know, sort of a party. We could have some cookies, and your aunt Lil, and . . . well, whoever you want to invite."

His mother, Verna, took up the task. "I'll make my coconut cake. Oh, Ricker usually saves some back from the shelves for us, but you still can't always buy sugar. I don't know where I'll get any, what with the Lamarges' wedding last month. Oh, if I hadn't given my sugar coupons for that wedding cake, I'd have plenty for a coconut cake and some punch, too."

"Just make coffee, Mom," Wilbur said. "Then you won't need as much sugar."

"Oh, you drink *coffee* now!"

"Well, hell, Verna, the boy's been to war. What did you think, he'd be drinking fruit punch in the trenches?" And with that, both parents were off into their familiar, compact world of bickering and picking at one another and everyone they knew. It was generally good-natured. It was the way they communicated with each other about the world as they saw it.

Garnelle looked toward Wilbur and made a face of recognition. "They're off at it now," she said. "So what were you smiling at, really?"

"Just picturing the way you always used to romp on me when I'd come through the door."

"Well, that was before you were hurt."

"So? I missed it, was all."

"Well, it didn't seem right."

Wilbur reached toward her with his left fist balled up so one knuckle stuck out prominently. "It seems more right than you looking away every time I talk." He jabbed at her arm right below the triceps, where it would get a good "frog" going.

"Hey, you!" Garnelle whispered, menace on her face.

"Hey, what?" Wilbur jabbed again, more forcefully.

Garnelle rubbed at her arm and bit her lip. She seethed between her teeth. "Stop that, Wil-Bum!"

"Make me, Gar-Bage." He nailed her arm with a bruising knuckle.

She plunked at him with a fist of her own, and he deftly caught her hand in his, grinning. "Ouch. Stop it, you!"

"Children, what are you doing! Garnelle Virginia Fielding! Hal, stop this automobile. Stop this minute and have a talk with her."

Hal looked into the rearview mirror, which he'd aimed squarely at Wil, and for a moment saw the soft face of the boy who'd left them not so long ago. "Leave them alone, Verna," he said.

"See what you did, Wil? You made Mother upset." Garnelle cocked her chin toward him, not a speck of regret on her face.

Wilbur reached toward her and tipped her beret off her head. "Mom, let's do have a party. Maybe you can get this munchkin to help out. Clean the yard or something suitable."

"Oh, Wil," Garnelle said, "that's your . . ." Her face blanched. "Job." Her eyes widened before they filled with tears.

"Knock it off, stupid," Wil said.

"I'm sorry," Garnelle said, and turned toward the window.

"I said knock it off."

"Oh, Mother, I'm sorry," she said. Her face reddened, and a tear rolled down her cheek.

Verna's face was wet, too, and Wilbur was overcome by them all. Even his dad sniffed suspiciously. "Look, all of you. It's not like I'm dead. I've got legs, for cripes' sake. I've got one arm that still works fine. I just want y'all to stop acting like—like I'm some kind of broken toy or some ugly baby you can't stand to look at."

"Wilbur, that's not what we think," Verna said. "Hal, tell him that's not what we think."

"Your mother's right, Wil. We're on your side. We just want to help you . . ."

"Well, stop. I don't need help. I don't want help. Just—" He paused. Their faces were so wounded. He had pronounced himself guilty, knowing he'd lived and so many died; now he added his family's confusion and misery to the load. "Just let me do things, and if I need a helping hand, I'll ask. Hell—I mean shoot—Mom, I can tie my own shoes. One-handed."

"Well," Hal began, "as long as you know we're glad to help. Just ask if you need it, that's all we want. Just don't be afraid to ask."

"Sure enough," Wilbur said.

Garnelle smiled. But the pity and guilt and horror he saw in her eyes made his stomach lurch. Wilbur turned away from her sickening smile. He wanted to punch her again, but this time square in the face—cave it in, maybe, or at the least change that expression. "Are we there yet?" he said toward the windowpane.

THE YOUTH FOR HOME CLUB had shrunk to Marty Haliburton and about four girls. He kept them busy making sure, among other things, that Mrs. Beaudrin's dishes were done. While Raylene finished drying dishes one day, he swept the floor. Mrs. Beaudrin snored from the parlor.

"Raylene, you know I've prayed about this." Marty said. "I don't want you to misunderstand God's will for your life. I'm truly convinced of it. Pray it over."

"But I always believed God meant for me to marry Wilbur Fielding."

"Do you think God would want you married to half a man for the rest of your life? Wilbur's a good old boy, but you've got to listen to the leading of the Holy Spirit. There *is* no higher call for a woman than to be a preacher's wife."

She lowered her head, brushing at her skirt. "That's true."

"Say yes, Raylene. I *know* what God's decision is. Now the only thing left is for *you* to do the Lord's bidding. Don't say no."

She sighed and smiled. "Yes, Marty. I'll marry you."

"You realize you'll be called upon to make sacrifices for the Lord Jesus? You have to accept my calling as your ministry in life."

"Yes, I do." She giggled at the permanency of those words.

"Well, there's not another girl in this town righteous enough that I'd even consider her," he said, and smiled, patting her hand. "Let's go tell the good news to our folks."

I was more alone in that little apartment than I had been before Garnelle came—crowding made it more fun; now it was lifeless. I had to wait for Gordon alone. No one at the plant knew him beyond what they'd heard from me. Only Garnelle could say to me, "He *is* good-looking," and mean it. In the one photograph I had of us, his face was in a shadow; you could see nothing but his uniform and me in a big sun hat holding a little American flag in my hands. I had the telephone company take out the line to save money, but it made me feel lost—untied.

Today after the news was over, I put on some work trousers and a pale green sweater that I'd just bought from MayCo, got my bicycle, and headed for the beach. This time I didn't stop at the hills. I rode until

I hit sand and took off my shoes and pushed the bicycle until it didn't want to move through the sand. Breathing hard, I pushed up the hill, digging in with my toes. I leaned the bicycle against a black rock with hairy green growths all over it and kept walking toward the water. It was closer than I'd ever gotten to the actual ocean. It smelled wetter here, fishy and sour like vinegar, but darker.

The news reporter had said Peleliu. Taken. It was ours. But at what cost? *He's there. I know it's Peleliu. Gordon, be safe on Peleliu.*

Seaweed hung on rocks, smelling not so rancid and more familiar, looking like shreds of dried and blackened tar. The sand beating all the shore plants against the rocks on the beach in California turned them black and dry as well. I moved several steps closer to the water. The tides moved like blowing lace against the breast of sand, leaving bubbles that became pocks. Never the same, but the same.

Sand stuck to my feet as if it were glued on. The lip of a wave came toward me like a warm tongue. Lapped my toes. A newer, fresher one swirled around my ankles. A chill spray made me rub my arms.

I stepped one more pace toward the blue edge of the earth. The height of the ocean was over my head, and it looked as if a huge bowl would overturn and spill across me. Spray hit my face, and I licked at it. Waves pulled the sand out from under my feet and set it in a new place; it slipped away, like the friends I never wanted to leave behind at home, while those I tried to leave behind kept surging toward me. Mother's letters came in waves, telling me to come home, to stop "living in a dream world" and come "back to reality." I don't know what was unreal about California. I just worked and shopped and ate and slept. I had friends here who liked me; maybe that was imaginary, but maybe Mother just couldn't imagine that decent people might like me. To her, they probably weren't decent people in the first place. I faced the sun as it dropped, unmoving, until the tide's action had covered my feet in sand. The sun glanced off the surface; I licked salt water on my lips; the sky turned apricot yellow tinted green at the edges.

A wave lunged toward me, much higher and faster than all the others. It swelled up my calves and curled around my ankles, dragging filmy moss around them. My pant legs got wet. I could go back to Texas, where I wouldn't be so alone. But I had to wait for Gordon. Garnelle? I hadn't heard from her since she left. Not a note. The Fieldings had money. And she'd always been popular. She used to tell me about her mother and the things they did together. The only things I ever did with my mother were to take care of Deely. The least Garnelle could do now was answer my letters; I sent her two a week.

Mother's latest letters accused me of going to bars and picking up sailors, of dating different men every night of the week. I was working only to gain money, she knew, filthy lucre to be spent in wantonness. I could hear the conversation now: Garnelle would say, just in passing, that we tried the Cherry Kissed nail polish; Deely would declare she was worried about my soul, and Mother would conclude I was dressing in red satin cut high-up-to-here and low-down-to-there, tight as a sausage case. Garnelle might tell that we'd jitterbugged in Mary Jane Elmore's parlor—no one there but five girls and Mary Jane's baby boy, because her husband, Jake, was a Seabee—and that would confirm that I'd become a hootchy-kootchy girl at a juke joint at the end of some railroad spur. I've had so many of those one-ended conversations with Mother. If she was going to think the worst anyway, I might as well just go down to Mr. J-J's Dime-a-Dance Hall and have some beers.

I threw a rock into the waves. It slipped without a ripple into the lunging water. I walked back up the beach to go home. Mother didn't know my real secret, and therefore her condemnation had nothing to do with Gordon, or learning to lindy hop, or wearing red nail polish. It had to do only with me.

Wilbur begged his mother to keep her party simple and postponed it twice. He was hoping just to fade back into life in Sabine, rather than have to make some kind of entrance. The less attention focused on himself, the better. But Mother would not listen, and acquiescence was the only path left to him.

Marty Haliburton showed up three hours early the day of the party, with a leather case held closed by brass clasps. Somewhat unprepared for anyone to arrive that early, Mrs. Fielding invited Marty in, to learn he had come to discuss "urgent business" with Hal and Wilbur. She left the men alone and returned to the kitchen, where Garnelle was decorating cookies with frosting.

Marty walked in carrying a cane, not leaning on it but swinging it with each step as if to point to his foot where to step next. He sat on the porch across from Wilbur.

"Where'd you get hit?" Wilbur said.

"Oh, just the foot," Marty said. "Nothing much."

Hal Fielding coughed and stretched. "He never actually made it into uniform, did you, Martin?"

"Well, no, sir. But I was going to go. I would have made it if it warn't for them Nigras."

There was a long silence. "So I hear," said Hal. "Cigarette?"

"No, thanks. So. Well, that's the very thing I come to talk to y'all about." Marty shuffled through some papers he was producing from the case. "If I hadn't had some resources to draw upon in a crisis like that, like you yourselves have no doubt experienced setbacks and all in life, well, I'da been up a creek without a paddle. If you know what I mean."

"No, I don't, rightly," said Hal.

"Well"—Marty flushed dark red—"you know the war's bad enough. They got Krauts over to Pflugerville. Then we got the colored here. Mostly they stay pretty low, but there was some bad riots last year. Talk is that there's trouble spreading all over. I heard some old colored boys went on a terror and savaged a white woman over to Lafayette, and to cover their tracks they shot up the place. Did a couple thousand dollars' worth o' damage. It was a real nice house, too, like this one."

Wilbur flashed a look at his dad. "Marty, what you got in the satchel?"

"Protection. Just one hundred percent guaranteed, pure-D protection, sir. You got to think of your families if anything comes along. Could be anything. Could be war, which you already done had a taste of. Could be riots—that's what they call 'em—two police and fifteen colored killed in one day down to Atlanta. And there was that dance-hall fire in Oklahoma. Of course, y'all wouldn't have nothing to do with a dance hall, being good Bab-diss and all. To my way of thinking, and I'm sure you agree, the Lord taught them a lesson. It's only so long He'll abide folks caught up in sin."

"What kind of protection?" Hal said.

"I'm talking about insurance. The kind where, for a mere few dollars' premium each month, your loved ones are protected from ever seeing the wolf at the door of the poorhouse. I'm talking about rebuilding this nice home you got here should the next hurricane come this way instead of Kirbyville. You heard about that one? No? Well, there's fifty or more people, all with families, living in the streets and in alleys, wishing they had some insurance. Families tore apart, you know. Some dead, some's houses up and blown to Oklahoma. Had to go down to the poorhouse, and got turned away 'cause it was full. All on account of no insurance."

" 'Zat so?" Hal Fielding said, running his fingers through his thin, mouse-gray hair.

"Well, Mr. Fielding, y'all just think it over and let me know. I'll be back later for the party, but I just couldn't let you all go on this way. Y'all are my friends. We go back. I couldn't sleep thinking about it, but I didn't want to bring it up in front of some of the gossips in this town."

"That's real neighborly of you, Haliburton."

"Yes, sir." Marty got to his feet and shook their hands.

"Say, John Moultrie was by a couple days ago. Asked about you. Wonder if you'd seen him?"

"No, no. He ha'nt been around my place," he tossed over his shoulder.

"You still living with your folks, aren't you?"

"Sure enough." Marty was making tracks.

"Well, reckon he knows how to find you," Hal called out, "if he wants to bad enough."

After Marty was down the road some distance, Hal turned to Wilbur. "You know, them there Haliburtons is real pillars of society. Salt of the earth." Wilbur smiled and nodded. Anytime his dad used less than perfect grammar, it was completely intentional. "I hear between them and the Bandys, they are the mainstays of the Five C's Club." Hal flicked his cigarette off the end of the porch.

Wilbur laughed aloud. He put his hand over his heart and recited, "Coon, Collards, Chit'lins, Cracklin' bread, and Coffee."

"Don't forget corn."

"That's six."

"They figure it don't count if it's liquid."

"What'd the sheriff want with him?"

"He didn't say."

Wilbur didn't mind too much that there were almost all girls at his party. He would like to have had Frosty Summers around, but Garnelle gave him a hug that she said was sent from Frosty to him. Marty returned with Raylene on his arm, the two whispering and Raylene avoiding Wilbur's eyes. Opalrae Summers came, carrying a pound cake.

Late in the evening some of the kids put some music on the wireless and started singing along in the dining room, where Wilbur's mother had put out cake and lemonade and several kinds of cookies and homemade pralines. Wilbur felt exhausted. It was still so much effort to speak and smile holding his face normally. It wanted to pull down at the left corner of his mouth; sometimes the damaged nerves restricted his speech with a sudden jerking of his face sideways. It was annoying having to think about something that had always been natural.

Withdrawing, he leaned against a doorjamb, staring into the dark parlor. There was a single gas lamp, turned low, in there—barely enough light to see outlines of the furniture. The kids stayed near the kitchen and dining room. In the dark parlor the piano began to play. He peered into the shadows, rubbing at the bridge of his nose with his fingers. A feeling akin to an electric charge ran through him from the knees upward, making his breath come with difficulty. A girl with long brown hair sat on the old claw-footed stool, poised at the keys. She had a filmy dress that moved about her as if it were part of the specter; the lamplight reflecting off her hair made a halo effect. She played "Fairest Lord Jesus," pausing at the middle octave F when it stuck, then continued, ignoring the missing note.

He stood without moving, barely breathing, until the song was done. She moved her hands up an octave and played the song again, then stood and turned. She jumped, startled to see him standing there, watching and listening. Wilbur let out an audible breath. Delia Summers. He forced himself to smile. "That was really nice," Wilbur said.

"Thank you. You should have let me know you were there," Delia said.

"How come you aren't in the kitchen with the kids? You'll miss the cake."

She looked angelic, her eyes glistening at the corners with tiny images of the gaslight, her skin smooth as milk glass. She seemed to glow with a light from inside.

"Oh, I had some, thanks. It was just peaceful in here. I've always admired your mother's parlor. So well decorated . . . tasteful. It feels homey." She touched the top of the old upright piano, her fingertips resting on the lace of the dust runner. "I suppose I was feeling lonely. It's not the same as before with everyone gone."

"It sure isn't."

"I suppose——" she started, then cast her eyes downward.

"Do me a favor?" he said.

"Yes?" she said with a deep sigh.

"Do you know 'Silent Night' on the piano? Could you play it for me?"

"But it isn't Christmas. Besides, that's a German song."

"I know. But it's a Christmas song, too. I don't think Christmas has borders that way, do you?"

"Well. Of course not. Do you have a hymnal?"

"Sure. It's page—" He stepped toward the piano, stopped, and turned up another lamp, this one brightening the room considerably.

"One-sixty-one." She smiled. "I've played it from our hymnal at home."

Delia Summers played "Silent Night." All four verses. Wilbur stood behind her and watched with the intensity of a voyeur. Now and then he sang some of the words. On the last half of the last verse he rested his hand on her shoulder.

"Welcome home, Wilbur," Delia said, looking up at him.

He leaned over her face, smoothing her soft brown hair with his hand, and kissed her.

For three days and nights without stopping, Gordon stayed at the microphone of the radio station. He slept with his chin on his arm, the earphones still alive, while it grew around him from a portable set balanced on a boulder to a small shed topped with palm fronds and a long-range antenna.

"Neh-hecho-da-ne," a voice crackled in his ears. "You guys awake?"

"Hey, Billy," Gordon answered. "How's things on Tinian?"

Billy spoke in Navajo. *"Got some birds on the ground here. They got more watchers than I've got fleas. Lotta potatoes on board."*

Gordon said, "You told me that yesterday. You just trying to stay awake?"

Billy switched to English. "Yeah. I'm so tired I slept through a loose shell going off."

"Listen to what I heard. Old man Jimmy King translated the 'Marine Corps Hymn.' Take this down and pass it down the line. Anybody else on this *big singer* listen up, too."

"No kidding? Hang on, I broke my pencil."

"Here goes." He began to sing loudly into the mike: *"Nin hokeh bikheh a-na-ih-la . . ."*

A lieutenant stood next to him, listening, puzzled by the sound but respectful of the tune. When it was done, he took him by the shoulder and said, "Son, get yourself some sleep and a shower, not in that order. Oh, and hey, mail call came. You better check with Gagliotti. I think they called your name."

"Yes, sir."

"You going to cut that hair?"

"Not unless you order me to, sir."

"Just asking. Beat it."

"Yes, sir."

When Delia strolled home after church with Wilbur Fielding, she noted the potency in the air. It was early spring, but warm, and already the magnolias were in bloom. Cornflowers turned their sullen blue faces in one direction against the wooden fence that lined the road leading to her house. She'd given up driving, she told him, after her sister took her car to California and foolishly sold it for the price of a new dress. She believed that the Bible warned against having life too comfortable, since that would naturally turn a person away from God. Cars were part of that.

Three weeks later she came into the living room after saying good night to him at the doorway. "Mother, Daddy?" she called. She dashed to their bedroom, tapping at the door before pushing it in. "Wilbur and I are engaged."

They drove in Wilbur's automobile to Beaumont that week and picked out two plain gold bands. And, to Delia's surprise, an engagement ring she could wear immediately with a pair of diamond chips set beside a tiny diamond in a "sparkler" setting that made it seem larger. When he put it on her finger in the car, she squealed with delight and hugged him. "Oh, I'm so happy, Wil," she said, and tears shone on her cheeks.

"I'll be true to you," Wilbur said, smiling.

"And I, to you . . . dear," Delia said. She tipped her head demurely at the endearment.

Bobby Lee Baker hadn't been any help at all. He insisted the letter by itself wouldn't stand up in court without a witness to cross-examine, confession or no. Yes, a soldier's last words were taken as sacred as scripture. But just saying Marty Haliburton had a can, and finding a can, didn't put him in the building either; anybody could have a can like that. Moultrie needed a witness willing to hand over his friends and stand up to a defense lawyer's grilling to boot. Sheriff Moultrie motioned a new car to the side of the road and pulled up beside it. "Well, it's Miss Garnelle back from the western front! Good morning, Miss Fielding," he said.

"Hey, Sheriff," Garnelle said. "I wasn't speeding, was I? I'm so rattled in this big old thing of Wilbur's. He lets me drive it, but it's just too big for a lil' old girl like me to handle."

"Naw, that's all right. You were scootin' right along, though. I guess we better put up a speed limit sign now that we've got ten or twelve cars in town."

"Oh, Sheriff, you're teasing me," Garnelle said with a grin. She tucked her chin down and set her manicured and dainty hand on the windowsill of the car.

"Miss Fielding, I'd really like to talk to you about something. Maybe just clear up some details about a little thing I've been worrying away at." He was out of his car, with his elbow resting on the window frame over her head.

"I've got a blueberry pie here for the WMU."

"You think they'd miss it for ten minutes? This is pretty important. I'd like to get this settled. If you'll just follow me to my office, it'll just take a minute. I want it to be confidential, you know."

"Can't you just ask me here? I'll try and remember anything you want me to. I can't guarantee anything stays in this silly head of mine, though."

"Oh, I don't imagine you're that silly. It's not the kind of thing you'd easily forget. Besides, I already pretty much know the facts. I just want you to confirm what I've heard from the others that I've asked." He put his foot on the running board and leaned toward her. "You ever hear from Miss Maggy Ann or Miss Neomadel?"

"Why, Sheriff, you heard about Neomadel, didn't you? After her daddy went wild, she . . . well, she went and lived in the boardinghouse. Last we heard, she'd gone off to Lafayette with some sailor. They weren't married."

"Shame."

"Yes, sir. No one's ever heard from her again."

"Maggy Ann? How about her? You hear from her?"

"She married C. Dub Taylor, and they took off to West Virginia as soon as high school was out. You were there at the wedding." She giggled and blushed.

"Sure, but I don't keep up with the family, 'specially since both her folks died afterward on that bus trip to Beaumont. That was while y'all were off to California. Reckon you've got her address?"

"No. They weren't really . . . well—*our* kind of people. What is it all about?"

"Well, I want to know who else was with you that Halloween night, before Pearl Harbor, when y'all held that bonfire."

"Gee, that's forever ago."

"Try," he said. She had quit simpering. He waited two full minutes while she said nothing, then tried again. "It's better if it's all out in the open, Miss Garnelle. I know about the gasoline. I figure sometimes some kids can act crazy without meaning to. It doesn't mean they're bad kids. Who brought the matches?"

"To—to the bonfire? Oh, I don't know. It was going before I got there. I'm sure of it. Yes. It was already going. I just watched for a while and went on home."

"Were you sweet on the Bruellers' boy back then? Or did that start later?"

Her face reddened, and her lips trembled, pulled in tight at the corners. "Why, Sheriff, I don't know. A young girl can have a crush and it doesn't mean anything much. Was he there? It's been a long time; I don't remember it at all."

"Who else was there?"

She tipped her head, stared at the roof, and shrugged. "It was too dark to see."

"Well. I'm sure the ladies are missing that cake you brought by now."

"Pie. Blueberry pie."

"Yes'm. Anything else you can remember, you'll tell me?"

"Why, of course. Bye, y'all."

Mother and Daddy wrote me about Deely's big news. I waited until Sunday afternoon and called them from the Rexall store. Mother said she and Daddy were happy about the arrangement. "Although," Mother added, "I am sorry that Delia felt she had to settle for a cripple. It's probably because of her having had polio. It made her sympathetic. Still, she could have waited for the other boys to get home."

"She's always been . . . sympathetic," I said.

Daddy took the phone from her and added, as if he were completing her thought, "Well, Fielding'll make it somehow. As long as they don't go on the government dole, it'll be all right."

"I guess so," I said. I tried to maintain a note of happiness in my voice. "That's good news, all right."

"Yes," Daddy said. "Well, here's your mother."

Mother continued, caught in the string of thoughts between them. "But if that makes her happy . . . well, Delia always was a nurturing person; liked to take care of any old stray cat."

Wilbur was the only boy in town who'd air up your bicycle tires without giving you static about it. "Mother," I said, "Wilbur Fielding's not a stray cat. He's a pretty nice boy." There was a deadly silence on the other end.

"What do you mean?" she said.

"Nothing—just—well, I always thought he was a nice person." I could never in my life remember Deely taking care of anyone or anything. "I think he'd make a nice husband."

"Oh. You do?"

I stammered, "Delia knows what she's doing. She wouldn't have said yes if she didn't think he'd make a good husband."

"If you're feeling jealous, young lady, you can just cut that out right now."

"I'm not jealous, Mother."

"I hear something in your voice. What did you think? That you'd marry Wilbur?"

"No, ma'am."

"You just sorry it's her and not you?"

"No, ma'am. Not at all." Maybe. Yes. Mostly. Partly something else. Maybe that wasn't such a bad idea. "I just work here with all these girls, and sometimes we talk about all the boys that aren't coming back. Maybe I'll never get married. Maybe I'll always be . . . lonesome."

"Oh," she said. The tone in her voice changed. "Oh, honey. Well, don't you worry. You're a pretty girl. Boys will start noticing you."

"When they come home."

"When they come home," she said. I knew she was nodding at the phone, reassuring it.

"Bye, Mother."

"Good-bye, Frosty. You be careful there. Don't worry, you'll be fine. Now, here's Delia."

Deely told me every word and nuance of expression she and Wilbur had shared since the first time she laid eyes on him after he got home from the hospital. "You know what this means, too, don't you?"

"No," I said, "what?"

"Someday he and I will inherit that house." Then she said good-bye, and just as I'd returned the same, Deely said, "Oh, and Mrs. Raylene Haliburton—did you know she and Marty have married?—she is going to be my maid of honor."

I put down the phone after telling her I was happy for her and stared in astonishment. Wilbur must have lost more than an arm in the war, to be engaging himself to my older sister. I had long ago put aside my former crush on him. After all, most of the girls I knew thought Wilbur was pretty smart. He was older than us. Good-looking. His family was richer than we could imagine. I just never expected him to go for Deely. Mother and Daddy thought of him as a cripple, like Delia was "settling" for some kind of damaged goods. He was Deely's age, I guess. The more I thought about Wilbur and Deely, the more something swelled in my chest that threatened to cut off my air supply.

Hal Fielding reached into his overalls pocket for his smokes and tipped the pack toward Moultrie. "Using ready rolls now. Last longer. Hands shake too much to roll 'em."

"I see. Well, sir, what can I do for you?"

"You know, John, that my family and yours go way back."

"Yes, sir. Cousins somewhere along the line."

"And we've supported you in every election. Backed you up in every decision. It hasn't been that long since you thought about running for governor. I was hoping you'd still entertain that thought."

"You're getting at something."

"My girl, Garnelle, came home all upset. There's no need for this to go any further. Whatever you got to do in your line of work, you leave her out of it. I spent my life raising up exemplary children. Honest, decent, true sons and daughters of the South. Why, there's not a man nor woman in this county that'd say word one about me or my kin. Most of them, I own the land they're living on."

"Yes, sir. I reckon that's true."

"It wouldn't do any good to pursue some drawn-out old case about nothing, not when elections are a-comin' up. Whole thing could fall by the wayside. Are you hearing me?"

"Loud and clear."

In July the papers said we had taken Saipan and Bougainville and now Guam. I added them to the list by the radio, under Tarawa and Kwajalein and Eniwetok—names you could break a tooth on. We were turning out machine-gun parts for the newest Mustang P-51s faster than we'd ever worked before.

The first Saturday in August, I took a lunch and bicycled out past the factories and rows of camouflaged buildings with their silly canvas houses and cardboard trees, to where the small path led up a hill toward the bluffs. At the top, where I could see the vast Pacific Ocean lapping at the beach, I didn't unpack but just sat on the weeds and watched for a while. A breeze carried the salty, bronze air, warm with seaweed mingled with remnants of fish left on the beach by tumultuous water or lazy fishermen. It also brought the fragrance of flowers down the side of the hills.

It's hard to say how I knew that day I'd be going home. I hadn't heard from Gordon, not even one small postcard since he left. I got asked to date all the time, but I never accepted. I made up lists of excuses not to do whatever the other kids were doing.

I'd built a new kite. It was about twice as big as the first one—a little harder to get the strings balanced just right, but by midmorning I'd launched it, and it was holding steady over the hills. I took my shoes off and left them with my bicycle on the path above the sand. I saw something in the clouds, the way they were heavy and wet-looking this morning, that brought me back to being a kid again. Something about the energy of the storm, lying just behind the dark gray curtain of cloud, was too familiar. It took me to an August afternoon two years ago.

I could hear my own voice on the wind. "Mrs. Jasper, I came here to help you clean house. I can sweep and mop and wash the windows. Mrs. Jasper?" I repeated my first statement, louder, as if her ignoring me was a sign of losing her hearing. "Sunday school is having a be-good-to-them-that's-unfortunate workday. I'm getting started early."

"Your mama know you's here?"

"No, ma'am. Mother and Daddy drove to Shreveport to get Deely some arch supports."

"What makes you figure I's unfortunate?"

"I don't know. I figure you seem like you're tired. And you got no kids here to help you out."

"My chil'ren's grown. I don't need no help."

"I won't be trouble. I'll sweep off your porch. See? You got leaves there in the corners. Might be spiders under there."

Eventually I swept the porch and, under her careful supervision, dusted the furniture. Then I was sent home, baffled and more than a little hurt. I filled out my "Ministry Record" card, showing what I'd done as far as ministering to someone in need. I proudly signed my name at the bottom. The next day was Sunday, and once I'd turned in my card I slipped out of Sunday school after roll call and across the wet meadow grasses to Missionary Way Evangelical Tabernacle, sliding in beside Mrs. Jasper during the call-to-meeting prayers.

But by Monday the very air of Sabine, Texas, had changed for all time as far as I was concerned. All day long at school something was wrong. Dead wrong. Other kids snickered when I was in their hearing, turned away from me, pointed darting eyes and fingers at me. At the last hour of school, during World Geography, Miss Epplethorpe called on me to read aloud, and when I stood, two boys in the back of the room grunted—accompanied by odd noises of scooting chairs and dropping books—and laughed into their hands.

Miss Epplethorpe rapped on her desk at the front of the room with the tipless wooden pointer and ordered them to stand and tell the class what was on their minds instead of whispering behind everyone's back.

"He says," Beans Bandy started, "he says he seen Frosty going to the nigger Bab-disses' church, Miz Epplethorpe."

Marty laughed, red-faced. "You started it, Bandy."

"Did not."

"Boys! I've warned you before. Don't you know gossip's a sin?" Miss Epplethorpe bristled like a cat in a dry thunderstorm.

"Yes'm!" they said together. Then Beans said, "Marty there says to me, 'What's the difference between a nigger and a Summers?' And I says back, 'I don't know,' and he says, 'They don't neither.' Ma'am. That's all that was said, ma'am."

The whole classroom rioted in laughter. Even the girls laughed, in two ways: openly and loud or shamefacedly shaking with squelched laughter behind their books. The jeering went on forever and forever. The only girls I could count on were not in this class: Garnelle had Rhetoric this hour, Maggy was ill, Deely was probably ironing a box pleat in some woolen sweater in Home Ec.

Miss Epplethorpe was ashamed of us more than any other human beings she had ever had the misfortune to know, she said, and she laid into me as the cause of it all. After a scolding that shook the windows of the room, most of the girls were in tears. I glared at all of them, as stone-like as if I were mute and devoid of all feelings. I was sent out of school with a note to my parents.

Later I got the whole story from Coby and Farrell. The way they told it, I could picture Junior Jasper, striding through the sawgrass and brambles, parting the weeds like a smooth black boat on its way to take the message of my shame to the people who could hurt me with it the most. I hated him and all of them. Those dark-skinned people. The ones whose presence I'd counted on, felt a part of. They'd thrown up the color of our very skins as a reason to fling me to the lions.

I had wanted to hurt them in the one place that was closest to my heart—and which, if only for that reason, I believed was closest to theirs. The people at Missionary Way Tabernacle. And so I watched without protest. I had the corn liquor from the mason jars with everyone else, and I watched that old building turn to ash.

I wanted to stay in California forever. Except I was no longer part of something; I was like a rejected link, tossed out in a bin. With all my first friends gone, I seemed utterly anonymous. I moved to the water's edge and knelt right there in the wet sand, rocking back and forth, aching, holding the kite's stick between my hands, pressed together as if in prayer. If I let out all the string, would the kite blow out across the ocean and keep going? Would it go to where Gordon was, so maybe he would see it and know it was from me? Trouble was, the string tethering it to the ground was what kept the kite flying. Without its connection it would never stay aloft.

"CENTRAL? Is this Mayvis Plinkle?" I said.

"Yes, ma'am, it is," came the voice.

"This is Frosty Summers. Could I have my grandmother Summers's exchange?"

"Well, hello, Frosty. Sure you could, but she's not home. I saw her come from Ricker's and go toward the dime store. Of course, she might be over to Mildred Somes's house. You know Mildred has those gallbladder attacks." She settled into a tone of voice that was comfortable and slouched, the way I could picture her sitting in the armchair in the exchange office. The springs were gone out of the back of that chair, so it stayed in a permanent posture of recline.

"Do you think if I call Mrs. Somes that Grandma will be there?"

"I'll try it for you and not put you through until I find her." I could hear the dimes mounting up on this end if I was to get entangled in one of Mayvis Plinkle's wild-goose chases. "Mildred said she's at the Beaudrins' making potato salad with Eldeena for a church supper."

"Mayvis, would you try the Beaudrins' number for me?"

"Sure, hon. How's your mama doing? All the family?"

"Fine." When I got through, I wasted no time. "Grandmother? Will you keep a secret for me?"

IT NEVER OCCURRED to me to speak to the aged man holding forth three seats behind me on the bus, and it had nothing to do with what color either of us was. He was talking a bit loudly; his hearing must have been on the wane. Pushing my nose into a book, I unfocused my eyes and let his voice carry me far away. It wasn't just a dialect; the sound of the man's voice was a steamy delta afternoon, hot, many-flavored, and thickened with okra and filé. It was hiding in the grass to hear the railroad tie loaders singing, chanting, grunting, their hard labor and melodious accompaniment ripening the air. Its rhythm hinted of a place of French Acadians, where over time r's were swallowed until they became cottony and long and overstressed vowels rolled out like the delta waters, muddying the flow enough that it took experience to navigate the nuance. That's what it was. The shadowy way of telling what must go unsaid.

I was going home to tell them how I was not acting wild or rebelling against anything. I'd tell them so they'd understand and things would be fine. The war, I'd say in deep earnest, has changed everyone it touched. I really had gone to fulfill a calling: to do without sweets and stockings and get skinned knuckles and tired, flat feet assembling machine guns. Praying that every bullet found a mark, that every belt from this factory was made perfectly and wouldn't snag or jam and leave some boy defenseless in the sky over the ground forces on Peleliu.

The bus rolled steadily eastward, and I closed my eyes. My heart and mind, baptized in the old man's healing cadence, began hearing a woman's voice, rich as warm cream, aiming—through the languor of a hot Sunday morning—toward God, with some gospel song, a cappella, resounding against the walls of a clapboard church house.

The land started to ripple up, and the dry flatlands of north central Texas gave way to the hill country, the last change before the pines of home. First we'd cross Angelina County. I remembered that yellow sign at the county line that just said, in big letters, DRY. Going the other way, toward California, there was a sign that said SALVATION AWAITS, a second that said THOSE WHO TRUST IN, and a third, posted by some wisecracker: a red-and-gold billboard for Jim Beam whiskey, hammered into the ground at just the right height, square in front of the hand-lettered one that proclaimed, HIM.

We passed a truck farm with a fruit stand next to the highway, a mountain of watermelons lined up before it. Those would be gloriously sweet Texas melons, warm from the sun, not cold in a store, red as a wound inside, covered with white-green skin that would explode with a crack when the knife popped it like a pressure chamber. Bloodred against white rind and black children inside in rows. You gulp them down with the fruit, and red runs down your chin.

As the sun went down, the bus made a stop at a gas station about twelve miles outside of Lubbock. The scent of cattle manure mingled with the acidic smell of petroleum. Giant grotesques of hopper-grass bugs scattered across the landscape thick as a plague, seesawing up and down, slurping out oil with those long tongues attached to elliptical heads. The odor, sulfurous and thick as second-run molasses, I'd been told, was the smell of money.

When we stopped, every passenger lined up for the toilets, and those already finished hurriedly paid out for Dr Peppers and bags of oily, stale potato chips to eat while the gas tank chugged. As the bus rolled onto the highway again, a young woman with two little kids fussed in whispers to one and settled the other one in a seat with a pillow. The bus was quieter, emptier, too. I could move if I chose to be friendly, up front where the woman was trying to hush the children. This was not the factory; as a white woman I could not go where I would rather: to the back where that old man looked toward the glass and into his reflection.

THE SHRILL WHINE of brakes heralded the bump and turn of a raised parking lot. At four in the morning the bus station at Sabine was lit with a single shimmering cloud of bugs. A towering pine tree crowded the tiny bus station. The air was dense, as if hurricane or some other damp calamity lay in wait. It was always like that. On jellied knees I moved off the last step of the bus; in my hand was a small envelope, containing a small lined sheet on which I'd listed everything I intended to say to my family.

The porter from the station had taken upon himself an air of overanimated busyness as he saw to the organizing of "bags on, bags off" carts. I'd seen people act like that in the factory in San Diego. Flapping wings and strewing feathers, not accomplishing a thing except leaving a mess for someone else to take care of. He fluttered a chipped clipboard in the air and hooted to no one in particular, "Number one-oh-niner, dimbarkment re-eady!"

I studied him for a second through road-weary eyes. Beans Bandy. A lot fatter, but still Beans. I hadn't thought of Beans since high school. I had just assumed he got sent overseas or was 4-F and worked at the mill. That's all anybody did here in Sabine. I turned my head, thankful that—as far as I could tell—I looked very different than when I'd left town. Time enough to meet old acquaintances later. After I'd plunked down at my grandmother's house. Had a bath. Called Mother.

Midnight in a car was just traveling, but midnight in a bus station was dreary. Condensation outside the glass formed a barrier on all the windows; opening the door was the only way to see exactly where I was. I could see the lights of Main Street—three constantly blinking intersection markers, along with a cadre of moths and mosquitoes from the front walk—and it occurred to me that the blackout must have ended. Standing at the station door, I felt a chill tighten the skin on my arms. I shrugged my shoulders, breathing in, trying to shake the feeling that too much time had passed and I was desperately late for something. Closing the door again, I stepped over a fat palmetto bug and went to the luggage cart, now nearly empty. I snagged my two bags off the cart, avoiding Beans.

I hoisted the largest one of my suitcases like a soft duffel bag— which it wasn't—over my shoulder, swung my purse over the other, and picked up the smaller bag. Then, suddenly, Beans Bandy looked straight at me, with no recognition in his eyes. I felt like a refugee: displaced, unknown and unknowing.

Outside the tent Corporal Benally shared with three other Marines—all radio operators—Corporal Judson Beattie had lettered a sign: NO TAN ATOLL—NO BEER ATOLL—NO GIRLS ATOLL. Gordon sat under the sign on a stack of green ammo boxes, rereading a small stack of letters.

Gordon had fought on six different islands by the time Iwo Jima was taken. He'd stopped cutting his hair before he'd even said good-bye to Frosty. The first time a mail plane landed, he'd received ten letters from Frosty, along with three from his mother and aunts, who sent their short notes all together in single, puffy envelopes. His chest had swelled with emotion he found hard to define when he read Frosty's letters. She wrote of little things happening at the factory, of her sister's marriage. Of her loneliness, of missing him. He smiled. At last he was allowed to write back to her.

The war was still raging, but he was no longer behind enemy lines. Allied soldiers were still clearing out some of the caves of Japanese soldiers here on the island, but for the time being he was to stay put and forward code-spoken radio messages in Navajo to and from other islands. It grated against his need for action, for movement, to sit by a radio idly sweating, eaten alive by mosquitoes, waiting for a message that might not be coming.

Gordon put the letters in his footlocker and took the picture Frosty sent of herself to the radio shack. Against the post that held the antenna upright, they'd all tacked pictures of the girls they left at home. He tacked Frosty's picture up next to another one.

"That your girl, Benally?" Beattie said.

"Yeah. I asked her to marry me."

"Well, try not to look so het up about it. You can always call it off."

"It's not that. It's just sort of hard to remember feeling that way."

"Yeah."

"You got a girl, Beattie?"

"Yeah. Sweet little Annie. We got hitched right before I left. I guess it does kinda feel like I dreamed all that."

"Oh. I'm glad for you."

"You're just worried. She'll wait for you, man. She will. She looks like the waiting kind."

Gordon nodded. He ached inside and didn't know why. It was the only feeling he could find. Just a tugging ache through his middle that started from the scars across his ribs. There was nothing else in his heart but a dull, thumping sore.

Beattie said, "Write her another letter, bud. You'll feel better."

Gordon nodded. He wasn't sure where to start. Usually something about everyday life was appropriate to begin with. Life on the island was tedious beyond anything he could have imagined. For the first weeks it was hot and dry. Then one day a little cloud appeared on the horizon and rose with the sun. No bigger than a sheep alone on a hill, it ambled across the sky until about three o'clock. Then the sky opened up, and the rain fell as if it wanted to wash the blood from the sand in one vast deluge.

Rain started to fall, a gentle, warm rain, the kind that sounds like bacon frying. I always cry when rain hits my face. I immediately rush outside myself and become some poor urchin in a Dickens novel—lonely, starved, cold, shaking and crying even in balmy southern showers. I trudged through the dark quiet of the town. A dog bothered at a fence, running back and forth at its edge, snapping without putting voice to its bark. The rain softened and slurred everything.

To the rhythm of my feet and the jouncing bag on my back, I practiced my speech again. The closer I got, the more I began to doubt my fortitude. My chances of remaining in one piece. I wish I could have brought Gordon with me. I might need the Marine Corps to get me in the door alive. I could have waited until he came back from the Pacific and he could have gotten the time off. One of the things he told me that night before he left for the Pacific was that I'd never find the peace I needed until I made peace with my family. I told him Lizzie Borden once made pieces of her family, too, but he didn't get it.

By the time I reached Grandmother Summers's front porch, with its single, mothy, yellowed light, my hands were red and cramped into claws I doubted would ever straighten out. I let myself into the house with the key she kept on the gas meter. She'd told me on the phone she would be visiting her sister in Lafayette and had closed up the place, but I could stay the night if I'd be *careful*. The screen door swung on rusty hinges, the sound moving some deep chord inside me as meaningful as a church bell on a still morning. Feeling my way around the wall next to the kitchen door, I found the light switch and turned it. A small low-watt bulb hanging from a cord lit the room. To Grandma it was a testimony to her having electric power, instead of the gas lamps that burned at my folks' house.

Grandmother Summers wasn't the kind of person just to open her house to people—even grandchildren—but she was happy to help with anything that would needle my mother in any way, providing, of course, that she'd be able to face her friends at church afterward. Daddy was her only child, Mother her darkest burden. I was welcome to stay in her empty house precisely because Mother wouldn't like it that I did.

I opened every window without holes in the screens where mosquitoes could come through. They were packed two or three to an inch on the glass at windows where the screens were tattered. I searched for the matches in the holder by the white porcelain stove and struck one, touching it to the burner, glad the gas and water had been left on. Grandmother could be miserly sometimes; she'd been known to shut off the gas for a week's trip, claiming she didn't want anybody to think they could just come in and cook themselves supper on her nickel. Searching for her tin of tea, I opened a cupboard and saw a photograph thumbtacked to the inside of the cabinet door. It was Deely, standing in front of the car she gave me. In the picture it still had all four of its fenders. Deely was pointing proudly to the car with one hand and to her chest with the other.

I fell asleep in Grandma's spare room, contemplating how I was going to tell them I loved a man. I'd describe him so they'd see him through my eyes. They'd understand him the way I do, and they'd see me as an adult, making grown-up decisions every day. Choosing to love a man who was everything anyone would want in a husband. Honest. Quiet. Loving. Not a part of any group of people they had ever in their lives complained about. Not Irish or Catholic. Not German or Lutheran. Certainly not Jewish. Though most definitely a caramel-skinned man. *If only he'd write me,* I thought.

I thought of Gordon facing those enemy soldiers he told me about, holding his finger to his lips as if he were one of them, so that they thought nothing of his presence. I wondered if I could manage to lull my parents into believing I was one of them, so that I could escape unscathed. In the end, of course, Gordon hadn't escaped. He'd been tortured, rescued by fellow Marines only after everyone he knew was killed. He'd survived, but he had the scars.

When I awoke, it was well past sunrise. Sunday. The air smelled so familiar, as if it had moved over to make a place for me. I did not hop from bed and hurry to get ready. I planned to miss church and "arrive" after it started, to give myself a few minutes alone. It felt wrong and sneaky and wonderful to amble around Grandmother's house, not getting ready for church.

I stood away from the starched piqué curtains at the parlor window, watching determined people trudging their way to church. Familiar forms went by, some pious, some gleeful. A few greeted one another. An automobile eased down the road: the Rickers' new Chevrolet. I'd heard about it from Garnelle. I watched until it turned the corner at Washington Street. From Grandmother Summers's house I would not be able to tell when my parents had arrived at the church; they walked this route only to pick her up on the way. After the human traffic thinned, it was replaced by a catahoula hound, squirting every fence post and blade of grass he could find.

When I knew it was late enough that they all must be at church, I checked to make sure everything in the house was exactly as I'd found it—I didn't want to hear later about what a mess I'd caused—then closed Grandmother's door and put the key back on its rusty spot on the gas meter. I wondered whether she'd know I'd taken her up on her offer. The sun was warm on the back of my head. The suitcases fit into the grooves in my fingers that had been embedded just before dawn. I'd even put on the same dress: rumpled, travel-weary, awake, and ready.

The house had shrunk markedly. So small compared to the apartment complex and the factory. As I entered the yard, I knew there was a hair's-breadth chance some head cold or other ailment might have kept Mother or Daddy home. I lowered the suitcases, took a deep breath, and tapped at the doorjamb with the strap buckle on my pocketbook. The house didn't answer.

There was no lock on the door. It had been recently painted: just the door, not the jamb or the walls. When I opened it, a whiff of the metallic smell of paint mingled with Daddy's shaving soap and shoe polish, coffee grounds, and the warm copper-colored fragrance of "our house." I left the bags on the porch.

Deely's stuff was gone from our room, replaced with Opalrae's unfamiliar belongings. On top of the radio in the front room there was a little framed picture of Deely and Wil in nice clothes, her holding a bouquet of flowers. In the kitchen I ran water to get a drink. It was automatic to let the water run for a few minutes until it came clear. "It's like I'd never left," I said aloud. The screen was still torn over the kitchen sink. Never stand at the sink to drink, Mother would scold. For a few minutes I watched a fly senselessly beating its head against the window, before I drained the glass.

I returned to the front door and hefted my suitcases, then went to the door of my old bedroom. Opalrae had taken over the room. Too soon for that. Taking the suitcases back outside, I sat on the front step. Elbows on my knees, I studied the gravel and waited.

They came around the corner of Washington, Mother and Daddy with Opalrae between them. I turned my face slightly and shielded my eyes as if I were watching something down the street. After a few minutes I heard "There she is!" in Opalrae's voice. I turned toward them, and they were smiling. Waving. My heart sang. I raised my arm to wave and went to meet them.

So glad to have me home. *So glad*, Mother said. After all this time. And how you've changed. And look at your hair, it's so short. So stylish. And your figure, why you're just pretty as a movie star. Look at that, are you wearing powder? I declare, Frosty, but it looks real nice on you. What a smart dress, too. Those set-in sleeves? You did that stitching there? That color is so flattering. We'll have chicken and fried okra, and you don't have to peel those potatoes, Opalrae will do it. Would you like to just set the table instead? Here, let Daddy get that for you—get that, Earl—have a seat, honey. Wait till you see Raylene Haliburton, she's big as a house and due anytime now. And, oh, won't Delia and Wilbur be happy to see you after all this time—be careful not to look at his arm—maybe you could just make some tea, there.

It was home the way I'd barely dreamed. I kept thinking something was going to happen. Someone was going to say something, teach me a lesson I'd not soon forget. Or was this the welcome for the prodigal? I settled Honey Doll once again on the pillow of my old bed.

There was no time, no reason, really, to explain anything to anyone.

I WAS PUSHED BACK into my spot on the line of our family as if I'd never left. They couldn't wait to hear about the factory. They couldn't get enough of tales about all the girls singing and eating fudge. I never mentioned the brown arms and legs. I never mentioned that we lindy-hopped until eleven some nights. It was good to have me home.

Wilbur and Deely were shining and happy, polished-looking. Tidy and starched on a humid day as only Deely could do. Deely talked with Mother at great length about planting her winter-greens garden while I wrote a letter to Gordon, telling about my trip home. Opalrae asked me to show her something in a magazine that was the color I remembered being Cherry Kissed, so she could picture how it looked to have red nails. Deely didn't seem the least interested in my being there. She acted as if nothing had occurred but her marriage to Wilbur.

That night, along with the addition of Wilbur Fielding and Garnelle—who came because Wilbur did—our old places in church felt crowded. I had brought only the soiled and rumpled dress I'd traveled in, expecting to find the two I'd left in the closet still there, but Opalrae and Mother insisted I'd taken all my clothes with me. I ended up wearing one of Deely's skirts—so threadbare I thought the least little crooked place on the wooden pew might tear through it. Mother didn't own a blouse, since she was never caught in anything but a one-piece dress, and Deely was too "slender"—flat-chested—to help, so Daddy had handed over one of his work shirts and I tucked it in and wore it as a blouse. "Thanks," I told him. "I'll wash it and iron it for you right away." He looked more bothered than was necessary, and his eyes followed my hand as I took the shirt.

Deely sang loudly during the hymns, giving it her all. As she sang, she unwittingly beat out the pulse of the music with her knees, causing her entire frame to surge, wormlike, to the beat. It would have been comical if I'd been in the mood to laugh at her. Everything I was supposed to aspire to, she had become. But I wouldn't trade places with her for anything.

Deely took her place in the pew next to me amid a heartfelt-sounding chorus of *Amens*. Praise the Lord she's finished. How far I had gone from this little cloister of folks.

After we ate the pot roast and carrots, after the dishes were done and only the smell remained, my family let loose its surging stream of reasons I should stay. In fact, Daddy said, the very strength of my yearning for California and being on my own was a sure sign that it was not God's will but most certainly the pull of Satan drawing me toward ruination. "Only sin can make you want something that bad," he said. "The only way to fight sin is to deny yourself the things you want most. Deny, or God will take them from you by force. Otherwise you are putting false idols before God."

"Of course not, Daddy," I said. Besides the ninety dollars in Honey Doll, I had tucked fifteen dollars in nickels and dimes into an old sock and tied the ankle end, in case I needed change for Laundromats and telephones on the way. It made me feel good to have the heaviness of it in my purse, and I figured a sock among many socks in my reclaimed drawer would escape discovery by Mother or Deely or anyone.

I tried to stand my ground. I had a fellow, I told them. A boy who said he'd come home to me. And, of course, this was just a visit; I had *things* in California. But if I was going to get married anyway to that nice soldier boy, Mother said I ought to stay home and wait for him here. "That's what most girls would do. Spend as much time with your family as possible, because after you are married you'll regret it if you didn't. Of course," she claimed, "we've kept your room the same." She actually smiled when she spoke to me. I hesitated saying anything definite, but they kept on until I heard myself agreeing that I would be staying in Sabine.

The next Sunday, Brother Miner came and pumped my hand before the service, and when he started preaching, he seemed to be staring right at me the whole time. My neck felt wrenched, but I dared not move. Under the layer of condemnation he was spinning, a single twitch or odd movement would flash alarms screaming "guilty!" No one moved. Not a fan stirred the dust motes. As he emphasized his last few words, he began to point at individual people, as if convicting and sentencing each to hell with one stroke of his powerful, corpulent finger. He glared at me, straight in the eyes, and I looked right back at him. What I saw in his eyes was accusation, plain and simple, God's one-man posse, jury, and executioner.

Sometimes I thought sarcasm was my new religion, and I practiced it regularly, albeit quietly. He was telling about some young people being led straight to hell by an Oklahoma square-dance caller with big feet, there to be forever listed alongside the sinners of Sodom and Gomorrah. If this preacher was thinking that the threat of sulfurous, fiery hell awaiting wandering young people who fell away (meaning me), lost like seeds on hard ground (meaning California), betrayed by the lusts of the flesh (meaning earning wages in a job for which I wore trousers), was going to bring me to some critical juncture here in this hard-shell church, when I had already lost all my future hopes out from under the bed . . . well, it would take more than his gnarled and hairy finger to do it.

They sang forty-seven verses of "Just As I Am" for the invitation. Before it was done, every person in the church had "gone up"—stepped forward, to the front of the church. It was a place to declare yourself a sinner and throw yourself on God's mercy. A place also to announce your intention to join the church, after which there was a vote from the church members to let you in or not.

As a small child I'd gone up to get saved in the First Southern Baptist church in Orensville, then again to get baptized when we moved to Turkey Creek. Later, when I learned about boys and what they've got that Deely and Opalrae and I don't have and why, I had gone up to ask God for a clean heart. As I sat in class and Miss McCormick, pale and intent, unveiled the wonder and horror of what girls' bodies were all about, I gripped my lower lip between my teeth to keep from gasping aloud. She assured us it was God's plan for us. I remember the blanched look of her face, the sinking feeling in my stomach, the dreadful urge to pass water out of pure shock, as if that mordant flow would cleanse away the coming catastrophic one.

How could all the world revolve around such a repulsive, indignant act when I had been taught and devoutly believed that Baptist religion and well-pressed laundry would set a girl's course in life? I was angry, and also consummately curious, which meant—in the only logic known to me—that I was also guilty. So I went up in church and made up a story to my parents about what brought me there. I hated my blooming figure. Hated that I couldn't lie on my stomach for the stretched and knobby pain in two places on my chest. I hated Deely for being flat, Opalrae for being too young to understand. Deely's reaction to my woe was to sneer and click her tongue against her teeth at my shame.

And now I went up again, my inner burden more painful but less well defined.

THE NEXT SUNDAY I walked boldly to the Missionary Way Evangelical Tabernacle's new building and stepped right in. A sign over the door had the name of the church, though it no longer proclaimed "All Welcome." But a few people greeted me with smiles and a handshake when I arrived. I sat in a pew near the wall and thought about the window where Mrs. Jasper had shown me my crown of rolled hair.

The service was a short one. Junior Jasper did the preaching that day, and he was good—so good I felt myself sway to his words, sinking into the rum-butter cadence, the melodic canticle of scripture. He just read from the Bible without adding to it. The people hummed "Amen," "Yes, Jesus," "Oh, Lord, come on down." The room was already looking a little scuffed from use. But the floor didn't creak. And there weren't as many windows as before, so I couldn't see the field I'd crossed to get here, the field that spread like a great gulf in my mind.

I felt interrupted by the end of the service. I went to shake Junior Jasper's hand but waited until the room was empty.

"Good to see you again, Miss Summers," Junior said, more or less ushering me toward the door. "How do you like our nice new church house?"

"It's really fine, Junior."

He put a key in the padlock that hung over a small hasp on the outside of the door.

"You're locking the door?" I said.

"Well, just for safety's sake," he said, and smiled.

"Have you-all been robbed?"

"No, ma'am. But since Brother Blye passed, we've voted that it's best to keep it locked unless we are all hereabouts. Just so nothing can happen like that again."

"Who was Brother Blye?"

"Oh, don't tell me you forgot?"

I shook my head.

"Brother Blye. Luke Blye. He always gave you such a troubling. Didn't want you around and said so, right out. Don't you remember?"

"Oh. He's passed on?"

Junior bowed his head. His face went from friendly, pastorlike, to stony. "By his own hand, unfortunately. Hanged himself. From the beam down the center of the old church building. The post where we hung the lantern. Set the place afire before he kicked off, too."

"Afire?"

"Yes'm. Lit her up with gasoline and climbed on two stools stacked up. Kicked 'em down."

My eyes filled. My hands shook, and I stuffed them into my pockets. "He lit up the church?"

"We couldn't really figure out why, though. Except maybe he didn't want his ghos' hanging around haunting; he lit it up so we had to build a new one. Found two empty gasoline cans in there, after it went out. It would have gone completely down except for the rain that night. Fact was, we had to tear her down anyway."

"Why, Junior, why?" I said. I sat on the single step made of concrete. Loose aggregate scrabbled the top of it. One gas can. I remember only one. Marty tossed it through that window, where I first saw my hair in a coiled crown.

"Why, Miss Frosty, were you partial to old Brother Blye? Tell the truth, some folks think it's a blessing all around. You see, he was always so fierce. Crazy, some said, even Grandma. She's known him from the old days. They beat him crazy. Made him walk in chains. Wildened him like a dog beat almost to death and woulda been better to kill it than leave it alive and wild. Snapping at every little mosquito like it was about to hurt him. Now, he's on th'other side. Gone home where the Lord can patch up the hurts. Take out the stingers. He didn't kill himself. Life killed him long before. Just didn't have mercy enough to put him under."

"But the fire," I said. "How did *he* set the church on fire?" I couldn't turn toward Junior's face. My whole being was trembling. "What makes you think it was him?"

"Brother Blye 's angry at everything in the whole world. He took his mad out against other folks than who did it to him. It wasn't safe to be mad at the folks who hurt him. Just like a bad dog: can't attack who beat him—he'll get more and worse. So he attacks something else. Some quieter dog. But it's all right in the end."

"How? How can it be all right?"

"Just is. The old church house was a slave quarters off a plantation big house used to set off in that field there. Brother Blye the last one around remembered. Except my grandma. And she ain't mad anymore. New church gets built. Folks put the past behind. Luke Blye always knew that church as something else."

"You mean Brother Blye was a slave?"

"That."

"And what else? Miss Ronelle, too?"

"Grandma had her reasons for everything she done."

SOMETHING HAD TO BE done, all right. There were no two ways about it. Junior Jasper had been seen talking with that Frosty Summers in front of the moving-picture theater. Standing right in the street. That evening the radio announcer had told a cleaned-up version of a fuss-fight going on in Toullange. Eighteen colored people made to get down off some school bleachers, they said. Sent home, tails between their legs, they said. But word by the singing-gourd vine had it that two folks were dragged from their houses and lynched that night. Their houses, hovels that they were, burned to the ground. A child—a four-year-old child— maimed with a butcher knife, a little girl forever to go through life without her right hand. And there were the raised brows, the notes left in the bottle tree. Notes picked up and passed along—notes whose forms were of broken clothespins, bent wires—worries caught and spread like fever.

And here was that white girl Frosty Summers. No matter the years since she showed up in church with her hair on end; no matter how innocent it started. Junior and his sister, Esther, were all old Ronelle Jasper had left of family; they had to be protected from what she might bring without knowing. All Ronelle's other kin were dead, gone, or in some prison in Huntsville as good as dead. It had made her feel good, all this time, to see that odd white child come sit by her side. She'd told her friends it didn't matter one hoot if that little scalded thing showed up at her elbow or not. She wasn't no white child's mammy to coddle and soothe—long done with that kind of work. But she'd still liked the girl's upside-down way of seeing things, as if she was so blind everything came to her real clear.

That girl had no more sense than to talk to Junior in the middle of the day in the middle of the street in the middle of town, rubbing people's noses in their own hate and spit. Making 'em want to murder and take up a butcher knife and take off a child's hand. Ronelle had to put a stop to that before something happened here. So she sent Junior to the courthouse to brag in front of the old men playing checkers about that gal Frosty setting spang in the middle of the Missionary Way just free as you please. Junior got his eyes bruised and a rib broke, but the white folks turned her back into the fold, kep' her away. And the rumors turned, like a vine growing on a fence, the fruit of it bearing on this side or that. No one hanged. No one maimed. Things back the way they belonged for a while.

JUNIOR RUBBED the back of his head and turned his hat around in his hands. "It's more than just being a slave. The way it kills a man on the inside and leaves him hollow. Standing up but just drained out and dead inside."

"I don't think Brother Blye lit the church up," I said. "I think it was someone else."

"Don't matter. All for the best. Everything works for the best for them that loves the Lord. Says that right there in the Bible."

"Think that's true?"

"Yes'm."

"I don't."

He stood and stepped down from the concrete step. I followed, my broad hat in my hands, the ribbons dangling.

"Folks got to have hope, Miss Frosty."

"All those boys that have died in the war. I figure they all hoped they wouldn't. And old Brother Blye, I figure he hoped he'd never be a slave."

"I hear you's betrothed."

"Yes. His name is Gordon. Lance Corporal Benally. Only now he seems so far away I can't picture his face. I'm scared I'm not really in love. That the war did it, made us crazy."

"No, not likely."

"Could have. I keep looking at this little Kodak of us in front of my apartment, asking myself if that is really me."

We reached the end of the dirt road where brown-eyed Susans clustered against a teetering fence post. He said, "When you see him again, you'll know."

"I hope so."

"See what I mean?"

I smiled. Junior was my same age. He seemed so old. So like an older brother. "Junior," I said, "he isn't white."

"Sure enough?"

"He isn't Negro either."

"What then? Chinaman?"

"He comes from an Indian reservation. He's Navajo. He was a radio man in the Marines. Got wounded and sent back to teach new recruits. He knows about electronics. Radios and things."

"Indian like in the movie pictures?"

"Sort of. He says about a tenth of what you see in the movies is real. Maybe less. He's really handsome. But he's brown. I figure my folks will kill me or both of us when they find out."

"That why you're hanging around here?"

"Hm?"

"It's on toward dinnertime."

"Sure enough, it is." The air hung around me, dense with the smells of magnolia and sweetbrier. "I'd better make some dust fly."

I walked home at a quick pace. Plain as a bell ringing in my head, I could hear the voices of Delia and Raylene echoing out of the past. It was that Halloween morning. They came, hand in hand, and each of them took me by a shoulder so that we made a kind of circle.

"What do you want?" I demanded. "I have a biology test in thirty minutes."

"We came to talk to you. To pray for you and lay hands on you," Raylene said.

"Well, get your hands off me. And if you're gonna pray for me, do it somewhere else. I don't need the likes of you trying to tell God what to do with me."

"Frosty, you're my sister, and I care deeply about you," Deely intoned. She had that eyes-to-heaven-like-a-Madonna-statue look on her face she wore in church all the time. "We have to pray for you. We have to."

"Get lost, both of you," I snarled.

"God will forgive you," Raylene said.

"For what?" I wiggled out from under their grasping hands.

"For running off to the Nigras like that. It isn't right. It's as wrong as wrong could be."

"You don't know anything," I said. "You don't know. Those people like me. They care about me and they act nice to me. They are my friends. You two sure aren't. All you ever do is call me names."

"Those Nigras weren't nice to you."

"Yes they were. They are. Right this minute they're just as kind and sweet as none of the white trash in this town ever thought about being." I turned, again flinging Delia's frail arm away from me, hating the cloying way her hands touched me, too soft, too complete. "They are the nicest people on earth!" I headed for school.

In a voice I'd rarely heard her use, Delia belted out words toward my back. "What makes you think, you stupid fool, that they have any choice?"

My feet moved in a rhythm. I hate her, I hate her, I hate her, I hate her.

And that night had been the Halloween party. I spent the whole day replaying every last thing I'd ever done or heard from the people at Missionary Way Tabernacle, every expression on their faces, every blind, dumb-head thought that had ever gone through my mind. And Deely was right. By the time the Bandys and Marty had offered me their taste of moonshine, I was so angry I could have burst into flame from the inside out.

I WAITED UNTIL my tears had dried on my cheeks, then worked up a cheerful smile before I swept open the screen door. I rammed my hands into my pockets, where they trembled, so I began fidgeting to disguise the shaking.

"Where have you been, young lady?" Mother demanded. "You been down to that Nigra church again? You know good and well—"

"Yes, Mother. I'm sorry I'm late. I heard they built up a new one, and I just wanted to see it. And Mrs. Jasper's grandson Junior was preaching."

"Preaching? What?"

"Straight from the Bible. Like it was Paul the Apostle himself extolling and exalting. There wasn't anything wrong with it. Just straight-out preaching. More like reading right out of the Word."

Mother looked tense. "Like reading," she said. Her mind was some-where else. "Well, get in the kitchen and get some biscuits up. The stove was plugged, and I had to stop everything and clean the tube. We've got to fill out this supper table, because your sister Deely has gone and in-vited Brother and Miz Miner to dinner. Didn't have the decency to let me know until just now, and she's got the gall to lay around and stroll this way with them, while I've got to get home and try to cobble up more supper than I've got out of thin air. I'm going around back to hunt some poke salad. Slice those two tomatoes from the icebox real thin and spread 'em on a plate so it looks full."

I watched my mother in her Sunday dress and apron with little green apples embroidered on it, bent in search of poke growing along the back fence. She prodded the grass with a stick. Her mouth moved angrily. Her face was blotched and red, the way it got when she ham-mered at Daddy or shrieked at us, blistering our backs with the razor strop she kept in the pantry. And as I turned the biscuit dough and kneaded it "seven perfect times," I felt separate from her for the first time in my life. My mother was angry, and not only didn't it include me—this time it didn't even touch me. It was like she was in a glass bot-tle, fussing around furiously but no more affecting my life than the lightning bugs I'd trapped every summer night in another lifetime.

Mad as she was at Deely, in less than fifteen minutes she would have the poke in a pot—with some fatback if we had it or bacon grease if we didn't. And she'd greet the Miners with a smile. I glanced at my mother's face, the jaw that was always set, the tight cords from her ear-lobes to her collarbones stretched against the skin tight as a clock spring, the protuberant lower lip. I remembered Grandmother Summers's odd threat I'd heard over the phone all those years ago. Junior's words sounded in my ears again, so clearly it was as if he were standing there watching her. "Can't attack whoever beat him, so he attacks something else. Some quieter dog." When her words broke the silence, I hardly reg-istered that they were directed at me.

"Frosty!" Mother yelled. "Answer me when I talk to you, you hear? Are those biscuits in the stove?"

"Mother? Did you ever in your life get anything you hoped for?"

Mother looked stunned. Her jaw dropped, and she stared at me. As I watched, a panoply of emotion moved across her face. "What kind of fool question is that?" she said accusingly.

"Just a serious one. Junior's sermon ended up being about hope. And I was thinking about it. How most folks don't get much they hope for. Did you?"

"Well." I saw raw anger bristle in her face, then soften. The taut straps linking her jaws to her collarbones vanished for a few seconds. Then she spoke quietly. "You can't go around your life waiting and hoping for something. You got to see to it yourself. No one else is gonna look after you."

"God is supposed to." I could feel the tines of her tortoiseshell comb.

"Well," she said, and the look on her face gave place to curiosity.

"I think with all that's going on in the world, it can seem like there isn't much hope."

The tiny opening that had begun forming moments before in my mother's armor now shut tight. "There's Delia and the Preacherses. Mind your own business and get that table set, and don't be talking any of that California nonsense at the table or I'll wash your mouth out with soap. Be sure you let the Preacherses take chicken first in case there isn't enough. Just 'cause the ration is over don't mean I've got money to feed every soul in town that Delia decides to drag home when she isn't paying for it." She went out the door, smiling.

I took a stirring spoon and pushed the greens into the boiling water. The bacon grease she'd flopped in from the can on the warming shelf above the stove formed a waxy scum on top of some of the leaves, letting loose as they met the hot water.

Marty had just finished meeting with a county inspector and was walking around the church building alone. Siloam Springs Baptist Church had termites in the vestibule. Dry rot in the opera seats three rows from the back. The cost of repairs would throw a wrench into his plans to start up a building program. He opened the side door and took the closest seat to the pump organ, where he could see both the doors at the other end of the long room. The curtain over the baptismal was tarnished with ribbons of the amber colors of the soil from which the well water was drawn. It was better when they used to baptize once a month in the Sabine River anyway.

He had a little folded pad of paper in his chest pocket. Feeling for it, he took the pencil from behind his ear and next to "termites" wrote "curtain."

He had Raylene type up a little agenda for him to take to the trustees' meeting, because he intended to press the issue and get some progress done. It was about time they added on a real kitchen and a couple of new Sunday school rooms. There was no reason for them to have only a hundred or so members—only half of whom showed up at any one time—when First Southern was running close to three hundred now that the war was going strong. It had to be this shabby building. The congregation just kept wanting to spruce up the same old building, when what they needed was new space and money to build it. He had to make a statement, put his foot down where it counted.

At any rate, it was a good thing he was now treasurer of the trustees. A small committee made up of two deacons, Brother Miner, two of the laypeople, and himself, the trustees were charged with taking care of the building and everything that took place in what he liked to call "the facilities." Night before last he'd convinced them they were shirking their responsibilities to let the building go without insurance. Insurance needs had been overlooked in this town, and he was setting that right, one street at a time. Brother Miner had signed on the bottom line just in time. The county man came and found termites the very next week. He'd call a special meeting right after suppertime.

Marty yawned. Too many nights in a row without more than six hours of sleep. That baby cried around the clock, it seemed. Raylene cried with it sometimes. To get any peace at all he slept in the car last night. The coming night would be no better. There was another Klan meeting at eleven. Since the riots in Beaumont there was good reason to keep vigilant. Some people said the Klan was dead, or at least asleep. But as long as American citizens like him cared about their families, it would live.

Marty closed up the pad of paper and returned it to his pocket. He had a couple of visits to make. Elmer Jones was over to the infirmary at Kirbyville, recovering from the lumber mill accident that had cost him an arm; then back to old man Fielding, to try to get him to sign a fire policy even if—Marty chuckled under his breath—he had to wring his scrawny neck to do it. The man was the hardest sell he'd encountered yet. Then he had to get to the Bandys' to find out if old Bart Bandy was coming to the meeting tonight or had turned against them on account of something he'd said about Farrell wanting to marry some Japanese girl—and to see if he could keep that idiot Beans from showing up and making a mockery of the whole thing.

He stepped up to the pulpit and ran his hands around its edge. A smile crossed his face.

In February of 1945 Lieutenant Ditterman signed Gordon Benally's orders to be posted stateside. The fighting was still raging, but his count was full: Gordon had 172 points, far more than the 85 needed to get back on friendly shores. He was ordered to stand down for a flight to Hawaii, then San Francisco. Given a thirty-day leave, he would have a month's freedom and return to Camp Pendleton, to take up training where he'd left off. Corporal Beattie gave him a ration of trash about it all, too, filling his duffel bag with coconuts and hiding all Gordon's things in a filing cabinet.

"Come on, knucklehead. Where'd you put my underwear?" Gordon said, holding Beattie gently but firmly in the crook of his arm. "I can make you talk," he said, laughing. Gordon rattled his knuckles on Beattie's head for several seconds.

"Name, rank, and serial number. That's all. You just lost your own stuff. Don't blame me. You've got yourself a bad case of short-timer's disease. Brain stops all function. All you can think of is getting home and smooching that girl. Eating your mom's fried chicken."

"My mom doesn't fry chicken."

"Goat, then. Whatever she makes. You Nava-joes ate every last dad-burned goat on this floating turd of an island. Let me loose."

"Not till you tell."

"Think you can wrestle me? I took All-State two years ago."

"I know I can. Come on, man, I'm gonna miss my boat."

"I don't know. Swear."

Gordon dropped his hold, and Beattie fell to the floor, unready to catch himself. "Have it your way," he said. He dumped the duffel bag of coconuts onto Beattie's rack, went to Beattie's footlocker, and started filling the bag up with *his* clothes and toiletries.

Beattie grabbed him from behind. "What do you think you're doing?"

"Packing."

"Fine, sure. Filing cabinet. The one with the empty bottom drawer."

"Thanks," Gordon said, and went to retrieve his things.

"Think nothing of it," Beattie said. He worked on putting his things back in order. More than twenty coconuts were still scattered on his bed when Benally brought his duffel bag back into the room. "Well, bunkie, I guess this is it," he said. "You don't want to miss your boat."

"So long," Benally said. "After thirty days I'll be hanging around the radio shack at Pendleton. Maybe I'll catch you on the airwaves."

"Yeah, yeah, yeah. Say, who's that walking by over there?"

Gordon turned to look over his shoulder, and when his head was turned, Beattie took a coconut in each hand and dropped them into the open lip of Gordon's duffel bag. Grabbing the pullstrings, he hoisted it up, yanking it tight, and twisted a quick, hard knot in the strings to hold it shut. "There, that ought to hold until you reach Honolulu. Say, kiss one of those 'hula-hula' girls for me, bunkie."

"I've got a girl," Gordon said.

"It's just a kiss. Oh, the heck with it. Get going."

"You act like you're gonna miss me." He grinned.

"Beat it," Judson said.

Gordon waved his hand with dismissal. "Give my love to Tokyo Rose."

The trip to the States felt eternal. He slept through Hawaii. Dreaming. Home. Nothing familiar in San Francisco either. He bought a road map at the airport and started on his way. Walking, hitchhiking, ever toward the morning sun. Lukachukai. Spring-on-the-Plain. Gordon wore his medals proudly on his uniform, but it didn't always guarantee him a ride, even though it was against the law to pass a man in uniform with a thumb extended. His face had darkened to a deep bronze from weeks in the Pacific sun. His hair was tied with string in a Navajo bun, a waterfall above the tender place on the back of the neck.

On the last leg of his journey he begged a ride with a family all the way from Blithe, California, to Holbrook, Arizona. He hung around the post office in Holbrook for a while, then went to the gas station downtown where he'd worked as a teenager. Uncle Bill came in about three or four in the afternoon to get some gasoline and shook his hand for five full minutes when he saw him. Billy's mother and sister, Aunt Loma and June, sat in the bed of the pickup with a dog and four puppies cradled between them. They told him he could have one if he wanted, as a welcome-home present.

His mother saw the pickup truck coming from a long way off. She had no way to know how or when he would arrive, only that he would. She didn't run but started walking to meet it, not moving her eyes from the truck's windshield, stumbling over stones. She didn't open her mouth but held her arms up when it stopped and Gordon opened the door. She stood, trancelike, holding her arms toward him, shaking with happiness.

When he got inside, his uncles told him about the ceremony she'd planned. June told him about Billy Tsosie. Billy had come back eight weeks earlier. And they'd held a Blessingway for him, too. But when it was over, Billy went around eating rocks and dirt and sticks and sheep dung, until some doctors from the Veterans Administration came and put Billy in a straitjacket and took him to the hospital in Gallup and locked him up.

Gordon had never before raised his voice to his uncles. But none of them, not one, was listening, no matter how loudly he said *no*. Seething inside, tired of the arguments, he threw a saddle on a pony and rode to Crooked Knife Wall, where Na'atlo'ii was supposed to be herding sheep. She at least would understand. All the kids who'd been sent, taken, or forced to go to the Christian School in Crossroads knew what it was like, walking between two worlds.

Na'atlo'ii had gone to school, too. She knew you could not cross the old ways into the new. Besides, he thought, what did those old men know of war? When had they fought anyone but the white government and once in a while some Hopi? Those battles were simple by comparison. What did they know of Japanese cruelty and the sounds of mortar fire? What did they know of rounds that misfired straight up and came right back down on top of your own men? Of torture with knives and razors by Japanese soldiers wanting answers to questions he didn't have? What did they know of nightmares and the strange sweating that overtook him night and day? All they talked of were ghosts following him, holding his pant legs and throwing ashes in his coffee, sand in his eyes, and who, if allowed to hang on long enough, would bring witches' attention and certain death. "Ghosts," he muttered. "Old religion for old people." Instantly his left side went into spasm, the claw of some unseen hand twisting at the knotted scars across his ribs. He kneed the pony impatiently.

The old, dun-colored pony picked its way across rippled red sand, dotted here and there with needle grass and snakeweed. It snorted and jerked its head against the bridle, moving reluctantly against the wind. Gordon spotted a curved trampling, here and there an odd hoofprint out of the knobbed pathway. Sheep. Na'atlo'ii must have led them around the wall. The water at Crooked Knife must have dried up again. The echo of the horse's hoofsteps against the wall came back at him, so clearly it sounded like someone was following him. Crossing a brushy low spot, his horse jerked its head, trying to reach the ground with its nose. Gordon swung his leg over and hopped down. "Hello!" he called.

"What you yelling at, Hashke?" Na'atlo'ii's voice spoke behind him.

"I didn't yell. I was looking for you."

"You kinda come back rude. Marines don't teach you any manners?"

He smiled and turned his head away. "Thought you might be up here. Your auntie said you had her sheep headed this way."

"You better go on home. They'll be coming soon."

"Who's coming?"

"Your mother sent for three Singers. Everyone is coming. Even some Apache girls from Albuquerque that I used to know in school."

"I'm not putting up with it."

"One of them's pretty cute. You might like her. Part Hopi, part Apache. She's got that mixed-breed look. Kinda cute."

"Na'atlo'ii, they expect me to just go back to being something I never was. I only let them do the Going Away ceremony to make my uncles happy. I'm not going to sit around and let them—"

"Your mom paid a lot for a Coming Back dance. And here you are."

"I was coming back anyway."

"You weren't coming home until they did the dance."

He squatted in the shade of a short piñon tree and scraped up rocks. Tossing them around in his hand, he let them fall singly back to the ground. They each made odd indentations in the red silt. She was talking like an old woman. "You sound like you've—" he started. He gritted his teeth, biting off the words "gone native," so that he uttered them only in his mind. He watched her feet, unsure if she'd heard or not.

Na'atlo'ii whistled to her dog. "I've got to get going," she said. "These sheep got appointments. Big dinner in a couple days."

"I guess you heard about Billy."

" 'S too bad about him. You know, your mom cries a lot."

"Why? What for?"

"Go home, Hashke. Gordon." She whistled more shrilly, and the dog jumped and ran, circling the sheep two times, nipping at a couple, starting them downhill. Na'atlo'ii pointed down the wash with her stick, and the dog troubled the sheep, biting their legs, moving them down. A couple of goats with noisy bells on their necks clattered out of the herd trying to lead the way and get away from the dog. Bleating animals, kicking dust, scuffled past Gordon where he squatted in the shade. Na'atlo'ii looked at the ground, passing close by Gordon. "Somebody wants to marry me."

Gordon stood and rubbed the red sand from his hand on his pant legs. "Who?"

"I guess if it really mattered, you'd have said 'Oh, no' instead of asking who. I guess I made him wait until I saw you again, but your feelings aren't here anymore."

"Na'atlo'ii, it's just that I haven't had a minute's peace since I got back."

She moved away, whistling at the dog, waving the long stick. Her wide skirt swayed as she moved. Her hair was long, a single braid hanging down her back.

Gordon picked up the reins the horse was dragging, its nose to the ground where it lipped at some mossy rocks, and tugged the reluctant animal with him. He walked farther up the wall. From that vantage point he could see the dirt road that led from the highway to the fork where his mother's hogan sat near a crooked corral. Near it were three dilapidated vehicles. One of them belonged to his mother, the other two were Aunt's and Uncle's. Like smoke growing from kindling just lit, dust was billowing up from the road behind a string of old cars and pickup trucks. From this angle the hogan looked like a Japanese pillbox.

Angry, Gordon yanked the horse's bridle and started walking toward the gathering. His mother hadn't waited for Gordon to agree, she'd just invited everyone anyway, hired Singers and who knows who else.

He'd survived the war. This was simply not necessary, but Mom wouldn't listen. He might as well have tried to talk to the couch.

That evening, as the sun started to go down, the Enemy Way began. Gordon became again Diné Hashke' Yitah Deeya': Fierce One Who Walks Among Enemies, clan of Hashk'aa Hadzoho, born for Tabaahi. They kindled fires and laid wet blankets on them. They bade him drink something warm and bitter from a gourd. They took his clothes and tied two bundles around his neck. A bag of corn pollen, a secret medicine bundle wrapped in leather. The women had vanished, hiding.

A circle of old men, some so feeble and blind they had to be helped to stand, began to pray. The oldest ones were men about whom he'd heard stories. Famous Singers. Gordon had truly walked among enemies, behind their lines, crawled sometimes, known their blades with his skin. Scars told their stories. Each man touched him, fingered every mark made by the enemy, passed over him with eyes blind to the day but that now saw something beyond the firelight. He began to recount everything that had happened, all he'd seen, all he'd done.

The fire crackled in its pit, snapping at the shadows that surrounded them. He inhaled. His head swam. The stars moved. Fear began to prod him, dance around him, jerk his legs out from under him. Unable to stand, he sank to his knees. The head Singer, Tom Begay, began the first important Song. Homer Nightbird started drumming. Gordon shook with the feeling of thousands of fingers clutching at him, pulling his skin, trying to take it from him. The old men nodded. Sang. Drummed. Ghosts wanted his skin to wear, to come back to this world and torment living people.

Faces swirled before him. Ghosts of Japanese soldiers, throats slit and pulsing blood, cried at him, their voices bubbling through black foam. Ghosts of the Americans who had died next to him raged over-head, under his chin, between his thighs. They curled around his arms and legs, angry that he'd lived, demanding his body be exchanged for their dead ones; slithering, coiling, blood dripped from them and wiped on him, staining his skin. Red stripes appeared on his chest.

Exhausted, Begay passed the chore to the secondary Singer, and

Long Nose sang. His voice was higher, louder. At the second verse of his first Song a shooting star careened through the sky over their heads and disappeared in a bright feather of sparks. The ghosts wailed and howled. Gordon's entire body dripped with blood, but he held his head erect, his eyes open. He could not appear sick. Not asleep. Not dead. Together, all the men sang. Gordon opened his mouth to sing, too, but what came out was a horrible shriek.

Coby Brueller came. Holding his helmet, which appeared to be full of blood-soaked rags, he called out pitifully, "Take. Take this. Will you take this for me? Will you, Benally?" And when Gordon only stared ahead, ignoring Coby's pleas, the image loomed a hundred feet high into the starry night, bared its teeth, and raised the helmet, dumping its contents upon Gordon as he sat on the floor. The rag was a huge American flag, battered and torn but vividly colored. The cloth tumbled slowly, slowly, until it came to rest between his feet, and thick red liquid dripped from the helmet, staining the soiled white stripes, turning them black. The face of Coby grew as large as the moon, glowering at him, its eyes leering, lusty. It drew away with a wolflike howl that came from the back of the head. Blown away by a mortar shell, it was a skull inside out, clacking teeth at him, rolling its eyeballs. Then it left him.

Medicine bundles were opened, their contents held and prayed over. Herbs were shaken against his skin. Sand poured upon his head. Gordon swayed. Tasted sand. Dawn appeared and came a second time. The first Singers had to rest, but others kept up the prayers. Gordon shook inside. When night came again, the last of the prayers began. The singing went on until the moon had crossed the sky and was resting against the lips of Turquoise Mountain.

"We have finished," Long Nose said. "It is finished in Beauty."

"Finished," Tom Begay said, too. "It is finished in Beauty."

Gordon looked down at himself. If there had been blood on his skin, it washed away in a great flood of sweat. He wasn't sure. There was a dark brown stain on the sand all around the place he had sat for those long hours. There was nothing but a trace of smoky sweat. He was weak, hungry. So tired.

His uncle led him to his mother. She had prepared a bed of clean, sweet hay and new blankets. She left him a large tub of cool water to bathe in, and clean clothes, and a bed. Gordon forced himself to bathe. That small task took every shred of will and determination he could call upon. He felt more shattered than when he was first taken to the army hospital. Carefully, he dressed in the fresh clothes, holding them to his nose, inhaling the clean smell of wind and sun and life. He slept.

When he awoke, it was midday, and the party had already started. Sheep were roasting on spits in front of his mother's house, and people had come from the whole clan bringing food and blankets to sit on.

"Son," his mother said softly, "you found the new shirt?"

She would mean the ceremony. She couldn't ask him, but she had to know. She had pressed Gordon's uncles to make sure the right thing was done so her son could come back from war, to stop being a warrior. But to say the words might bring back the ghosts, which might not have gotten far enough away yet.

He smiled and set his hand on her shoulder. He couldn't deny what he'd seen. He felt different. Lighter. Free. The memory of war was already far removed from life. As it should be: back in its place, the old way. Living people and dead people had to stay apart, to avoid doing mischief in each other's worlds. At last Gordon breathed deeply, feeling his sides, free of that clutching spasm; death was gone.

Frosty. He couldn't feel her presence anymore. She was as gone as the ghosts. He hunted through his things for his wallet and, taking out the little photo of them, stared hard at it. He recognized himself. He remembered standing next to that fence and asking a passing stranger to take their picture. Frosty's face was hidden under the shadow of a hat. Her legs were sticking out from a blowing skirt. He hunted for her features in the dark under the hat. His heart shuddered. She was gone. The old people would say it was always a mistake to bring a woman into your life when you are at war, no matter that he was on leave when he met her. As soon as he could, he would have to find a way to get to the telephone at Chinle to call her. Shake loose of some of this stuff from the old people. Not all of it, though.

After he ate, Gordon fell asleep and slept, untroubled, until long after sunrise the next day. Friends and family and Na'atlo'ii's two girl-friends from Albuquerque ate and laughed and slept and ate more. When Gordon woke, they lined up to shake his hand, patting him, welcoming him home.

M onday I felt headachy from the moment I opened my eyes. I told Mother I was going walking. The wind that blew that day didn't all come from one direction but seemed to curl and eddy around buildings and trees, ruffling my hair first one way and then the other. All of creation seemed confused and disturbing. I ambled through town, amazed at how different it all looked. How faded. Small. Oddly sinister. My initial peace at deciding to stay here was eroding. I needed something I couldn't find.

Without realizing it I had topped the Knob and gone past Ricker's Grocery, beyond the two-story houses, where smells of laundry touched the air. I found myself at the old cypress stump and cut across the weedy lot to Mrs. Jasper's house. Mrs. Jasper sat fanning herself on the front porch in a slumped rocker, wickerwork standing out from the chair's frame like giant whiskers. Her head rolled around when I approached.

"Hello," I said.

"Who there?" She stopped fanning, searching the area, it seemed, with her nose. "Who's 'at saying hello?"

"Mrs. Jasper, it's me, Frosty Summers. Don't you remember me?"

"Frosty. Oh, sure enough I remembers. Can't see in this bad light. Cloudy. Mighty hot for a cloudy day. Could rain pretty soon."

I looked at the sky. There was not a cloud anywhere in the dull blue bowl of heaven.

"How's that Frosty doing out there in California? Hear she's building bombs or some such. Lands, bombs. Sure enough?"

"I build machine guns, Mrs. Jasper. Machine guns for fighter planes."

"You like doing that?"

"Well, it's a job. I like having my own place. My friends. I'll be going back soon."

"Sure enough? They need more machinery guns?"

I sat on the top step, my elbows on my knees. My hands were shaking; I folded them together as if I were about to pray. "Yes, ma'am. I suppose they do. Mrs. Jasper, I have to tell you something. I have to tell you about something I did a long time ago that was horrible."

Mrs. Jasper frowned and puffed up her cheeks, and for a moment I thought she hadn't heard me. But then she spoke, and her voice was strong and clear, almost loud. Not the tired, ancient whisper she'd been using. "Not to me, you don't."

"But, Mrs. Jasper, you don't know what I did."

"Don't matter. It's all the same."

"What do you mean, all the same? I—"

"No, no! Don't you go opening nothing bad here to me. Then you make me the bearer o' it too. I got my own burdens to carry. You just—"

"But this was—"

She raised her left hand with finality. "I won't hear it, Frosty. Now, hush."

I stood, fingering the yellowed folded newspaper on a small table by the only other chair on the porch, an old wooden-legged rush chair with the seat dangerously caved in. A pair of old-fashioned spectacles was laid on the paper, thick with dust, as if the wearer meant to come back but got lost in years somewhere. She must have just put them aside one day. Useless.

"You think," Mrs. Jasper started, her voice slow and quieter now, ominous in its tone, "you think you the only woman in the world got a load to bear? You think no one else in the world got trouble?"

"But this isn't trouble I *have*, it's trouble I *caused*. I want to make it

241

right. I was mad. I did it to you and to all the Nigra folks in this town. Only I wasn't mad at them, or you either. Just took it out on the wrong ones."

"My grandgirl Esther done got married. Name Davis now. Probably see a great-grandchild before I go home to Jesus."

"I really have to tell you this, Mrs. Jasper. It was a long time ago."

"Frosty Summers, you never done nothing to me. And if you think you did, and you're suffering so, well, it idn't like you got away with nothing, now is it? That's why you got a soul, so's your sins will prick you in it, like settin' on a pincushion of guilt. I got me a great-grandchild comin'. You know what that feel like? What that mean to me?"

"No'm, I guess not. But——" I felt tears close up my throat. My nose ran, and I sniffed.

"Don't matter." She leaned forward, her metallic breath coming toward me. Her swollen, gnarled hands worked over the end of the cane as if she were finding something startling there. "Don't matter, 'cause I'll be dying soon, and I'm long past ready to go. And I'm telling you, for all I seen on this earth in all these year, it don't matter, Frosty, if you set in wait and th'owed a body in the swamp. You take it to the cross, child. Don't you be taking it to ol' Miz Jasper to feel sorry for you or to go shake the Lord's shirtsleeve when I gets to heaven to make it good for you. You go on and make 'mends and don't look back. Hush, now, hush. The onliest thing that matters is that great-grandchild and what chance she got in this life." She pulled out a wrinkled, embroidered hanky, thinned with wear, and wiped at her eyes. "You always been some kind of child, Frosty. Always looking around with them sharp eyes, acting like you didn't know what going on half the time. Only thing you never did see was what color a body was. Underneath, you mad as a wet hen most your life. Ain't hard to get mad in this world. No, sir."

"Mrs. Jasper," I started. My mind went a hundred directions at once. "If I tell you this——"

"You just want a good scolding? What you think I been giving you? Now, you just hold up your head and wash your face. You ain't the first woman, nor the last, that's got a load to bear. And when it finally get too

242

heavy, you takes it to the cross. You gotta keep taking it, until someday you leave it there. And if you don't . . . well, then, that's your burden. You just ask the Lord. He'll tell you. Now, I thought you come over here to visit? You seen Junior yet?"

"Yes, ma'am, Mrs. Jasper. Heard him preach yesterday."

"All right, then. Amen. Amen, honey. Lord's been good to me." Her face was full of peace. A hint of a smile tugged the corners of her mouth upward. Her eyes searched the ceiling of the porch blindly. Her ankles were swollen so tight they looked as if they would split. She coughed, a rusty hinge of a noise, not liquid and drowning like Mr. Fielding's cough but a solid, dry, choked sound. "You hear that? Got a lung affliction. Ain't TB, but a few thinks it is, so I stay home mostly. Cain't walk on these old feet anyhow. They done give out, too. I's just settin'. Waitin' for Him to call."

"Mrs. Jasper? Could I ask you, please, to sing to me?"

The lady laughed, and that started a long jag of coughing. "Young peoples. Always so selfish," she said. "I tells you, Frosty. You sing to me. About time to repay some of what I done for you. You sit here and sing right out loud to me. Sing 'Angel Band,' that's what. 'Oh, come, angel band; come and around me stand . . .'" I took hold of the note where she left off. Closed my eyes. I tried hard to sing well, though my throat kept clutching shut and my lips hurt and jerked out of control.

When I got home that day, as if God had finally heard, there was a letter for me in Gordon's handwriting in the mailbox. He'd gotten back stateside and was getting out on leave. *He's coming home, he says, coming here to see me. We'll marry and leave this place. Or leave first, and get married on the way.* Gordon was coming. In thirteen days.

WHILE I WAS GONE, Daddy had been promoted. Now, instead of just unplugging septic lines, he worked for the official Sabine Sanitation and Public Works office. He didn't push a cart around with stinking tools hanging from it, "like some Irish Tinker," or dig ditches and run new pipes, but walked sedately to work in a gray-blue fedora,

243

where he made sure that other men unplugged septic drains and put pipes in ditches.

Part of my family's new prosperity, a 1939 Ford, sat in the yard. Daddy had to take off work to drive Mother anyplace in it, and this morning he washed and waxed it and took it to fill the tank with gas. The day Gordon was due to arrive, the rest of the family was going along to drive Deely and Wilbur to the doctor in Toullange. Deely was ecstatic because she thought she might be pregnant. I could not tell if Deely felt a warm nest heating up her insides or not. I couldn't ask her.

The whole town knew that Gordon was coming. My betrothed would come, and we'd plan a little wedding like Wilbur and Deely had. I prepared them to meet him . . . sort of. The bus would not be arriving until after they started the drive to Toullange. I told them I'd fix supper, not to worry. It seemed better if he was in the house when they got home. Something about the picture of him walking through the front door into them, like an innocent victim in some murder mystery, chilled my bones.

In the bathroom I kissed my fingers and used a trace of pink to brighten my cheeks. I felt sparkling in a new dress, inside and out. Just before I left, I felt under my normal socks for the tied-up one. I hefted it a couple of times, loving the feel of it, liquid and rich with the weight of dimes, and put it in my purse. I checked the folding money ironed flat and slid into the lining of my suitcase; all was in place. I could go with him today if he wanted. All I had to do was collect a couple of things in this suitcase, and we'd take off and start our life together.

Thirty-five minutes early, I plopped myself into one of the hard seats at the bus station. I watched the room. It was almost one o'clock. The face of the old clock hanging high on the wall grinned at me with anticipation, its throaty innards ticking away boastfully. Beans Bandy was pushing a flat broom with bristles that curled away from its edges like a giant handlebar mustache. He whistled distractedly, the same little snitch of a tune over and over.

I wiped my palms with my handkerchief. It was sodden by the time

I heard the bus's engine downshifting into the parking lot, the sound as familiar as if I had taken a thousand bus rides and entered that lot a thousand times. When the door finally opened, I felt overcome with a push toward it. A very old, very tiny woman emerged. Mrs. Brady. She used to seem large and ominous when I was little; now I wondered what it was that seemed so intimidating. Like someone in a slow-motion film, she alighted from the bus's bottom step, helped the last inches by Beans and an unidentifiable form behind her. When the figure appeared in full and the sun showed his features, it was Gordon. He adjusted his cap, looking nervous as he stepped around Beans and Mrs. Brady. As he reached for the door, I pulled it from the inside.

We were alone, and he swept me up in his arms. An impossibly long time passed as we kissed. Warmly, desperately familiar, and yet strange. "Oh, Gordon, how I've missed you."

He sighed, closed his eyes, and a look of pain crept across his features. "I didn't mean to do that." He stepped back from me.

"What?" We were still standing close together, but not touching. I thought I could feel his heart beating from where I was, across the six inches or so of air between us. Tension moved into the space.

The door opened again, held by Beans stretching his round form over the bent frame of Mrs. Brady. She caned her way slowly across the threshold.

"What just happened, I mean," Gordon said, too loudly, I thought.

I stepped back half a pace. Beans and Mrs. Brady were both occupied with getting her far enough through the entrance so that the door could be shut. She was muttering the whole time, too quietly to be understood, but suddenly her voice grew louder. "Now, you go get my portmanteau, little boy, and don't you drop it. Go on. I don't need help. Go on, boy."

Beans stammered, "Y'all wanta sit in the waiting area, Miz Brady?"

"I'll wait for the portmanteau. Do you think I'd come all this way and leave it behind?" She waved her cane toward the door, and Beans followed.

245

Gordon touched my elbow lightly as he moved toward the row of chairs. I tried to look into his face, see his eyes, but couldn't. He whispered, "Come sit and let's talk."

"What's the matter?" I said, reaching up to touch his shoulder. He pulled himself away, this time so obviously that I knew it was intentional.

"Frosty," he said. There was a pleading in his tone this time. He looked me square in the eyes for a split second as he sat.

I watched the girl in my new dress sitting on the old chair. The dress was red and white. Tiny stripes, like tiny parts of a flag. A thousand stripes, all of them going away from me in many directions. "Gordon," I began in a hushed voice, "I'm so glad to see you. I'm sure we can convince people to accept us if we both act like it doesn't matter."

"Like what doesn't matter, Fros?" His fingers held his garrison cap across one green-trousered knee the way some people would slip their fingers through the pages of a book to mark their place until they could come back to it.

His skin looked darker than I remembered. His eyes still had that warmth, but there was distance there, too. I said, "Our love is stronger than any differences."

He looked somewhere into the wall over my shoulder. "Love is strong."

I told myself I could relax now. He'd said he loved me. But the air felt sharp and hard between us. The whole scene was still being played out by two people I was watching from a corner. The seat cushion was dark green canvas that had been painted and sat in too often, and now at the corners it was frayed and splitting. Where the edges opened, sandy-colored stuffing was bursting out. I adjusted my skirt over the frayed place.

Gordon took my hands in his. I squeezed warmly, and the pressure from his hands increased. "Frosty, I came all this way to tell you, now that I'm out of the Marines, I'm going back to the reservation. You and I don't belong in each other's lives. I see that now. It was hard to see before. But that was a different world."

I felt my head spin. I tried to crush his hands and shook them. "This is the same world. It's the same place. How can you say we don't belong together? It's the same, Gordon. It is."

"I went home. I had to live there awhile to see."

"Someone talked you out of it? Some girl you never bothered to mention?"

"No. I've always been honest with you. No person talked me out of it. But I began to understand things. I can come to your world for a while, behave in your ways. I can even live there. But you cannot come to my world."

"Because I have freckles? Is that all this boils down to?"

"You have no idea, do you? I'm trying to be mature about this, to see the longer picture."

I shook my head. The world was crumbling around my feet. I was sinking into the morass that was Sabine. I smelled the diesel from the bus. I dropped his hands and picked at the lint poking its way out of the chair. Mrs. Brady was scolding Beans. For someone going on a hundred, she was loud. Beans's mouth opened, and he responded, but nothing he said made sense, as if my ears could hear it but my brain could not decipher the sounds.

"Frosty." Gordon's voice was gentle, warm. It was that same tone he'd used that afternoon when we slept together. "Let me explain."

I whispered through grinding teeth, "No. All that needs explaining is that I gave myself to you. I trusted you, and you're dumping me like yesterday's garbage. I knew you would do this. I knew it."

"I'm not just dumping you, Frosty. This is not an easy decision. You cannot come to my world. Let me show you something." He leaned forward, reaching under his uniform jacket for his back pocket. He took out a billfold and opened it, lifting out a tiny, broken-edged photograph. "This, Frosty, is my mother's home. I want you to look at this. Look closely."

"I see it," I said, taking the picture. "So? It's a little round hut."

"It's not a hut. It's a hogan. It's how we live. The floor is dirt. The walls are dirt. When it's cold, the fire inside makes your face black, but it grows warm when you bring all the sheep inside to sleep around you. The agents give a few people wood houses to live in, but they're cold, and when the wind blows, they fall apart. The sheep don't like them. You would have to give birth to our children in a home like this. It is our way, my way. You must be Indian to understand. You have to be Diné."

"We don't have to live like that. Dirt floor. I—I mean we—we can live in a town. We can have an apartment like in California. You told me you grew up in a town. What's wrong with California? That's what we planned. You could stay in the army. Or work in a store. We can visit your mother. We don't have to live there. Look—look here what I've got." I gave the picture back to him and hauled the sock full of dimes from my purse, defensively, as if I planned to strike him with it. "Just because you asked me. Since I've been here, I saved up almost fifty dollars. We can buy your mother a flock of sheep."

"I never asked you to do that."

"Yes you did."

"No. I said she would ask how many you have. It shows you come to the family from a good clan, that you are honest and you work hard. It is your fortune to bless the clan with. Sheep or horses are there if they are needed."

"This doesn't make sense." *Don't leave me, Gordon. Don't leave me* here.

"I guess not. The elders were right. You can't know. Frosty, you have no clan."

Pain taking hold of me, I sobbed. "I could. I was *going* to buy a sheep."

Beans Bandy was suddenly near. "Hey, fella. It's ready to go."

"You're going?" I said, also too loudly.

"Yes," he whispered.

"Just like that?" I dropped the sock of dimes to the floor, where it slumped in the same shape as my soul. "You never gave me a chance," I said. "You could at least have given me a chance."

He lowered his voice until it became a feathery sound, like a breeze coming through a tiny crevice. "I won't ask you to come with me. You can't walk in my ways. You can't." Then he turned, stiffened his back, and adjusted his hat on his head.

"Gordon," I said, "I'll wait for you."

"No. Go on with your life, Frosty. Go with your own people."

"I hate you."

Gordon's back was toward me; his black hair, tied in a strange kind of knot over his collar, gleamed in the light. He paused, as if he might say something else. Then he walked out the door. I was aware of Beans staring at me as if I'd lost my mind. Having *him* look at me like that made me feel dirty and beaten.

Gordon's bus pulled sluggishly away. When I stood, I was overcome with nausea, and I stumbled toward the door and hung my head over the garbage pail that stood outside it. It reeked of cigarette butts and the toxic, winy odor of decaying fruit. Five or six bright flies hovered between my face and the top of the can. My insides lurched for a few minutes, but nothing happened.

I cried in great, wrenching sobs during the entire walk home, so that when I got there, and saw my reflection in the window of the front door, I would not have recognized myself. The tiny red and white stripes of my dress were rumpled and smeared with tears. I don't know how long it took me to stop crying. My handkerchief was long since too wet to be of use, and childishly, sullenly, I wiped my nose with my sacred white gloves.

Back long before I expected her to be, my mother enveloped me when I came in. The unmet space that had been mentally prepared for "Frosty's fellow" made her instantly uneasy. First she said, "What happened? Where is he?" Then, as I was trying to form words with my lips, stiff and tortured from the distortion of crying, she wailed, "Oh, no! Oh, no, he's been killed. Oh, lands. Oh, lands' sakes alive. Oh, Frosty, honey. Oh, baby, come here."

And then she was everywhere around me, cuddling, pushing me into her upholstered rocking chair, wrapping me in the quilt that lay over the back of the sofa. The day was steaming with afternoon heat, but I let the quilt stay on my shoulders. "No, no," I said. "No," again, was all I could get out.

"Oh, lands. Deely, get your sister some coffee. Get her some water. Something. Can't you see he's been killed?"

"Oh, Mother," said Deely, "I'm going to be sick again."

"Can't you think of someone else besides yourself for once? Can't you see Frosty's fellow's been killed? How would you like it if Wilbur was? Well? Get some cold water, Deely."

Deely stood, wobbled a bit; then her eyes opened wide, and her hand covered her mouth, and she ran toward the bathroom.

Mother said, "Oh, lands. Just you stay here and I'll get some, Frosty."

"No, it's not that," I said. "It's not that!"

Then she was in the kitchen, and I heard all kinds of water running. She was filling more than one glass. Then I heard the hollow echo of the teakettle filling; on top of that, flushing from the bathroom roared through the pipes. Deely was coughing. Then Deely was retching and coughing, and the toilet flushed again. By that time my mother had appeared with two enormous glasses full to the brim with water.

"Drink this, baby. You'll feel better."

"Mother, I can't," I said. I was tumbling through the air, holding the arms of the rocking chair. Gordon wasn't dead but gone. Gone as good as dead. And I'd given myself to him. It wasn't just the sex. I'd made him a place in my inner self. A vast and angry emptiness, red and torn and wounded, remained. Mother. Mother.

"Now, go ahead." She pushed the glass to my mouth. I tried obediently to sip from the tumbler. I'd only met the bus, the words formed in my mind. I had to say it. I'd met the bus and he came and said "I love you" and then tore me in half. "Did they send someone to tell you? Oh, lands. Daddy's gone back to work. I'll have to telephone Daddy."

"No, don't call Daddy," I said. "Wait. Let me explain."

"Well, I have to, sweetie. I have—" And the words broke off in midsentence as she hurried to the phone in the hall, as if she'd ordered herself to make the call and that separate self had leaped to do so. "Mavis, get me the Septic Department. Well, whatever the title is, just connect me. This is an emergency. No. I'll tell you later."

Mavis would listen, and it would be all over town in less than five minutes. I heard her ask for Daddy, heard her frantic speech explaining to Charlotte, the secretary. Then she got so quiet that she had to repeat things two or three times. I slumped down into the quilt, covering my face with it, my mouth open in a scream that would not find voice.

Deely walked into the room. "I'm sorry, Frosty," she said. I didn't look up. She moved around the room. "I'm going to have a baby," she said.

I raised my head at last. Numb. I had to say something. "That's nice," I offered.

"Yeah," she said. "Wilbur's really happy."

"That's nice," I repeated. Deely would become, God help us all, a mother.

"Don't you want to know when? September twenty-ninth."

Mother came into the room. Her face tragic. Eyes moist. Her spirit keen. Her hands full of a tray set with teacups and the sugar bowl and spoons. I don't think I had ever in my life seen her serve anything on a tray. That old thing had hung inside the pantry on a hook since we'd put the door on the pantry. She had always just balanced the cups on saucers or plates or handed them to company, turning them gingerly at the last second she could possibly hold them without burning herself. But here was a tray. For me.

I put down my glass of water, shook off the quilt to my sides like great wings, and accepted the teacup from my mother. I could not say he left me. If they wanted to believe he'd died, all I had to do was shut up and not explain. They'd never met him. There would be no telephoning of consolation to devastated parents. No cards or letters of condolence. It was too far, too foreign, to think of reaching all the way to Arizona. You might as well have told my mother to write a letter to Madagascar.

I sipped the tea obediently. It was weak and sugared. The cups were that old set of delicate china she used to let us play with because Grandmother Summers had given her that set; she must have hoped we'd break them. We never did; so awed were we with the petal-like delicacy of the china, we treated them like fragile flowers. Mother was making soothing noises. I couldn't understand what she said. Deely left the room, and the toilet flushed, and Mother clucked pity for Deely's condition.

When I finished the tea, my entire dress was heavy with sweat and tears. As it began to cool, I shivered. The only thing I managed to say that was true was "I wish I'd known before today, when I was supposed to bring him home." Trembling shook me from the inside out; I cried again. Mother soothed, and Deely vomited. When Daddy came home from work, it started all over again, until I was wrung and senseless and shattered. I went to bed at around seven o'clock, and it was noon before I opened my eyes the next day.

THE FIRST FEW DAYS after that, people around me paused and fixed their eyes on me with looks of pathos. I hated them for it, and I hated Gordon for making me the center of that kind of attention. I hated myself for falling for him and his line, for being like girls at the factory. I hated my ridiculous thinking that ours wasn't just some wartime romance, that it was something real and lasting. I hated people's eyes and avoided them, looking toward the ground when I spoke. And now that my mother had the story in her head and on her lips, there was no going back. To say "Oh, by the way, that wasn't real—I just pitched a fit" would have humiliated her in front of people, and the fury that would follow was unimaginable.

I wrote my landlord in California and asked him to keep my things in the storage room there, said I'd send for them as soon as possible. I couldn't think about getting my money from the bank yet. Meanwhile, I resigned myself to Sabine.

Garnelle commenced trying to set me up on a date with Danny Poquette. Danny got out early for having a nervous leg. He didn't like to talk about where he served, but we all figured it must have been something awful. Then Deely told me how she found out he'd been a cook in New Jersey the whole time. "But," she said, "his nervousness is due to his sensitive spirit." Hadn't Gordon endured horrible things and not returned shaking like a Model T?

Danny came one afternoon and hung around like a stray cat, waiting, I guess, for someone to invite him to supper. I watched him as he sat on our davenport, talking about some new car design with my daddy. He wanted something called a "flathead," he said. Gordon once told me that a friend of his had punched a man for calling him a "flathead." Anytime Danny tried to sit still, his leg started twitching again. He had a pretty nice-looking face, but he was still shorter than me. Deely kept asking me if we'd gotten "serious" yet. I tried to imagine waking up to him and his jitterbugging leg for the next fifty years. Or ten days. I just wished he'd hurry up and finish his iced tea and go home. I'd let Danny kiss me good night, finally, the week before. It encompassed all the glorious passion that kissing a pop bottle would have had, and there was no Dr Pepper to show for my effort. Danny kept a little piece of chewing gum in his shirt pocket, and when he wanted a kiss, he'd roll the tobacco out of his cheek and chew the gum a few seconds. Invariably, his leg would start to shake, but we'd kiss, perspiring with the strain of the action more than the ardor of it.

Daddy and Danny went out to the yard and started talking about cars again. Everyone in town either had one now or was planning to get one. Daddy came in and said, "Well, Danny wants my advice about a car he intends to purchase, so we're going to look at the Chevrolet dealership. Christine, is my good white shirt ironed?"

SILOAM SPRINGS BAPTIST CHURCH had workdays twice a year. For Deely to get herself placed in charge of part of an event, a job that more or less made the rounds of any female married person in the church, wasn't unusual. What she did, though, was to have everyone come in pairs, which she called subcommittees. She wanted each subcommittee to work on each project that was scheduled. If there was any woman in that church who could nag people into action, it was her. I had a funny feeling when she assigned herself and Wilbur to pair up with me and Danny Poquette. I guess all subtlety was forgotten, and the church women were not going to rest until we were shoved up the aisle. The army missed a real bargain not drafting Deely Summers Fielding. She'd have annoyed Rommel into the sand.

On Saturday I showed up at seven-thirty in the morning, just as Deely had arranged, to get a head start on the day's heat. Danny got there at a quarter to eight with some paint buckets and rollers, and we talked a bit about where we'd start. It was nearly eight-thirty when Mr.

and Mrs. Wilbur Fielding arrived, tight-lipped and smiling, a blue haze of electricity bristling between them thick enough to slice.

"Thank you, dear," she said icily, when he held the car door for her. "Hello, Frosty. Hey-oh, Danny-oh." I watched her looking stunned as a rabbit at first, then her face flushing dark. Deely was just showing with the baby now, still able to hide it with a long-tailed shirt. Wilbur had his hand full of bundled sheets to use for drop cloths, balancing the pile with his short arm. Delia said, "You kids come get these old sheets to lay on the floor. I'm just going to grab a powder-room break," and oozed from him into the church building, where I heard her saluting other folks inside. It wasn't long before Wilbur and I were more or less shuffled into the role of painting the walls, while Deely kept Danny busy bringing us cans of pale green paint. She spent the morning mixing, stirring, and dashing into the rest room every now and then.

Before long I was smudged head to toe with paint speckles from working next to Wilbur. He was having a little trouble left-handing the brush, but I wasn't about to complain. I laughed at the bigger globs that slopped over, and we switched places so that I was on his right side and the paint had farther to go. "We make a pretty good team," Wilbur said.

Delia's voice came through the door ahead of her face. "Wil? Oh, kids? How about Danny and I go pick up some sandwiches at the diner? We've all been working so hard, and Danny said he'd buy because he felt he hadn't been pulling his load. Well, I was going to insist we all go together, but obviously y'all can't go anywhere like that. Good night, you two are a mess. We'll bring sodas, too."

"Here, Danny," I said. "You take this ladder and paint, and I'll run to the diner."

"Now, Frosty," Delia said. "I won't have you behind the wheel of a car. That's a man's place. It's too dangerous." She said the last as she tiptoed out the door.

Wilbur turned toward the paint bucket in front of him. "Frosty, would you mind stirring this up again?"

"Sure," I said. I stirred the paint. Whipped it, nearly. "Do you want me to pour in the rest of the other pail?"

"She thinks I really don't notice."

"It's nearly empty."

"Like part of my mind is cut off, too."

"Well, of course it isn't."

"I thought it would be different, is all."

I wanted to shake him and scream *How could it be different? She's Deely!* but I just shrugged.

"You know, I always meant to tell you, I think you were quite brave, going all the way to California to build planes. I really admire that."

Sunday, a Sing-spiration Service was followed by Dinner-on-the-Grounds. There's nothing like a Southern Baptist potluck dinner, every woman in the church trying to óutdo whatever dish she brought the last time. We toured the potluck tables, congratulating each other on the work done the day before as we went. Deely collected me and Danny to sit with Wilbur and her next to Raylene and Marty. Garnelle sat with us, an uneasy seventh.

Raylene rocked their baby, looking distracted. She carried a huge diaper bag with her, and a pocket of it was stuffed with envelopes, all addressed and stamped. She told me she wrote lots of letters. Marty shot her a look that I couldn't read.

"Well," she said, straightening, "we pay taxes to have mail delivered every day, and I think they should deliver every day, that's all. Why pay for something you don't use?"

"She puts a single letter or envelope or bill in the mailbox every single day, instead of saving them up. I swan. She writes letters to places just to make the mailman stop," Marty said. Marty never stopped talking. He talked about insurance, the weather, where everyone was since war broke out. He'd heard Farrell Bandy had gotten stationed right on Okinawa as part of the forces air-bombing Japan. Marty said for his part in the war he liked to sit along the side of the road at sundown, take aim at anyone who walked by, and holler out "Halt! Das ist ein American. Up-n-ze-arms, Krautzenheimer!" Everyone laughed at the way he said that, just like the kooky German rats in the picture cartoons. "One time," he said, "I did that with this thirty-ought shotgun in my hands, and the fellow walking down the road was one of the Schoenzes who'd moved here in '34 from down by Pflugerville. Schoenz starts screaming *'Nein! Nazi, nein!'* and running around like a chicken with its head cut off. He took off down that road faster than he'd ever moved before."

It used to be so funny, the way Marty said things. I watched Garnelle and Wilbur and Delia across from me and Danny. There was a tired, faraway look on Wilbur's face. I remembered a place out behind our little house—a little cubby I'd made, wiggling under a sagging hickory and through hide-itching weeds like a quail. Once I got inside the cocoon of it, it was safe. I could put a bush I'd pulled up in front of the opening and be certain no one could find me.

"Frosty," Delia said, "will you pay attention? Danny asked if you'd like him to walk you home. Honestly."

H ere you go, Sheriff," Verna Fielding said. "There's a nice big piece of devil's food cake. I made it myself."

"You don't say? Thank you, ma'am." He found a seat next to his wife, and they watched the children playing in silence. He leaned over to her and said, "You know, angel, it seems like I ought to ask that Summers girl some questions, but it doesn't seem right, with her bad news."

"Can't it wait, John? She's awfully torn up lately. Just shrunk up to skin and bone."

"I reckon it'll wait. If you get a feel for when she's able, let me know. I just don't want her to leave town again before I talk to her. County isn't gonna pay to bring her here nor send me there just to ask some questions."

Thursday I was at the WMU sewing circle in the basement of the church. Mrs. Fielding had recently joined Siloam Springs to be near her children. Even though she'd been a mainstay at First Southern all her life, now she was the new chairman of the Siloam Springs WMU. She made sure there was plenty of nice coconut cake and strong coffee.

My clothes didn't fit anymore; I'd lost some weight, I guess. Every dress I had hung loose on me, so I'd pulled some of my work trousers on and stuffed my blouse into the waistband. The buttons were supposed to be done so they could make one size uniform fit about four sizes of girl. I was on the smallest button. I could tell that the ladies were uncomfortable because I had on trousers.

Mrs. Fielding said good afternoon to me, and her eyes traveled down and back up again as if she were a boy checking me over. Then she smiled, and said, "Oh, that's like Garnelle's uniform she brought back. Well, how clever of you to wear something practical to work in." I searched her face for signs that it was one of those silken stabs like Deely was good at handing over. "Honey," she whispered as I returned for the last couple of slices of cake, "I saved you a nice big one. You're going to positively blow away if you don't put some meat on those bones. You just go right ahead and have that last one for yourself."

"Thank you, ma'am," I said.

Mrs. Brady was there, rolling bandages like it was her calling in life. Mrs. Brady muttered something to Neomadel, and then, as she did so often, suddenly increased her vocal volume beyond her strength and burst out with "And they just sent some old colored fellow to tell her, too! Isn't that a shame? Sent some old colored boy to tell her news like that in a bus station. Of all places."

All the women's eyes were on me. My mouth opened, dumbfounded, and I left the room. I walked all the way home. For a while I thought my heart would just quit, it hurt so. I walked into the kitchen and out to the back porch, where I sat on the top step and stared at the sticker bushes near the railroad track. I had to leave this place. I didn't feel half as brave as I did when everything was before me, and the only frightening thing was staying in Sabine.

I WAS LISTENING TO A Glenn Miller tune on the radio when, like so many times before, a voice broke into "Pennsylvania Six-Five-Oh—Oh-Oh," with a news flash. I had one of Mother's delicate china cups in my hands; I'd been moving the set to dust the top shelves and was standing on a kitchen chair. *President Roosevelt has died.* The cup hit the floor. I reeled above it. I stepped from the chair and sank onto its seat. My faraway father, living in the White House he was saving for me—oh, come, angel band. I leaned my head into my arms on the counter, feeling the crunch of china under my shoes.

"Mother and Daddy," I said at supper, "I have to go to California to get my clothes and things." I felt the words, knobby, heavy, on my tongue. *I have to get away from here before I explode.*

"Can't someone just mail it to you?" Opalrae asked.

Of course they could. "None of the girls are left there that knew me. I don't know how to get the apartment manager either. It's only a bus ticket. Two weeks. It's not like I'll miss school or anything. I have to get my stuff—my savings bonds—if I'm going to stay here for good."

"Maybe the trip will do you good," Daddy said. "Give you time to think things over. Cheer up."

"Maybe so," I said. "I'd like to see the ocean again."

Mother was fingering a little hole in the tablecloth. I focused my eyes on the hole. "Can't you just go down to Port Arthur?" Mother said. "I'm too tired for all this."

"You don't have to do anything, Mother. I'll take care of everything. I just have to get my stuff," I said. She nodded as if it made perfect sense. It didn't even make sense to me. Apparently there isn't much you can't get away with if everyone knows you are grieving.

I AWOKE EARLY and left a note on the kitchen table that I had gone to the church to do some soul-searching. That, at least, they would support, even be comforted by, and most likely leave me alone with my thoughts for a while.

I loved the smell of church in the misty dawn, heady with the memories of souls saved and ever potent with the Holy Ghost. Old wedding-candle wax and hymnbook covers, faded flowers, the moving of the Spirit, tears of joy and sorrow and guilt . . . the smell of God's sweat. Kneeling on the floor in front of the little cross on the pulpit, I sighed. A squirrel called, like a rattling squeak, from the big magnolia tree next to the side door by the organ. I heard him jump from the tree to the roof and run across it. It sounded like someone had rolled a cannonball overhead. I got off my knees and went to the window. Leaning against the frame, I scratched at the blackout paint with my thumbnail until I had a hole I could see through to the magnolia tree.

Unsatisfied, I ambled home. Mother was in the garden, fussing aloud, beating at the ground and the plants with a hoe as if she were wiping out sin on the earth. I went to my room and counted my dimes again. If I left Honey Doll on my bed, I decided, it would look as if I intended to return from California. That way, if I did return, she would be here; if not, she was the price I'd have to pay to go. I took a couple of ten-dollar bills from her middle, about half the dimes from her legs, and then smoothed her stuffing. She was thinner, shriveled, like me. Pressing her dress neatly, I settled her on my pillow. I sighed. But at least it would be possible, I thought, to write Opalrae and ask her to mail the doll just for the sake of a memory.

I'd go back to my job. I'd get my apartment, see which of my friends were still around. I'd have a party to welcome myself back to the fold, with popcorn and soda pop. I'd invite the girls from my line, whether I knew them or not. We'd laugh all night and jitterbug to my radio.

"Don't talk to strangers," Mother said, suddenly behind me. "And when you get there, you just pack everything up and get back on the bus."

"They won't hold the bus for me while I do that, Mother. I'll have to take a later one in a day or two. I'll call you when I get there to let you know I arrived safe and sound."

"Yes," she said. "Well, you sure you don't want Daddy to ride you to the bus station?"

"I'm sure. I've got forty-five minutes before it comes. Plenty of time. Say so long to Opalrae for me when she gets home from school?"

She nodded, looking at me hard, then turned and went back to the kitchen, muttering.

Suitcases in hand, I looked back when I stood on the edge of the porch. At the end of the yard I turned once again, wishing I had a Kodak of the house. I ran all the way to the bus station.

On the bus I kept thinking about rolling a cannonball across the roof of the church; it was all right to be a squirrel if you were born a squirrel. So far I'd only found out things I wasn't. Mother must have known I was really leaving for good. That's why she acted like she didn't care. Just go and get it over with. Maybe I wouldn't go to California. Maybe I'd get off somewhere else. Change my name. Backtrack up north somewhere, where people talk like Sharmayne. I stared at the suitcase at my feet. I heard Dr. Fine's voice in the back of my head, talking about my "prospects."

Alone in the bedroom, Marty Haliburton was taking the heads off matches with a penknife, dropping them into a coffee can. When he had most of the boxful decapitated, he poured them into a shoe box, lining them up in a row with his fingers so that they formed a chain. Then he lit one more match and held it to one end of the chain. One at a time they burst, spraying glowing bits of sulfur around the box. He smiled. *Just like a fuse.* The shoe-box lid smoldered and flared; flames shot two feet above the desk. He grabbed the closest thing he could swing, the pillow off his bed, and beat at the flames that danced across the room, skidding to the floor, clinging to the pillowcase. Sweat covered his face; he breathed roughly, mouth open, of the smoke as he stomped the sparks, swatting at the desktop over and over with the smoking pillow. Finally he plunged his bare hands into the pillow itself, wadding it tightly, grimacing at the pain as he held it down the way one would drown another, at arm's length, with all his force. After several immobile minutes he relaxed and whisked at the smoke with one hand. He lifted the window and opened the bedroom door, moving it back and forth four times to draw air.

"Martin, what's that smell?" Raylene called.

"Nothing, dear. Just lit some matches in the bathroom. I'll open the windows, too." He pulled the sheet off the bed, wrapped the charred pillow in it, and peeked down the stairway. "Want me to take the trash to the dump for you?"

"Yes, Mother Fielding," Delia said into the telephone, "I understand. Yes, I used to drive. Not anymore. Why, no, not that. But after many hours on my knees I believe that God condemns automobiles as unnatural." There was a long silence. "No, ma'am. Yes, I'll be glad to do that." She hung up the receiver. How could that woman press her to drive alone across town? Cars were inherently against the will of God. Sinful. A woman driving was the same as a woman preaching, simply not an ordained function. And what with her weak legs, she only had to ask Wilbur, and he drove her anyplace she needed to go. It wasn't her fault Mrs. Fielding had loaned their car to Garnelle for some useless errand. She picked up the receiver again. "Central? This is Mrs. Fielding. Please ring Wilbur for me. His mother needs him."

Two-thirds of the way across New Mexico I awoke from a deep slumber, not aware I'd fallen asleep except for the crimped feeling of my neck. For the next couple of hours I watched scenery roll past my window. We crossed the line into Arizona. The bus stopped just before noon in the middle of nowhere. A sign outside read FORT DEFIANCE, and next to that was a triangular sign announcing THE THING??? with arrows pointing inside the building. We'd passed seven or eight similar signs warning travelers that no trip to Arizona was complete until they'd paid fifty cents apiece to see THE THING??? The building itself looked like it once had been painted white, but it was stained around the bottom as if it were wearing a dirty, reddish-brown skirt. Around the doorjambs it was marked with black handprints. We filed out of the bus, making the customary line for the rest rooms. THE THING???, I thought wryly, must just be this trading post itself. Indian humor. Gordon would have laughed himself silly. I smiled, too, at the thought. Charge white people fifty cents apiece to see themselves made fools of.

I had at least half an hour before the other ladies would get finished, and the driver was sitting at the counter working on a cup of coffee and a piece of cherry pie that looked too red to be real. I wandered through odd displays of "genuiN Indian jewelleries," boxes of powdered milk, matches, snow chains for tires, and photographic film. In a glass case under the cash register was an accordion-pleated box camera for sale. Dust had turned the camera and its accompanying price tag the same color as the shelf it sat upon. Five or six children with dark skin and tousled black hair scampered through the aisles, and two very ample women ignored them except to whisper something at them in a hissing sound, then turn back to looking intently at the jewelry in the case.

There was a stand of magazines and newspapers. I picked up a *Redbook* and thumbed through it, my eyes catching on some words. " *'I found him,' she exclaimed. After two years and three thousand miles . . ."* Some girl had been engaged to a boy in the Air Corps. From her home in Licking River, Tennessee, she tracked him all the way to the Bering Strait, doing odd jobs, hopping freight trains like a hobo, until she made it to Alaska. He met her, and they married on the spot, to live happily ever after.

My hands trembled. I was in Arizona, where Gordon lived. I could find him if I meant to. Outside, a handful of old pickup trucks were parked, a couple of horses milling between them as if they were vehicles, too. The air smelled of gasoline and motor oil, and I found a garage on one side, where a pair of greasy coveralls stuck out from under a battered Buick.

I walked away from the trading post to a little rise beyond the garage. There the slope fell away more steeply than on the other side, and it looked as if a vast sweep of land emerged from this little hill like the spreading of an antique red fan. The sky seemed immense. Bright blue, an ocean wide and crystalline clear carried puffed sheep across it as though they swam in the blue. At my feet, clumps of coarse grass made little islands in the red soil, and here and there a bush grew from a mound of dirt. There were no trees. No cactus either. Nothing in any direction except the voluptuous boulders in the distance, the red and redder ground, and the brilliant sky. The clouds moved quickly, but going roughly east, the wrong way for me. *I can find him.*

I went back toward the bus, stopping short at the bleat of a sheep. Around the other side of the bus, filling the tank on an old pickup with the crank sticking out the front like it was permanent, was a Navajo man. He looked something like Gordon, but older, heavier. He had on a huge black hat, like the kind actors wear in the cowboy movies, only this man hadn't bothered to crease the bowl; he'd just plumped it out like a big round kettle on top of a wide brim. His pickup had been made over, added onto with flimsy wooden poles, and in the bed of it a pack of sheep were bunched together. I could not tell how many were there, but they all seemed to jump at something at one time and struggle against each other.

"Wait here, just a minute, please," I said to the Navajo man, and ran as fast as my feet would go to the dining counter inside the store. "Mister," I called to the man behind the counter. "Mister, could I talk to you for a minute?" He was putting cheese slices onto white bread that sizzled in grease on the griddle.

"Yeah, what?" he said over his shoulder.

I buckled up my courage. "How far is it to Chinle from here?" This was the wildest thing I'd ever done or even thought about doing. "Is there any way to get there today?"

"I don't know. Half a day maybe. Mail comes every other day, though. You could get a letter up there day after tomorrow."

"Mister, I need a job worse than anything in the world. I'm trying to find someone who lives around here, and it looks like you could use the help. I can cook and make pies and stuff, cakes, you know, pretty good. I did lots of cooking back home, and cleaning, too. If you don't mind me saying, you've got a pretty grimy floor here. I'd keep the place spick-and-span. And if there's anything people will say about me back home it's that I'm dependable. I'll work cheap, too. I just need a place to sleep and a little pen, and it's just temporary until I find this person. Gordon. What do you say?"

"Temporary, huh?" He looked me over. "What the hell's the matter with you, kid?"

"I'm not a kid. I'm older than I look. I worked in the Morrison Kellogg Tool factory in San Diego. Line supervisor. I did every phase of ammunition production in thirty- and fifty-caliber rapid automatic— You can call my boss, Mr. Yount. He made me line leader after only a couple of weeks."

"You say you worked in a factory?"

"Uh-huh." I nodded eagerly.

"Lotsa gals doing that, huh?"

"I know everything there is about a machine gun. Firing range, accuracy, trajectory quotients. Delivery rates. I can learn anything about working here."

"What do you want a job here for, kid?"

"I'm looking for someone. He's supposed to live near Chinle. We

were engaged. I went home, and he was supposed to meet me, but . . ."
No, no, throw your own cannonball. "Actually—" I started again.

"Sweetheart, didn't they tell you?"

I could literally feel the blood rush to my face. "He's not dead. I've left home to find him, mister."

He scrunched up his face and for a few seconds flipped the sandwiches back and forth, flopping them onto waiting white plates, the bread centered in a faded blue ring that ran around the rims. He turned back toward me and said, "Look, kiddo, help here comes and goes, but there isn't much of a place for you to stay. There's a little room on the second floor here, you get to through that yella door. You can have the room and fifty cents an hour, three days a week. You gotta do like I tell you, though—no loafing around. The next bus'll be through in a week. You decide then if you're staying another week. Getcher stuff and lug it up there. It's a crummy little place, but it's safe enough, and no one'll bother you long as I'm around. There's aprons beside the freezer in the back there."

"Thanks, mister!" I called, already out the door. The bus driver was smoking a cigarette, talking to the pair of legs sticking out from under the car on the dirty garage floor. "Excuse me. I'll need my bags off the bus. I'm staying here. No hurry," I called, backing toward the gas pumps, "as long as you get them down before you leave. I'll be right out here." I motioned toward the pumps and clumsily waved to him, feeling light, as if my arms could lift me from the broken pavement.

The Navajo man was inside, paying for his gasoline. As he walked back to his truck of sheep, I tried not to stare at him, but I studied his clothes, his old truck, the giant mattress of wiggling mutton in back. Gordon seemed so close.

The only way I'd ever find him in this vast place of wide, eye-aching skies was simply to ask, person to person. I approached the Navajo man as he went to the door of his pickup truck. *Remember not to point,* Gordon had said. *Remember not to talk suddenly. Remember not to ask directly, but go around to the back door. Don't stare at people's eyes, it's insulting.*

"It might be nice weather today," I offered, trying not to look at the man. He turned his head to me as if startled, but his eyes didn't meet mine. "It would be good to find a man named Gordon Benally. If he's around here. Some person is wondering if anyone knows him." I felt like an idiot. If this man understood me, he was as likely to think I was making fun of him as anything else. I tried to look earnest without looking at him. I peered at the sheep jostling in the slatted pickup bed. "Maybe," I started again, a little louder, "maybe Gordon Benally lives around here. Somebody here might know him. He's from Chinle." Rats, I'm not supposed to throw people's names around like that either. You don't just go asking for someone by name over and over. How the heck do Navajo people find each other? "I'm looking for someone," I said again.

There was no response. I sighed and gazed at the cloud sheep moving overhead. And then it came to me. I rehearsed the way he'd taught me to change the emphasis of my words, so they weren't insulting or abrupt; then I spoke, louder, facing the man but with my eyes to the ground. "If some sheep are for sale, somebody could be buying sheep today."

Maybe he didn't understand English. I took a deep breath. "I'm buying five sheep today." I had no earthly idea what mutton was selling for. I figured maybe a dollar apiece. Maybe two. Gordon wanted me to give his mother some sheep. I had no idea why—some kind of dowry thing, I guessed—but if I had them, and found him, and gave them to him, I figured it might change things. I had my money saved up. I said, "Five sheep to give to Gordon's mother. He said she wants some sheep." Behind me I heard the *clunk-chunk* of the gas pump's nozzle being put back in the holster. A low voice said, "Five sheep, probably cost sixty dollar."

I stopped in my tracks and turned. "No, maybe you didn't hear. I only want five sheep, mister."

"Five sheep. Sixty dollar."

"Well." I felt my insides quiver. "I can't pay sixty dollars. How much is one? Maybe just one," I said again.

"One's fifteen dollar," he said.

I looked hard at the bleating jumble of dirty wool. What on earth was I thinking? I could not find Gordon in this place. It was just a little gas stop, for crying out loud. I couldn't put a sheep on the bus if I keep going. "Mostly," I said, "I need to find a man named Gordon Benally. And I need to buy sheep from someone to give to his mother." Should I argue with him? Tell him the math doesn't add up? Ask if he means a gold-plated sheep?

"Fifteen dollar," the man said again, crossing his arms.

A couple of children stood on the far side of the highway, a single lamb between them. Their raven-black hair flew in the breeze playing around the low hills. They both wore simple, plain pants and tunic-type shirts. They watched for a long five minutes or so as a car passed. My heart pounded, and the flush I'd felt in my face now seemed to envelop me.

I tried to calm myself as I approached the man with the sheep. "One sheep, then," I said. "I only have money for one sheep, if it's a good one. If it's still for sale, mister. I mean, if there's a sheep for sale." I looked squarely at his face and saw some kind of expression flicker across it. Maybe it was curiosity, or maybe he was laughing at me, or a combination of the two. He'd definitely softened in his appraisal of me. It was the same letting-down I'd seen on Gordon's face, as if somewhere inside a door opened up. I have no idea what I'd done that caused the look to appear on this stranger's face.

"Fifteen dollars. One goot one," he said, as if sealing the deal.

"I'll get my money," I said, and dug into the bottom of the heavy purse draped over my shoulder for the sock full of money. Thank goodness I'd traded some of the dimes for paper money. Turning so that my back hid my actions, I pulled out the small roll of bills and opened it, peeling off a ten-dollar bill and five ones; then, thinking of reducing the weight of the bag, I put them back and started counting out quarters and dimes. I put the change I was spending into one of my dress pockets, and by the time I got to fifteen dollars, it was swollen and heavy so that it pulled the dress awkwardly.

"Fifteen dollars," I said. "For one really good sheep. Best one you've got." I dug into the pocket and came up with a handful of change. The man didn't look at the money. He walked to the back of the truck and unwound a couple of loops of heavy baling wire from two of the sticks. He reached into the thick mass of sheep, laid both his hands on the back of one, and abruptly plucked it from the packed flock. The sheep all around filled in the gap, as if the loss of one made not a bit of difference in reducing the cramped conditions.

My sheep made a frantic bleating sound, which started up the others in a flurry that just as quickly subsided. The man was busy for a minute; with a few deft moves of his hands he formed a loop in a piece of cord he'd produced from somewhere and made a ring around the animal's neck. He handed me the other end of the cord, and I twisted it around my fingers, dropping a couple of nickels as I did. I poured the money into his hands. "You'd better——" I started, then began again. "Maybe a person should count this again. Someone should always count money two times, I guess." I picked up the nickels from the ground and fetched the remainder from my pocket. "With this makes fifteen, all right?"

He nodded and held his hands up to his shirt front, pouring the heavy coins into first one, then the other chest pocket. Still looking at the ground, he said, "It's a pretty goot day to sell some sheep," and tucked his hands into his pant pockets as he turned toward his truck.

The sound of a car suddenly downshifting caught my attention. The scream of rubber tires on the pavement—the sound of wasting—a thunk. My sheep pulled hard at my fingers, tightening the cinch and turning them blue. I yanked on it, unwinding, feeling the gorged flesh behind the string swelling with immediate bruises. The car stopped, rakishly angled against the squares formed by the gas pumps and the concrete driveway in front of the store. The two small children were now on the near side of the highway, and crying. On the road, wind pulled at clumps of reddened wool around a small, whitish lump, all that remained of their lamb. Near us a young man, blond and freckled, the kind Mother would have called sunny-faced, emerged from the car.

He looked around, curiously, at me, the man with the pickup full of sheep, the bus, and the trading post. He didn't look toward the children.

Disappearing into the store, he came back out striding confidently, holding a Coca-Cola bottle with ice chunks dribbling from its bottom edge. He drank it down lustily. The children both whimpered now. It was not crying like I'd ever heard before. It was as quiet as a distant wail on the wind, a breeze through bare tree boughs, as if the sound were underneath the air.

"Hey there," I called toward him.

"What's the word, chickadee?" he said, and he slumped to one side, putting two fingers over his belt and leaning on it like it was separate from his body.

"You just killed those kids' lamb."

"What? I didn't see any lamb."

"Right there in the road." I pointed, quickly caught sight of the Navajo man watching me, and put my hand down. "Over there. You killed it. At least say you're sorry."

"Well, ain't you the do-goodly-do-right. What're you, some kinda missionary?"

"This man here is selling sheep. You ought to at least buy those kids a new one. That one you killed might be all they had in the world."

He guzzled at the soda bottle, draining it and making some artificial movements like he was involved in sport, avoiding other players, twisting dancelike, and tossing the empty bottle toward a trash can near the far pump, where bees spun wearily. "And he scores . . . two more points for A and M. And they move up in the playoffs. Shee-yit, chickadee, if you want those ugly little gremlins to have a sheep, you give 'em one. Lazy Indians." He turned to the Navajo man near me. "Get off the government dole and get a job and buy your own lousy kids your own lousy pets."

The sheep seller had already gotten inside his pickup.

"You hear me, Chief? What's your name, Injun Joe? Get a job, moron."

Suddenly I tensed as if I'd been living on the verge of some huge explosion. At the top of my lungs I bellowed, "You low-life, misbegotten jerk. I wish you'd go lay in that road and I'd get in that car and run over you about fifty times until there's nothing left but a greasy smear of your slimy guts! You rotten creep. Get in that car and drive out of here before I rip your creepy head off your creepy shoulders and spit down the creepy hole. You jerk. You motherless, you—you *bastard!*" My mother's mouth seemed to have taken over my face.

He screwed up his face, glaring at me, and the peachy sunniness of his face flushed violet. "Witch," he said.

The worst thing he could have called me, here in this place. I shriveled up, feeling deflated beyond recognition. While I had been screaming at the man, I'd moved toward him, dragging my recalcitrant sheep with me, and the animal stood, chewing, its eyes looking dreamy, as if this were all very boring.

I looked at the hill behind me and the wide plain that spread below it. The knobby boulders, the bloodred soil. My sheep moved, pulling painfully at my fingers. The Navajo man was in his pickup, and the engine started. The two children sulked toward the trading post door. Shaking with spent fury, I stepped backward as the young man spun his car in loose dirt and bolted onto the black highway. A cloud of orange-red dust hung behind him. My sheep made a noise that sounded like irritation, like *baa-ad.*

When I got the cord off my fingers, I thought they would burst. I half led, half pulled the sheep toward the two children. My face hurt. My eyes stung. My heart made a single clunking noise I could actually hear. "I'm sorry for what that man did," I said to them. "I'm really sorry he was so mean. Here, you can have this one. I know it's not your little lamby, but it's a pretty good one. I guess you need him more than I do."

I held the string out to the children, and they shrank from me like I was some kind of evil thing. I looked toward the man sitting in the pickup, wondering what he was waiting for. "That man there, it's his sheep. He wants me to give it to you. Here. Take it, kid. Yes. That's right, take it." Finally one of the children took hold of the string. Neither of them looked up.

I walked back to the running pickup truck, staring hard at the door handle. The man inside seemed to be watching the clouds. I said, "I really don't have any more money to spare. I have to get to California. I guess this must all seem kind of crazy to you, because it's pretty crazy to me, too. If you know Gordon Benally, mister, please tell him some-one is looking for him. But now I don't have any sheep to give his mother. So it—it doesn't make sense for me to stay here. I'm—some-body is going to California—to a job there." *I should have brought Honey Doll.* My lips clenched hard. The stupid sheep was baaing loudly, and the children patted its head and back. Walking toward the bus, where the other passengers had already gotten seated, I looked back. The Navajo man was staring at me. Gordon said not to expect anyone to look me in the eyes. But Gordon was just a dream. Just a long time ago, a dream, a wailing on the wind, under the air.

It was thirty miles or so later that I realized I'd never said anything to the man at the counter, no "Thanks for the job" or "I'm leaving now" or even "I'm the craziest person you'll ever meet." I just walked away. In this very day I'd done nearly a dozen things I'd never done in my entire life before. "Missionary," that jerk had called me. Of what? Vengeance?

Raylene Jeanette Smith Haliburton," Raylene wrote across a sheet of paper. She wished she had beautiful stationery with her name scrolled across the top of it. She had lovely penmanship. It was a good thing, too, with all the correspondence she had to do. She sat in Delia Fielding's front room in the house they rented behind one of the big two-story Ladies on Potomac Street. It gave Delia a nice address, but it was still just some servants' quarters in the olden days. Raylene had driven there that morning after dropping Marty off at the insurance of-fice he'd opened in town, a corner room in the lawyer's office. It was down in the two-story district, too, near where she expected to be living before too long. Marty said he might take up real estate, too. The two professions went hand in glove, for if people bought houses, they needed insurance for them. Before long she'd be living in one of the Victorian Ladies. Maybe she'd rent *their* servants' quarters to Delia and Wilbur.

Her baby was in the car, sleeping. She'd left the motor running. The baby slept very well in the car. He was fretful other times. But she could always count on him having a nice long nap on a blanket in the back-seat of the car. She listened to the hum of the engine for any sound of crying. All was quiet.

Garnelle returned from the kitchen, carrying peach cobbler and iced teas on a tray. Delia brought napkins and spoons. "Well, let's just enjoy this," she said. "Then you tell us your news."

"Oh, I can't wait," Garnelle said, sparkling. "Danny Poquette and I are engaged!"

"Oh?" Raylene said with a hopeful lilt in her voice.

"I see," Delia said. She smiled, her chin lowered. She placed spoons on the saucers of cobbler, passing them to the other two women. "Praise the Lord. I'm so truly happy for you, darling." When she raised her face, her eyes were glittering.

Garnelle stuffed a large bite of cobbler into her mouth. She nodded. "Oh, and take a look-see at this!" She tugged at a little chain under her collar and pulled it up. "I have an engagement ring." She held it out. They cooed and clucked their tongues appreciatively. "Mama said I shouldn't wear it until she can get a proper announcement printed in the paper. It's coming out this Sunday. I'll be wearing my ring in church."

"Is that a, what, a quarter carat?" Raylene said, squinting as if she could barely see it.

"Well," Delia said, "I know mine is an eighth. Here, let's compare. No, I believe it's just a hair different from mine. See. They're almost the same. So when's the date? You know, Frosty just left to get her stuff in California. She'll want to come, seeing as she was so close to Danny and all. You're not planning it before she gets back, are you?" She took a bite of peach slowly from the spoon.

Garnelle straightened her back. She smiled. "Well, that's a secret for now, Delia. You'll find out soon enough."

"Oh, tell. Tell," Raylene said.

"No chance. Isn't that the baby crying I hear?"

"No." Raylene went to the door and looked at the car through the screen. "No. Still asleep. Believe me, if that baby were to cry, I'd know. I declare, I hear the least little pip from him and can't sleep until he's happy again. Motherhood is an all-encompassing occupation. You'll see, Delia. You'll see."

Delia stood. "More tea, Garnelle? It doesn't have to take up your entire life. More cobbler?"

"No, thanks."

"Well, I have news of my own," Raylene said. "Before long, my Martin will be handling real estate in addition to the insurance business. But before that, Martin will announce this decision Sunday. Since you girls are my best friends, I just have to tell you." The two young women leaned in toward her. "Martin has surrendered to preach the gospel. Of course, everything else will be just piecework, and I'll be helping with simple paperwork so he can devote himself to the Lord. He's being ordained by the deacons Sunday night."

I walked eighteen blocks to the apartment building, only to find that my key didn't work in the lock. I pounded on the manager's door. "Hey! Yoo-hoo!" I called.

Mr. Abregos answered his door, scratching his generous belly, looking as if he'd been asleep. Inside, a radio blared. "Turn that down!" he yelled over his shoulder. "I can help you?"

"Frosty Summers. Number twenty-one? I paid the rent in advance and sent you a letter asking you to store my stuff, and now my key won't fit. You'll have to let me in."

"Can't do it. Figured you wasn't coming back. I ain't in the business to be keeping empty rooms. Got lots o' GIs coming here to work, no place for 'em all to live. What you paid I can get double or more. Rent's up."

"Where's my stuff? What did you do with my things?"

"Oh, that I got here in a storage. All the keys is different now. I'll unlock it for you." He fumbled in a grimy-rimmed pocket in his trousers and pulled out a large ring of keys.

Following him down a narrow concrete walk to the storage unit, I said, "You have any other places for rent? I need a place to live."

"I got number three opening up end of the month. Two bedroom. It goes for seventy."

"Seventy dollars? Mr. Abregos, this isn't fair. I can't believe you gave away my apartment." It might as well have been a thousand and seventy.

He found the key and opened the storage room door. Five haphazardly stacked boxes with "Summers" written on them in pencil sat in a spidery corner behind the door. Shiny garden-slug trails made crosshatching across the fronts of the boxes. He shrugged. "There you go."

"If you don't have any places for rent, I don't know where I'm going to put it. How am I going to carry this stuff?"

"I could charge you something for storage."

"I can't pay it. I don't have a job."

"I could sell your stuff."

"Look, Mr. Abregos, what do I have to do?"

"You should figure you owe me for storage and keeping your mail."

I put my hands on my hips. "Look," I said, "I was a good tenant. You had lots worse."

"Ah, you was a lot of trouble. Who knew if you was coming back?"

"I wrote and told you I'd come back."

He made a chewing motion with his mouth while he thought. "So here's the deal. You can leave this here free of charge until you find a place. So? I'm a nice guy. Everything square and fair."

"Thanks. I owe you."

"Yeah. You owe me. Just taking down your mail was giving me arther-iters."

"Oh, come on now."

"You got all those mean letters from the person in Texas. I had my eye on you. I read one of them, and I kept a watch out in case you was as bad as all that. You was all right as long as I kept that colored fellow away."

"What do you mean?"

"I found out the name of that boy that was always after you. Took care of those letters, too. I knew no good girl was wanting letters from coloreds. Figure it's my responsibility for all the girls here working away from home. Look out for 'em some." Gordon's letters. He had written to me. Mr. Abregos passed along Mother's letters and kept Gordon's from me.

He let me look through the stuff in the boxes, and I picked out one of the little novels Garnelle had left behind. I'd taped my bankbook inside the back cover. The novel had a reassuringly fat feel to it. Then, aggravated and tired, I left the complex and started walking toward the Morrison Kellogg factory. It took twenty minutes of explaining to get in to see Mr. Yount, and even then I had to be escorted by some man who came from the tin-sided office building, as if I hadn't walked through those gates hundreds of times. As if I was some security risk to national defense.

Mr. Yount wasn't any happier to see me than Mr. Abregos had been. "Disappointed" was the exact word he used. The only thing he could do for me was send me to the snack bar. They might have a part-time job I could have. "It's flat unpatriotic to hire women anymore. You know Congress declared it. Send the gals home and hire the boys that did their duty."

"I did my duty, too," I said, but he just shrugged. There was a place in the snack bar, working for nothing but tips. I needed income. I went back to Mr. Yount. "Please," I said. "I'll do any kind of work. Just try me. You know I can learn."

"Do you type?" he said.

"Sort of. Not very fast. But I can do math and—"

"Nope. Got men to do the financial stuff, payroll and bookkeeping. I just don't need any help in those areas."

"I work hard."

He looked at me and rubbed his head. "I could put you on in janitorial. You'd have to work at night. You have to be able to lift and move tables and stuff."

I nodded, although even *I* knew it was without enthusiasm. "The other thing, Mr. Yount, is that my apartment was rented out from under me while I went home to visit. I've got no place to stay. Is there a night watchman's bunk or—"

"You can't sleep here. No way, no how, no ma'am. Check the bulletin board in the hall there. There's usually someone with a room to rent or something."

So I was back. But instead of being a line supervisor, I scrubbed bathrooms, I swept. I mopped using a big bucket with a squeezer on the side that more often than not caught strings of the gigantic mop in its teeth. After working until six in the morning, instead of going to my complex full of girls trying to win the home front, I had to walk to a little room behind a house. It was made out of an old garage, closed in. The bathroom was just a toilet and a sink. I had to use a garden hose to fill a washtub to take a bath. Cold.

I was there two days before I called Sabine. Mother answered the telephone. I stood in the telephone booth in front of the Rexall store, sweating and trembling even though a chilly breeze hurt my ears. I held the door for strength. "Mother? I just wanted you to know I got here. Yes. No, everything's not fine. No." I told her about the apartment being gone.

"Well, just get your stuff you need and come on home," she said.

I took a deep breath. "I found a job. It's a real good job. In the same factory. And a nice room to rent. I'm going to stay for a while. Just a while, Mother. It will be all right. I don't want you to worry about me."

"Is that so? Sure enough. Well, you do what you think is best." She hung up abruptly.

I hadn't had time to tell her my new address. I was alone in California.

THREE DAYS LATER I decided to ask Deely to mail Honey Doll to me. At the pay phone by the Rexall I called Deely and Wilbur. Delia couldn't come to the telephone. She was hysterical, Wilbur said. They had been having tea or something, the three of them. Raylene had gone out, driven home, went to take the sleeping baby into the house, and found him dead. The doctor said it might have been fumes from the car. He gave Raylene a shot of sedatives and kept her knocked out until after the funeral. He'd ordered Delia straight to bed, where she was miserable. "She's asking for you," he said. "She wants to have you home."

"Really?" I said. "Me? What does she want with me?"

"She said—well, she thinks you're going to come to some calamity out there. Wants you home so the family can be together. She said God told her you were in serious trouble."

"Maybe when my rent is up, at the end of the month."

"Oh, and Garnelle is getting married."

"Great. Who to?"

"Danny."

I stammered something dopey for a few seconds. "Tell her I'm really happy for her. Maybe I'll be home before Christmas."

D elia moaned in the bed, crying out "Oh, Jesus," for hours on end. After four days Wilbur began to give up hope and called the doctor to see if there was a mental hospital she could be sent to for help. At her bedside the doctor said—phone in hand—he would ask for the asylum in Toullange. When she heard them talking about her as if she were a child in another room, she sat up and straightened her hair. She blew her nose, put on her wrapper, and got up from bed. She nodded to Wilbur, holding Ronny, wet and irritable. She said, "Dear, where are my manners? Please excuse me. May I offer y'all some coffee?"

It took her an hour to convince the doctor that she was only suffering a sort of setback. Finally she assured him that Wilbur would be there to call again if it was needed, and he left.

"Wilbur, darling? There's something I have to discuss with you."

"Just take it easy, dear. The doctor said you should rest a few more days."

"I really will go crazy if I don't tell you. Put Ronny in his bed and sit here. Please?"

When he returned, she began to cry. "Cars are nothing but evil. Oh, that darling baby! They kill people! Listen, listen to me. When I had a car, I had to drive everywhere, taking care of things for my family, running the other girls around town. One night— Oh, this is terrible. You'll want to divorce me. One terrible, awful night, there was a storm. I hit something in the road. And the next day I found a piece of someone's shirt stuck to my car."

"You mean you hit a person? Did you report it to the sheriff?"

"Well, no. I was too afraid."

"Of what?"

"I don't know. Afraid I'd go to jail. Afraid Mother and Daddy would—"

"Well, maybe it was an animal. Just a dog or something. You said it was night?"

"Wearing a calico shirt? I think it was that old Nigra preacher. The paper said they found him in the sump by the foot of the Knob. That's where my—my accident happened."

"Damn it, Delia! Why in God's name didn't you tell someone? If this were to come out now, our family will be ruined."

"Because I was so afraid. I was afraid, darling. Terrified. If Mother and Daddy knew, if anyone knew—oh, my life would be over. It was the fault of that evil, evil car!"

"Listen to me, Delia. You must never, ever speak of this again. Do you understand?"

"I just couldn't go to jail. I was so dreadfully scared."

"Do you understand? Never say a word. You dreamed the whole thing. It was a—a hallucination, because of Raylene's baby dying. People have hallucinations. Delia, promise you'll never say it. Promise!"

She shook her head, putting the backs of her wrists against her eyes. Her hair hung in oily strings. "Oh, *please* don't divorce me."

"I have no intention of ruining my family with a divorce. It was the fault of that evil car. But it's gone now. Pull yourself together. We still have *our* baby." He reached into his bureau drawer and took out a pack of cigarettes he kept there in case his father came over and had run out. "This'll calm your nerves. Daddy says it helped him to settle after the war." He took out a cigarette and put it to his lips. He lit it for her and held it. "Now, we're not going to say anything more about that. Here. Try. Just a little puff at first."

I worked so hard I forgot what day it was sometimes. In May, on the eighth day of the fifth month in the Year of Our Lord Nineteen Hundred and Forty-five, the German Axis quit rotating. The skies over San Diego were filled with planes, doing loops and formations and trick maneuvers. The newsman said they couldn't find old Adolf Schmadolf. People were in the streets cheering and having a big debate over just how to do him in when they did. Personally, I thought they ought to load him in the bomb-bay of a B-17 and drop him on Berlin.

My job was numbing, mindless, even more than the assembly line had been. At least there I could think about the lives I might be saving. Now I was only mopping up other people's filth. I was still inside Morrison Kellogg Tool Company, but the men who worked there referred to me as "the cleaning lady," making me sound decrepit and ancient and worthless all at once. It felt altogether strange to be here without any purpose other than emptying ashtrays.

The other cleaning "lady" was a Negro man named Alfred. He read a lot of books that I think the library must have thrown out, because they always looked coverless and ragged, subjects I wouldn't have read for love nor money. Today, while we were filling the mop buckets with clean water, he said to me, "Did you know that words have a history, just like people?"

"I guess," I said, not in the mood to banter with him. He liked to get my goat just to show he could. I didn't dare argue with him; I knew I couldn't win.

He stuck his mop in the bucket, releasing a dark slick on the clean water. "In olden days the word 'Negro' used to mean just a servant. Any servant. Any color. Did you know that?"

"Are you just trying to rile me?" I said.

"No, ma'am. Just think it's interesting. You and me is both Negroes." He said it with a smile. But there was a bite behind his words just like Deely always used. That glint in the eye.

"Thank you for the education, Alfred." I thought about that all night while I was mopping and dusting. I thought about being a cleaning lady all my life, like some colored women are. They cleaned or cooked or took care of other people's children. Any of their men who got jobs had to work at the mill in Sabine, only they never got the jobs that involved riding on a wagon or deciding anything. They got the ones where every fourth or fifth tree that was felled maimed or crushed someone to death. Their jobs were the ones that involved something filthy to be handled, something dangerous that might blow up, or something sharp and quick that could cut off a piece of a man. There was no reason I couldn't at least get back on the assembly line, except that I wasn't a man. They already had plans to retool back to machinery for some use other than war. All I could do was work down there with Alfred, who was one smart character.

Tuesday two different men from the factory asked me on dates.

280

When Bill Scott asked, he was polite and all, but I said, "No, thanks. I've got a boyfriend." He looked so disappointed I was immediately sorry. And I didn't have a boyfriend at all. *I should have been nicer to him,* I thought. *I'll never meet anyone if I don't date.* Then, as I was walking out the gate, Herb Fontana, a guy with greasy hair and glasses, approached me. "Hey-dee-ho, girly-o. How's about a fellow showing you a good time?"

Even though Herb Fontana had dandruff I could smell, he could be a nice person. Maybe I was just getting more popular. Maybe I'd have lots of dates now. He didn't give me time to answer. "Pick you up at nine tonight, girly. Wear something to do the town in, and I'll take you out, treat you special."

"All right," I heard myself saying. He pushed his fedora so low on his forehead he had to lean back to see. I felt excited, getting ready that night. I finished ironing my blue dress and unplugged the iron from the light socket over the kitchen table. I wished like crazy that I had a party dress. At nine o'clock I sat in my room on the lone chair, waiting. At nine-thirty a hand rapped at my door.

Walking away from the apartment, Herb put his arm around my waist. "You're one sophisticated girly, I can tell right off the bat," he said. "How do you take your gin? Neat?" I shrugged. As soon as we rounded the corner, he squeezed me up tight, which seemed awfully fast for someone I'd only said hello to about eight times. I pulled back from him. "Hey, come on, sugar," he said, and pulled me so hard toward him I couldn't walk straight. We went on another block like that. My side hurt.

Maybe I'd distract him with conversation. Deely always said I was no good at the art of fetching conversation. How could a girl have a date, she'd lecture, without conversational skills? "I was thinking maybe someday I'd go to law school."

He laughed, saying nothing. We walked on.

"Yes," I said, "I believe a woman with prospects could overcome a lot of hardships, provided she's determined and works hard. I'd like to do well. What are your future intentions? Do you plan to stay in Morrison Kellogg when the Pacific war is over?" I could smell his hair, slick with freshly doused Three Roses. When he grinned at me, I could smell his mildewy breath, too. The moment I realized that, he flattened me up against the wall of a building and kissed me with rubbery wet lips, smelling of must. I recoiled as much as I could, trying to turn away from him. He pinned me roughly, kissing at my face. When his tongue poked at my lips, which were pinched tight, I gagged, tasting spoiled milk.

"Come on, gal, give up a little. I got somethin' for you you're gonna like. I know how you bright girls like it done. Feel that?"

"Let me go, Herb. Cut it out. Stop. That hurts. I don't want to do this."

"Sure you do. Come on, gal."

"Stop calling me 'gal.' *Quit it.* I thought we were going to a movie."

"Let's get down to what you really want. I know *what*, and I know how to give it to you." He slammed himself against me, and I felt a protruding brick from the building punch into my shoulder. "That's it, fight a little. Love to feel 'em squirm. Wiggle all you want to, that's what makes me chug."

He kissed me again, wet and sticky on my chin. Somehow I drew in a breath and screamed. It was so dark, so awful dark, and the whole city smelled of mildew and rotten milk. I pushed at him, pounding him with my fists for all I was worth. Worse than any movie where the guy kisses the girl and she melts in his arms; this was a masher, doing far more than kissing me. I saw a shadow and heard footsteps approaching. "Help me!" I called.

Herb clamped his hand on my mouth. I felt his hand plunge between my legs, bunching my dress and ripping the skirt half from the bodice. I jerked at his hand on my mouth.

"No! Help me, somebody! Oh, God, make him stop!"

And just like that he did. Herb rose in the air momentarily and went backward, lifted and propelled by the uniformed arms of two men with MP bands around them. "Leave the lady alone," one of them said. "She ain't in the mood."

"Mind your own business," Herb said. He whisked his sleeves like he was brushing crumbs fallen from their hands. "Just one of the gals from the factory. You know how a bright gal likes it, kind of rough." He grinned his mildew smile at them. "She's just the *cleaning* gal, fellas."

The two Marines looked me over. "Don't look like she's bright to me," one of them said. And suddenly I knew what he meant. I thought he'd meant I was intelligent. He meant bright-colored.

I was mortified. Furious. "You—you moron! Wolf!"

The Marines looked from me to Herb Fontana. "We'll walk you home, miss."

Back at the apartment I locked my door and piled every scrap of furnishings against it. I even put the coffeepot on the stack. With a choice between Bill Scott or Herb Fontana, I'd picked swamp scum.

In the morning I looked at my face in the shiny metal handle on the door of the only cabinet in that tiny room and said the word "Negro" aloud to myself. I said it several times. I said "Nigra." Then I said "nigger." The word hit my ears like a blow by some unseen hand. "Never again," I said toward God, who now lived just above the ceiling in this room. "Why can't a person just be a person? If a red-haired man made a pass at a blond girl, would they hang him?" I shuddered so hard I thought I would fall down. Herb Fontana's hideous face kept flashing on my eyelids.

My feet felt like stumps. Light poured in through the venetian blinds. I crawled back into bed and closed my eyes, but I couldn't sleep. My head ached, but I had no aspirin, so I put my shoes back on and walked to the Rexall. I watched over my shoulder every step of the way.

"Help you, sugar?" Millie said. Millie was older than I, pretty but in a too-much-lipstick-and-mascara way. Mother would have said "cheap," but I wouldn't, not anymore.

"Have you lived here awhile?" I said, trying to look pleasant, not as desperate as I felt.

"Well, all my life, sugar. What's the beef?"

"Nothing. I just want a new job." *I want to change the world.* "Something men wouldn't want to do."

Millie stopped wiping for a minute. "Cooking, cleaning, having babies—they don't want to do those. They don't want to pay you to do 'em, either. That's why they invented marriage." She laughed. "What's a girl to do? If you got any money, you could go to beauty school. You know how important a girl feels when her hair looks nice? And how bad she feels when it doesn't?"

"That's it. I could work in the daytime and make people feel pretty." I went on, surprised at my own words. "I thought I'd go to college someday, but that isn't going to work out. If they'd let me pay on account, I could go. Do you know of a school like that?"

"ABC Beauty College on Griswold. I got a kid sister went there."

"Did she like it?"

"Sure."

"Does she make money? I need to make enough to live on and quit mopping floors."

"She got killed in an auto accident before she graduated."

"I'm sorry."

"Me, too. She was my best friend in the whole world. You got any sisters?"

"Yes. Two."

"Well, then you know what I mean."

I studied a sprinkling of sugar crystals on the counter next to the sugar dispenser in front of me. Millie didn't keep the place as nifty as Sylvia had. "I guess so. Thanks, Millie. On Griswold, you said? Up or down—I mean, right or left from here?"

By noon I was signed up. My heart thundered as I put my name at the bottom of the payment form. My plan was to work at the factory all night mopping and slopping, as far from Herb Fontana as possible, and go to ABC Beauty College during the day. I'd get done by fall and leave the factory behind. There was nothing unpatriotic about earning money, I didn't care what Congress said. If President Roosevelt were alive, he'd tell them all *nuts!* Fixing ladies' hair might not be law school, but it had to be better than mopping, maybe even better than assembling machine guns.

July brought unrelenting heat to San Diego. In the second week of August two bombs ended the Pacific war for good. Strange how anticli-

mactic, even inevitable it felt after the fall of Germany. After the surrender was signed, I dreamed that the yellow and orange demons who'd
been feasting on human flesh for the last ten years suddenly put down
their knives and forks and wiped their lips with damask napkins. By
September I was almost done with beauty school; men who had collected their service points started heading stateside. The rest stayed on
to form the Occupation force. I knew without a doubt that even my job
as a Negro would soon vanish.

ordon got up one summer morning and walked from his
mother's house to the trading post at Chinle. He hung
around there until the next day, hoping to come across one
of his uncles. Finally he asked the man who owned the post where
Archie Lefthand was. Archie was the janitor, the most dependable way
to get a message to people. He asked Archie to pass the word around
that he needed a job. Then he went back in the store. "I'm good at electric wiring and stuff. Radios—I can fix any kind of radio. I'm a veteran;
got my honorable discharge papers. You know anybody who needs a
radio fixed? I've got to work at something. Make some money." He had
to get out from under his mother's and uncle's friendly staring, get some
breathing room that didn't smell of sheep.

"We send it all to Gallup."

Gordon nodded. Then he started walking to Gallup. In three days
he was there. Along the way he'd had no luck finding food, and he was
hungrier than he could ever remember being. The first Navajo person
he found, he greeted. "Say, Hasteen, anybody around here got some
extra food? I'm looking for a job."

"Don't you speak Navajo?" the man said.

Gordon nodded and repeated the phrase in Navajo.

"No food here," he said. "Try over there." He jerked his head in the direction of a little diner.

He stood amid cans of garbage overflowing with flies and greasy paper and knocked. A fat, greasy-looking white woman opened the door. "Get lost, you!" she yelled. "I told you to quit coming around here or I'm going to call the police. Take off, or I'll get the shotgun."

"Lady, I haven't been here before. I'm looking for a job."

"That's it. I'm going for the gun."

B y summer's end I'd finished beauty school but found only a part-time job on the weekends. I couldn't get enough hours to make the money I needed to leave my mop and bucket behind. Every day it got harder to force myself to get dressed for my night job. The first night in October, though, when I showed up to clock in at Morrison Kellogg, there was an envelope in my card slot. Inside it was a pink piece of paper: *"Due to circumstances beyond our control, your position is no longer necessary to this company."* How did they think they were going to get by without someone cleaning up the mess every night? The next morning I showed up at Mr. Yount's office, to find he wasn't there anymore. Sue, who used to always hang around outside his office with a pencil stuck over her ear, said he'd gotten a promotion, so I was going to have to wait for a Mr. Taylor. A whole hour and fifteen minutes passed before he showed up. He got tight-looking around the neck when he saw me sitting there.

"Hello there, Mr. Taylor," I said. "Good morning."

"Good morning, little lady." His accent was from East Texas or northern Louisiana.

"I need this job, Mr. Taylor. I've got another part-time job, but it's only fifteen hours a week. I can't afford to get fired. You've got to have someone sweep and mop and do the bathrooms. You can't run this company without someone cleaning up."

"Oh, I know that, missy. It says your services are no longer needed. Can't you read?"

"I read just fine. Why did I get this note in my pay envelope? Are you saying I'm not doing a good job?"

"You'll find there's an extra two days' pay in there."

"You didn't answer my question."

"Well, aren't you the rude little gal? Y'all been away from home too long, lost all your manners? No wonder you ain't married yet. Skinny old maid like you without manners a-tall. Your mama ought to be ashamed."

"My mama has nothing to do with this." I walked back to the janitor's closet. Alfred was there, too, and he had an identical pink slip. Standing next to him were two young men. One had an obviously new tattoo on his forearm reading U.S. NAVY. The other said, "Say, boy, why don't you show us where the mops and stuff are kept? We just got jobs here."

"Yeah," the first said. "We're on the career path now. Gonna start at the bottom and make a clean sweep of things!" They laughed, patting each other on the back with loud smacks.

Sometimes, I've been told, God works in mysterious ways. By the time I'd gotten fired, I owed the beauty college two hundred dollars. I was a part-time beauty operator. I lived in a garage. I had almost no income at all. I should have been praying like crazy, or packing and walking to the bus station. Instead, I went to the movies.

It took a ten-block walk to get to the old theater where Gordon and I used to go. The matinee was thirteen cents, and I splurged on popcorn and a bottle of Coca-Cola that was so cold a little ring of frozen pop clung to the inside at the top and made it trickle out slow. It was the best thing I think I ever tasted in my life.

The show was an old one, though—*Jezebel* with Bette Davis and Henry Fonda. Bette Davis was Julie, a southern belle with a wild streak a mile wide and then some. For two entire hours I lived in another place and time.

It was still sunny when I stepped into the lobby; light streamed through the big glass doors. For a second I was a little girl again, my memory come to life. The lobby was red-carpeted, with shiny brass rails and chandeliers. As I studied the gilded plaster decoration on the ceiling, someone honked a car horn outside and the noise brought me back to the present. A help-wanted sign was tacked up next to the front door. I took a deep breath. I picked it up, went to the snack bar, and all at once I had a new job.

We ran an afternoon matinee every day except Sunday, and two on Saturday. My old friend Zoe from the plant worked there, too; we talked a lot about the old days, and we watched movies for free to our hearts' content. The double feature started at seven, and sometimes I wasn't out of there until midnight. The other ushers complained about that all the time, but it was so much easier than dragging that huge mop around all night that I thought I was in heaven. Part of the time we even got to put our feet up. After cutting hair all morning and mopping all night, that was wonderful. They gave us bags of popcorn after the matinee if there was some left so they'd have room for the fresh, and after the late show you could have all you wanted. I carried it home in my coat pockets by the bagful on the days I ran out of groceries before payday.

MR. ABREGOS HAD returned my mail to the post office; they tracked me down, miracle of miracles, and I started getting mail again. One day I got a string-wrapped bundle of letters the post office must have been saving. Amid the circulars and stuff came a terse letter from Mother, with a column saved from the newspaper on how to clip coupons to save money on groceries. That would do me worlds of good if I ever got to where I shopped for groceries anyplace besides the refreshment counter at the movie house.

Garnelle included at-home cards in her wedding invitations. She wrote to tell me that Danny had gotten a job as a shift boss at the mill, and he was chairman of the deacons at Siloam Springs. Garnelle got herself a new electric vacuum sweeper and a pop-up toaster that browned bread all over at once. She sent me two letters in one week detailing all her wonderful furniture and household things, plus a clipping from the paper's social page. *"Mr. and Mrs. Daniel Poquette have rented a new house on the road to Kirbyville,"* the column in the local paper said. *"Danny's smart in business, more than I ever realized,"* she wrote. *"I've got a gas stove with a heat shelf, and it's white porcelain. It's just beautiful. Everything comes out so perfect in it. Just the other day I made a custard pie."*

I stuffed a bite of supper into my mouth. Popcorn. I used to dream about it, smell it while rich kids ate it. Now I hated it, but it stopped my stomach from grumbling for a little while. Especially if I drank water and not sodas. What I wouldn't give for a piece of custard pie.

Gordon found a sign in the window of a Sanders, Arizona, hardware store that simply said WRANGLER NEEDED, SPRING ROUNDUP, SEE INSIDE. The work was hard—he'd forgotten the long days of roundups—but the food was plentiful, and it was provided in addition to small wages.

In the middle of roundup, John Ford's movie crew came through Four Corners with a company doing some fill-in shots. He needed Indians who could ride horses and fall off them convincingly, he said. It was their second trip to the reservation in as many months. On Sunday, when he had a day off, Gordon stood in line to top off a slue-footed mare. He promptly hit the dirt, and after dusting himself off he approached the director. "Sir, I don't ride too good. But falling off? That I do convincingly, sir."

The man looked at him. "Go over there and get into makeup and costume. Do like you're told, and we'll give you fifty dollars. Can you read English?"

"Sir, I was a radio technician in the Marine Corps. I read pretty good."

"Well, then. Maybe we'll give you some lines to say. You yell it in Cheyenne, if you know how."

"No, sir. I don't speak Cheyenne."

"Oh. Anyone here speak real Cheyenne?"

The line of Navajo men around shook their heads. One of them laughed. For a moment Gordon saw the chance of making fifty extra dollars slipping out of his grasp. "I speak real Navajo, sir. It sounds just like Cheyenne. There's only a few words different. No one will really know except another Navajo talker, and there's not too many of those. Everybody goes to regular white school now."

"That so? Navajo sounds just like Cheyenne?" The men in line nodded enthusiastically. "You, you, and you, old man there, go to that tent. The rest of you can wait over there as extras. You'll be given costumes if we need you. We might need some bigger crowds."

"When do I get the fifty dollars?" Gordon said.

Cowboy pictures. The week before Thanksgiving we ran them every show. It was better than "gumshoe week" by a mile, but I was in the mood for something funny, and I was tired of heroes who got their courage from killing each other and thousands of Indians. I wanted Cary Grant to knock my socks off being witty and dashing and kissable and charmingly stumbling. Friday after Thanksgiving they opened with a new one at the one o'clock matinee, but not a soul showed up. Since Mr. Peabody was paying Rory, the projectionist, and two usherettes, Zoe and me, he made Rory run the picture in case someone came in late.

I sat right in the middle of the best loge seats upstairs, thinking about maybe quitting this job. I was finally getting enough clients that I could pay my rent from my beauty operator job, and I could work more hours if I quit ushering. The salon was a long walk from my apartment, but there was an apartment right over the shop for rent. It was really cheap, but if I smelled of sulfur from permanent waves drifting up from the salon, I'd be fired from the movie theater. I dropped my flashlight.

"Ssshhhh!" Rory hissed from the booth overhead. "Keep it down, you!" He laughed.

I found the flashlight and pointed it right back at the booth into his eyes. Rory was a pimply kid who I suspected cut classes to work here. He snuck chocolate bars from the counter and ate them like they were going out of style. My mother would have accused him of having diabetes and a tapeworm, and given him one of her diarrhea-inducing tonics to cure that habit. I turned the other way—I could be fired for not telling on him—but I was so hungry myself I couldn't blame him. If they'd been giving away extra candy bars, I would have been first in line. I just couldn't steal them.

"Knock that off!" Zoe yelled from the floor-level seats directly below me. "I'm trying to watch this picture. It's the only time I'll ever get to sit and enjoy it straight through, and you two monkeys are messing it all up."

"Sorry," I whispered over the balcony rail. At that second I looked at the screen, pretending to pay close attention. The camera closed in on a terrific Indian battle. By this time I knew from Gordon how fake it all was, so I was barely registering what was going on. Then I noticed the face of one of the Indians. He was yelling with a rifle held over his head in one hand, holding a dagger maliciously in the other. He had curious scars across his ribs and one arm. Movie people rarely paid attention to their Indians; heck, the Beautiful Indian Maiden in this story was some actress with blue eyes and a phony black wig. But this Indian shouting at the camera had long, sleek, black hair that didn't look fake. He had eyes that looked like they came from the past and saw into the future. *Gordon.* The soldiers were fussing about the "Cheyenne," but the Indians in the picture had to be Navajos. I left the balcony and went to the lobby.

"Hey, cover the snack bar, will you?" Mr. Peabody said. "I'm going to the can. I'll be upstairs if you need me, in the office."

"Sure," I said. I put my head on the counter and sighed hard. I felt so lost.

The next weekend it looked like rain. The Friday-afternoon matinee had just filled up with rowdy little boys wearing iron six-guns and knotted kerchiefs around their necks when I closed the magenta curtains to return to the popcorn counter. As I went to get a new box of corn kernels, I tipped over the tin of salt, dumping the whole thing on the floor. I sat beside the pile of white salt crystals, and a sound like a single deep sob came from my chest without warning.

A voice said, "Why so blue? Was it the way I said my lines?"

"Sorry," I mumbled, grabbing a great wad of paper napkins and drying my face. Through the leaves of white paper I saw him. "Gordon," I said.

He nodded. "I'm an actor. Like Clark Gable. They paid me fifty dollars to yell 'This director has got rocks in his head!' and we got to massacre and pillage and squeal like little girls."

"I thought I'd never see you— What are you— That was *you*? I mean, I *thought* it— It looked like you. They shot you, and I couldn't—" I wanted to throw my arms around him. *Remember, he's the one who came and kissed you and threw you away.* It was a feeling I had grown used to, but it was a lot easier to feel it without him in front of me. "Look at your hair!" I finally said.

He turned and touched it. "You like it? You know, they got Mexican and Jewish guys in women's wigs and headbands reading all the important lines. Except that one. I got a close-up and everything."

"It's really . . . Indian."

"The real thing. Can we go somewhere and talk?"

"I have to mind the counter. Gordon?"

"Mm-mm." He stood, looking uncomfortable, studying the candy in the case.

Why did you hurt me; what are you doing here; why am I so lonely I can't think of anyone but you; what do you really want; are you here to hurt me again? "So, um, did you grow your hair out for the movie?"

"No. It was a personal thing. You see . . . well."

" 'Cause I just got through with beauty school. Cut hair part-time." I laughed nervously.

"I called that town where you lived, and the telephone operator told me you went to California. She said you'd gone right back to where you were before. She asked me if I wanted to talk to your parents, but I said no. I figured if I came back to this neighborhood I might find you. The apartment manager told me how to get here."

"So . . . why? Why go to all that trouble to find me?"

"I thought—I believed I couldn't live on the reservation with you, that we were too different. What I found was that I couldn't live there without you."

"So you think I've been waiting for you all this time?"

He didn't answer. Looked hard at the carpet. "No. I mostly intended to apologize. To tell you I'd realized I was wrong. Sometimes I— I feel sometimes like I'm not Navajo anymore, yet I'm supposed to feel everything the old people do. On the reservation so many people are starving to death. Even the veterans can't get work. Can't even get the handouts the government promised. Can't get nothing. I ate garbage from somebody's trash cans in Gallup."

I made a racket with the popcorn maker, positioning myself behind it as if in defense. "You expect me to feel sorry for you? I was supposed to have a husband and a house and a family by now. Maybe a car and a—a dog, too. I waited for you and prayed for you and dreamed about you, and . . . I wrote you a hundred letters, and you never answered one. And you dumped me like a hot potato."

"I don't want you to feel sorry for me. I'm trying to say I thought I was meant to stay there. But I'm not. I can't live there at all."

"So you've finally got room for me, is that it?"

He thought for a moment, smiled. "I'll bet you cried when they shot me in the movie."

"You don't know that." I *loved* you, you dope.

"Do you work here every day?"

"Except Sunday."

"Can I come see you here?"

"It doesn't cost anything to come through the front door."

"I mean, *see* you."

"I guess."

That evening, getting ready to go home, I opened the bin under the popcorn maker. I ate garbage before it even got to the trash can.

HE CAME EVERY DAY. Sometimes he got work picking up scrap at construction sites. In less than three weeks I went back to the hilly shore with Gordon. We pooled our meager money; Gordon picked out two tomatoes and an orange for each of us, and a small package of saltines. We watched the waves without talking for a long time, wrapped in coats, a blanket over our legs.

As the sun started to go down, he stared intently ahead. "You don't make kites anymore?"

"I never have paper. When Garnelle lived here, we shared expenses."

"You don't eat too good sometimes."

"I guess I don't eat too good most times."

"This lunch is the same as you shared with me once."

"I hope that's not the only one you remember."

"It is."

He didn't remember the sandwiches I trimmed the edges of? The cupcakes with icing made into curlicues with a spoon so carefully? "Why?"

"All the other lunches you had plenty. It's easy to share when you have plenty. That one you and Garnelle had—this was all you had, and

294

I could see that. I remember this lunch because I first saw you on the inside. I think I began to love you right then."

"I don't think people who have plenty share that easily."

"Maybe not. You didn't ask if I needed food or had more than you did. You said 'sit.'"

"I gave you an order and you had to obey, huh?"

"Hey, I'm a good Marine."

"So how come when I was there alone you ignored me?"

"I didn't think we knew each other well enough to talk alone. You know, for your reputation."

My reputation, dingy as it was? "Look at that sky," I said. "It's glorious."

"My mother said you can live in her house anytime you want."

I turned to look at him. "Well, thanks . . . I guess. Why?"

"She heard about you and Big Bill Tsosie's sheep. He skint you good—fifteen dollars for one old sheep—and then you gave it to some little kids and you didn't have any more. Stuff like that gets around faster than anything. Uncle Bill said it was a woman with hair like a sunset in the rainy month, and the boss in the store said her name was something like Cold Water. I knew it was you."

"How did she hear about that?"

"One thing Navajos do real good is talk. It's our national pastime, like baseball. So she said, 'Maybe this Cold Water Woman isn't so bad for a white woman. Maybe you should think about that instead of being sad all the time.' I told her your name was Winter Morning."

"She told you to look for me?"

"Yeah." He picked up a handful of sand and gravel, sifting it through his fingers until only small pebbles and bits of broken shells remained in his hand. He piled that to the side of his right knee and picked up another handful, holding it. "There's old folk around who think only bad things about white people. They've never known any but the bad ones."

"Sometimes people aren't intentionally bad. Just ignorant."

He shrugged. "Ignorant people with power. Happens a lot."

A thickening in my chest made me sit up. I nodded, putting a slice of tomato on my last cracker.

Gordon brushed at something on my chin and smiled. "I've got news; I got a job today. Found Corporal Beattie—Judson Beattie. A guy I used to share a tent and a Betty Grable poster with. He's in Carmel. He's opened up an electrical business, wiring up houses. He's got more work than he can handle, and he says I can start Monday. I can be an apprentice, then a journeyman. Just have to buy a couple of tools. By next month I can support . . . us."

"Us?"

"If you're still interested in the husband and family. I know where I can get a pretty good dog."

"With long ears?"

"The husband or the dog?" He dropped the handful of sand.

"I'm not picky."

He nodded, and smiled broadly. His cheek made that slight dimple. "I'll get you money for groceries as soon as I get paid."

"You're not asking if I need it or want it?"

"No. Make a list. Get a newspaper if you want, so we can fly a kite. I'll find you some sticks."

I QUIT THE movie theater the day after Gordon made good on his promise for the groceries. I hung around the salon, picking up walk-in clients and answering the phones. We talked about weddings one afternoon. I told him about girls at the factory that walked down to the justice of the peace on their lunch breaks and got married. All I cared about was being connected to Gordon, permanently and quickly. He didn't stand much on ceremony either, and he said in his hometown, weddings were sometimes as simple as telling your family you wanted to marry so-and-so, then moving your clothes to your new house. He said if I ever got tired of him, all I had to do was put his shoes outside, and when he came home he'd know it meant to start walking. Of course, I'd never do that.

The day before my wedding I wrote a sincere letter to Mother and

Daddy telling them about my plans. I bought myself a peach-colored dress with a silk flower at the waist. It had white cloth tucked in like little petals at the shoulders, and a tiny, pearly button at the base of each petal.

On the way to the justice of the peace at the county courthouse, we stopped, and Gordon bought me half a dozen white roses. We stood in line behind three other couples, and it was over just like that. I thought about Deely and Wilbur, standing at the pulpit in Siloam Springs Baptist church. About what Mother might have said to me on the day of my wedding. I wanted to put them all completely out of my memory, but I couldn't. I longed for them to be here with me, to celebrate and make a cake and throw rice.

A couple of weeks later as we sat down to supper one night, Gordon stared at his plate without moving. "What's wrong?" I said.

He shook his head. "Frosty, I never thought I'd refuse any food, because I know what it's like to starve. But I . . . can't eat this."

"I thought you liked pork chops."

"I do. It's not the pork chops. It's the rice. It's like having a mouthful of maggots."

I ran from that place, down the street toward the factory, pressing my feet hard into the sidewalk. People stared at me in my apron, so I whipped it off, crumpling it, sopping my face with it. After a while I was so exhausted I had to go back. I'd never love him again, I knew that. This had been a colossal mistake. All that remained was to get a divorce.

When I got back to the apartment, I avoided his eyes.

"Where did you go?" he said. "I couldn't catch you, couldn't find you." He laughed nervously.

I gritted my teeth. "I have never—in my entire life—heard anything so nasty. When did you ever have a mouthful of maggots?"

"I'm really sorry I said that. All the rice was just getting to me."

"You never said anything about it before now. How come it's different tonight?"

"It's not different. I thought I could stand it if it was only once a month or so, but, Frosty, you fix rice five or six days a week. I hate rice."

"It's what I've always had," I said. "You want potatoes instead, all you had to do was ask!"

"I don't like potatoes either."

"A balanced meal has to have a starch group. How are you going to get your starch group? I've studied it in Home Ec class. There are your four food groups, and we're supposed to eat them all."

"Who says? The pork chops are real good. And really, I'm sorry I said that. Sorry."

"I'm going to bed."

"Go ahead." He turned away from me. So I cried myself to sleep, and he sat on the kitchen chair—only two feet away from the bed, but the gulf between us felt like a valley of live alligators.

Deep into the night I awoke, still wearing my dress and socks, to a scuffling sound. I reached over the bed for the string on the light. "Gordon?" He was writhing in the floor; then he sat up quickly, flailing at the air, looking about as if he were lost. "Gordon, what is it? Are you sick? Say something."

He said on the edge of the bed, drenched in sweat. He unbuttoned his shirt and waved the sides of it to cool himself. "I dreamed I was back there, held by the Japanese. They gave me rice still boiling from the pans. When they held the bowl to my face, it was soured and full of maggots with little black heads. They jammed it in my mouth, hot like that, and put a rag in too, so I'd have to swallow it all. They watched and laughed. When I vomited was when they cut me."

My heart shuddered. "This was a dream?"

He sat like a stone for a long time. Finally he said, "It was a memory."

"Come here," I said, holding out my arms.

"I'm not a child. Or an old woman."

I saw the muscles in his chin tighten. "You're a soldier whose wife won't ever cook rice again. And I need you to hold me." I rested my cheek against his neck and whispered, "I love you, Gordon." We slept with the light on, but I woke every few minutes, it seemed, to make sure he was sleeping soundly.

FOR TWO MONTHS we crowded into my egg-crate apartment. I cut hair four mornings a week at a shop eight blocks from Lomita. Gordon bought a car so he could drive me to work and go from job to job. Judson Beattie, Gordon's friend, figured out a way to build himself a house in a new development that opened up, and they were going to work together and build us one, too. Only the bank manager took one look at Gordon and me and told us they were out of the home-loan business, "even for GIs. Sorry. You'll have to go elsewhere." Gordon accepted that, as if it happened to him all his life. After finding out, Judson and his wife, Anne, went with us to the bank and signed affidavits on the man's desk about how we were decent people, how he needed his chief electrician to live near the business office. He didn't mention that their office consisted of one end of their kitchen dinette. So the bank loaned us money for a house. We moved in and rolled around in it like marbles in a shoebox for weeks.

There were times when I was home alone and all was quiet except for the sounds of new houses being built a block or two away. I read a lot of magazines, and one day I saw an article in *Life* on "the poor in America." Under the title was a picture of a house that looked like my home in Sabine. *Poor? It was better than the boxcar.* I closed the magazine and looked around the room at my beautiful white walls, at the upright Frigidaire holding Coca-Colas and tonight's meat loaf. I may have been sitting on an apple crate, but we had a porcelain toilet, and there were no possums in the roof or copperheads under the porch. It wasn't until now that I began to understand the depths of what must have been my parents' despair. Suddenly I felt as if I needed to get outside these plain white walls.

Every day on my way to work I walked past Browning's Bargains and Second Hand. It was in a line of stores with hand-painted signs, shabby fronts, and dim lights inside. I'd never been in them, preferring to browse empty-handed through Woolworth's and Montgomery Ward and dream of things I might someday have. My feet carried me to Browning's, it seemed, in defiance of my own pride. It smelled of mice. Dust. Old cigarette smoke. Used clothes were piled on tables made of planks and sawhorses. An old Victrola supported a tray of glass trinkets positioned to catch the single beam of light from the front window. I spent an hour mentally making a list of things and prices. Garnelle and I should have tried this place, I thought. There was a perfectly good coffee table—better, at least, than suitcases and a board. I moved an old racoon coat off a chair and sat in it to test the springs. That was when I noticed that on the coffee table was a cigar box marked "All 50 cents—piece." Old jewelry, single earrings, broken watches, odd sparkling things were all jumbled together. Underneath a cameo pin with a huge crack down its face I saw the tines of a hair comb. I pulled it out and held my breath. It was not the same as the one I'd lost—my mother's only treasure from so long ago—but it could have been a cousin to it. This one had twelve blue-gray pearls, not graduating sizes, but all the same, all in a row. I felt in my pocket. Thirty-eight cents. I'd planned to buy a soda before I went home. I found the only person in the store, an old man reading a paper, smoking, sitting behind a glass counter full of chipped statuettes. "Mister?" I said. "This comb is fifty cents?"

"No. That's in the wrong box. It's supposed to be a dollar—dollar fifty."

I suddenly felt like I was buying a sheep in the high desert of Arizona. "Everything in here is covered with dust. Business isn't very good. I'll give you thirty cents."

"What are you, a thief? A vagabond? Come in just to insult me?"

"No one's in here shopping but me, and it's late afternoon. Thirty cents."

"You got thirty cents?" He held out his hand.

"Have we got a deal?" I put my hands on my hips.

He rolled his eyes and made a gesture toward the ceiling like he was reiterating some long-standing argument with God. "For this I work night and day, to have cutthroats come in my shop and steal my merchandise. All right, lady. We got a deal."

I hid it in my sock drawer, next to the dimes.

BEFORE LONG WE bought ourselves a brand-new blue-and-yellow-flowered divan. We sat on it for a long time that evening, just thinking. All at once—as if it were the most normal thing in the world—he said, "Let's visit our families. I want you to meet my relatives."

I caught my breath. "Someday, sure."

"You don't want to go?"

"Oh, sure enough I do. After things slow down at the shop."

He nodded. I watched his face. He said, "I have a chance to get an extra job this weekend. Six hours or so. Maybe we can get some bedroom furniture. A frame to put the mattress on."

In the morning he kissed me good-bye and said, "Got to make some money for my honey to spend." I could hear him whistling as he backed the car down the drive.

Watching him pull away, I lingered at the open door. I put aside all thoughts of seeing any of our relatives, going back to visit our pasts. Without those things, I had never felt so ultimately happy, so warm inside. I sighed deeply. We owned nothing but a mortgage and a divan, but we had so much more than our things. Sitting on the divan, I flipped through a magazine while I watched the hands turn on the clock until nine. I called my doctor's office. The doctor said if I was going to travel, I'd better do it now, because in a couple of months he would advise against a long car trip. We were going to have a baby.

I stepped out onto the slab of concrete by our back door, which we grandly called our "patio"—nobody had porches here in California. Trucks and loud machines with scratched yellow noses barreled around each other in a strange dance of new life. The sky was a shade of blue I'd never seen before. My heart had suddenly enveloped the earth. My soul clung to the sky. I held my arms, grasping my elbows tightly, hugging my baby.

There were no clouds. The day would be warm. Just a few more minutes until I had to get my nurse's shoes on, the ones I wore to do hair. Gordon had put white polish on them last night and left them on a newspaper by the door. On the toe of one of my shoes a red-and-black bead of a ladybug arched her wings, clamping them under red glass shells that parted in the center. She must have flown in when I opened the door. I picked up the shoes and watched her fly away.

For four hours I made marcels in old ladies' hair and thought of how to tell Gordon the news. That afternoon I made a cake from a recipe I got from one of the operators at the salon. I set the table using my thumb to measure the forks and knives one inch from the edge. I laid out napkins. I made fried chicken with ground red pepper in the flour—hot, the way we liked it. A sound at the door made my heart jump, but it was only the mailman.

The mail was a circular from May Company and one other envelope: a letter from Mrs. Wilbur Fielding—Deely—addressed to Frosty Summers. No "Miss," no "Mrs." I stuck it in my apron pocket. No one from Sabine had written me since I wrote to tell Mother I married Gordon. Deely was certainly trying to make a point of some kind. I mulled over what it might contain while I peeled potatoes and diced them against my thumb, dropping the cubes and pyramids of potato into boiling water.

Odd, Gordon mentioning families, and now this. I would wait to open it until he got home. Anything Deely had to say to me would be easier once he was here. *She's not going to ruin this day,* I thought, and checked the clock.

Four-thirty came and went. I turned the burners off. I turned them back on. Five. Five-thirty. I turned off the burners and dished up the food onto plates, trying to avoid the scorched bottom of the carrots. I opened a piece of tinfoil that I had cleaned and saved in a drawer, wrapped it over Gordon's plate, and set it in the oven. At eight o'clock I sat in front of my plate and started picking at food, but after three bites I lost my appetite. I washed the pots and pans. Dried them, instead of letting them air dry like usual. I closed the drapes. When I sat again at my place, staring at the plate of cold food, I crossed my ankles and heard the paper in my pocket make a noise. I took out the letter and leaned it against the salt shaker.

At eight-thirty I called the Beatties' phone number. Anne told me her husband had been home for two hours, even though they'd worked late that evening. Judson was taking a bath. She went and asked him for me, but he didn't know where Gordon was. I covered my plate again and put it in the oven next to Gordon's. At nine I opened Deely's envelope.

"Frosty," it began. "Not sure if you care or not, but a person ought to know. Your Mother has a brain tumor. Sincerely Yours, Mrs. Fielding." I let out my breath. I felt as if dense cotton batting had been stuffed into my brain. I didn't cry, but I couldn't breathe. I should have waited for Gordon. I put the letter down and, doing it, tipped over the salt shaker. I pushed the salt around in little paths on the Formica with a finger. Covering up the gold glitter flakes, my finger traced and piled the salt. I heard a sound at the back door and glanced at the clock. Nine forty-five.

Gordon dropped his work belt near the washing machine, instead of hanging it on the wall as usual. He stayed there, in the dark, for five full minutes, making no sound at all. I pushed the salt into a trail that went around in a spiral. "Gordy?" I called.

"Yeah."

"Are you coming in?"

"Just a minute. Yeah. In a minute."

I sat frozen at the table. My ankles curled around the legs of the chair. My knees quivered. I called out, trying to sound cheery, "Gordon? Come on. I have dinner saved in the oven for you." Getting the plates calmed my nerves. I poured water into a glass and commenced the usual war of wills with the ice-cube tray from the icebox. It seemed dark in here. I went to the living room and turned on the lamp that sat on the floor—where someday we hoped to put an end table—next to the divan. Even with the kitchen lights on it cast strange, elongated shadows on the wall, clownish and spooky at once. "Gordy? Everything all right?" My words stopped short at the sight of him. I sucked in my breath.

"I'm not hungry. I'll eat it tomorrow."

"What is going on? Why are you so late?"

"We had to stay to finish the job. They were supposed to give us another day, but the job boss said to get it done today or he wouldn't pay. Then Judson comes to me and says how he's got this new job that starts the day after tomorrow. Only *I* should take a few weeks off. Well, I can't, I told him. I've got bills to pay. And he says he's real, real sorry, but I can't work on this one job. It's nothing personal, but he had to guarantee an all-white crew or lose the job. And I said he should have told them to take a hike, but he said it's business. Just business. That was when I popped him in the mouth."

"Oh, Gordon. What did he do?"

"He got mad. Told me I was fired. I've lost my job."

I closed my eyes, squeezing out the dim light. When I opened them, images of the shadows on the wall and the filaments in the lightbulb combined into monsters with glowing innards overlaying everything I saw. "Apologize. Call him. We'll go over there and apologize. I made a cake. We'll take it. You can tell him you'll take the three weeks off. We can make it as long as you can work again after that. Please. Apologize."

"It's not that easy. This all happened in front of the whole crew. He's not likely to let me back; if he did, it'd mean losing their respect. It's like in the Marines. You mess up, you're done."

I said, "But no. *No.*" Something I hadn't felt in many, many months came over me—that clawing pain in my side, a demon's teeth and toenails hooked into me. "Judson and Anne are our friends. Please call. I'll call." I rushed to the telephone.

Gordon's hand reached over my shoulder and held down the receiver while I was dialing. "That's not all. I've already spent the money I made. There isn't any left. Everything seemed to be going all right. I thought I'd get paid next week just like always, and I could pay the house payment out of that. There isn't any money left."

"What did you buy? Take it back. You can take things back and get your money."

"Not this. It's too late. I was so foolish. I'm so sorry." He sat at the dining table, defeat pushing down his shoulders. He seemed physically smaller than I remembered.

I took the tinfoil from his plate and mine. One of the pieces ripped in half. A symbol of our waste. I would save it anyway, roll the torn sides together and pinch them to make a seam. Something was still missing from his story. "Gordon? How come you're so late?"

"I told you."

"I called Anne Beattie. Judson was home by six-thirty. Where have you been?"

He didn't speak for a minute, holding his lower lip against his teeth, his eyes closed. "I went . . . I got crazy. I went to a bar—thought I'd get drunk. Maybe start a fight and somebody'd kill me. You could have the GI insurance money. At least dead I'd be worth something."

I struggled to keep control. "How could you think that? That I'd rather have money than you? We can make it. We can."

"I've done a terrible thing to you. Talked you into marrying me. This is no way for you to live. I've seen the way people look down at you when they realize we are together. I've seen . . . the way they look. That bank teller, saying we couldn't even have a GI loan, which I was promised, and looking at you like you were—" He dropped his head into his hands.

"Stop." The phone rang. I left the table and answered it. Facing the wall, I said, "Hello?"

"This is Judson, Frosty. Is Gordy around?"

"Yes," I said.

"He's not still PO'd, is he?"

I glanced at my husband. "I don't think so."

"Everything okey-dokey there?"

I cleared my throat. "Yes."

"He tell you he cleaned my clock?"

"I'm sorry."

"So am I. Listen, I know it's late. You two going to be up for another half hour or so? We'd like to come over."

"Sure."

"Keep the porch light on. We'll bring the coffee."

"Sure enough," I said. And hung up. I went back to the dining table. The salt was still in the spiral I'd made. "So did you?"

305

Gordon said, "Did I what?"

"Get drunk?"

He laughed shortly and shook his head. "No. If I'd been in uniform, they might have served me, but not like this. I figured if I couldn't get into the bar, I'd have a heck of a time getting some fool to kill me. And if I really got drunk, I might forget why I came and fight back. So I just sat in front of it. Waiting. I don't know what for. Waiting until I had the courage to go home, I guess."

"Do you want this heated up? The carrots have about had it."

"I just can't eat. I'm sorry. It all looks—you went to a lot of trouble. Flowers on the table and everything. And chocolate cake. Is—is there some occasion I've ruined?"

"Judson and Anne are on their way over."

"Why?"

"I don't know. And we're going to have a baby."

He scratched his head thoughtfully. "Oh, Frosty." He came to me and held me. The doorbell rang.

GORDON DROVE BESIDE ME, patiently holding the steering wheel, now and then changing gears with a methodical motion of his hand. We had a two-year-old Plymouth with beige-and-green seats and wide whitewall tires. It was smooth, buttery yellow outside, and we packed it full of little gifts for people. Judson and Anne had been so understanding. They cheered with us over the news of the baby, and Judson said, "No wonder you were so panicked. You should have said something." Gordon squeezed my hand tenderly, holding it between both his hands. And Judson promised Gordon his job back in three weeks. But he loaned us a hundred dollars until then. "Not a loan. Just an advance," he said. "Business has been good." And he had a second piece of cake.

They stayed until eleven. While we talked, I mentioned I'd just learned that Mother was sick. Gordon immediately said, "I'll take you to see her"——in front of them, so there wasn't any way I could say anything but yes.

On the road we sang to entertain ourselves. He knew a verse and a half of "Johnny Got a Zero" and sang them repeatedly, laughing when he got to the middle of the second verse and started back at the beginning. I taught him the words to "We'll Work 'Til Jesus Comes." Then he sang the Marine Corps hymn in Navajo. "Did you know that song saved the world?" he said.

I remembered him saying "it's a language thing." I'd seen enough war movies to think the song was probably a secret code that the soldiers used. "I believe it," I told him.

"Someday," he said, "when it's safe and long past, I'll be able to tell you what it means."

Sometimes I watched the land surging toward us and imagined that the wheels under the car were big cogs in a machine that was pulling the road through like sheets of black tar. Now and then I'd just watch Gordon. We were stopping in Arizona to see his family on the way. All I saw in my mind were movie Indians in feathers sitting in a circle under the skins of a tepee. I couldn't bring myself to ask him what it might really be like. I didn't try to think what it would be like to walk into my parents' house either.

We ate hamburgers in Flagstaff. From Route 66, past Winslow, Arizona, Gordon turned north on a paved road with no name or marking on it. After about five miles he slowed again, turning west on a gravel road, at the end of which was a gas station and a little place that billed itself "Moccasin Mac's Café."

"These two buildings," Gordon said, "are a town called Wolf Creek. You don't want to eat at that café, though. It's just for mail."

I laughed, nodded, but couldn't talk. It wasn't as if I hadn't seen Arizona before. But I hadn't seen it at all——always intent on where I was going rather than where I was at the moment.

Driving through this strange and wide land, I breathed with my mouth open. I held the armrest on the door with burning fingers, afraid

307

of the emptiness of the sky around me. It was like seeing a shaved dog. Naked earth. Too much distance. The whole place looked vulnerable. In need of trees. So red. I wondered if the term "red man" had come from the soil more than the skin. There was nothing red about Gordon's skin. But the ground here reminded me of old blood. It made me shiver, deep in my core.

He turned the automobile onto a dirt road—a trail, really—with the same confidence he'd shown turning into the parking lot at Von's groceries on Coast Road near our house. After a few miles of bumping along, he stopped. We waited as dirt settled around the car.

We'd come to rest in front of a small brown building, familiar and odd at the same time. I had called them mud huts once. To my surprise we walked past it to a square, yellow-painted wood house, with two concrete steps in front of the door. Gordon's mother and aunts waited inside. But we did not knock. We stood at the foot of the steps, and he stretched his arms and said, "That was a long trip!" He patted his stomach and said, louder, "Some folks are real hungry. I hope these people are expecting company and made plenty of stew." He winked at me. "I hope they're looking out the window curtains at this Winter Morning, Cold Water, *nozhoni* woman and think she looks pretty hungry."

The curtains jerked to life, the door opened, and three short, heavy women descended the steps, circling us, patting our arms and shoulders, smiling, all talking at once. I smiled, too. The women wore their hair in buns, exactly like Grandma Summers. They wore calico blouses and plain wide skirts, gathered up at the waist around their heavy middles. The only thing they wore that would not ordinarily have been found in Sabine were heavy silver and turquoise bracelets on both wrists, like cuffs; they were wide and intricate and expensive-looking, as if they had dressed up for the occasion.

"Come in, Hashke, come in this house. This is the bride! This is the Cold Water woman. Oh, Hashke and Cold Water, eat something, eat something!" They surrounded us like a covey of little brown hens, pushing us all through the door, practically at once.

Inside, the place was spare but clean. Linoleum on the floor, woodstove in the corner. Barely different from many a place I'd seen in Sabine, converted and modernized but basically the same, standing on the same spot since *that* land was taken from those Indians.

Gordon's mother served us Coca-Colas, straight from bottles that had been kept on ice for us. "Hashke, you cut your hair," she said to him as she presented the Coke.

He nodded at me and said, "It's a nickname, like calling someone 'Shorty.' " Then, to his mother, he said, "Had to get a job in California. I didn't want to be a movie star forever. Too much trouble."

They all laughed. "Cold Water is polite. She'd make a pretty good Indian," she said again.

"Not too bad," he said, smiling at me.

His mother dished up lamb stew and some kind of fried biscuits, and the four of them talked and talked until I felt sedated by the food and the sound of their voices. Soft. Gentle. Now and then they'd break into Navajo, and I'd lose the gist of what they were saying, or they'd make some comment about something that happened to someone they all knew and laugh. It was no different from sitting at the steps of the courthouse and listening to the old men chattering away or at the WMU receptions full of ladies reminiscing about folks they knew, people who'd moved or died or married.

His hand pushed me; I lifted my head from the wall. "I'm so sorry. I didn't mean to fall asleep," I said.

"We can go to sleep in here," he said, nodding toward a door.

"Where are they, your family?"

"Gone to bed. They said you must be tired. Aunt Gladys said you look like you need to buy some pretty cloth."

I stood and fumbled with my feet; one of them had gone numb. "Where are they? In this room?"

"Out in the hogan. They said they will sleep there tonight, and you and I can have the bed in here. They have some puppies in the hogan that need to have people around."

"Oh. Puppies."

"Come on, sleepyhead."

"Why should I buy cloth? Don't they like my clothes?"

"No, Frosty. She could tell you were pregnant, by the way you walked and fell asleep. Pretty cloth for a cradle board. They were all tickled about it. Tomorrow you get to meet the whole clan. By the time the sun is up, they will all know."

"Are we going to have a cradle board?"

"No. But we can get a pretty cloth blanket."

By midmorning the next day people had accumulated in the house and yard of Gordon's mother like leaves blown up in a wind. They brought meat and breads, sodas, ice in a big iron tub, boxes and bales of hay draped with beautiful handwoven blankets to sit on. Little kids were running everywhere. Old ladies sat in circles and talked, fanning themselves. Not understanding the language, I could still tell that everyone was having a good time. They were dressed in marvelous clothing, bright-colored long dresses and shirts. The men wore cowboy boots, and everyone, even the tiniest child, wore heavy jewelry. Some people looked at me suspiciously or curiously, but most smiled and held out a soda or spoke to me, waving their hands, to which I could only nod and smile. Gordon's mother came to me and said, "Now, you can call me Bernice. You can be my daughter-in-law. Come and make me some bread."

What could I do but follow her? Very slowly, she showed more than told me how to do this bread. So I copied her hands, side by side, under the watchful eyes of about twenty other women, all laughing and sometimes nodding at me. After a while the process grew hot and tiring, dropping what looked to me like beignets into hot lard, time after time, watching hers puff just right and mine swell up like balloons. They nodded with appreciation at Bernice's bread. Every time one of my little fritters would swell and pop, women would sigh audibly. Finally we had huge bowlsful of the breads, and when we appeared with them in our arms, children and dogs rushed at us, the men on their heels.

All the other women had been cooking, too. They'd made stew and chili beans and had bowls of tomatoes and cantaloupe and peaches, then more pans of stuff I didn't recognize. We used the breads for plates, and now I could see how having it come out flat and chewy was the object.

People who got the ones I made had to break the top and pile the food inside it, hoping it wasn't too brittle to survive a bite or two before it crumbled.

The men all stayed in one place in the shade of the house, the women clustered in the shade of trees nearby. The children swarmed everywhere. A few young people, who ignored the children completely, mingled together. Those had to be the unmarried ones, young men making time with girls, just like after-church socials, boys hanging around hoping a girl'd go for a walk to watch the sun set. After people got down to eating in earnest, I searched the men for Gordon.

When I finally saw him, it was at the table—an old door suspended on two barrels—where the food was laid. He was talking to a woman, standing in front of her; all I could see of her was long hair and a magenta skirt. He nodded and turned around, a pleased look on his face, and walked over to one of the old men carrying slices of cantaloupe in both hands. I watched him, in case he looked for me. Then I glanced back at the table, and I saw the young woman he'd been talking to. I saw her eyes follow him, haltingly, as if denying to herself what was so plainly on her face. And that face. How truly beautiful a girl she was, even-featured, with perfect eyes and chin, her glistening hair thick and radiant in the sun. For a moment I was filled with panic as I saw him approaching me, with her close behind. When he introduced us, I tried to greet her the way Gordon had taught me, but she laughed and said, "I speak English."

Na'atlo'ii. It sounded a bit like "Natalie" when Gordon said it. An old friend from school. "Oh," I said. "School? Nice to make your acquaintance."

"Don't worry," she said, laughing, "that was a long time ago."

Still, I saw what was in her eyes. As she walked away from us, Gordon knelt by my hay bale. "My mother wants us to live here," he said. "She's asked me about six times today. Offered to set you up with your own herd of sheep, too," he added laughingly. "This is a pretty good outfit. Not bad to be part of it." He grinned broadly. "Said you aren't one hundred percent *beli-gana*—white—after all."

"That's really nice of her. I don't know, though. We just bought a house and all."

"Don't worry. It just means she likes you a lot."

The party went on into the night. People dozed where they were, little kids sometimes curled right up with each other or a dog. I lost sight of "Natalie." I helped Bernice make more bread for another go-round after the sun went down. Then there was more eating and laughing, and some of the men beat rhythms on overturned buckets, and women danced. "Natalie" came to me and tried to pull me into the line of women. I said, "I don't know this one."

"Come on, it's easy," she said. "Watch my feet."

I couldn't keep up with her feet, but it was fun. When I got tired, I took a cup of water and sat near some older people, a man and a woman, who pretty much ignored me until suddenly the man spoke directly to me. "That dance is pretty hard."

I said, "I didn't do a very good job."

"That's like a lot of things. You think you can do it, walk in someone else's steps, but when the drumming starts, it's harder than it looks."

I nodded. "I'll try again later."

"Gordon is a son to me, to all the old people here. He is one of us. Even for a good person, it's hard to walk in someone else's steps. Gordon belongs here. He is Navajo. You have your own ways."

I fought the urge to face the man. "Gordon is teaching me. . . . I've learned new ways."

"New ways are not good. The *beli-gana* way is not our way. Let him come back to his people where he belongs." The man left without waiting for me to answer—it felt rude, in my way or theirs.

In the gap he left on the bale, another man tapped his fingers lightly. I recognized the voice of the man from whom I'd bought a sheep so long ago. "Not everyone likes the idea of marrying a white woman. Some of the people will accept you, some won't." Gordon's Uncle Billy. "It would be easier if he stayed here and acted like a good boy, easier for us old ones. But you can't change what's in a man's heart, and I don't think Gordon would last long if he lived here. Not right now. He needs to be where you are, someplace away where he can remember us, not live with us."

"ey, Poquette, you ol' Philistine, come on in here and set a spell." Marty rose and shook hands with Danny. He sat again at a small, well-used table in the basement of Siloam Springs church.

"Hey, Haliburton, Brother Miner. Bandy, what're you doing here?"

"I's on the committee, too. Building and Grounds," Beans said with a snort.

Marty continued. "Brother Miner here was just going to open this meeting with a word of prayer. Then we've got a lot to attend to."

Brother Miner prayed for guidance in the service of the Lord. He leaned back on his elbows, propped on the arms of the chair, and tipped it up on the back legs so that the whole thing seemed precariously balanced toward the wall of the church basement.

Marty started. "As you men know, I've recently answered the call to preach."

The three of them said "Amen."

"Well, there's always more to that than standing in the pulpit three times a week. It greatly concerns me that we go about the business of bringing souls into the Kingdom of God."

Beans Bandy said, "I thought you said we was gon' have coffee."

"Garnelle didn't come, Beans," Danny said. "She ain't here to make the coffee."

"Shoot," Bandy said. "Wanted some."

Marty went on. "Now, I'm not saying the Siloam Springs sanctuary

313

isn't fit. No, sir. No, I'm saying we have to keep with the times. Spruce 'er up. Keep it looking like a house of God ought to look. Folks oughta know we're a first-rate church."

Danny nodded, his lower lip engulfing the upper one. "I hear First Southern has gone and painted the inside of their sanctuary white. Laid carpet down the aisle."

"Well, now, that's what I'm talking about," Marty said. "I've seen it, and it looks spectacular, real spectacular. You're going to have some of the less dedicated ones going over there just because of how it looks. We can't afford that."

Brother Miner frowned and set his chair back on all four legs, leaning over the table with his elbows. "This church has been light green inside for at least thirty-five years. Maybe more."

Marty pressed his fingertips together. "Brother Miner, I think a whole new building is what we need to draw people in. How can we know how many have passed us by, simply because there's more room at First Southern? I know it's too soon to hope for that, but we could shine it up some. All I am asking is some white paint."

Miner shook his head. "You put this up for a vote and there'll be a four-hour business meeting next Wednesday. Guaranteed." He had already tendered his retirement letter, but he didn't want to be caught in the tailwind of some hair-splitting decision like this, at least not until he'd completely stepped down from the pulpit.

"Well, that's why the trustees need to take the responsibility. Make the decision. We can't be hindered by having to vote on everything. Besides, if we go ahead and do it and somebody doesn't like it, what are they going to do? Paint it again?"

Miner shook his head. "You ought to think this over."

Danny shrugged. "I don't know. Maybe it is time to update things. I heard the Methodists are thinking about putting robes on the choir."

"Hell you say," said Beans. "That'd make 'em look like a box full o' judges." All four laughed. Beans roared. "I said a good one."

"All we want, Pastor," Marty continued, "is your agreement. These

314

boys and I will do the work. Have it ready by Sunday morning. Fresh, clean, sparkling white."

"I can't back it, Brother Haliburton," Miner said. "Not without a vote."

Danny looked up. "If we go around and talk to people before Wednesday night, get some interest going, we might be able to swing the vote without it taking too long."

Marty said, "Every old granny in the county will show up that night, even when she hadn't been here in ten years, giving her two cents about keeping it the way it has always been. I just know it's easier to get forgiveness than permission." He watched them as he lowered his voice and leaned forward. "Brothers, I'd like to talk to you about a way we can have it all."

After two days we were on the road again. I was anxious to get there but terrified, alternately sweating and freezing as we drove. I told him the names of people I thought we could count on: Garnelle, Junior Jasper, maybe Opalrae, maybe Raylene.

"What about your own family? You said you have a grandmother there."

"I don't know. She always took up for me before, but she's awfully worried about her social standing. She wants to be in the Daughters of the American Revolution."

"Never heard of them."

"It's a club. They have tea parties to congratulate each other on how many Founding Fathers—first Americans—they have in their bloodline and how 'old' their money is, even if they don't have it anymore."

"If a grandmother says it's important for you to know, then it is. I

315

believe a heritage is important, too." He laughed. "She'll be glad to know you've married into a family that goes back ten thousand years, whose land was half the continent. A Son of chiefs and warriors—generals and colonels—who fought and won wars in almost every generation, including this one. Their songs are still sung."

"There's a chance no one will let us in the door."

"Tell them I've spent all my life in the sun. Cowboying. Arizona is where they make the movies. People still ride horses. Maybe they won't notice."

I nodded. Maybe he learned as a child that if you didn't understand people, a quick smile and a friendly shrug sent a message of harmlessness. It was better than my solution as a child, to pretend stupidity until people considered me an idiot. His plan sounded too simple to work.

I told myself I was coming to set things right. To see Mother, make her understand me before she died. To make amends, too. I could recall the feel of her legs moving beneath her dress, as I was very small and holding on to her, calling her as she moved away. Surely this time she would turn around and say something.

When we hit the western border of New Mexico, Gordon said, "You haven't said a word for miles."

"I was thinking that we could just turn around now and go home."

"You wrote them we're coming, right? If you're worried, we'll call them in the next town. See how they react. If you want to go home then, we'll go."

"All right," I said. "That's a good idea."

"Let's talk about names for the baby."

"Sure," I said. "Sure, let's do. Were you thinking about baby names?"

He talked a long time about names of members of his family . . . Navajo names, and what they meant to the person who carried the name. "It's all real important," he said. "Sacred."

We telephoned from Albuquerque. Mother wanted me to come, she said. They wanted to meet my husband. And Opalrae was getting out of hand; maybe I could straighten her out, steer her back on course. To me the whole thing vibrated with tension, like the ambush scene from Gordon's movie—invited in, surrounded, then slaughtered. They knew only that "my soldier" had been found alive after all. I had let them believe that he'd been lost like some others had, in the paperwork and bedlam of a long and bloody war.

The road rushed toward our car, faster, faster. I crossed my arms, holding tight to the warm place in my middle where our precious baby waited. I felt so like I was risking its little life, taking it to this place where we were going.

"You tired?"

"No," I said. "Why?"

"Why don't you stretch out? Here, put your head on my knee and sleep?"

"I don't know. I'm not tired, just . . . bored. Why don't you tell me a story, one of those about magical people and animals?"

"Have I told you about Changing Woman and the Twin Heroes?"

"No. How come her name is Changing Woman?"

He thought awhile, tapped his fingers on the steering wheel. "I don't know. Anyhow, First Man and First Woman found a baby on a mountain, and she grew into Changing Woman."

"What did she look like?"

"Who?"

"Changing Woman. What mountain was it, a real one or made up?"

His brows scrunched down. Someone passed around us in a black car, traveling fast. "I don't know. This is a story about her twins and how they fought the—"

"How did they find her?"

"I'm trying to tell you."

"I just wanted to know what she looked like."

"You're kind of grouchy."

"I'm getting sick. Stop the car." Gordon pulled the car off the road. I stepped into the sand and walked away from him. My head was spinning. The fine silt filled my shoes. Burrs seemed to jump at me from invisible weeds, twisting themselves into the ankles of my socks. I didn't throw up, but I needed to put my feet on some soil that wasn't moving.

When I went back to the car, Gordon was leaning against it, his arms folded, chin resting on his chest. "Feel better now?" he said, looking up.

"Guess so." I spent the next hour picking stickers from my socks.

"Look there," Gordon said, thumping the map. "Next town is Loubock."

"Lubbock," I corrected.

"Don't you feel like singing some more? You're awful quiet."

"I guess not."

"I meant, you're awful quiet for a white woman." He grinned, rubbed my neck with a hand.

I shuddered involuntarily. "It's going to be trouble, isn't it?"

"Naw. I'll behave. No scalping or face paint."

"I'm serious."

"Don't worry. Compared to a lot of things, this is nothing. Look," he said, and abruptly pulled to the side of the road again, "you and I have a pact. You can count on me no matter what. I'm counting on you."

"They'll probably have rice for supper."

"Then you'll know how hard I'm trying."

We stopped in Tyler for gas and a bathroom, and Gordon said, "Maybe we should buy some meat, a big roast or something, as a gift."

"I already have gifts for them. I'm afraid they'd think that was . . . weird." A little while down the road I said, "How come we didn't take meat to your mom?"

"She has meat. Doesn't like beef from the store. She says they don't butcher it right."

"But shouldn't I have brought her something?"

"She showed you how to make kneeldown bread, and right away you made enough for the whole family and the dogs, too. You acted respectful. Best thing a mother could want."

"Some mothers, I guess. My bread wasn't very good."

He chuckled softly, nodding. "She liked that, too." A few miles later he said, "You know, I was thinking, being the son-in-law, it might be better for me to sleep somewhere else. Some people's mother-in-laws don't ever want to lay eyes on them, like they're poison. If she's hard for you to get along with, she may hate me already."

"Garnelle will let us stay with her if things get bad."

"It might be all right for *you* to stay with your parents, just not *me*." The road surface changed for a minute, humming at a different pitch. "Maybe this is a good time to cheer you up. I got this to surprise you." He handed me a tiny box from his pocket. "After all the trouble I got into before we left, I have sort of mixed feelings about buying it. But not about giving it to you. This is what I spent my paycheck on. I couldn't take it back."

I'd never asked what he did with the money. Not because I didn't care but because that night was so emotional that when I remember it, all I do is sigh and worry.

"I know we got married sort of on a wish and a prayer, but I know your people put a lot of store in stuff like this. I want you to wear it— let them know what I think of you."

The box had an engagement ring inside, a yellow gold band with a clear, sparkling stone in the middle and two more on each side. "Wow," I said. "Look at that! This isn't real, is it?"

"It better be. It came with an insurance appraisal. It's got the date of our wedding inside. You're not mad, are you? I hope it fits. I put a string around your finger while you were asleep. Do you like it?"

"*Yes*, I love it. It's beautiful. And it fits. But I'm scared to wear it. I might bump it." Relief flooded through me, but along with it came worry: what were they going to think, that we were rich? That was almost as sinful as being a deadbeat. "We'd better not say anything about how you came to have this vacation," I said. "Honesty is not always the best policy with them."

"Frosty, have you ever just tried to talk to them? To your older sister? You're both adult women. Maybe she's changed. I think you'd be happier all around if you cleared the air with each other."

"I'll think about it," I said.

"You going to tell them about the baby?"

I held my hand out so that the sun caught the diamonds and flashed stars across the ceiling of the car. "Only if it seems as if things go well. Something like that might upset·them."

"Those people are hard to figure."

ON WEDNESDAY we had passed a faded sign that said WELCOME TO THE LONE STAR STATE, then hit Sabine late Friday morning. The sun was intensified, as if the humidity in the air were a great magnifying glass and we were trembling ants, but my feet were freezing cold. In the gas station we changed clothes—Gordon putting on his best, which was his uniform—before we went on. On Main Street we stopped to make the turn at Delaware, and as we did, I saw a familiar form going into the dime store. "Stop, Gordon. There's Garnelle."

I caught up with her next to a row of fabric bolts in the back of the store. I shouted her name, and she turned. "Frosty Summers! Oh, it's you! I just came to buy some material to put new curtains in my kitchen. Lands. Have you just gotten here?"

"Yes. I spotted you and made Gordon stop."

She looked nervously about. "Gordon? He's with you?" There was a strange greenish-blue cast to the left side of her face.

"I wrote Mother and told her when we got married. I can't believe she didn't tell everyone. He should be here someplace." I glanced over my shoulder.

"But, Frosty, that was *California*."

Gordon approached sheepishly, having followed me at a much slower pace. "Hey, Garnelle," he said, and put out his hand.

Garnelle looked around, then pressed his hand lightly, leaning toward him with that almost-touch of a cheek. "Well, what a surprise," she said. "Are you two married? I could hardly believe it when Delia told me." Much softer, she said, "Are you really?"

Gordon looked a little embarrassed, but he was the one to ask her right up front if he could sleep at her home. "My Aunt Gladys warned me that a man who looks at his mother-in-law can go blind. I'm not sure, but I'm not willing to risk it."

"Oh, certainly, as long as Danny agrees, of course." There was a pensive look on her face. But she laughed merrily. "Better get my shopping done. Bye, y'all."

"Garnelle," I said, "you haven't told us how to find your house."

She was already down the aisle when she said, "You can't miss it. We're halfway to Kirbyville off the east fork. You'll see a little yellow house right near the lane with two rows of red geraniums up the walk."

Back in the car and headed toward Mother and Daddy's, I said to Gordon, "She looked strange. Sad or something, don't you think?"

He tipped his head. "I don't think she was as happy to see us as she said."

"Turn here." My heart made a knob in my throat when we slowed to a stop at the yard in front of the little house that used to be mine.

THE SOUND OF THE CAR brought them all to the porch, with stiff hugs for me and swift handshakes for Gordon. Grandmother Summers sat on the rocker, refusing to acknowledge either of us. Deely and Wilbur were there, and it warmed me deep inside when Gordy took one look at Wilbur and snapped to attention and saluted him. Wilbur returned the salute a little sheepishly with his left hand, and then they shook hands.

"Iwo Jima, Peleliu," Gordon said.

"France," Wilbur responded.

Daddy and Mother looked uneasily at Gordon. Finally Mother said, "Well, I didn't spend all morning cooking to let it go to waste."

Saying I wanted to wash my hands, I slipped into my parents' room. Under the pillow on Mother's side I slipped the tortoiseshell comb with blue-gray pearls. I peeked in the door at my old room. There was a place near the window on the yellowed wallpaper where a bleached V pointed upward to a bare nail. Eight hair ribbons that belonged to me had been hanging there when I left. All traces of my life were gone except for some vacant whitened wallpaper shadows. There were no clothes left in the closet except Opalrae's things.

Mother and Daddy and Grandmother Summers sat at one side of the kitchen table, Delia and Wilbur and Opalrae on the other. Delia held their baby, Ronny, and a bottle he worked on contentedly during supper. Gordon and I sat the end opposite Daddy. Their faces were strained, tight. There was roast chicken and corn on the cob, greens cooked with bacon, and a huge bowl of dirty rice.

After several quiet minutes, Gordon spoke with a smile. "It looks like it might rain."

"Are you a Christian?" Delia said abruptly.

"Dear," Wilbur said to her.

"Well, it's a question. Just conversation," she said.

Gordon said, "I went to Christian school for ten years."

Daddy said, "So, Gordon. Where exactly are your people from?"

"Arizona, sir. Some from Utah and Colorado, but my mother and my uncles live in Arizona."

"He worked as a cowboy before the war," I said.

"No foolin'?" Opalrae said. "Roundups and gunfights and everything?"

"Well," Gordon said carefully, "there aren't gunfights anymore. But I've worked a few roundups. Mostly it's just hard work. Fixing fences, digging holes, herding . . ."

"What do you do now? For a living, that is?" Daddy said. He had one eyebrow cocked.

Grandmother Summers humphed, then said, "Roughneck."

Gordon nodded. "Sir, I'm an electrician. I worked radios in the war, and they taught me all kinds of electrical work."

"So what's that pay nowadays?"

"Sir?"

"You able to support my daughter, or is she having to work to support you?"

"Daddy," I said. "I've never supported him. I just *want* to work a little bit longer."

There was an edgy silence. I felt Gordon's shoe touch mine twice.

I said, "I saw Garnelle this afternoon. Said hello just before we got here."

"Don't even speak to me about that woman," Delia said.

"Why on earth?" I said, looking—without thinking—at Wilbur. His face appeared positively tortured.

Delia continued, "She ran off on Danny. Left him. Packed up his stuff and threw it outside and got a lawyer to divorce him. Broke his heart, is what she did."

"She had a right, Delia. He was unfaithful," Daddy said while concentrating on peppering the food. "Last I heard, she took him back and they're still in that house together."

Delia pointed her fork at him. "Nevertheless, she broke his heart. He didn't deserve it."

Wilbur searched the faces at the table. "Now, dear. Garnelle told me she's decided to forgive and give him another chance. Frosty, tell us about your adventures in California. You finished with beauty school? Think you can make me beautiful?"

I laughed. "It only works on girls." Gordon laughed, too. Mother looked up. She had not touched her plate since she sat. Delia left the room to put Ronny to bed.

"Opalrae," Mother said, "is that nail polish I see on your hands?"

"Only clear, Mother. You said I could wear clear."

"Go take that off this minute."

Opalrae groaned and left the table, shrugging her shoulders childishly.

"Mother, Daddy," I said, "Gordon and I were thinking, you know, this house is full, and we'd hate to put anyone to a lot of trouble. I was thinking maybe we could stay at Delia and Wilbur's? If that's all right with you two?" There was another minute of silence, so thick we could hear Opalrae moving things around in the bathroom.

"They haven't got enough room for two people. One, maybe. Not two," Mother said.

"Mother," Wilbur addressed her, "we can fit them in if they want to stay with us."

Gordon said, "I will be happy to stay with you and let Frosty stay here and visit with her parents. She's come all this way to see them. That's what's important."

It seemed as if everyone nodded. *That's what's important.* How could they refuse?

Mother looked back and forth from Gordon to Delia. "Well, Wilbur will be there," she said. "So it's all right."

Grandmother Summers looked up abruptly. "Who's going to carry me home? Earl?"

"Mother," Daddy said, "Opalrae should be the one. She drives the car."

"I have to do everything," Opalrae mumbled. "C'mon, Grandmother. I'll get you home."

Grandmother Summers stopped by Mother's chair and toward the back of her head, said, "Chickens have come home to roost." Then she tossed her chin in the air like Deely used to do.

"Don't you go one bit over twenty miles an hour, young lady," Daddy said.

We all retreated to the front room. I put a record on their phonograph. Over my shoulder I said, "I brought this for you. It's the Old Time Gospel Hour Choir." We sat, reverently listening to every note. Sweat ran from my hair down the back of my neck. I wish they could all hear Julia Green sing. How twanging and off-key the Gospel Hour Choir was. Hillbillies hooting out the words to a hymn with no gift for rhythm or voice. When the music was finished, we breathed a collective sigh.

Brother Haliburton?" Danny Poquette said. "We've got us a serious problem."

Marty rolled himself out the door. "Hold it down. Raylene just got the kid asleep. Is this about that shade Frosty Summers come back with? 'Cause I got more than that to worry about. We just had a meeting. You heard they voted down the painting and the new pulpit I had in mind? Just want to fix it up, instead of buying new. Where were you? Another vote coulda changed things."

"Gol-durn Garnelle told me they were at the Summerses I went to take a look at that buck myself. Been keeping an eye on 'im."

Raylene came to the door. "Hello, Danny. Martin, honey? You-all want some lemonade?"

Marty turned to her. "Sure, sugar. Bring us some lemonade. That's a good girl. Run 'long while we talk some boring business." To Danny he said, "Maybe, just maybe, we can kill two birds with one stone, so to speak." He paused for a moment, then smoothed his hair with both hands. "I got a special sermon to get ready for Sunday, and I want that place painted for it."

"Let's round that boy up and get him to paint it," said Danny. "She says he does 'lectrical. We could get him to do that, too. Wire up a couple of lights."

Marty nodded slowly as the idea took root. "Electrical?" He grinned. "Yes, sir. That'll do. If we can't convince him to help with that, we could take that old boy on a nice, neighborly hunting trip. Maybe some night fishing, maybe down to the blackwater swamp between Attouyac and Little Sandy Bayou."

"Hard to see down there," Danny said.

"Reckon. Thank you, honey." He took the lemonade from Raylene. Passed one to Danny. When she left, Marty continued, lowering his voice. "Maybe both. Do the work, then go hunting. A fellow could get lost, and there'd be no one to blame even if he got some wires crossed."

Danny drank, then shrugged. "I don't know. What if he won't go?"

Marty straightened up and slapped his thigh. "Well, Brother Poquette, it's just a little friendly hunting trip. We'd do as much for anyone."

325

The telephone rang. Daddy went to it, and I heard him say, "That so? Sure enough? What repairs? Well, all right. I see. We were wondering. So that's it. Oh—oh really? Mm-hmm." Then he came into the front room with an odd look on his face. "Wilbur, Brother Poquette would like a word with you."

Wilbur listened silently. When he came back into the room, he said, "Delia, fetch our son. We best be getting home." Deely looked confused, but she didn't argue with the tone in his voice. Both of them said good-bye more to the house than to any person.

When they'd gone, Daddy spoke to the air in the room, "Seems there's some work needs doing, and Danny heard from Garnelle that you're doing electrical. The boys want to know if you'd help them put up a light in the church."

Gordon looked up, surprised. "Well, yes, sir. Where's it at?"

"They'll be along directly to carry you up there."

I looked from Daddy to Gordon. It felt like loose electricity was charging through the room. If it was simply work to be done, why would Wilbur have acted like that?

Gordon said, "Right now?"

"Unless you've got other plans."

"No, sir." He looked at me with no expression. "I'll just change clothes, if that's all right."

Gordon hung his uniform on a hanger inside the car. He brought his special rubber-soled work shoes to the porch and sat on the steps to change, carefully putting his spit-shined black ones under a chair near the door. I searched his face, wanting to say to him "Be careful" or something. When at last he looked at me, he squinted his eyes for a moment, a tiny communication that was ours alone. I raised my brows, and he smiled.

Marty and Danny barely said hello to me. They talked loud and long about electricity, and Beans kept interrupting everything. Then they all got into Marty's big car and drove away.

DADDY SAID, without looking at my face, "Come in here and sit down."

Mother sat at the table, her hands clenched together as if in prayer, but the knuckles were yellowish and the skin between them was scarlet. Her bottom lip was tucked tightly under her upper one. Her chin was so taut the cords under the skin made white places.

"So," Daddy said. "What's this boy's background? The one you're running with?"

"We're not running, we're married. His name is Benally. Gordon Benally."

"What kind of name is that? Eye-talian or something?" Daddy said.

"He's from Arizona."

"Looks a lot like the Cajuns around here."

"No."

Daddy bristled. "Looks Japanese. You're hiding something."

"No, Daddy. He's American. Fought in the Pacific Theater the whole time. He was wounded, too. He has a great job, and we've bought a house." I felt condescending. I wanted that tone to leave my voice, but there it was. "He's from Arizona. We met in California at a picnic. Garnelle was there. She'll tell you."

"Garnelle's told us enough already," he said.

Mother's jaw muscles quivered under the skin of her neck. "Garnelle," she said. She started shaking. Her head jerked to the side, and she clamped her jaw tightly. She didn't utter a word, but her eyes stabbed at me.

Daddy spoke for her. "Suppose you tell us, young lady. Well, not *lady*. Suppose you tell us, are we supposed to believe this was the boy you were going to meet before?"

"Gordon was found. Missing, but found."

Daddy was off and running. "Damn. They'll say *anything*, I tell you. Anything. How nice you look. How good your cooking is. Anything, just to get you to marry them."

"Daddy, he's not some Communist trying to infiltrate the country. He's an American."

"What in hell kind of name is Benally? That doesn't sound French to me."

"Navajo."

Their faces dropped with mixed expressions of shock and confusion. "What?" he said. Mother slapped the table with her hands.

My brain was cottony and feverish. A loud buzz filled my ears. "He's American as they get. He's a radio specialist. A corporal in the Marine Corps. He landed at Guadalcanal and Eniwetok, and on Wake Island he was captured and tortured. When he escaped, he was shot, and with the help of some Marines he crawled back to the American lines. They sent him to California to get well and to train other radio operators. He's a hero, Daddy. An American hero. The only thing strange he eats is pizza with too many olives, Daddy. He likes *The Wizard of Oz* and Laurel and Hardy movies. I love him." The cotton wadded into my brain must surely be visible now, bursting through my eyes and ears. I wondered for a second if I would have a stroke from the pressure in my skull.

"Those things aren't important. Can't you see that? Is he a Christian, Frosty? Does he go to church? Was he baptized? Is he South-ren Bab-diss?" Daddy's face distorted in rage.

"I—I think he said Presbyterian."

Daddy pounded the table. "Sprinkled! That's not baptized. We won't see you married to some colored, Catholic-ismed idolater. Unequally yoked. *Unequally yoked!*"

"Presbyterian," I said weakly. "We go to church, but the only one close is Methodist."

Daddy simmered, dark red, his face screwing up before me. "I don't care what you call it, it's a dad-damned Catholic red-skinned Indian. Good Lord. God-d-damn! Couldn't you go down to that jack-black church and at least find a *Christian* nigger? Whadda you been doing? Taking off to who knows where and consortin' with niggers. She's probably carrying some colored yella pickaninny right now, jack-full—" The words left him, stymied by fury.

I had never seen Daddy so mad. Mother, it was her constant state, but him, never. We all stared hard into the tabletop. The silence deafened me. The screen door hadn't shut completely, and a breeze pushed it in place with a thunk. The noise caused me to jump, even though I saw the door move. Not since I left here had I thought of myself as if I were a spectator to my own life, and I fought the urge to back away.

Mother seethed. Her jaw set hard, she grimaced and slurred out the words, "I'll call sheriff."

Everyone turned toward her at that minute, and the absurdity of it made me roll my eyes. I almost smiled.

Daddy breathed heavily. "What else you hiding? What else?" And with the last question he struck violently across the table and slapped my face. The chair I was sitting in rocked back and hit the wall. For several seconds I sat paralyzed except for the trembling of my hands and feet.

Mother opened her mouth and——fighting to get the words out—— said, "I'll never be able to hold my head up in this town again. Couldn't you think about anyone but yourself?"

The pressure in my head released itself in a low moan. I walked unsteadily toward the front door and went through it. All I could think of was finding Gordon and leaving. I started down the long sidewalk to the little gate and heard repeated banging from the house. The door opened behind me, but I kept going, not turning around. The splintered remains of the Gospel Hour Choir record came flying out of the house in my wake, hitting the backs of my legs like it was shot from a rifle. I stopped long enough to twist around and see drops of blood forming, and was filled with some kind of satisfied relief. Physical pain annulled the other kind. It always did. I squeezed my hands into fists, kicked the gate askew, and kept walking.

The hush of the hour hung over the town. Before long the sound of an automobile approaching behind made me slow and move to the side, and I was angry that they'd come after me so soon, as if apologies would change anything, as if I'd accept one.

"Hey, there," a man's voice said. "Frosty, honey! What you been doing? Steal a watermelon and get yourself a load of buckshot?" It was Junior Jasper, driving a car.

"Oh, no," I said. "Well, something like. Not . . . just a little accident." I tried to smile.

"Too hot to walk. I got Mr. Ricker's auto here to take to gas 'er up 'fore he goes down to Beaumont. Plenty of room."

"Well, I don't want to get the seat covers messy."

"Right here." He leaned across and flung open the back door near me. "I'll open this sack." Junior reached over the seat and pulled up a sack, took out a box of cornflakes and a bottle of orange soda. While I held on to the door handle, he pulled the bag apart at the seam and flattened it over the plush seat. I watched his hands, his long, long fingers like a newborn baby's, longer than the palm. "There you go. Best sit in the back, so folks'll know I'm just giving you a ride."

I was in the seat only a second when he started down the road. Before I could say a word, I lost my composure and broke down in great, gulping sobs, childlike. I felt the car swing lightly to one side of the road, heard the engine go through a couple of gears.

"Oh, Miss Frosty, I'm sorry, whatever happened," he said. "Looks like you went a couple rounds, too." He extended a hand toward me, and I held it, squeezing his fingers with thanks. After what seemed like a terribly long silence, he opened the glove box, offering me a tightly folded, faded blue plaid handkerchief. "Good, I thought there was a clean one here. I hope you at least got a taste of that old watermelon." He smiled, then drove me the long way around town, finally pulling up at Ricker's.

By that time I'd gotten hold of myself, a little bit. "I can't stay with Mother and Daddy. Will you show me where Deely and Wilbur live?"

"Sure enough, Miss Frosty. But, if you got the time, could you see my grandma first? She'd be happy you stopped in. It'd give you a chance to wash up."

I found Mrs. Jasper in bed, breathing as if every movement of her lungs was a massive effort. When I told her who I was, she said, "Hand me that picture in the frame there on the bureau. That one of all the people. Frosty? You recollect my grandson, Junior? This his wife, Marie. That their chil'ren, Beau and Arnella. This his sister, Esther Davis. She got a husband over to Macon County, Georgia. Got me three great-grandchil'ren, now. The baby is Eleanor Roosevelt. Esther's back in that house behind."

"Hello, y'all," I said to the picture. "They look real fine, Mrs. Jasper. Real fine. How are you?"

"Esther's man got a job in Macon. Only she come here to look after me, and now she can't get home. I told her get while the getting's good, but she don't listen. Just stubborn. No sense waiting around for me to die. Ain't like I can leave her no money to get home on."

"Mrs. Jasper, don't say that. You aren't going to die."

"You hush that. Don't be talking the Lord out o' taking me home. Been waiting too long. Now, who's that with you?"

"I'm here alone. Junior had to run along."

"Is that Frosty? Where's Junior? I thought that boy was in here. I told him to get that there, and . . . I told him. Where's Gramma's long-tall boy? You see that picture? Eleanor's the baby."

"Yes'm."

"She got to get that baby home to Macon."

ay, there, that's real fine," Marty said, flicking the light on and off two times. "Done real good work." He smiled at Gordon and looked at the other men. "Now it's time for some fun. Y'all know plenty 'bout huntin', boy, don't you?"

Gordon shrugged. "I've hunted some. I should get back to Frosty's folks, though."

Beans Bandy laughed and said, "I'll let you borry my old gun."

Marty said, "I told them we might go hunting. Just let Frosty catch up on old times. I'm sure she's got girlfriends to see. Why, my Raylene was just awaiting your arrival to show off the new baby. That's how things're done here."

"What do you hunt? Deer?" Gordon said.

Danny slapped Beans and Marty's shoulders simultaneously. "We got critters here to hunt you wouldn't imagine. All's we got to decide is, are we crick hunting or dry hunting. It makes a difference. You paddle a canoe?"

"No. Never did."

Beans said, "I thought you was a Indian."

Gordon ignored the comment. "I'd like to get my old Marine Corps boots out of the trunk. Not mess up these. I'll catch up to you there by the filling station we passed."

Next to the boots in the trunk, he had his service dagger and the bayonet he'd taken off a Japanese soldier, which he used at home for poking holes in plaster to run wire in old walls. He slipped the dagger into his belt and fiddled with the bayonet for a few minutes, finally slipping it into the top of the boot with the belt hook over the top of the leather where it was hidden by his trousers. It didn't show, and it made him feel ready. He really wanted to make friends with Frosty's people; going hunting was a good way. He made a note of the angle of the sun, the length of his shadow, then went to join them.

At the edge of a stream the four of them got into two small skiffs. Gordon sat in the rear of the one rowed by Beans. Marty and Danny took the other one. They headed upstream into thick trees, where the water opened wide and looked shallow. "What are we hunting?" Gordon asked.

Danny eyed him carefully. "There's a thing we got hereabouts that's the best eating you ever had in your life. Better than ham and steak put together. And we don't want a little one, they're too skinny," Danny said. The others laughed. "Or too big a one . . . where it's all tough. What size, would you say, Brother Haliburton, is the best size gator for fillets?"

Beans grinned and snuffled noisily. Marty whistled and thought a moment. "I believe ten foot is the best. You've shot gator before, ain't you, boy?"

"No," Gordon said. He wondered if this was a "sand trout" hunt. He'd taken three set builders from a movie crew once, who'd seemed friendly and good-natured, on a sand-trout hunt. It was all in good fun. He'd just go along with the joke, they'd laugh at him, he'd be a good sport, and it would clear the air. "What's it look like?"

"Oh, you can't miss 'em. They got a long nose and a knobby head,"

Danny said, "and a tail that whips back and forth. You've got to watch out for the tail. That's the dangerous part. Wouldn't you say that's the dangerous part of a gator, Brother Bandy?"

"Right likely," Beans said. "Nothing else on one will hurt you. Just the tail. Keep your eyes on the tail." He laughed, then slapped his fingers across his own mouth. "Got to be quaht. Don't wanna scare them big'uns away."

"Right," Marty added. "The little ones will hang around hoping you'll feed 'em, but the big ones will take off if we make any noise. Are we almost to the spot, Brother Dan?"

Their boats parted trees and hanging moss, entering a strange world of leggy growth and imperious birds who looked down from wadded nests as if they were the true heirs of their kingdom and the people were a sort of intruding gnat. Floating logs bumped the boat hull, then drifted by. A soft, cool stillness surrounded them. The beat of birds' wings, the cry of some animal too distant to see, filled the air. The seriousness of the hunt descended upon the men.

After a while Danny said, "This is close to the spot where I've bagged two in the last year. If you get one, Gordon-boy, you can bet the Summerses will be eating for a month and thanking you the whole time. What we're gonna do is let Brother Marty out here on this little island, see?" The "island" he pointed to was no larger than a good-size chair. "And you, Gordo, you take that one around the bend there. Then me and Beans will circle yonder through the cypress and see if we can round any your way." He maneuvered the skiff toward some dense trees.

Marty waved and said in a loud stage whisper, "This'll get you in good with Frosty's people."

Gordon did as he was told, stepping out of the skiff onto another small island, not big enough to sit upon and far too wet to try. He crouched with Beans's pistol at the ready. Danny looked up at him as the skiff settled and said, "Now, here's how we get them thinking there's food in the water, something struggling. It's sure to bring a couple." He slapped the water with the oar. A few seconds passed, and a great vibrating boom, muted but intense as if it came from under the ground at Gordon's feet, answered it. "There. That's a big one. Any luck, there'll be a good-size gator along any minute now. If you can't shoot 'im and he tries to make a run for you, you hang on to his tail—don't worry about the rest of him."

Gordon nodded, and the men in boats disappeared into the shrouds of lacy moss. Within a few seconds he could no longer hear the soft, rhythmic slicing of the oars. A bird soared, long and stretched out, across the canopy of leaves over his head. No gnats biting. Something called overhead, a hauntingly clear, two-note birdsong. He sank onto his haunches, listening. He smiled and thought to himself, this was indeed a sand-trout hunt. They would let him start to worry, maybe even let the sun go down, then come back and laugh.

He inspected the pistol they'd loaned him. The sight was bent; the barrel itself was bent. The cylinder barely turned, and when he tried to pry it open to check the loads, it wouldn't move. Carefully peering down the business end of it, he could see there was only one bullet left in the gun. He worked the cylinder, notching the hammer back and forth until the live round was next in line for the chamber. After a few minutes he shifted his weight. At that second another vibrating boom echoed through the trees. A log, propelled by some eddy or current that didn't ripple the top of the water around him, came drifting by. Gordon tried to hook it with his toe, thinking he'd tip it on end and see how deep the black water was around him. Even if this was an island, the water might just be ankle deep; that'd give them a good laugh, stranding him on an island he could have walked away from.

The log gave under the touch of his toe and moved on, rolling. One side was mossy, the other black. It was impossible to see where the sun was. There were no shadows under the trees. All was cool, green, black, and wet. The darkness deepened, the air going bronze and hazy. Strange, flickering lights appeared above the water's surface. Gordon shifted around until his ankles got tired; he decided to take a step at the edge of the island and see how the slope went underwater. For some minutes he gingerly tapped at the edge of the island with his toe. It felt solid. He placed his foot at the spot and put more weight on it. With a sudden splash he was neck deep in the murky water. Grimacing, he looked at the pistol he'd managed to keep overhead. Knowing it probably wouldn't fire anyway, he tucked it into his belt. He faced what looked like the nearest shore and started to swim toward it.

The water was inky, and thicker than a moonless night. From nowhere a large snake swizzled past him, causing him to hold his breath. Branches clawed at him from below. He tried to reach the knife in his belt and found himself tangled, the water plants stiffer and harder than seaweed. The weight of his wet clothes pulled at him. He tried to duck his head to see his boot but couldn't. He felt for the knife and came up with it at last, gasping. A branch caught him. Blood ran from his left arm and made a red slick just under the oily-looking surface of the water.

He hacked at the weeds snarling his legs, then started again for the shore, swimming with the knife in his hand. From his right side the water began to move toward him, weeds coming in clumps like tiny green pebbles on a mound. He treaded water, watching this odd clump growing, coming closer. Behind the clump of bright green pebble grass, two large eyeballs emerged from the water as if they were suspended on stalks. Less than a second later a set of jaws rose up, shunting the clump of green off to one side, revealing a vast pink gullet and two rows of dog teeth that belonged on some monster from the beginning of the world. The jaws smashed down, inches from his hand; then the thing dipped under the water and vanished.

Gordon's heart raced. He swam for the shore with all his might, but he was not a good swimmer. He'd only done a little playing in the waves of the Pacific Ocean. There'd been no black water, thickened with unseen—

He felt a jarring crash and a sudden jerking on his foot. Before he could inhale, he was pulled under, whipped around and around by some powerful grip. He felt the animal at his chest, bending him double, as if trying to coil him into a ball. The alligator thrashed, twisting his leg mercilessly, making Gordon want to scream. He clutched at it, hacking uselessly with the knife. Then suddenly he caught the thing in the joint of one leg, and it arched, flinging him out of the water. Drawing a gasping breath, it let go of his foot and circled, partially submerged, then charged directly at his head, at the last second rearing its great fangs again, spread wide. Holding the knife hilt in his fist, Gordon shoved his whole arm into the mouth, and when it tried to slam shut its jaws, it jerked and roared, stunned by the blade pinning its mouth wide open. Gordon pulled his arm free and swam. The alligator writhed and bellowed, frantic.

Gordon caught hold of a great root of one of the strange trees forming the canopy overhead and wedged himself into the gaps of its legs, using them to scoot himself far above the water's surface. There he found a place to stand and watch the monster fighting for its life, plunging to the depths and surfacing, gurgling and desperate. For several minutes the struggle went on, and then its trips to the surface slowed. At last it disappeared below the black water. Only when the surface had not been broken for at least fifteen minutes did his heart begin to calm. "Hang on to the tail," he said aloud. "Good joke, you boys. Come on out now." A bird cried over his shoulder. A small furred animal swam toward the tree he was in, saw him, and turned and swam away without a sound. It was too quiet.

Gordon pulled the bayonet from his boot and held it ready. He felt for the old pistol, but it had been lost in the water. There was no corn pollen under his shirt. A snake had crossed his path. He was so far from the old things that kept him safe. Even in the jungle in the Pacific, he'd held to faith in some things. He felt abandoned and afraid. He moved his perch on the tree to a place where he could, if he angled his legs right, almost sit.

Coming back from Porter Lane, I found Deely's house almost by accident. I'd stopped at the Phippses' to ask where they lived and saw Deely across the yard by a small house two doors down. I tried to look happy to see her. I wished Gordon would come back. "Delia, yoo-hoo!" I called. She turned, and I hurried toward her.

"Delia, I'm so glad I found you. Listen, the boys have taken Gordon hunting or something. I went by the church, and they're not there."

"Well, that's none of my business, I'm sure."

"I wanted to ask you if Gordon and I—I mean, if we can still spend the night here."

"I don't know. Ronny is pretty fussy. He doesn't like it if other people are in the house." She walked toward the back door. I followed her, uninvited. She turned on the stoop, one hand on the doorknob. "Well," she said, "come in, then." Deely wandered around, stepping quietly, fiddling with things.

Ronny was sleeping on a blanket she'd put on the floor by the divan. A fan on a bookshelf moved the air over him. Patting the baby, she sat beside him, straightening her dress. "Don't you just love my wittow Wonny?" She pressed her hands against the hairpins in her hair, which had been pulled back into a matronly bun.

"Yes, Deely, he's a real sweetie-pie. Does he sleep through the night yet?"

"Pretty much all night now. At first I just never slept. Not a minute's rest. But there was never a day I didn't make it to church."

"I guess you'd know more about that than I."

"You talk different now, you know? And your hair is so short and . . . well, *stylish*." The way she said it, it was no compliment.

"How's everyone been?" My voice dipped. "Mother—is it really true? She didn't say anything to me about her . . . illness."

"No, but it's true. More and more she has days when she can't talk. Or she talks, but it doesn't make any sense."

I nodded. "So it's not, well . . . immediate?"

"They took her to a specialist in Beaumont. Daddy told me he didn't want her to know."

This felt so imaginary, like a scene from a movie. "Is she happy about Ronny?" Would she even understand about my baby?

"Well." She cut her eyes toward the door. "Mostly. I mean, she says

337

to me, 'You'll always love your first one the most,' but then she won't change his diapers, and she says 'because of . . . *you* know.' Isn't that just ridiculous? Does she think boys' diapers change themselves?"

Silence moved tangibly between us. *The first one.* I said, "Do you think you'll love him the most? More than your other kids, if you have them?"

"I don't know. I expect it's true, if Mother says."

My eyes fell on a magazine opened to an add for toothpaste, a girl smiling, with stars on her teeth. I sighed. "What happened to all my things?"

"What things?"

"Clothes. Things. In our room it looked like nothing was left." No evidence of the years I had cocooned in the tiny room next to Deely. "I thought I might get my old doll, is all."

"Oh, Mother was horribly mad when you wrote you weren't coming home. She said she told you it was time you get yourself home, and you just passed it off like you were happy to run wild. Did you date a lot of men?" Then she looked straight at me. "You're going to have to confess everything if you want to be forgiven.

"Frosty, we've all been praying for you, that you would follow God's will for your life and just come home. See how God blessed me with my witty Wonny?"

I sat on the floor next to the sleeping baby. "Did they take my stuff to the swamp?"

"Oh, no, they would never do that. Not where hoboes could get it. Please try to understand how we beseeched God to restrain you from evil."

"Aren't we grown-up enough to be honest with each other?"

"Honest," she said wistfully. Then her face hardened. "They burned your clothes."

My mouth opened and closed twice. "Everything?" The fan pushed my hair around.

"Back of the house, in the trash barrel. Mother tore them up for rags, but she said she couldn't bear to look at them. So she poured pork grease on everything and lit it up."

"My senior yearbook? Did you save my silver spoon? My hope chest had those embroidered pillowcases we worked on, you and I together." She jumped abruptly to her feet and left the room, returning with folded cloths. She placed them in my hands without a word. "Honey Doll?" I said. "Did you save my doll, too?"

"You don't need an old filthy rag doll anyway. Why, I wouldn't want it in this room, with my witty-bitty Ronny-wonny." Delia stood and raised the window. It stirred but did not cool the air. Mosquitoes gathered at the screen, leering in at us. A katydid sang outside. "I'm going to sit here and have a cigarette."

"You smoke?"

"Mother and Daddy have accepted it. After all, I am an adult. And I took it from Wilbur. He always has a couple of cigarette packages around the house. Picked it up overseas."

"Why would you want to do that? I haven't seen him smoke."

"It's to calm my nerves. Besides, it's just a habit. Like some people collect cookbooks." Delia struck a match and made a production of lighting the cigarette, blowing the smoke toward the open window, and fanning it through with her hand. "Raylene and Marty have another baby. A little girl, but not very pretty, if you ask me."

"Isn't there anything of mine left? I came here wanting to make amends. I'm trying, but I feel like—"

"Well, it's your own fault. Mother and Daddy believe you've thrown away your life."

"I've done the same thing as you, found a nice guy and settled down."

"Wilbur is from the finest family in the county. I hardly think you could call Gordon the same. All that hanging around the Nigras was bound to rub off." There it was. She sucked on the cigarette and blew smoke directly into the room while she eyed me closely. "The things Mother told me you were doing out there, sometimes I thought you must have been possessed by the devil. But I know what's behind it all. You were always jealous, because I needed help. You knew if you kept Mother and Daddy worried and upset, they'd pay lots of attention to you." My mouth hung open. She pulled on the cigarette again, making a little kissing sound. She breathed the smoke out against the window screen, and the mosquitoes vanished for a few seconds. Ronny stirred and made noises. Her tone softened. "Being a Christian, of course, I'd forgive you if you just apologize."

"You want me to apologize? For what? You were the one manipulating; everything in this family revolved around you from the first I remember."

"Ha!" she said dramatically, waving the cigarette in the air, making me think of Bette Davis. "From the minute you were born, it was all about you. 'Don't wake up the baby, Delia; don't touch the baby!' Before you were out of diapers, you were so spoiled! Then Opalrae came along and knocked you off your high horse, and you were the one being sent outside for touching the baby. Then I got sick, and when a little help and sympathy was asked from you, you pitched a fit I still remember."

"What on earth are you talking about?"

"When I came home from the hospital."

"That wasn't about you, Delia. It was about my dog. *Our* dog. Don't you remember?" For the first time she took her hot, furious eyes away from mine. The smoke she was making turned my stomach. "Look," I said, "I cut hair. You're too young to wear yours like Grandma Summers."

She inhaled sharply. "Grand*mother*. Besides, 'let not your adornment be with braiding of the hair and putting on—' "

"That verse is not about hairdos. And if it is, that's one long braid you've got wound in a circle anyway; you're going against your own advice." When she touched her bun but said nothing, I went on. "You'd look nice with a shoulder-length bob. My shears are in my suitcase at Mother and Daddy's, but I could use some sewing scissors." I looked at the stitches on the pillowcases, remembering each and every one. I searched her face. "Deely, I never resented you for being sick. I guess I did resent the way Mother always made me responsible for your schoolwork and stuff. You know good and well that half the time you were faking."

Her eyes darted toward the door. "I was not."

"I don't mean intentionally," I said, "but it was a way to get out of stuff you didn't want to do."

"So? You did it, too."

"I didn't either."

"You snuck off and hid all the time. You hid in the sticker bushes. You hid in the outhouse. You even hid under the house one time."

"Didn't you ever just want peace and quiet? Didn't you ever just want to get away from Mother? From everything?"

"I find my solace in the house of God."

"Well, I don't. I find God in the house of God. . . . You faked being sick because Mother would bring you stuff and then close the door and let you sleep. Only you weren't asleep; you played paper dolls and read books and then laid down every time she came in the room. Then you acted like you were so holy an angel had to wash his hands before tapping you on the shoulder, so no one at church bothered you either."

Delia shook her shoulders, dragged heavily on the cigarette. "Well, aren't you the little tattletale?"

"I'm not telling anybody."

She stubbed out her cigarette carefully against the side of the package, spilling some ashes and unburned tobacco. She set the butt on the package while she picked up the crumbs with her moistened thumb. "I'm singing in church again Sunday—solo. Wilbur says I have the nicest voice."

I tried again. "Let me do your hair for it. You'd look great."

"Wilbur likes my hair modest. He says it's becoming."

"Gordon likes mine any way I want to do it." Before the words had even left my mouth, I could see Na'atlo'ii's long mane flowing gently behind his shoulder.

"I can't see Mother and Daddy letting you get away with this for long. Bringing a colored man here. Like you were proud of it, flaunting it in their faces. You should have just stayed in California. You said you were going to get your stuff and come home, but you stayed there to wait for him. Wouldn't you be mad if someone lied like that to you?"

"I never thought about it that way."

"Sister Raylene told me that Brother Marty once admitted to her that if you'd have stayed around, he might have married you."

"Marty? I'd rather have myself skinned."

"You could have been married to a preacher. I can't think of any

341

higher calling for a woman than to be a pastor's wife. I keep praying Wilbur will hear the call, too."

"I'd rather go live in the swamp."

I saw the fire return to her eyes. Defensively, she pursed her lips. "Imagine the spirituality in a house dedicated to the Lord; imagine the prayer vigils, the constant leading of the Holy Spirit. Haven't you ever thought what sacrifice it must take to surrender to the ministry? Sister Raylene has that privilege alongside Marty, but it could have been you."

"Maybe I know Marty better than you."

"If that were true, you wouldn't be so critical of him. Why, he spends every moment he isn't working on a sermon taking care of the old people in the congregation." Ronny woke, scarlet and screaming as if he'd been pinched. Deely opened the diaper bag and started making a flourish out of changing a wet diaper. "The thing we really have to worry about now is saving Opalrae. I've asked everybody to pray for her. I'm worried about her soul."

"Oh, *stop*. Just stop it. Delia, stop saying that everyone's soul is in danger of hell every time their opinion differs from yours." I took a breath. "It's not up to you. I've got a right to my own thoughts. I've got a right to my own husband, and house, and family. So does Opalrae. It doesn't have to be like yours. You aren't God's messenger of damnation."

"Well, aren't you the uppity little thing?" Ronny wailed in her arms, and Deely tapped the bottle he had worked on before he slept against her wrist, smelled it for spoilage, and stuffed it into his mouth. The baby gulped with relief, as if his hunger had been painful.

"Every time I turned around, you made up some lie to Mother. I saw you once watching while I got whipped. After that I never cried again. Because I knew you enjoyed it."

"Liar," she said. Then suddenly she burst into tears. "*Liar!* I never enjoyed it. But you were so wild. You just did anything you wanted, and everything was so hard for me."

"So you had to hate me for that?"

"Sometimes you did stuff just to remind me how sick I was."

"Sometimes you acted sick and pathetic just to get Mother riled at me. She believed everything you said." I felt my own tears rising, pooling in my eyes, blurring everything. "I was a kid. Playing and having fun is what kids do. You can't blame me for still playing even when you couldn't. Would you tell Ronny *he* can't play ball because you didn't?"

She wiped her eyes and nose with the edge of the towel on her shoulder, then leaned Ronny upon it, where he immediately produced a loud belch. "Wonny wants to play ball, doesn't he?" she murmured to him. "Need some more num-num?" She turned to me again, stared a long time, then looked down. "But you did flaunt your—your development."

"Because I wore a bigger brassiere than you? I have bigger shoes than you, too. I saw you one time put rolled-up socks in your bra."

Delia blushed pink, then deep violet. "No you didn't." She searched my face. "That was just to see what it was like."

"You wore them for a week. You could have seen what it was like in a day."

After a tense, long pause she smiled. Then we both laughed, nervously. But we laughed together. She patted Ronny's back. "'When I was a child, I spake as a child.'"

"So we were a couple of kids. We don't have to stay childish," I said.

"No, we don't. Old things *are* passed away." She put her arms around my neck.

I hugged Deely.

The baby's slurping filled the silence for several more minutes, then he nodded drowsily. She put him down on the blanket again, and said, "So. You go to work every day? Like a man?"

"I go to work like a woman. A couple mornings a week. Plenty of girls do. And every other Friday I cut hair at the old folks' home downtown. Volunteer."

"Oh? Do you witness to them?"

"I don't want to save their souls. I just want to do their hair." I thought I detected the faintest smile at the corners of her lips. "Where's Wilbur? Did he go hunting with the others?"

"He said he had work to do. And I should pray for everyone concerned," she said.

"Concerned with what?"

"You know. Hunting. It can be dangerous. He said he'd never believed in hunting when you could just buy beef. He said he wanted no part of it."

"He never knew how poor we were. I used to wish Daddy'd hunt something."

"Daddy worked very hard to support us."

I nodded. He did work. And he hated it, I remember.

We spent the better part of an hour talking like old friends. It was amazing to be on the same side for a change. Still, it wouldn't do for me to stay with her and Wilbur. But Delia did offer to smooth things with Mother and Daddy.

I KNEW THAT WHEREVER Gordon was, he would be okay. He had the car, after all, and if he needed, he could sleep in it like we had on the trip. But I didn't want to be left sleeping in the cypress stump if he didn't get back until late. So I let Delia do what she did best. The sun was going down when she called them. All I could hear was her end of the conversation; she said, "Well, I don't think so," and studied me closely. "I don't know, Mother. But it would be obvious by now if she were."

Mother and Daddy greeted me with a sort of embarrassed silence. Mother asked me to peel cucumbers in the kitchen, and when I turned toward the sink, she said, "You skin your legs on something?"

"Yes, Mother. Something like that," I said.

"I told Opalrae to let you have your old bed back. She can sleep in Delia's. It'll be like old times. Make you feel at home."

"Sure enough," I said, nodding. *I don't want to feel at home here.* I pressed my arms against my sides. "Mother, are you well?" I whispered.

"Why? What'd they tell you?"

"Delia said"—I paused—"you have a tumor."

"T-sh." The sound accompanied a wave of her hand. "Well, forever more. I had a little stroke. Not serious, the doctor said. As you get older, it's first one thing and another."

"Are you all right? Is it getting well?"

Mother waved me out of the kitchen as she started washing dishes, saying, "You go visit with Opalrae. You two need to talk."

Opalrae, however, was busy doing calisthenics in the bedroom. "Hey, there," I said.

"Hey, yourself—*twenty-five*," she said. "Heard Farrell Bandy came home with a war bride you're gonna want to see. Just like you and whoosis."

"Gordon. Listen, Mother thinks something's bothering you."

"*Four, five, six*—that so? *Eight, nine*," she went on breathlessly. "Danny Poquette thinks my figure is really hep."

"Does Mother have a brain tumor?"

"Don't know. She went to a doctor in Beaumont. Daddy says she's fine. Delia thinks she's going to die any minute. '*Leven. Twelve*. Louise Bandy's mama says Mother had a nervous breakdown, just like a movie star."

"Everything's all right with you?"

"Working on my waistline, sugar. *Eighteen, nineteen*. You're not moving home, are you? 'Cause if you are, I get Delia's old bed, not yours." She tossed her hair from her face with a smile and winked at me.

"Want me to do your hair? You'd look great in an upsweep with some curls on top." That got her attention. I got my curling iron and a box of bobby pins from the suitcase and worked on her hair for an hour. The whole time she jabbered endlessly about the space between her eyebrows, the size of her nose, and how much she wanted a pair of nylon hose—so much that she had drawn a seam with a pen up the back of her legs to look like hose.

Every time I said anything serious, she flipped around in the seat, poked me with a finger, and said "You are the mee-ow!" and laughed. I finally gave up and concentrated on her hair, telling her how to get it to look like this or that. Opalrae looked a lot like Deely. Cuter, without Deely's sharp nose and chin. Same easy-to-handle hair—not like mine.

She grinned in the mirror. "I'm going to bicycle over to Louise's and show her. Tell Mother I'll be back in time for supper." I noticed she slipped out the front door without letting the screen touch the jamb, just the way I used to do, lifting up on the doorknob so the hinges wouldn't squeak. I never realized before just how sneaky that seemed.

I wandered around the yard, stopped at the garden fence, woven with dried runners from pea vines that had been replaced with rows of tomatoes that were about knee high and already setting small green fruit. From out there the house and garden looked small, even the train tracks narrower and less meaningful.

The sun stayed long, but the mist in the air took away the shadows and made everything hazy. By the time the fireflies realized it was evening, it was late. I went to get ready for bed, wearing a cotton night-gown that was nicer than some of the dresses I used to own. The house was dark, just a couple of lights burning. I was putting pincurls in my hair, and standing by the door, where I caught a glimpse of Mother moving about in her room. She pulled back the bed quilt and lifted the pillows to fluff them. Suddenly she sat on the bed and picked up the tortoiseshell comb.

As I watched, she rocked back and forth, holding it to her cheek. "Frosty," she said softly. "Frosty, why did you do it?"

What, Mother? Why did I steal it? Why did I bring it back? Or why all the thousands of things that I've done to make you unhappy? I waited for her to come to me, say something—not thank you, just *something*. She put the comb in her hair with one hand and touched it, holding it against her head. Her shoulders jerked. Then she took the comb down and opened the drawer in the bureau where she kept her underwear and pushed it way to the back just as Daddy went in their room to go to bed.

Opalrae came in, noisy, talking nonstop. "I'm really tired," I said. "Let's talk tomorrow. Good night." I lay there in the dark—the train rumbled by, and down aways the whistle blew—remembering my mother calling my name and rocking back and forth.

W hen the moon rose, Gordon felt a slight breeze. It carried with it the faintest smell of food. Animals seemed to be moving about in the darkness, uttering strange cries and flapping wings that didn't belong to the big graceful birds he'd seen during the day. With darkness the insects came, returning Gordon to the jungle, the grit of sand replaced by grit of dead plant matter that chafed in his clothes. He put the bayonet through his belt and felt his way around the trunk of the tree. By moving across the "knees" of one tree to another, he got closer to the smell of food—almost fifteen feet, he reckoned—before he ran out of tree. There was still a lot of black water before him.

This had stopped being a sand-trout hunt. The boats had not returned. Gordon played over in his memory all that the men had said, everything leading up to the alligator's attack. Danny had hit the water with an oar, saying something about calling them to eat. So Gordon's falling may have alerted the big one that came after him. A breeze, strong enough to move his hair, cut through the darkness, again parting the smell of decaying vegetation with the unmistakable aroma of fried chicken. Gordon's mouth watered; he turned in the direction of the breeze and eased himself into the water.

He held the bayonet in his hand as he swam, terrified he'd drop it. Abruptly his feet stumbled onto something below him, and he kicked at it, rising from the water, standing hip deep. He stepped forward gingerly, bayonet outstretched, crouching toward the surface. If the ground under his feet fell away again, he would avoid the kind of splash that would call up another alligator. The shallow floor led him to a ledge where pine trees took over from the cypress, and he slipped into them on dry ground. Mosquitoes attached themselves to every inch of his face.

A few steps farther in, he heard men talking. A campsite had been set up around a glowing lantern. Three figures hunched over, facing

347

each other. One of them laughed. The voice of Beans Bandy said, "Well, I'll piss to that!" and he walked away from the small circle of light. As Gordon hid behind a tree, he watched the man come toward him. In the dark, Gordon watched as Beans dropped the front of his trousers. *It would be easy to take him,* he thought, *like the Japanese soldiers.* Gordon felt for the lump at his chest, again disappointed that it wasn't there. "This isn't war," he whispered, then narrowed his eyes. "But a little of your own medicine wouldn't hurt." When he figured Beans was just about finished with his task, Gordon reared back his arm, the point of the bayonet balanced in his fingertips, and hurled it with all his might. It impaled the tree trunk Beans was urinating on with a resounding thunk, the hilt protruding just above Beans's right hand.

Beans screamed as if it had stuck him. "Jesus-aitch-Christ!" He ran back to the men and began shouting hysterically.

Gordon drew the bayonet from the tree trunk and slipped deeper into the darkness. The three carried their oil lantern and came to the spot where Beans had stood. Circling behind them, Gordon found the pail. It was full of fried chicken, covered in a dishtowel. At a low place where water reflected moonglow, the two skiffs were pulled side by side, towropes carelessly thrown to the ground. Gordon tossed the ropes into the boats and shoved them gently into the black water. Then he reached into the mound of chicken. He helped himself to as many as he could carry, tore the meat from one piece with his teeth, threw the bone back into the bucket, and rushed to the edge of the small clearing. Opposite the position of the boats he found an opening that led to the pathway they'd come down several hours earlier. He put the bayonet back into his belt and sauntered down the path, finishing off the meat, dropping the bones where he'd done with them. A bright, nearly full moon blinked through the trees, dappling the ground. If they were any kind of hunters at all, they'd follow him, and he'd have the last laugh.

Before long he came to a wide road; an hour later he discovered Garnelle's house, looking just as she'd described it.

"GORDON, WHAT ARE YOU doing here?" Garnelle said with her head stuck out the door. "I barely heard you knock. It's after eleven. Is Frosty with you?"

"Your lights were on. I used your faucet to clean up. Garnelle, I'd like to talk to you."

"Well—well, now's not a good time." She looked anxiously up and down the road. "Maybe come with Frosty, too, or when Danny gets back. I thought you were together."

"I got separated from the other men. I figured they probably can find their way back. I'm only asking you to give me ten minutes. Then I'll be going."

"Well"—her face softened—"oh, come on in. I suppose it's all right. What's the harm? Gonna come in? You'll get eaten alive by mosquitoes out there."

"Thanks. What I've got to say I can say right here."

"Look, you're not sore about things, are you? You've got to know how it is. If people found out I condoned you two in California . . . what the hell. If I leave Danny, my reputation will never survive anyway. Come on inside before we both take malaria. I'm truly sorry, Gordon. Really."

He followed her into the house. A few bugs had evaded the screen door and flittered at the yellow light hanging in the middle of the room.

"Be it ever so crumbled, as they say," she said, sweeping her arm around. "Have a seat anyplace. Danny said after they went hunting he had mill business over in Toullange that might take another day or two. Monkey business, likely. Anyway, we can catch up and talk. Are you hungry? I can fix you a sandwich." She went into another room and reappeared in a few seconds. "Coca-Cola?" She held cold bottles and an opener. He opened the tops as she sat. "I told him if he went, I'd be gone when he got back. Take a look at this." She pulled up her sleeve to show four deep bruises in a row and an opposing one on the other side. "And I've got a knot on my head that feels like he used a hammer this time."

"There's no reason for him to do that to you."

"That's what I said. Of course, he says it's only because I make him so mad. I figure to be packed and gone by the time he gets home. Want a sandwich?" She popped from the chair and left the room.

On the dining table was a large book next to a second, nearly empty, cola bottle. It was filled with pictures of young people. Most of the pictures had handwriting beside the photographs. Gordon stepped closer to the table. On the book a crumpled wet handkerchief lay next to a handwritten letter, folded once, that opened in an L. On the paper he saw the words "... *darling, how I miss* ..." and averted his eyes.

"Frosty know you're here?" Garnelle called from the kitchen. "See," she said with a short laugh, "Fros never was good with hints. If you don't flat-out tell her things, she may think you've up and hit the road for home."

"Word will get around. It didn't take an hour for word to reach her parents' home when we got here."

There was a sustained silence. Then Garnelle laughed. "That you're here with me, alone? Oh, you can count on word getting around. Somebody probably is already trying to put two and two together and ending up with five." She brought plates with sandwiches, setting one down in front of him. Under one elbow she had clasped a thin bottle. "Gin?" she said. He shook his head. Garnelle tipped the bottle over the neck of the Coke and filled it to the lip. Then she took a long drink. She tipped her head toward the book and letter. "I was just having a walk down memory lane. Catching up on a little correspondence, that sort of thing." A bit too quickly, she put the letter under the last page of the book. "Want to see Frosty in high school? This is the yearbook." She pointed out pictures of people, one of Frosty looking hesitant and pale. While she was flipping pages, a loose picture popped out of the closed sheets and landed on the tablecloth, facedown. "Oh. Here. I'll take that," she said, and reached for the picture. "It's nothing. Just an extra photo. You know how there are always extra photos—"

"Here," Gordon said, and picked it up. As he did, he turned the picture over. Coby Brueller's voice came to him, saying, *I'm going up* . . . and Gordon tasted salty grit in his teeth. He smelled gunpowder and sweat. He stared hard at the photo. "I know this man—I *knew* him."

"That's Coby's first uniform picture, from basic training. An old friend of . . . Danny's. I just keep it for sentimental reasons."

Gordon looked hard at the picture, then put it on the table. His fingers trembled. "Coby," he said.

Garnelle said softly, "He died in the Pacific—you knew him?" A single tear rolled down her face and clung to her chin. She felt around distractedly for the handkerchief. Gordon handed it to her. When she took it, he looked squarely into her eyes. "Thanks," she said. "Were you with him when . . . ? I don't want to know." She took a long drink from the Coke bottle. "His parents are real nice. I see them now and then."

"Corporal Brueller saved my life." He could feel the weight of the radio pack. "How far is it to their home?"

THE BRUELLERS LIVED in one of the Victorian Ladies that waited like southern belles on a tree-lined lane in the oldest part of town. Carl and Marie Brueller sat stiffly, anticipating Gordon's arrival since Garnelle's phone call earlier. Every few minutes Carl would turn to Marie and say, "If they left Kirbyville at half past nine, they should be to that curve at the Turkey Creek crossing by now, passing Ricker's by now. Probably near the school by now." When they opened the door, their eyes were pleading, puzzled. Hopeful.

Garnelle said, "This is the man I told y'all about. Gordon Benally."

"Come in, come in," they both said at once. "Please sit down. Young man, will you have some coffee? How about a nice blueberry cake?" They filled his hands with food.

"Mr. and Mrs. Brueller, I know it's late. I just wanted to tell you some things about your son, Coby, and I don't plan to be staying long."

"Garnelle said she found out you knew him, son. Anything you can tell us—" Mrs. Brueller began to cry. Her eyes reddened, and Gordon could see by the color of her face that before her hair had gone gray, it had been red. She was a sunset-colored woman, like Frosty.

He cleared his throat and sipped the coffee, put the saucer of cake on the lamp table. "He was more than just someone I knew. He was a friend. I only knew Coby for a few weeks. But I fought alongside him. He hated injustice and cruelty, and he was brave. I have this"—he reached into his pocket—"from him. It's not much, but it's from him." Gordon unthreaded three keys from a hard metal ring they were on, winding them around its tight circle until they came off and it clamped into a ring again. "It's a grenade ring. He pulled it, threw the grenade, tossed this to me, and said, 'Here, Benally, this is for luck. Keep this and nothing will happen to you.' He saved my life with this grenade." Gordon handed the ring to Mr. Brueller, who took it in his hand carefully, staring at it. "He took out an entire machine-gun nest. Which means he saved dozens of other lives, too. I wish I had something more to give you. But . . . well, we weren't in a place to give each other gifts. What he really gave me was my life."

"Wow," said Garnelle. "I've never heard you talk so much."

He smiled. The Bruellers were both crying soundlessly, staring at the metal ring. Clearing her throat, Mrs. Brueller said, "Would you like more coffee?"

"Thank you." He held forth his cup. "Sir, he never knew. He was just talking one second and not the next. He died a warrior's death. A hero's good death. My uncles would have written a song about me if I'd died so bravely."

The couple clasped each other and bowed their heads over their bundled hands. Garnelle was weeping, too, sniffling hard into a handkerchief. Mr. Brueller said, "Garnelle, we knew you were special to him. He was going to propose to you when he got back. He told us, but said he'd not asked you yet because he didn't want anything to happen."

"Maybe if he had, I wouldn't have got mixed up with Danny," she said. "Coby was always— I loved him."

Gordon said, "We need to talk of good things. Of living things. Maybe not disturb his memory with sad thoughts anymore."

"Yes, we do," Mr. Brueller said. "Yes. Will you stay here with us? We have plenty of room. Just us in this big old house. Plenty. Please, young man, stay and visit."

They held Mrs. Jasper's funeral early the next morning. It was vital to be prompt, even in cool weather. In summer, funerals in Sabine were held the same day as the passing.

Junior preached. And he sang. It was like Mrs. Jasper's voice came out of his body, but lower in range, rich and soothing. He sang "Soon I Will Be Done with the Troubles of the World," and we swayed back and forth, humming along, moaning, hurting. He burst out in a fast, hand-clapping "I'll Fly Away." When he got to the chorus, the congregation answered back, and the whole thing got jumping and happy, and it was a joyous funeral, a celebration, as if we were waving good-bye to someone going on a well-earned vacation.

Hallelujah and amen.

John Moultrie hung his gun belt and hat on two separate pegs near the desk in his office. Ronelle Jasper was the last of the three that death had called. Her passing marked a fading-away of the remaining living slaves in town, maybe in the whole county. Brutal murder, followed by accident, followed by natural old age. His wife had brought blueberry cobbler to the funeral—used every last grain of sugar in their house to make it.

He'd watched with pride over the tables spread outside the church, noting that his angel's cobbler was among the first to vanish. One of the treasures about funerals here, he mused, was the joy involved. It gave him a real sense of peace to think that when his time came, people would gather over fritters and hopping John and blueberry cobbler and relish their lives in the shade of a piney afternoon.

When the sun hit its peak at noon, he realized he'd seen Frosty Summers at that funeral. The general easy feeling he'd been enjoying left him. He opened his top drawer and looked again at Uncle Blye's watch.

By the time I got back from the funeral, I was starting to worry about Gordon. I couldn't find the shoes he'd left on the porch. I remember the time he told me that when I got tired of him just to put his shoes outside. But he'd left them there. If he'd come home in the night to get them, surely he would have wakened me.

I was about ready to trust Deely. Not necessarily Wilbur. Or Garnelle. But I didn't think Deely would have any idea where Gordon was, since Wilbur hadn't gone hunting. After a long time sitting on the back steps staring at the garden, I thought of the only person who'd help me look and not let personal feelings get in the way. *Sheriff Moultrie.*

I GUESS SHERIFF MOULTRIE looked like a ghost had walked in when I showed up at his house. His wife answered the door and led me to a little room where the man was bent over a table with a magnifying glass and a pair of long tweezers. He dropped the tweezers when he looked up at me, and the half-wound fishing fly popped out of its holder and fell to the floor.

He stood and smiled, then fumbled with the fly, poking his finger with the hook. "Going after some bass this time next week," he said. "Come on in and set a spell, Miss Frosty."

"Sheriff, I got married in California. Mrs. Benally now."

"Well, congratulations. I'd heard something about that. Forgot in the spell of the moment, so to say. What can I do for you, Mrs. Benally?"

"I think those boys, Beans and Marty and Danny, have taken my husband Gordon into the swamp. They said they were going to paint the church and put up some lights, then go hunting. I went by there, and the lights are up, but it's not painted."

"You reckon your man can't take care of himself against three of 'em, eh?"

"That's the problem. I guess he can. I guess it'll be just as much taking care as they force him to do." I watched as he mounted the parts back into the holder. "Delia fixed it so that I can stay at Mother and Daddy's. Gordon's got our car, so I know he can sleep in it if he needs to."

"You're thinking he may not come out of that swamp."

I nodded. "He'll be back for me. I believe there's already a rumor through town that he—that he's some kind of . . . Well, I know what those boys are like."

"I figure you do. Tell you what, little lady." He leaned up on one leg, reaching into his back pocket, and pulled out a wallet. "I'll be glad to go find your man. In return, you take a look at this here." He pulled out a thin, much-creased slip of lined notepad paper, unfolded it delicately, and held it toward me.

He was silent while I read the letter, signed by Coby Brueller. I looked at the sheriff. My hands were shaking. "What do you want me to do with this?"

"Just wanted you to read it."

"Sheriff, I . . ."

"I'll go get my boat and start hunting for your fella."

There was no way I could refuse Mother and Daddy's insistence that I attend church. Mother did not attend Sunday's service. Daddy insisted she'd be fine. She'd stay home and rest, fix us a little dinner. But when we left, she was sitting in the front room, nodding in a way that seemed to me to be unintentional. She didn't acknowledge our leaving.

At the door of the church I saw a man in uniform and a short woman with hair as black as Gordon's. The man picked the only open rose from the bush near the door and handed it to the woman. He turned, and I saw his face fully. Farrell Bandy.

"Frosty! Frosty Summers!" He dashed toward me and stopped abruptly, pumping my hand up and down with so much enthusiasm I laughed. He was so tall. His jaw was heavier, set over broad shoulders. Farrell said, "I guess it's too late to collect that kiss now, eh, Frosty? Come meet my wife, Kiroko. I guess all those years running shinney in the swamps paid off in one way, learning enough French to talk to her. She speaks French."

I said, "How do I say hello, Farrell?"

"Oh, she knows a few American words." Then he crunched my shoulders in a friendly hug. "Gosh, it's good to see you."

"You, too. I'm glad you made it home safe." Kiroko was pretty. Not the face I saw in my red-and-yellow nightmares clutching babies but white as fine china, sweet and exotic. "We'd better find a seat," I said.

Brother Miner sat on the front row, nodding proudly at his protégé. I closed my eyes for a prayer, and when I opened them, standing beside me, was Gordon. Filed in behind him were Mr. and Mrs. Brueller, Coby's folks. Gordon's uniform was fresh and starched and clean. He said nothing, nor did I. But he sat there, next to me. That was enough.

BROTHER HALIBURTON CLENCHED his eyes in prayer while one of the old deacons droned on about somebody's gallbladder opera-tion. He surreptitiously thumbed his Bible until he found the verse he wanted. There was one more hymn left to get his thoughts in order. He'd intended to set the stage for what he had planned next week, about how the early Church needed persecution to spread the gospel—how this church might experience calamity, too. Frosty Summers and that shade were bad enough, but, no, Farrell Bandy was parading into church with his Japanese wife. He'd let Brother Danny give the good news about the electric lights. It would all fall into place like it had been ordained. For God had another message in mind.

By the time the hymn was done, he strode to the pulpit, ready. "The sins of the fathers," he boomed, "I say, the sins, brothers and sisters, of the fathers, are carried, passed on, *sent down!* Unto the fourth generation. What we have in our midst is sin. Passed on. Sent down. Sin among us carried unto yet four generations, each one getting blacker. Meaner." He drew a great breath and said, *"More vile!"*

I HAD TO HAND IT to Marty, he really could preach. The walls fairly vibrated with the Scripture when he read, demanding God's judgment upon us all. His sermon was full of terrific allegories and poignant stories. If it hadn't come from his mouth, I might have believed every word of it. I heard and didn't hear Marty's sermon. Mostly I watched Farrell and his tiny wife, Mrs. Farrell Bandy. I thought once that he and I might become more than just pals. It was as if she'd filled a hollow, and once again there was one less link between me and Sabine.

I saw Hal Fielding take my daddy's shoulder before we got out the door and lead him to a corner. They stood in quiet discussion for some time; Daddy's face flushed dark, then faded. I tried to talk with Farrell and Kiroko, but I kept watching Daddy. Pretty soon Marty and Danny joined them. Their part of the conversation I heard, though, loud friendliness, was all. Daddy came to me, looked down at my shoes, and said, "You'll both be coming for dinner." Then he turned and went out the door.

"Let's go home," I said to Gordon as we walked down the road.

"Frosty, where are my shoes?"

I looked at his feet. He was wearing the old work boots, polished black, but broken and cracked as always. "I thought you took them away."

"I thought you tossed them out."

Daddy was walking up ahead and slowed down when he heard us talking.

"I didn't. I swear it," I said. "Last I saw them was when you put them under the chair."

While we were gone, Mother had cooked liver. Hard little black arch supports wobbled back and forth on each plate and defied being cut with a knife. Something that might have been gravy was drizzled over it. Pan grease, with flour and water mixed in, thin streaks through the orange-colored grease. Lima beans, corn relish, something she had concocted and fittingly entitled "greasy onions," and grits full of big uncooked lumps. I hadn't suffered any pregnancy nausea yet, but this supper was about to change that.

As I stared miserably at my plate, it occurred to me that food had always portrayed the anger among us. Really bad food—harsh-tasting and scorched beyond recognition or only partially cooked—was a punishment in and of itself. I remembered experimenting with whether it went down easier in several small mouthfuls or just a few larger ones, settling on smaller because having a mouth too full of something awful was likely to cause gagging.

Daddy said grace and kept talking once he was done. "Brother Haliburton gave a truly anointed sermon, Christine. Shame you missed it. God has really blessed us with him."

Mother said, "He's the best thing that's happened to this church in a long time."

Daddy watched Gordon. "Didn't you think it was a Spirit-filled message?"

I watched the two of them, wondering what was going on. Gordon said, "Yes, sir. He's pretty good at giving a speech."

Daddy said, "Why, the Word of God is never just a speech."

I thought I heard thunder. Gordon held his fork poised over the plate.

The lima beans had been cooked to a soft, pasty mash, barely distinguishable from the grits or the limp rings of onions. That's how it always started. Something you couldn't possibly want to eat. The slightest perceived reluctance to do so was proof of our stubborn and willful natures, sin at its most basic, in need of purging. I held my fork at the ready but couldn't bring myself to touch the food.

Mother spoke, her eyes fixed on the middle of the table. "Well? You people appreciate someone cooking all day, or you just so selfish you don't even notice when you've got good food set in front of you?"

Opalrae merrily emptied a bottle of Tabasco sauce onto her plate and began cutting liver into wafers. The telephone rang, and she jumped up so quickly her chair wobbled backward.

"Sit!" Mother thundered. "Daddy will get the phone."

"You know," Gordon said, "Frosty is a good cook. She makes an applesauce cake with raisins."

Opalrae said, "That's probably one of the kids for me. Is there more Tabasco, Mother? You know how I like it. Frosty, did you know Mother and Daddy have been thinking about moving in with Grandma? Of course, there's ghosts in her house."

"Opalrae, close your mouth," Mother said.

"Well, it's not a secret, Mother. Everyone knows it's haunted, on account of Granddad."

"Finish your supper. We'll not be talking of heathen things in this house."

Opalrae sulked, pushing out her lower lip in a way similar to Mother's, though on her it looked more cute than threatening. "Shoot, there's always something we're not talking about. We talk about the Holy Ghost. Can't believe there's one of those and not the other kind."

"Opalrae," I said, "what's that color called you've got on your nails?"

"Tawny Rose. Do you like it?"

"You know, I heard girls at the factory say that if you run your nylon hose, you can stop the runner with a little dot of nail polish. Only, one of the girls had walked up against a bush and got about twenty little runners, and by the time she finished putting nail polish on all of

them, her date told her he wouldn't go out with a girl with the measles."
They stared at me. Opalrae sputtered. Mother looked disgusted. "Don't
you see?" I said. "It's supposed to be clear nail polish, not red."

"There's only one thing a girl's after, wearing that kind of stuff,"
Mother said in a low voice. "And it's a sure thing where she took the notion."

I tried to smile. "Maybe," I said, "she just wants to feel pretty."

"Like cheap, dime-store trash. See what you did? Taking off to
beauty school and making a living turning decent girls into sluts."

I watched Gordon set his glass down without making a sound. "I
didn't go to beauty college to do that, Mother. I had to earn a living. All
the jobs were gone."

"Anyway," Opalrae said, a Tabasco-dripping crumb of liver on her
fork, "this old house is haunted, too. I can't wait until we move."

We were quiet. About the only thing that could get Gordon stirred
up was a ghost story.

When Daddy came back, the color had completely left his face.
"Christine," he said, "I've got to go to the church."

"Without finishing your supper?" Mother said.

"It'll have to wait. I'll eat it when I get home."

"What is it, Daddy?" I said.

"Somebody started a fire at the church," he said.

"Well, it's about time," Opalrae said, and sang, " 'Set my soul afire,
Lord . . .' "

"Hush your mouth!" Daddy said to her. "I mean a real fire. There's
been some damage." Without another word he strode to the front door,
took his hat from the hook, and left before the screen door had banged
against the jamb. We exchanged looks around the table.

Opalrae jumped up. "I'll get the car and drive Daddy."

Mother said, "You'll sit and finish your supper." She set her jaw; we
heard her draw a breath. "Frosty, you drive the car up 'n' p-pick up Father and ride him to the church."

I stood quickly to follow orders. She had never called him "Father"
that I could remember.

GORDON FELT UNCOMFORTABLE in the company of Mrs. Summers and Opalrae. He decided to talk, to keep the silence at bay. "Who would do that?"

"It's nothing," Mrs. Summers said. "The trustees just call each other . . . time a mousetrap goes off."

Opalrae said, "Somebody probably dropped a cigarette in the trash can in the bathroom."

Mrs. Summers glared. "What do you know about that, young lady?"

"Nothing." Opalrae pushed the lima beans around. "These beans are really good, Mother. Is that bacon in them? I was saying, this old house rattles and moans like ghosts . . . Hey, do you and Frosty live in a real house, or is it some kind of longhouse or something? I read where the Indians build these houses out of bark and stuff."

Gordon looked from one woman to the other. "You shouldn't live in a house where somebody has died."

Opalrae's eyes widened. She locked her gaze on the salt shaker. "There you go."

Christine bristled. All the features of her face moved, tightening against her skull. "Who are you to tell us where we should live? I don't see you footing the bill for us to go live with the Rockefellers."

Opalrae watched with gleeful shock, which she hid with a drink from her glass. Mrs. Summers abruptly slapped the girl a brisk and stinging backhand across the side of her face. Milk splashed, and her teeth hit the curve of the glass, and Opalrae was in tears. A red welt appeared so quickly on Opalrae's fair skin it seemed as if Mrs. Summers had had paint on her fingers.

Gordon stood, gritting his teeth.

"Go . . . get out. I don't care if you are saved. You—you colored, quadroon-yello' Nigra, you." Christine Summers writhed visibly, standing opposite him.

Opalrae shrunk toward the kitchen, hands reaching behind her back for the wall.

Gordon said something in a language neither of the women understood; it ended with " *'Iin-tziin!*" He went, at a near run, into the waning light of the evening.

OPALRAE TWITTERED behind her hand. "Wow," she whispered.

Christine Summers cleared the table without saying a word. When she finally spoke, she said to Opalrae, "You get . . . dishes washed. You started this. I told you to keep still, but you're too stubborn ever to mind. There'll never be a day people will see me having a colored at my supper table again. It's just as well Frosty is rid of that right now. We'll never hold our heads up again, but that's the end. Those kind just want what they can get from a white girl. And after Frosty gone and ruined her reputation, it's no blessed wonder. Never you forget that." She sank into a chair, trembling. "I need to set a spell."

Opalrae ran water into the sink and started scraping plates. She rubbed her nose with the back of her hand. "He was rude. Did he call you an 'Injun'?"

"You ever back-talk me at the table again, I'll take your head clean off."

Opalrae shrugged. "Do you think that was an unknown tongue?"

"Some devilment."

"I know it wasn't French. I've had a whole semester of French. And I heard Cajun before, and it wasn't that neither."

"Stop wasting . . . get that done 'n' get up to the church. Tell Daddy to keep Frosty there."

I found Daddy walking down Washington. The air smelled like snakes, that musty summer smell when we all secretly pray for the rains to start even if they bring tornadoes and hurricanes. "Daddy," I called. He stopped walking and held his hat over his face until the dust blew on by. He got into the car.

"Good thing you came," he said. "Take that turn next, and we'll pick up Brother Miner."

"Brother Miner? This is serious?"

"Yes. Maybe. Can you pick it up any?"

"Sure," I said, and stepped into the gas pedal. "Daddy, what's really wrong with Mother?"

"Oh, she's just worn out. She'll be all right. You learned to drive real good."

"Thanks, Daddy."

"I thought about you driving all the way to California by yourself. Thought about it a lot. No problems with the car?"

"Couple of flat tires. And it boiled over regularly. But I carried some jugs of water, and I never needed to wait long to get some fellow to change a tire. I could have done it myself if I'd had the time to learn. Practically had to chase them away. One time two boys in army uniforms had a fuss with each other over changing my tire."

Daddy nodded. "Figures. Here, slow down, he's come a-walking this way. Brother Miner, hop in." The pastor got into the car with no more than a nod to Daddy and me.

We passed the impressive stone-and-brick building of First Southern, standing there ghostly with its white columns in a row. We went past the Morgan House, where the only piano teacher in town lived. Her daughter had killed herself in the attic of that house before we moved to town, and people said while they were taking piano lessons you could hear her ghost walking overhead sometimes. "What's that smell?" I said.

"Drive faster," Brother Miner said.

"I smell it, too," said Daddy.

WHEN I TOOK the fork of the dirt road to Siloam Springs Baptist Church, the sun was below the trees, making deep shadows. I concentrated on picking out the thicket of pine that bordered the road, not hitting it with the bulbous nose of the car. I looked higher up through the windshield, and I jammed my foot against the brake pedal, stalling the car in its tracks. In front of the nose of the car was a roaring fire where Siloam Springs Baptist Church had stood.

As if a signal had been given, we all leaped from the car. Sabine's tiny fire department, three volunteers and a horse-drawn pump that had to have a hose laid to a stream or swamp to pull from, had already given up their labors. There was no water source anywhere near enough to the building to save it. Flames like jack-o'-lantern teeth snarled from the window frames.

The fire had a voice. It groaned and growled. It roared. Angry. Consumed. It seethed and sizzled. It smelled like a wood fire, but more. It smelled like dirt burning. I stood in my tracks as if I were ordered to stand still. Daddy and Brother Miner had moved closer to it and were trying to roust the volunteer firemen to action, to try to salvage something. I knew from where I was standing there would be no salvaging it. It was going up faster, brighter, with greater eagerness than anything I'd ever witnessed. The heat hurt my face. When at last I pulled away from staring, the air felt chill around me, as if I'd plunged my face into cool water.

In the darkness I could make out more faces. Indiscriminately clustered faces watched the blaze, detached from reality, open-mouthed. There was a chorus of "Oh" when the wooden walls sighed and the roof dropped in on the floor. Within fifteen minutes of that, one wall collapsed outward in an explosion of sparks that started a dozen little fires in the weeds lining the property. Shadowy figures stomped up and down in the weeds, putting out the tiny lights. Then, suddenly, it was out. Out as if a switch were thrown somewhere. Out and smoldering, puffing, small catches of long-hidden sap pockets whistled in the darkness.

We stayed there, appalled, helpless, until the moon rose over the hawthorns and an owl called from the shadows. Brother Miner stayed even after Daddy told him he needed to take me home.

When we got to the house, Mother and Opalrae were waiting. Mother wouldn't—or couldn't—speak. Opalrae said Gordon had gotten mad and left. She said, "He was crazy to walk away at night. Likely to get killed by some hunter. That's what Danny told me." She blushed deeply.

"He'll be all right," I said, and purposefully shrugged as if I hadn't a worry in the world, keeping my eyes away from Mother's stare. With every blink of my eyes, I saw that church burning, as if fire had overlaid everything in my life. "I'm going to bed. I'm exhausted."

Later, I whispered Opalrae's name in the darkness. "Just listen to this one thing. I know you don't want to hear this, but you deserve to hear it. If you keep flirting with Danny you're going to be sorry. He'd never be faithful to you either. And he hits Garnelle."

"He's nice to me."

"He's after you. He's flirted with Deely and me, too."

After a long silence, she said, "Why did you say I deserved it? Do you hate me?"

"You deserve to hear the truth because I care about you, silly."

I heard her sniffing in the darkness. Then she said, "Gordon's crazy about you."

"Did he say where he was going?"

"I just wanted a boyfriend."

Every little sound woke me through the night. Early next morning I slipped into the hall while Mother and Daddy were talking about the fire and had Mayvis ring Garnelle. There was no answer. Daddy insisted I drive him back to the church as soon as we had breakfast.

The giant magnolia tree next to the church stood its post over the popping wooden remains. Black and tarred on one side, still in full scented bloom on the other, it looked like a wounded soldier guarding a fallen comrade. Practically the whole town turned up at one time or another during the next two hours.

Marty walked around questioning every person there, whether or not they'd seen anything, as if he were the sheriff's personal assistant. Later the sheriff showed up and asked all the same questions. Marty came up to me when the sheriff walked around the back end of the church. He leaned in real close, like he had a big secret to tell me. "You seen that red Indian o' yours lately?"

"Why, Marty?"

"Just wondered, is all. Just trying to put things together. You got any idea where he's spent the night?"

"At Garnelle's. Mother wouldn't let him sleep in the house."

"Garnelle Poquette. Shame about that family—used to be real proud. Danny keeps asking the deacons to pray for her. Not even sure if she's really saved. Seems she's missing too. Don't want to think what that means, the two of them gone off together. Pray for 'em, that's all you can do, Sister Summers."

"Benally," I said, and reached out automatically to shake his proffered hand. He shook it, hard. When he walked away, I smelled my fingers carefully. His hand smelled of bacon grease, nothing more.

I walked to the place where the front door had been. Someone had tried to nail a sign lettered UNSAFE—KEEP OUT on the wall, but it fell to the black ashes and was smeared with gray. A skeleton of wooden framework stood, cagelike, burned ribs left from a barbecue after the meat was gone. The floor was dipping toward the basement. Pew ends lined up like headstones down the center aisle. Some tipped this way or that. All charred black. The wood of the pews themselves was thinner and had disappeared in the flames, but the coal-colored markers remained. Light cast through the magnolia tree in fluttering shadows; a hundred crows playing in the ash.

The Sunday school was intact, smoky but perfectly whole. The flame had been confined to the sanctuary. By the magnolia tree I stopped and looked through the window of the one wall still standing, slightly askew. I touched the window frame gingerly, leaning my head in as if to call someone who might be praying inside, wary of its giving way, tumbling me into the basement. Light from the sun caught a fragment of glass, melted, frozen like ice in the icebox, and shot a glimmer of a rainbow across the charred viscera before me. The tree moved in the breeze and cut off the sun; the rainbow vanished. Siloam Springs seemed so hollow, so vacant, so naked, as if all this blackness were its real character, disease revealed.

I leaned back from the sill and brushed the black on my hands. It didn't come off, just ground in deeper. At my feet was a piece of the window, a section of the frame where the individual glass pieces had been in rows of three between little wooden tick-tack-toe boards. I recognized one of the boards and picked it up from the ground. The glass was gone, but the pieces of wood together formed a perfect cross. I stood the cross in the windowsill. A slight change of wind pushed the lemony smell of magnolia at me. I felt lost. Like part of me—of my identity—was gone. When I turned, Delia stood right behind me, her face red, her arms crossed.

"This is your fault," she said. "You and Farrell Bandy. Bringing those people into this sacred house of God. And right after that sermon! The judgment hand of righteousness has descended upon us. Sister Raylene said the sheriff could rightly charge you both with a crime, marrying somebody not white. And *I* suspect there's more to this yet, since *he* was up here before it burned."

"Delia," I said. "I thought you and I—"

"It would have been better if you never came home. I hope you go away and never come back." She turned and walked off without the flaunt of hands or the chin in the air, just a firm resolve. It was the way she walked, so unlike Deely, so gripped with conviction, that hurt.

People gathered nearby until there was a small crowd. Sister Raylene told me that Garnelle and Gordon had run off together and Danny was gone to chase them down with a double-barreled shotgun. "As your sister-in-Christ, I had to tell you," she said.

"Folks, folks, join hands in brotherly love," called Marty. We made a big circle in the grass. Little kids, old folks. Every last person took a hand; I made sure I was between two little children, away from Deely or Raylene and Marty. Somebody started singing "Just a Closer Walk with Thee." Head bowed, I looked at my belly, pressed tightly against my dress. I mouthed the words to the hymn, making no sound.

After the song Brother Miner looked up, his eyes circling the crowd, and said, "God is here among us. He will clothe the lilies of the field; He will provide a place for us to worship. Tell them, Brother Haliburton."

Marty cleared his throat. "Folks, there are just two words I want to say to you on this glorious afternoon: fully insured!" The crowd cheered. "That means," he continued, "that it will all be rebuilt. Only we'll have a chance to update: repaint, repair, and repay. It will be newer, better, finer than before. We can be in a spanking new building by Easter Sunday!"

Brother Miner said, "Now, y'all know that I've already retired to be pastor emeritus. Brother Haliburton here has been filling the pulpit in a grand style already and is prepared to take the reins. And he's offered his services to coordinate the whole building project. He's going to take care of all the headaches for us as head of the trustees *and* as pastor."

Beans Bandy whacked at the screen door on the Haliburtons' back porch with an open hand. "Hey. Hey, you, Haliburton!"

Raylene came timidly to the door. "What do you want?"

"Marty here, Miz Haliburton?"

"He's taking a nap. He was up all night."

"Well, get his fat ass up. He owes me some money, and I come to collect."

"I won't have you talk to me so rudely. For that you'll have to wait."

She slammed the door and left him there. Bandy's face went dark with fury. He beat on the door again, relentlessly. "Open this door! I come for my money!" he shouted, punctuating each word with a fist against the door.

Marty appeared, quickly opened the door and the screen, pulling Bandy inside by the arm. "You know women don't understand business. Get in here, Beans, before you wake the whole town. Just having an afternoon snooze, boy. You know preaching is a 'round-the-clock business. And don't be fussin' at Raylene. She don't know any better. Ain't been right in the head since the baby died."

"Pay up, Marty. I got somewhere to go."

"Where's the cans?"

"Aw, they're around there somewhere."

"I told you to bring the cans back here."

"I tried. They was hot."

"Sister Haliburton?" Marty said over his shoulder. "I've got to go out for a while. Just a little thing Brother Beans needs me to take a look at."

Sheriff Moultrie carried a two-gallon jug of gasoline stoppered with a cork in the back of his old truck. The truck had room for at least four bloodhounds or two or three men in back, if that kind of thing were needed. Lately people were starting to complain that they weren't getting their money's worth from him. That just meant he was doing his job, he figured; there'd been no need of actual dogs in the back end for over two years. So he carried gas, extra cranks, rope, even a mule collar and harness, just to be ready for folks in need of a hand. When he spotted a figure walking down the road carrying two large metal canisters, he slowed his car. "Out of gas?" he hollered from the window.

Marty Haliburton started, then smiled. "Hey there, Sheriff."

"Out of gasoline?" Moultrie repeated.

"N—why, that's exactly right," Marty said. "I decided if I was going to fill up one, might as well take them both and be more prepared next time. Sister Raylene never remembers to fill up the gas. You know women. Think machines just run on magic."

Moultrie nodded. "I've got some in the back. I'll drive you to your car and fill it up."

"No, no, thanks. But that's real generous. I'll just fill these here cans." He kept walking.

The sheriff rolled his little truck alongside. "You coming from the church?"

Marty wagged his head. "Had to look at it again to believe it."

"Well, then, you oughta let me give you a lift, Preacher. No sense lugging them both directions. They'll be heavy coming back." He pulled to a stop, turning just ahead of Marty so that he was cut off from walking past by tall weeds. When Marty was inside, cans on his knees, the sheriff said, "That was a fine sermon you preached the other day."

"Well, sir, the Lord speaks, and I am but the mouthpiece for His word."

"Well, it seems like attendance is up. Folks think a lot of your preaching. Interesting cans you've got there. Seems like they've both got a dent in exactly the same place."

Marty looked at them and admired his work. "You know, I was planning to be an engineer before I heard the gospel call." He tapped on the can's bent shoulder. "That's so they'll fit on the running board of my old Ford. I bang an angle on this corner with a hammer and strap them down—gives me more room in the backseat and trunk. I've been doing that since my daddy first owned the car."

"Sure enough. And it fits right in there, you say?"

Haliburton nodded.

"I'd like to see how that fits. Maybe I'll do something like that myself. People always think I've got a jug of moonshine back there. Coupla gas cans might improve my image." He pulled up in front of the gas pumps at Phipps's Garage. As Haliburton got out, Moultrie said, "Looks like you got soot on your knees from those cans."

"Thanks, thanks for the ride." Marty saluted with the can in his right hand.

Moultrie's heart was pounding, but he smiled until Haliburton was out of sight in the mirror.

Mother outdid herself. Monday's dinner was everything she made better than anyone I knew. With Gordon gone it was fried chicken and grits, gravy, okra boiled with black-eyed peas, creamed corn and biscuits, all topped off with blueberry pie smothered in sweet cream. Every bite stuck in my throat. Every time my left hand came near the table, Mother's eyes fixed on my ring. She glared at it like it was a neon beer sign in a bar. While I washed dishes, I took it off and pinned it to the inside of my pocket with a safety pin.

The afternoon grew long and warm, lulling me to sleep. I hadn't eaten much, but still I fought the urge to succumb. In the summer a midafternoon nap was part of the house ritual. Opalrae was stretched out on my old bed, breathing heavy, so I took a *Life* magazine and went to the kitchen table with the remnant of my glass of lemonade.

In the front room, soothed by the rolling hum of a black electric fan spinning in its cage, Daddy was dozing on the divan. He could do that—had a talent to sleep for precisely the number of minutes he had left before he needed to head back to the Sanitation and Public Works office. Mother nodded over some embroidery she was doing. Needlework, like a thousand other things, was something I was only passingly good at and secretly disliked intensely. Watching Mother there, crewel frame in one hand, needle poised but frozen in the other, I sighed. Her stitches were jagged. Loopy threads stuck out everywhere, unnoticed by her.

The radio played softly; through the static someone was crooning the old hymn "The Upper Room." Tiptoeing into the hallway, I tried Garnelle's exchange on the telephone. Mayvis said she thought she remembered Garnelle telephoning to the Brueller family, and she added that it was a shame Garnelle didn't see fit to attend church anymore. Did I want her to try the Bruellers' exchange? I sighed. "No, thanks," I said, and hung up. I counted minutes to the nagging whine of a fly trying for all his worth to discern what was in the glass I held. I drained the last of the lemonade and let him have at it. The insect unfurled his long tongue into a drop on the rim of the glass and flew away as if he had been stung.

I peeked into the front room again. Mother's needle hand had lowered itself to her lap. Daddy's mouth was fully opened now, the way Opalrae slept. In that pose he looked as vulnerable and childlike as Opalrae did sometimes, as if Mother's storms caught him completely off guard, as they did the rest of us. I wondered what it was he felt for Mother. For any of us. I don't think it was anything even related to affection. I'd heard of men who deserted their families. How rotten could a home be, if this was one that a man stayed in?

A locust began to saw at the air close by. I let myself out the back door and sat on the top step. Sweat poured from my neck and trickled between my breasts. I pushed my blouse after the drip, to catch and stop the tickling. As I did, I leaned forward and caught sight of the rickety lattice that surrounded the porch. A few weeds had sprouted next to the rosemary Mother had planted in front of it, and they bobbed, tipped with tiny, lacy white flowers, in a breeze I could not feel. The lattice, meant to keep raccoons and skunks from under the porch, had fallen in on one section. The sun glanced off the window of the car Daddy kept at the side of the house and framed a large diamond shape of bright glare on the pushed-under latticework. There, as if the fallen wood formed an arrow, was a box. The corner of it was outlined, brushed by the glancing light.

Tentatively, I moved the wood screen and reached in for the box. I dragged it toward me and pulled up a layer of newspapers. The papers had a multitude of raised, leprous spots of green and black mold. Under them were my schoolbooks, my straw hat with the ribbon band, mashed and mildewed, one glove. My silver spoon. Tucked in between my Fort Worth pennant and a tea towel, relatively safe, was Honey Doll. I picked her up and brushed off her face. My throat tightened as I held her. The fabric of the doll was rotted, fragile as old paper. She smelled of mildew, yet I didn't see any sign of stains. Honey-money Doll. My escape. My salvation. I could no more have explained to anyone what was going through my mind than I could have recited the Gettysburg Address backward. I picked up the silver spoon, too, and put it in my pocket. I started walking.

I walked back into town and past Ricker's Ridge to Porter Lane, past the knotted cypress stump and the blue bottle tree, that "milk of magnesia" trap for ghosts. I turned after Mrs. Jasper's house, headed toward the footbridge across Little Sandy Bayou. Beyond the house and across the furrowed yard, I knocked at Junior's door.

A little boy opened it. "Daddy!" he squealed. "They's a white woman on the veranda!"

Junior appeared, at first apprehensive, and then he smiled. "Hey, Miss Frosty. This here's Tyrelle."

"Hey, Junior. Did your sister find a way to get home?"

"She's hoping to in a month or so. Soon's her man can fetch her. How come, Miss Frosty?"

"Where's she at?"

He looked a little shocked. "Yonder below. Her and her baby."

"Thanks, Junior. You take care."

"What you doing, Frosty?"

"Fixing things, Junior. Fixing things." I strode straight through the grassy weeds to the little house in back. Esther opened her door slowly, one eye peeking out before the door opened like a great sideways eyelid, revealing her entire face. "Esther," I said, "I'd like to talk to you, if you've got a minute. There's something . . ."

"Yes, ma'am."

I was going to make it up to someone, going to keep making it up forever if I had to. "You don't understand. Only if it's convenient; don't want to interrupt you. I— There's something I want to give you, for your little girl. What is her name again?"

"What's that, Miz Summers?"

"What's your baby's name?"

"Her name Eleanor Roosevelt. Eleanor Roosevelt Davis."

"That's a fine name. A great name. I've got something here. May I come in?"

She opened the door. "Don't seem like you need to go giving us nothing, ma'am. This child got everything she need." She stayed in the doorframe, not allowing me inside.

I continued rapidly, fearing that I'd lose my nerve. "I know, she's got a good mother and daddy. You're right, it's just . . . there's something of mine I've had a long time. And I'd like to do something to help you, on account of Miss Ronelle meant a lot to me. This doll, and what's in it, also means a lot to me, if you'd take it. It might take her someplace she needs to go." I held Honey Doll tenderly, the leaden arms and legs hanging like sullen rags, suddenly knowing I couldn't just pass over money any more than Esther's pride could allow her to take it. I looked at Esther's face and back at the doll. She looked darkly at the offering in my hands. No doubt could smell it, too. If you didn't know its contents, I guess it looked like a pretty shabby gift. I saw what I believed to be restrained anger in Esther's face. "Please, Esther," I continued, "let me explain. I know it just looks like a worn-out old thing but—oh, I'm not doing this very well, I guess—I want your baby to have this. Please?"

Esther straightened her back, looking hard as an iron bar, yet her visage held that complacent smile that by now I knew was just a learned response and that I found deeply irritating. Her nostrils widened as she inhaled. "Thank you kindly, Miss Summers. My baby too young for a doll-baby. When she need one, I'll get her one."

"It's Mrs.—Mrs. Benally. I got married in California. I don't think you understand."

"You husband's over to Miz Poquette's in Kirbyville."

"I know. But my name is Mrs. Benally."

Little Eleanor Roosevelt crawled between her ankles toward me. With one deft movement Esther swept Eleanor up in the other hand, holding her almost the same way I held the doll. "Thank you kindly," Esther said again. She held out her hand. I laid the doll in it.

"Well, then," I said, "I suppose I'll be going." I searched her eyes for several moments for some connection. They looked at me, glassy and

374

still and without discernment, as if she were a doll herself. "Nothing's what it seems like, Esther."

"Yes, ma'am."

"I know it looks like you don't have a choice sometimes. I know."

"Afternoon, ma'am." The door barely made a sound when she shut it.

Esther shut the door of her one-room house and waited until she heard the white woman's feet in the rattle grass at the edge of the yard. She stood near the curtain where it parted a little on its own and glanced through the slit, holding the squirming infant on her hip like a heavy bag of flour. She set the baby on the floor and looked at the tattered, filthy-smelling doll in her hands. With one sweep, twisting her whole frame, she slammed the rotten thing against the far wall.

Dimes sprayed like a handful of flung fireflies, as the doll split every seam and fray, pounding the coins so hard they bounced back on Esther's face and dress. She opened her mouth and looked around herself at the spangles of money paving her floor. Eleanor Roosevelt picked up a dime and immediately stuffed it into her mouth. Esther pulled it free with a finger, a loop of drool following the coin to her hand.

"My Lord." Hoisting the baby on her hip, she knelt to retrieve the coins with one hand, filling it until they spilled from her grasp. She went to the pantry shelf and pulled down a mason jar and dribbled the dimes into it. A second time her hand filled, and a third. "Ain't that just like a white woman?" she asked Eleanor. "Give you charity and make you feel bad in the bargain. I ain't even gonna spend this money. That's what. Gonna throw it away."

She kicked at the burst doll's remains on the floor. Then picked it up. Tied with string to the doll's middle was a slip of paper on which was written "In memory of Mrs. Jasper, who was a grandma to me when she didn't have to be." She plopped Eleanor on the floor again and pulled the first of twenty one-dollar bills and five ten-dollar bills from its belly. It was enough for a bus ticket. A *dozen* bus tickets. A chance to get home. To find Hector in Georgia and raise Eleanor on their little farm. "Grandmam," she said aloud. "Grandmam, is this you talking to me from hev'm? Is this you sending me home? I hear you, Grandmam." Tears started down her cheeks, and, once begun, she couldn't stop them.

Eleanor tugged at her dress; Esther knelt and clasped her hands together, appealing toward the ceiling, "Lord, why's it always got to be with a kick in the teeth? You know I can't throw this away. Why ain't anything just all one way or the other, good or bad? I can't throw this away. It's Grandmam! Eleanor Roosevelt, child, we're going home."

unior met me again coming back up the yard. He called out, "I got to go to the mill. Swing shift. Mind I walk with you a spell?"

I said, "I won't forget you, Junior. Nor your grandma, Miss Ronelle."

"She was fond of you, too. You ain't coming back, I take it?"

"No."

"Shame 'bout y'all's church. Heard it was a 'lectric fire. I know just exactly what it's like. Like all your foundations just up and tore asunder."

Electrical fire? I hadn't heard that. There couldn't be anything wrong with the wiring—Gordon had just put it in. "Hmmm."

He went on, "You just remember the church ain't the building, it's the people, and they all sinners. Musta been needing a good hidin'. Lord knows his business."

"You sure of that?"

"Yes, ma'am. Of that I am double sure. Y'all take care now."

"You, too."

ON DOWN THE ROAD I heard a car coming and stepped sideways a bit into the grass. The engine slowed, and a voice called, "Hey there, Miss Frosty."

I turned. "Hey, Sheriff Moultrie."

"It'd be a real favor if y'all'd let me carry you to wherever you're going. I need to talk to you."

"Me?"

"This time, Miss Frosty," he said, watching my eyes with a hound-dog look on his face, "it's official business. Right now is a good time to talk without causing undue gossip. Would y'all get in, please?"

I sat in his little truck, too close to the man to feel comfortable. There was a rolled-down package of Red Man chewing tobacco on the floor in front of my feet, and as we drove on, I looked at it as if I had to take a test on the exact curl and angle of every crease in the pouch.

"I'm heading up to the filling station first. Got to check on something I've got cooking." When we turned into the semicircle scraped into the yellow dirt in front of two glass-barrel pumps, he honked the horn, making a wheezing *you-gah!* with the bulb. He laughed. "It was all I could do to keep this bulb away from that Bandy boy and his ever-lovin' rubber drive. That kid collected anything that wasn't nailed down, and some that was. People complained all the time. Hey, Farley," he called to the man standing in filthy overalls and bare feet. "Did Brother Haliburton come by here 'n' get gas earlier?"

"No—howdy, Miss Summers—ain't seen 'im. How come?"

"Saw him carrying two big cans. Left him off right there by the corner. He said he aimed to fill those cans."

Farley shook his head. "Don't reckon he'da done that and not paid, and nobody's left me a nickel all day."

"Musta changed his mind."

"Must be," Farley said with a shrug.

The sheriff turned to me as we pulled away. "So how's married life?"

"Just fine. But this trip's been . . . Mother won't let Gordon stay at the house."

"Gordon seems like a nice fellow. Marine Corps and all."

"He is." I wished I knew where he was.

We drove on. Moultrie said, "Farley is a Klan brother with Mitchell Haliburton."

"Oh." Was I supposed to draw some conclusion from that?

"You know, besides being a sheriff I've been a deacon at Siloam Springs for nine years."

"Yes, sir." I was still thinking about the Klan and Mitchell Haliburton.

"They asked me to be chairman of the deacons a month ago, then held the annual election and decided I wouldn't make as good a chairman as Beans Bandy."

"No kidding? He's the chairman—*Beans?*"

Moultrie nodded, pivoting his head at a corner where he slowed to turn. "People do stuff you know has got to make the Lord just scratch His head." He stopped the truck next to the redbrick building of First Southern Baptist Church. Turning off the engine, he lowered his voice. "I will confess, I was so disappointed I'd about decided to move my letter to First Southern. Then this comes, and I figure they'll need me for a while, just to lend support until it's rebuilt. Who do you think lit up that church?"

Lit it up? "No . . . one."

"I don't think it was any accident myself. Just wondered what you thought about it."

"Me? Why ask me? I haven't lived here in a long—"

"That's just it. Thought you'd have a different point of view."

"I know Gordon didn't have anything to do with it. If he wired up the lights, they were as good as could be. He'd never make a mistake like that. He's careful."

"Y'all remember how the Lord spoke to Moses in a whirlwind?"

378

"It was a b-burning bush. I think Mother's expecting me at home."

"That's right. Anyway, God says to old Brother Moses something like 'Go tell the Pharaoh I told you to take those children to the Promised Land.' And Moses says back, 'Well, I can't do that, no one will listen, I ain't good at talking, and what if they don't believe me?' and God says to him, 'You just tell them I told you so, and they'll listen.' But it takes Moses a lot of hemmin' an' hawin' around before he gets up the nerve to tell anyone. Even though he got the word straight from the Almighty Himself in a miracle, he can't hardly bring himself to say the words.

"It can be hard to tell the truth, even when a person knows the truth. Reckon old Moses had to worry what would his family think? What would they do, laugh at him? Talk behind his back that he was selling them out or lost his marbles?"

"I guess so," I said.

"And you know, that's just what happened. He went through all kinds of rigmarole to prove he was honest, when deep inside he was honest all along. He was the only one with the truth. He mighta just give up, quit trying to convince 'em. They were just a bunch of gossipy neighbors, probably had annoying habits, bratty kids—what did he need dragging their sorry lot across the Sinai? He could have just slipped out and said 'They won't come with me, Lord, but I'll go by myself, and You and me will set up shop in a new land.' "

I laughed. Still, I felt tangled, as if his words were spinning together on the rim of a plate, and the stories and Gordon and fires and people in this town were all blending together.

"God knew Moses couldn't run away from his problems. Who do you think lit up that church?"

I tried to sort out the circle of things he'd just said. I could hear my own breathing. Sweat on my upper lip drizzled to the side; it felt like a fly had landed on my skin.

Moultrie continued as if he'd never expected me to answer the question. "I've got a pretty good idea who did. And I'm pretty sure you know exactly who did. In fact, I've talked to the county attorney—who was almost as hard to convince as Pharaoh—and here's the deal. See, I'm not talking about Siloam Springs. I'm talking about the Missionary Way Tabernacle. Because the person who lit up that church knew there was a man inside. Came to start it earlier in the day out of pure devilment, and old Luke Blye came to fill the lamps and surprised him. So this person figured one old dead Negro wouldn't matter to anyone and killed him for pure meanness, the way some people will kick a dog they don't even know. Soaked the poor old man with gas, hanged him, shoved the only hymnbook they owned under the door so it wouldn't open, and climbed out a window. Then he came back later with some kids he'd convinced to burn it down as a prank. It would have to be a fellow who was a pretty good talker, real convincing."

Sweat ran from my face so thickly I'd have sworn it was bleeding. His windshield had a long crack in it: green lightning frozen forever like a picture in time. Marty had been angry when he'd heard about me going to Missionary Way. "This'll teach 'em," he'd said.

"So the kids are out cuttin' loose. They've got moonshine they're tasting and cigarettes they're smoking, seeing what it's like to be bad kids even though every one of them's brought up in a Christian home. And when one that's real good at talking says 'Let's go here and do this,' they all do it without a second thought. Without knowing they're parties after the fact to murder." He took his hat off the dash and polished the band on his sleeve. "Then along comes this letter—that one you read in my den—confessing the whole thing. The Bruellers' boy, Coby, writes me telling how these knotheads get jar-faced one night and set a fire. That would be enough, except he gets killed being a hero for his country. I've got this confession naming names and everything, and the county attorney says I need just one witness, but it has to be a live, breathing human being who can be questioned by a council for the defense."

"I was going to be a lawyer once."

Moultrie drew a couple of deep breaths and got out of the truck. He came around it and opened my door, taking me by the arm, leading me to the door of the church. He held it ajar. "Take a look in here," he said. "Anybody home?" he hollered.

No one answered. I shrugged and stepped in.

"This," he said, "is where three or four times a week a bunch of sinners get together and try to overcome their natural ways, which is to be greedy, covetous, lying, carnal humans. Same thing goes on in church after church, all over the world—even where they call God something else, they're all trying to step up to the light and be better than what is the easy way out. So when one of them does something wrong, which I see a lot of in my line of work . . . well, it doesn't surprise me too much. It's only when one gets away with it because no one will do the right thing that it gnaws at me."

Echoes that smelled of limp Sunday flowers bounced through the air around us. Sheriff Moultrie was trying to get himself where I'd have to look him in the face. I pretended to take interest in the ceiling.

"You could write a letter, Mrs. Benally. You could write a long letter telling everything you know about the fire at Missionary Way Tabernacle. Because I think there was only one person intent on seeing that place go down."

My eyes hit the stark white cross on the wall over the indoor baptism pool. "I just watched. I only watched."

Moultrie looked surprised. Then he nodded very slowly. "I never doubted that. You see, the same person who did that one poured gasoline in just the places he wanted destroyed at Siloam Springs. All through the Sunday school building there was water all over the floors, and the shingles on the roof were swollen and wet so they wouldn't catch fire. At the end of the hall, where the sanctuary led to the little prayer room behind the organ, you remember that rug in there? Alligator could nest in that rug, it's so wet. This fire had a real definite beginning and a real definite end. Smoke went everywhere, but the fire stayed right where it was intended. And you hold the key to the whole thing. No one else can, or will, tell me about the first one. It's so long ago—and you were underage at the time—that you wouldn't be charged for anything. The county attorney will grant immunity, so you can just be a witness.

"Pointing the finger at the guilty party at Missionary Way implicates the person who torched Siloam Springs. The first fire is too old to go after him for, but there's no limitation on prosecuting for murder. And with the second fire goes insurance fraud and willful destruction of property, all tied to the same man. But none of it will see the light of day without a witness willing to stand up in front of the court of Pharaoh and all the gossipy Israelites and say, 'Here's the truth, the whole truth, the by-God truth.' Comes a time when a person with a conscience has got to do the right thing because it's right, no matter how hard it is." He settled his hat on his head. "I'll carry you home now."

He never said another word, even when I got out. Just drove away.

MY HEART SANK. There was no sign of Gordon, no car. Mother started in as soon as I walked through the door. "You know good and well what's going on over there. I want you to quit this nonsense and just stay home where you belong."

"He's coming back," I said. *He's coming back.*

"Anyone could see wh—what's going on."

I fingered the spoon in my pocket, putting my thumb in the bowl of it, marveling how it seemed to fit just right. "What's going on?" I said. Through the window I watched the sun lower its golden green haze over the backyard. I saw the first flicker of a firefly, so quick you thought you'd imagined a spark in the bushes. I went to the bedroom and started refolding my clothes.

Mother followed me. "Over to that tramp's place in Kirbyville."

"You know Garnelle's not that kind of girl."

"Everyone knows what you two turned into in California. You drove her mother nearly to the mental home. You see what he's gone and done? Gone found himself a new girl to fool with, just like that. You're better off. You know it."

"How is that better off? Why is that better than happily married?"

"You know what I mean."

I shook out a skirt. "No, Mother. I don't. You'll have to spell it out."

"You just go up this Sunday and get baptized again. That's what.

And you quit wearing face powder and act like a lady. And maybe the Lord will forgive you."

"I don't wear face powder. Just lipstick."

"Don't back-talk me. It's only a blessed accident that you ended up home where you belong. You get on your knees. Quit running around like some wild city woman."

"And what, Mother? Do laundry and go to WMU meetings for the rest of my days? I want a family." The word cracked in my throat.

"If you mind your manners, you might get a decent husband."

"Like who? Danny Poquette? After he divorces Garnelle for running around on *her*?"

"There's nothing wrong with Danny. Delia still thinks he's mighty fine. Just look how he came around asking after you, even after all you've done. And he's real nice to Opalrae. Loves this family."

"Mother, I wouldn't marry Danny Poquette for all the tea in China."

"You are the stubbornest, most willful, hardheaded girl that was ever born. What makes you think you're any judge of character? Got to go your stubborn, muleheaded way."

"Mother. I have a nice job. I have a nice husband who loves me and cares for me and supports me. We've bought a little house. I have a couch, for goodness' sake." *And a child.*

"Good heavenly days, I can't talk to you. To live like trash itself for an ever-loving davenport!"

I knew, as surely as I was breathing, that no matter what I did, my life would forever be a disappointment to them. Maybe that was the biggest reason I had for wanting to be something larger than anything I'd known. God help the child I carried, who would never, under any circumstance, be forgiven for being born. I said, "I have to use the rest room." I heard the sound of tires through the bathroom window.

Someone knocked loudly at the front door. The phone jangled next to me; I picked it up instantly, so that the ringing hung in the air. I tried to listen to the living room conversation at the same time. Garnelle was on the phone, talking fast.

"Not now," I said. "I'll talk to you later. I'll call back. Yes, they're here." I hung up.

"Miz Summers," Sheriff Moultrie said, nodding at Mother, "I need to ask you-all just one little question. I need to know if anyone here can account for the whereabouts of that fella your daughter came back from California with, the night of the fire. I got two witnesses that put him 'n' Junior Jasper near the scene of the blaze a few minutes before it would have broke out."

Mother said, "Sunday we were eating supper. Brother Haliburton called just as we sat down to eat. Opalrae, see if there's any coffee left."

I clung against the hall door, wondering what Moultrie was up to. If he knew I was there, was this an act? If he didn't, was he serious?

" 'Zat right?" he said. "Any reason he might have been gone for a while that day? Say, in the afternoon?"

"He's the one wired up the church the day before," Mother said.

"This is ridiculous," I said. "Just plain ridiculous."

"Well, hello, Miss Frosty. I got a call from Brother Haliburton. He's got a witness puts this fellow near the church, acting suspicious. But if y'all tell me that boy was with you the whole day . . . it's that simple."

"Well, he wasn't," Mother said.

Moultrie looked at me.

"He went to the church with Danny and Marty—Brother Haliburton—and Beans. We don't know what they did. They took him hunting or something."

"Where's he at now? I'd like to talk to him."

"I—I don't know for sure."

"I see."

"Humph," Mother said.

The sheriff held up a hand. "Now, Mrs. Summers, don't rile yourself. Brother Haliburton says the insurance company is down on his neck for the facts so they can settle the claim."

I said, "Who is your witness?"

"That Bandy boy, the one with the Walking Liberty headbone," the sheriff said. "It don't mean calling him a liar if he's wrong, you see. The kid don't think clear, maybe don't see too clear."

"Beans? Sheriff, you know——"

"Sister Frosty, I'm just searching for the truth. Preacher Haliburton also said he had word some Nigras had slipped up from Beaumont to light up churches around here. But there wasn't any sign of fires at any other churches around. If that fella comes back here tonight, I'll want to talk to him before you-all leave town. There's always a chance it was dry lightning, that sorta thing. It happens. Natural fire. Night, folks."

Opalrae returned with coffee, cold in the cup. She'd been standing in the kitchen door throughout the whole thing, mouth open, eyes wide and crinkled at the corners. She walked a few steps into the room and whistled. "Holy smokes!" she said. Then she laughed at her joke.

I TOOK ONE STEP back, then turned and went out the kitchen door as fast as my feet would move. Down the steps. I couldn't catch Gordon, so I did what seemed like the next-best thing. I ran all the way into town, toward the sanctuary of Grandmother Summers's house. A cloak of sweat formed itself around my shoulders and neck. My hair hung damp against my face. My skirt clung to my legs. I turned the handle on the doorbell. Several minutes passed before Grandmother's wary voice said, "Who's there?" through the closed door.

"It's me, Grandma. Frosty."

"What do you want at this time of night? Go on home."

"Would you let me in, please?" I heard the creak of a door on old hinges and turned in the direction of the sound. One of the neighbors craned her neck to see the porch where I stood. "Hi, Mrs. Wheating!" I called.

"Frosty, hush your mouth," Grandmother Summers hissed. "That colored with you?"

"If you mean Gordon, no."

The door opened, her head appeared and turned one way, then the other, eyeballing the porch. "Come on in before you wake the whole town."

"It's not yet eight-thirty. No one is asleep." I entered her familiar place. Welcoming and warm it had seemed in times past, dark and cool to the touch now. "Grandmother, I ran away. I don't know where to go or what to do."

"So you thought you'd come here?"

"I hoped——"

"I knew there was nothing but trouble coming when your daddy married that Connally girl. Them Connallys and their uppity ways. Raised her to be spoiled and pampered. I told him it'd bring the whole family down. And now here you've gone and brought this to our family. That boy lit up our church, Frosty—where I was bab-tized and married and hoped to be buried. Thanks to you, like as not, I'll never show my face in polite society again."

"I know my marriage is hard for you to accept. I only want to talk to you."

"Sure enough, your mother's having another seizure over that fellow of yours." She laughed, a menacing, mirthful noise. "Likely she's gettin' what she deserved. I'm washin' my hands of all of you. You'll not get a cent of mine. I've left it all to the church. Our dear little Brother Haliburton will raise it up to the glory of God. Your mother will never leave you a thing either. Earl signed over all her inheritance to the church Sunday school board."

"What are you talking about?"

"I know she's had a nervous breakdown from all your carryings-on." She left the room abruptly and went into a dark corner, toward the little room under the stairs where she stashed her sewing. In a few moments she appeared again, holding something wrapped in crackling old paper. "Here it is. Proof. I keep wondering if maybe I imagined everything, but that's why I kept this as proof." She opened the little parcel. "See there. There's the fact of it. Just lying around like they hadn't a care in the world."

In her hands on the paper were three spoons, identical to the one

I'd held in my hope chest, and now my pocket, since I was a sophomore in high school.

"It's time enough you knew, and I'm telling you the whole thing because I don't ever want you coming back bothering me about it. The Connallys used to invite people over just to show off their finery. Rub decent people's noses in shame, folks who live humble like the Lord commands. I took this from her, 'cause she had everything and didn't deserve it and was proud."

I stared at the spoons.

"Here. Take these. Take 'em out of my house so there's nothing here to go to that bunch. Where you think you got that other one? She always had everything she wanted. When she up and marries your daddy, the whole town talks how she'd gone below herself. Like the reigning queen of East Texas had taken the paupers' son for a husband. As if we didn't come from the oldest family in Virginia! But it doesn't matter how much blue blood you have when your only son marries into that kind of family. Well, I'll tell you, the Great War came, and those Connallys lost their shirts and the box they came in. Your mother was left high and dry with only your daddy's income. Got herself in a family way with Delia, starts to act a Christian, but it doesn't last.

"It was just a matter of time before she laid that baby on my doorstep and took off. Then, lo 'n' behold, she's swelling with you. Her sister ran off with that drummer—the Watkins man. Vanilla and the devil—that's what he sold. *She,* your mother, got caught in the arms of another man, moaning and groaning how sorry she is she's going to have another baby and can't run off like her trashy sister. You changed all her plans—stuck her feet in the ground and made her stay. I always was partial to you for that. No need in her running off and ruining your daddy. Course, now you managed to do that yourself. It wasn't a year later that the Connallys informed them they were cut off. Famine Irish. Blood will out."

"But the spoons?" Her house closed in around me. Dark. Musty.

"Her folks died—influenza—not a day apart. They were laid out in the parlor—the big one, mind you; they had two in their house. Called one the 'library.' Had two maids serving tea in there. Wouldn't allow coffee in their house—that was beneath the likes of them, too. All those spoons spread out like a rooster tail, showing off how much they had. That kind of pride needs to be taken down a peg or three. Sure enough. Most of them disappeared by the time it was through. I got six of 'em."

I held the spoons and looked at them closely. They were heavy. Deeply carved and pierced through the handles, dense with curled stems and tiny roses. "These are beautiful."

"Hmph. I expect you'd think so." She snugged her bathrobe around her middle, jerking the tied belt tight with a snap. She went to the kitchen, and I followed her, hunting through my addled head for any-thing worth saying. "I always hoped you'd be the one to show her. *She* always favored Delia. Did you know that? That third girl—I won't say her name—pure trash."

"How do you figure Mother was going to run off? She's never said anything to me."

"It isn't the kind of thing she'd naturally talk about. I know. I just know, is all. I know because that's just the half of it. The man she was running around with . . . was a Nigra."

My jaw moved up and down, not sure what to respond, for a full minute. Finally I whispered, "I came here to ask you if I can spend the night."

"No. I won't have you sleeping in this house after what you've done. Ruint yourself. You get on out of here. Go home."

"I can't go to Mother and Daddy's."

"That's your own kettle of fish. Go on."

"Grandma," I said.

"Don't 'Grandma' me. You can't settle down and act right, you can just get going. You're holding the only thing I'm giving you. Bring-ing the last load of shame on the Summers name. You've been warned and scolded, but nothing nor nobody was keeping you here." She shook her finger in my face. "Broad is the way, young lady. Broad is the way! Narrow the path that leads to the Lord, and few there are that take it.

Now, take them spoons and get along. I don't ever want to see any of you again." She pushed through the kitchen door and toward the front. She stood by the door, holding it open. She leaned toward the screen and shouted, "You see this, Eldeena? She isn't staying here. Go on, Frosty."

I stopped on the porch, standing in the way as she tried to close the screen door. And I took a breath. "Say, Grandmother, I once had to look up Jamestown in school. You know the James Ratcliffe you say you're descended from? Next time you start listing your blue-blood relatives to impress the crones in the WMU, tell them the Jamestown James Ratcliffe died when he was twenty-four years old. Without a wife. And Ratcliffe wasn't even his real name. He was a bond slave, Grandmother, indentured by his own free will."

MY FEET CARRIED ME automatically back to Mother and Daddy's house, each step calling out mockingly, *blue-blood, blue-blood.*

Mother had a romance with someone besides Daddy, and he was colored? It took only a drop of blood to be labeled colored; for all I knew, that man's coloring may have been merely a matter of reputation, the same way I was called bright in California by that Herb Fontana. And yet it had been enough to provide grist for my grandmother—pretender to the American throne—for her entire life.

Miraculously, Mother and Daddy had gone to bed early. Opalrae was sitting up in the bedroom with a paper novel hidden inside a movie magazine. I slipped into my old bed and watched her for a few moments. "Opalrae," I said, "if you want, you can have my curling iron. I'll trade you for your fountain pen."

"No kidding? Jeepers, sure!"

"Ssshhh. You want my stockings, too?"

"You are the mee-oww!" she whispered.

"Good night, honey," I said.

"Jeepers," she said.

IN THE DEPTH of the night I got up and went into the bathroom, where I thought frantically and wrote slowly with Opalrae's fountain pen on some white paper I took from her dresser drawer. I had written two and a half pages when I heard the house creak with wakefulness, warming in the sun. Afraid of being caught, I went back to the bedroom and picked up a dress and some underwear. Then I took off my nightgown in the bathroom and laid it over the papers, then bathed and washed my hair. I did up three rows of pin curls. Then I wrote several more sentences. At the bottom of the third page I signed my name. I folded it all together, creased them against the washbasin, and pushed them into my dress pocket, where they kept the four spoons from making a wrinkle. I pinned my rings inside there with an old diaper pin that was on the windowsill, rusty and ignored against the dark crevice where it had slipped some years before. I looked at my suitcase: clothes, a few beauty supplies.

Mother came in and found me, gave me one of her tight-necked stares, and said, "Get in that yard and hang up that wash before it goes to mildew in the basket!" When I moved, I put my hand in the pocket on the front of my dress so the four spoons didn't rattle.

In the backyard I straightened and pinned bedsheets that had been washed yesterday, on the clothesline. I took a long time with each one, watching my hands move on the fabric, securing the stained wooden clips as if the hands were some separate, robotic machine that was no part of me. From within the billowing garden of white I peeked at my mother, standing behind the glass over the kitchen sink. Mildew coated the sill of the window; it looked as if it had been painted woolly black. I remember chasing that everlasting mildew with bleach powder and steel wool until my fingertips were raw. I could hear Mother complaining to no one about something at the WMU meeting. My mother, who might have run off with some man not my daddy if I hadn't come along.

Suddenly the door opened, and Mother went to the garden. She bent over at the waist, where I could see only the landscape of her back above the dead pea vines. A row of sunflowers, just starting to form heads, was all that stood between her and the world. Those tearing claws in my side left me, re-forming themselves into a new, sodden pain in my throat. "Mother," I whispered. *Turn and see me.*

She stood as if she'd heard and came quickly toward me. She said, "Baby carrots! They'll go good with pork chops." She hurried up the steps of the back porch, the door bouncing behind her. I pinned up the sheets. Mother called through the window over my head, "I want you to talk to Opalrae this very afternoon. I want you to tell her the wages of sin."

"Yes, ma'am," I said, nodding, "I will." The morning air was pleasant and dewy. Seedpods had sprouted on the mimosa and hung like green flags under the last tired blossoms.

Opalrae came banging through the back door, leaving it ajar and letting the screen door slap into place loudly. "Hey, you kid!" she hollered toward me with a giddy little wave of her hand. "Like my hair? I used your curling iron and did it all myself; I read how in a magazine." As she bounced off the steps—the nine wooden ones had been replaced while I was gone, by seven, made of concrete—a waft of perfume came toward me, crowding the smell of the Snow-White laundry soap from the clothes on the line, and she never looked back.

A breeze ruffled the sheets, and I noticed a pillow slip coming loose. I held it in my hands, a kite shape, lifted in the wind. It pulled and tugged at my hands. As I looked into the turquoise-blue sky, another puff of wind, stronger, opened the pillowcase and billowed into it. It whipped from my grasp as if it had been waiting some immense stretch of time, eagerly, joyfully. It sailed to the tops of the trees, over them, and disappeared.

Mother opened the back door and looked sternly at me, pushing her lower lip out reflexively. "Delia, I want you to walk to Grandma Summers's to get a box of things she's got for the WMU from her porch swing. Well? Answer me."

"Mother, it's me. Frosty."

"I've told her to watch for you."

"Yes, ma'am. I'll get them for you." I started down Washington toward town. I couldn't give Sheriff Moultrie this letter—this terrible confession. Could I? I pulled the letter from my pocket, as if to throw it to the wind, but there was no way to be sure it would fly fast enough, far enough, not to find its way to the hands of someone who knew this town.

As I walked, I tugged at the bobby pins clamping my hair against my head like a cap. Before long I had a fistful of them tucked into my pocket. Here and there the yellow soil glared, sulfurous and sore from having been recently scraped over with the road grader. Off the sides, grasses and seedling oaks clambered at the edges as if they were jostling each other to get to the road first. I cut through the short path that took me past the burned remnant of Siloam Springs Baptist Church.

In the black stubble of weeds I picked up a piece of glass and brushed it off. It was smoothly melted, stained gray and cloudy. I held it up to the sun, then tossed it toward the tarry-smelling timbers. Where it hit, a grasshopper leaped from the ground and landed a foot away. Then I fished it up again, dropping it into my pocket with the spoons and hairpins. Every time I closed my eyes to blink, I saw that pillowcase, a white kite, running like a lamb across the blue sea of sky. I moved faster, my ankles tight and cramped.

Out front of Ricker's Grocery, Marty and Raylene Haliburton were looking over some vegetables. My heart pounded with a racket I knew they must hear. "Hey-ho," I called in a friendly, not-running-away-from-here tone of voice. I couldn't catch my breath.

Marty looked up quickly, as if caught at something. "Miss Frosty," he said. There was a velvety tenderness in his voice, a sharp look in his eyes. The letter in my pocket felt as if it weighed five pounds. *Implicate,* Sheriff Moultrie had said, my letter would implicate and indict Preacher Haliburton. He said, "Heard the sheriff is about to close in on the Nigras that burnt the house of God."

"What? Who?"

"Two of them from across town. They'll probably hang, if there's any justice in this world. I'm ready to testify to the damage they done, if need be."

I raised my chin and looked squarely into his eyes. I'd told Junior I was fixing things. Giving Esther Davis money wasn't any more than a little sugarcoating on my soul. I knew Marty as sure as I knew the fabric of this place. A squirrel chattered impudently in a pine tree, hanging by three of his feet and holding a large pinecone in his front paw. My hands made fists, stuffed in my pockets. I took a deep breath and said, "I'm taking a walk. Drying my hair."

"God bless you, Sister Frosty," Marty said. "And tell that boy of yours, if you ever see him again, that we're still willing to take him on another little hunting trip. If he's not too busy sowing those oats."

DOWNTOWN WAS QUIET. A dog fussed at a blue jay. At the post office window Mayvis Plinkle's grandson Pervis was selling stamps, my old job. "I want to buy an envelope and a first-class stamp," I said.

"Whatya mailing this for?" he said. "The sheriff's office is across the street."

"I want it mailed," I said. "I just do."

"Sure must be true about people in California, got so much money they just throw it away."

"Yes," I said, handing him a nickel. "Must be. Thank you." I put the letter in my pocket.

I started humming a line of "Have Thine Own Way"—the pulse drumming in my feet making it seem martial and stern, an edict rather than a plea—all the while fingering the safety pin in my pocket with my right hand until I got it open. I slipped my ring onto the "married" finger of my left hand. From over a fence another mockingbird yodeled, calling out his territory. I walked faster and faster until I came to the bend in the road that headed south, snaking toward Kirbyville and Garnelle's house.

I pulled my fingers through my hair, coaxing it into shape. A battered wooden picket-sided truck ambled toward me from the direction of Kirbyville. An old man and his white-haired wife squinted toward me and waved, that courteous way of strangers passing, slowing as they passed to keep the dust down. As the road curved farther toward the south, a tiny breeze came up from my back, pushing me with the lightest of touches. It felt good to have the wind ruffle my hair, tossing it around my face. The sound of wind in the pines made me think of the ocean, the way the water never stopped rolling on the sand. Close your eyes and an automobile engine could become one of those larger waves that broke farther from shore and surged foaming upon the sand, tugging it from under you.

Suddenly a car moved toward me, crossing the middle of the road. Sun gleamed off the windshield, and I couldn't see who drove it. I stopped in my tracks. The car stopped, too. The engine shut off. The wind pushed the dust behind the car as if it were still moving. Gordon leaned his head out the side window. I went to the passenger side and opened the door. I saw his eyes go to the ring on my left hand.

"Were you coming to me?" he said without looking toward my face. His lower lip moved tightly against his teeth, as if he were steeling himself for a blow.

I couldn't make a sound come from my throat, but I got in.

Gordon turned the key, and the car rumbled to life. "I'll go with you to get your things."

"No. They're just things. Things can be gotten again. Just keep going, and don't look back. We'll turn into a pillar of salt or something."

When we hit the paved road, he said, "I drove Garnelle to a train station in Toullange. She's going to stay with a cousin in North Carolina. She gave me an address and said if you'd write, she'd be grateful."

LIGHT DIFFUSED IN the mist that meandered through the soughing pines. I could smell the river. A storm would follow. When the smell of the river came this far, it meant there was probably a hurricane close to shore somewhere east of Port Arthur.

The highway stretched before us like a gray ribbon. For two days I watched the road from an angle where the bump over the headlamp made a V, and all the bushes beside the road were rushing to get behind us. Finally the car came to a halt. "Why are we stopping?" I said.

"Out of gas."

"Why didn't you get enough gas?"

"I did, Frosty. That was two hundred miles ago."

"What is this place?"

"Reservation."

"Are we going to see your mother again?"

"No. She'll want us to stay three or four days, and I've got to get back to work. We'll come back to see her in a few months. After the baby comes."

"Baby." I leaned my head against the glass. All at once I questioned the wisdom of my decision to leave everything behind. I wanted clean underwear, a different dress. I had dripped ketchup on the front of this skirt while eating a hamburger yesterday, and it looked tacky. I could smell myself. "What are you doing?" I called to Gordon.

"Putting water in the radiator. Frosty, why don't you get out and walk around a little? Eat something. I bought you those peaches you wanted."

"They taste"—*like Texas*. "Not sweet enough." Gordon paid for the gas. He got back into the car, started the motor, and sighed, staring at the floor between his knees as if he'd dropped something. Then he worked the gearshift, and we started moving. I gazed out the window. After a few minutes I turned toward him. "Where are we going?"

"It won't take too long."

I nodded. We traveled over a long dirt path, which as far as I could tell led from nowhere to nothing. After forty-five minutes he stopped the car.

"This is it." Gordon stepped from the car and walked up a small ridge of rock. Tufts of dried grass rimmed it like fringe.

I didn't have anything to say to him, but I didn't want to be alone, not even for five minutes. When I caught up to him, he was sitting on flat rock, his shirt folded neatly beside him, hands on his knees. Around us, bare horizon circled haunting rock formations, floating in the distance like ships tethered in a bay of red soil. The wind moved, carrying a sound as if it sang through trees, though there were no trees in sight. The song came from the grass. He stared into the distance, lost in thought. I walked, consumed but not thinking: numb.

My feet moved me up the stone streaked with yellow and brown. It sloped toward the sky. When I had gone quite a bit higher than Gordon, I came to a stop at the edge of the rocks. I could see him behind me, still deep in thought, a sort of praying that takes more focus and energy than I've been able to concoct. In front of me a vast valley swept like a church fan. On one side a ridge of serrated hills was lined with colors like ribbon candy, tans and peaches and shades of gray. To the other side a wide green rectangle, bulging with trees and bushes, disappeared in the distance. Below, the drop must have been two or three hundred feet.

I paced as far to each side as I could go. Satisfied that I'd found the steepest prominence, I stepped to the edge of the stone and spread my arms away from my sides. I leaned into the wind, and it held me. I was a kite held aloft by the singing wind, a patch of color against heaven, square arms of an airborne crucifix. I closed my eyes. I heard the grass. The sound circled around the blue sky, calling the sheep clouds. I felt a tug on my waist.

Gordon whispered, "If you jump, we'll both go off. I'm not letting go."

"Who says I'm going to jump? You always know everything, don't you? The inscrutable Indian."

"Cut that out."

"It's true. You think you've got it all sewed up. And you make every decision, no matter how much it hurts. No matter how much it hurts me."

He was indignant. "I never wanted to hurt you."

I lifted my arms slightly. " 'Oh, I love you, Frosty, but we can't be together. You have no clan.' You think that didn't hurt me? And 'Oh, I love you, Frosty, but let's don't get married so you'll be free to go on.' I begged you. And then you didn't write. At least I thought you didn't. And this trip I told you I didn't want to come, but 'It's for the good of your family, Frosty,' like you know what's for the good of everybody alive. And all it accomplished was hurting me." I leaned into the wind, feeling it lift my arms.

I felt Gordon's arms spread, too, right behind me, close enough that his bare chest touched my shoulders and back. "I'm sorry," he said. "I thought it was—wished it was the right thing. Sometimes I'm wrong. But you know I didn't intend to hurt you."

I felt his arms trace mine to their every inch. His hands extended beyond my fingertips. His feet moved forward, touching mine on the outside edges. I said, "I just don't know if I can stand to face it all." The weight of the letter in my pocket pulled me toward the canyon.

"What do you have to face?"

I closed my eyes. "There are some things I've been scared to tell you about me—scared you'd leave me. I've put it all in a letter, to Sheriff Moultrie, but I haven't yet sent it. If I send this letter, there's a chance I'll have to come back and testify in court to a murder." Tears flowed down my face and arched away from my chin, salty rain on the dry canyon.

Gordon wrapped his arms around mine, twirling them like branches, out to our sides. The wind sang, pressing against me, shoving me backward against him. He whispered in my ear, "This place is called Needle Grass Hill. It is the place where Wind is born."

"What do you think people would say if they find us at the bottom?"

He breathed in and out two times, deeply. "White people would say I pushed you. Diné would say the spirit of my dead father walked up here and took us, or tricked us, and we went to him. I love you, Frosty. But I will not be left here alone again. Don't think, whatever your sadness is, that it is all about you." A stiff breeze forced us back a step.

"It wouldn't be to leave you." In the vast expanse below, a darkness hovered, the shadow of a cloud on the floor of the world.

Gordon said, "If you step off this place, the only one you leave is me." After a little time he said gently, "Your body came with me, but your mind and soul stayed there."

I sighed.

Gordon continued. "Garnelle told me everything. Could you have stopped them, even if you tried?" Suddenly a large black crow swooped over, calling loudly, three times.

"The point is, I didn't try. I've been running around thinking I could be more, somehow special, do something valuable. When my life has really been about *not* doing something important. Sheriff Moultrie thinks Marty knew about the man in there, maybe put him in there. And he believes Marty burned down Siloam Springs, too, for the insurance money. Marty, who's a preacher."

"And you feel like destroying yourself because Marty is a criminal?"

I shook my head. "No one will ever forgive me—for telling the sheriff about it. Don't you see? There is *no* right thing to do!" Forever cast out, like a dirty rag. I gulped for air childishly. "That's not all. My grandmother told me that before I was born, my mother had an affair. She said the man was Negro. She could have meant that I—I was his child."

"So?"

"What if people found out?"

"Who cares? Besides, it's not true. Some people think all white people look alike, but I can tell the difference."

"Deely said she wished I'd never come back. That I'd never been born." I scuffed pebbles off the edge with my shoe. "Mother blamed me; I kept her there, and she hated me for it," I said. *If the sins of the fathers pass on even unto four generations, what of the sins of the mothers? Are they as eternal as the voice in the grass?*

I felt a shiver sweep through Gordon, and he swung his arm down quickly, shielding my eyes from a crow that hovered overhead. Gordon twisted suddenly, turning us around to face the car. He loosed his grip, and I took a step away from him.

A sudden shift of the harsh wind pushed me toward him—toward the edge. "Gordon! No!" I shouted, throwing my arms around his chest. I saw his eyes open wide, heard him gasp, caught off balance. "No!" Swaying over the earth, with every ounce of will I possessed, I sank my rear toward the ground behind us, trying to weigh us down. He fell to his knees, and my feet flew between them as he grunted in pain. We landed on the crest of rock.

"Don't you think I know?" he shouted, bending over me. "Don't you think I know how much easier it can be to die than to live? Don't you think I wanted to die, when they came at me again and again?" He turned, sat beside me. Our feet hung over the edge of a mountain big enough to give birth to the wind. My skirt blew up, and I slapped it down with one hand. He was panting, rubbing at his knees. I sobbed, leaning down into my lap, aware that I couldn't bend in the middle; there was a thickening there. I heard the cawing of the bird and turned my head.

"Don't look at it," he ordered. With a soft voice he said, "Frosty, I know what it means to choose to live when living is the hardest thing. I know those people better than you think. I see how that guy Marty twists words and makes everything seem right that's wrong. I know that Beans character is a dangerous fool. When I was little, my parents would say, 'Children, be good, or dangerous fools will toss you off the earth.' Here you are, ready to be tossed off the earth for something done by some dangerous fools. You lived so close to them you couldn't tell what they were. You didn't know enough about them to see the disguise. It's only now, since you've lived farther away, that you understand. Their costumes are thinner than you thought, not so convincing. Come away from the edge more.

"If you don't speak up, maybe more people will suffer someday, much worse. The people who will be hurt now will suffer not because of you but because they are led by dangerous fools."

My mouth moved before I could get the sound out. "Do you and I really belong together? Deely said it's against God's plan for us to be together."

"Isn't it a little late to ask that?"

"My folks certainly don't think so. And your mother and your uncle told me they want you to come home. One man said I should let you go, like I had you in a jar. That girl, Natalie, *looked* at you."

Gordon smiled gently. "Na'atlo'ii was my first love, when I was still shorter than she was. I came to this hill to say good-bye—to that life, to my people, to this land. Never, *ever,* do I want to say good-bye to you."

I leaned into his arms, and we shuffled ourselves farther away from the edge, holding each other. I pushed my face against his chest, listening to his heart. "Gordon, I tried so hard to do what was right, to see beyond what people said, but I feel like everything—*everything* I've done is utterly wrong."

His arms wrapped around me, tightly, silently desperate. "So you question our marriage?" I could feel his breath, warm against my neck, tickling the small hairs behind my ear. The air surged around us, assailing from every side, cheated in one way, rejoicing in another.

"We've only started. It isn't ever going to be easy."

He said, "What do you want to do?"

I looked over the edge of the hill. The crow was gone. "More than anything, I want the world to be a better place because I've been here."

Gordon waited a long time before speaking. "I think it is. But I know what you mean. That's a lot to ask of life. Maybe all anyone can do is choose the best thing they can. Neither of us chose bad things that happened in the past, but we can choose the good. Can't we choose each other?"

In his eyes my reflection stared hopefully back at me. "Yes, Gordon, we can."

The cloud's shadow had moved, darkening one of the jagged escarpments that jutted from the flatland. Even though the sun was still bright, the now-full moon beamed at us from a few degrees above the horizon. I breathed in the newborn wind and felt a quivering in my womb. I saw the earth below moving away from me, like a wave, pulled from a force beneath its surface. I was so very present, so aware of feeling and knowing everything at once, freely choosing to let go of the tether, freer than a kite in the wind on the rock where Wind is born.

Reaching into my dress pocket, I pulled the four silver spoons from it with one hand. With the other I took the lump of soot-blackened glass that for so many years had let the light into Siloam Springs Baptist Church. I threw them all to the wind, without looking to see where they landed. I said, "Remember how you told me in the car that names are important, that names have power? Well, I even wrote Frosty on our marriage license because it's the only name I've ever been called and I thought it didn't matter. But it does. I have another name I've never told you. All I've ever been called is a silly nickname. This is about knowing the truth. About honesty. My real name is Philadelphia."

His smile warmed my soul. "It means love." He put his hands on either side of my face and stared into my eyes. "Now everything makes sense. Frosty never fit you; how could you be a winter morning with sunset hair and skin? A name has to fit you, or you never fit in." He kissed my forehead. Then Gordon shook out his shirt, put it on, and started buttoning it.

The top button of his shirt was still open, and I went to fasten it for him, pressing my hand against his skin at one of the scars on his chest. Our skins were the same there, where my hands have browned in the sun and his chest is always covered by a shirt—underneath the same, like Dr. Fine's favorite Bible verses. Suddenly they made sense, how in the eyes of God it doesn't matter if you are Ronelle Jasper or Wilbur Fielding. *When it all gets sifted in the end. When the sand falls.* I said, "Gordon, if this baby is a girl, I want to name her Hope."

After an hour's drive we came to a place called Holbrook, where I pushed the letter through the lips of a squat blue mailbox. Two more days and we were home in California.

The first morning I awoke back in our house, I forgot for a few moments where I was. When I got up, I made coffee and packed sandwiches for Gordon's lunch box. I kissed him good-bye and stared out the back window to the little patio, my eyes fixed on a leaf dancing in the breeze across the concrete.

By now Esther and Eleanor Roosevelt Davis will be in Macon. By now Sheriff Moultrie has gotten my letter. If he's good to his word, by now he's got Brother Haliburton in jail; Sister Raylene will be in the doctor's office under sedation. Delia will be taking care of their baby, no doubt ironing her diapers while frantically smoking cigarettes and blaming me for the inconvenience. Mother and Daddy will be cursing the day I was born, wondering where they went wrong. Junior Jasper and any other people who might have been blamed for the fire will be relieved, though the threat of the Klan may still be real. And every last one of them will know it is because of me.

READERS' GROUP DISCUSSION QUESTIONS

1. Frosty clearly loves the congregation of Missionary Way—a source of escape from her turbulent situation at home. What factors in her life compel Frosty to destroy the very structure that seems to bring her solace?

2. Frosty's depiction of the South is rich with sensory imagery—smells, colors, and tastes. What colors run through her story and what symbolism is attached to each? Why does Frosty describe her surroundings in these terms?

3. What does the word "water" in the book's title represent? How is water used as a symbol throughout the book?

4. On page 210, Frosty describes a fruit stand on the highway stacked with "sweet Texas melons." How are "black children" used in this fruit metaphor, and why?

5. What is at the root of the attraction between Frosty and Gordon? Does their future seem to hold a "happily ever after"?

6. Grandma Summers and Gordon both experience forms of prejudice—Grandma reveals her own feelings of resentment at the end of the novel. How have both characters reacted to the prejudice they have faced? Does one seem more justified? For whom do you have more sympathy, and why?

7. At first, why doesn't Gordon tell Frosty about his time in the Japanese internment camp? When he finally does tell her, on page 298, she responds with compassion. How does he respond to her kindness, and why?

8. The men who take Gordon hunting clearly have a destructive plan in mind, but what is their true intent? Do they want Gordon dead? How do their actions toward Gordon in the swamp compare to the act of burning down Missionary Way as young boys?

9. What makes it so difficult for Frosty to do the right thing in the end? How has she changed from being self-centered (as with her plan to rescue children so she will be heralded as a hero) to self-sacrificing?

10. At the end of the novel, what dynamic is present in the relationship between Frosty, her mother, and her sisters, Opalrae and Delia? Frosty and Delia seem to come to terms with each other—how convincing is their reconciliation?